Praise for Kerrigan Byrne

"Byrne weaves in such undeniable thrills and a sweeping sense of all-consuming passion that you may just end up falling for the story against your better judgment."

—*Entertainment Weekly* on *The Duke with the Dragon Tattoo*

"Another winner in a stellar series."

—*Library Journal* (starred review) on *The Duke with the Dragon Tattoo*

"Deliciously dark and dangerous historical romance . . . done to perfection."   —*Booklist*

"Readers who feel guilty about craving the thrill of a Victorian bodice-ripper will appreciate the moral reassurance of Byrne's sensitive characterizations."

—*Publishers Weekly*

"Exceptional and compelling."   —*Library Journal*

"The romance is raw, edgy, and explosive. . . . The path they take through adversity makes the triumph of love deeply satisfying."

—*Publishers Weekly* on *The Highwayman*

"A truly mesmerizing series that highlights dangerous heroes who flout the law and the women who love them."

—*Library Journal* (starred review) on *The Hunter*

"Dramatic, romantic, and utterly lovely."   —*BookPage*

Also by
Kerrigan Byrne

The Highwayman
The Hunter
The Highlander
The Duke
The Scot Beds His Wife
The Duke with the Dragon Tattoo

HOW to LOVE A DUKE in TEN DAYS

KERRIGAN BYRNE

St. Martin's Paperbacks

To every survivor.
#metoo

This is a work of fiction. All of the characters, organizations, and events portrayed in this novel are either products of the author's imagination or are used fictitiously.

First published in the United States by St. Martin's Paperbacks, an imprint of St. Martin's Publishing Group.

HOW TO LOVE A DUKE IN TEN DAYS

For information, address St. Martin's Publishing Group, 120 Broadway, New York, NY 10271.

www.stmartins.com

ISBN: 978-1-250-31884-8

Our books may be purchased in bulk for promotional, educational, or business use. Please contact your local bookseller or the Macmillan Corporate and Premium Sales Department at 1-800-221-7945, ext. 5442, or by e-mail at MacmillanSpecialMarkets@macmillan.com.

Printed in the United States of America

St. Martin's Paperbacks edition / September 2019

10 9 8 7 6 5 4 3 2 1

$\mathcal{A}$CKNOWLEDGMENTS

Since I began to chase my dreams to be an author, I've been lucky enough to gather a tribe of truly incredible women with whom I share this journey. I used to think that these fierce and wonderful female friendships and business relationships were rare and precious. And they *are* precious, but I was wrong about them being rare.

Throughout history, women have been supporting, elevating, protecting, and loving each other. Though our strict definition of the word *tribe* may have changed, the overall connotation has not. We need our tribe to survive. And as I look around at the wonderful change that is happening through and on behalf of women, I'm so happy to be here to see it.

Thank you, my ladies, for helping me to survive.

Thank you, Cynthia St. Aubin, for your tireless encouragement and your trust and bravery in the face of unthinkable adversity. You are my beacon and my safe place. I loved going through this crazy year with you. My person.

Thank you, Staci Hart, for your gigantic open heart and for the most precious resources you offer me with abandon: your time, your strength, and your many mad skills. Your generosity and your friendship are gifts I treasure beyond words. This entire project would have immolated without you.

Thank you, Christine, for the incalculable hours you spend on my behalf. I admire the living shit out of you and I owe you everything.

Thank you, Monique and the team at St. Martin's, for having faith and patience and being the engine that puts my stories into the world.

Thank you, Janna Macgregor, for the bitch fests and the brainstorming.

Thank you, Claire Marti, Kimberly Rocha, RL Merrill, Ellay Branton, Eva Moore, Kimberlie Faye, Dawn Winter, Janet Snell, Lori Foster, Penny Reid, E.V. Echols, Nikita Navalkar, Maida Malby, Martha DelVecchio, Marielle Browne, Cindy Nielsen, Kelli Zimmerman, and the many others who are there with a quick read, an opinion, a word of encouragement, a shout-out online, a hug at a conference, and some wonderful words I get to read for fun.

Just . . . thank you.

PROLOGUE

L'Ecole de Chardonne
Mont Pèlerin, Lake Geneva, Switzerland, 1880

"Do you know why I called you to my study at such a late hour, Lady Alexandra?" Headmaster Maurice de Marchand's hand disappeared beneath his imposing desk at her approach, but Alexandra dared not glance down to note it.

She didn't want to imagine what his hands were up to, concealed from her view.

Besides, liars looked down. And a liar she was about to be.

She'd always hated this room. The overstated opulence. Damask everywhere. Splashing together in garish reds, oranges, and canary yellows. Even at this hour, one felt the need to squint against the visual onslaught.

"No, sir, I do not." She summoned every lesson in deceit and temerity she'd gleaned from the Countess of Mont Claire in four years, and met the shrewd gaze of the headmaster with what she hoped was clear-eyed innocence.

Objectively, she understood why so many of the girls at de Chardonne found him handsome. With patrician cheekbones and an angular jaw, he portrayed the kind of sartorial elegance found in ladies' novels. Alexandra thought his neck too long on his strong shoulders, an effect exacerbated by a diminutive chin.

Her friend Julia had once mooned over his brooding, dark eyes, comparing their color to a rich, black Croatian stout. But Julia, she'd long ago decided, was incessantly ridiculous. And if Alexandra had to compare his eyes to anything, it'd be whatever Jean-Yves, the gardener, fertilized his hothouse orchids with.

Julia had obviously forgotten about his penchant to lash the girls' palms when they misbehaved. It wasn't kindness in his eyes she noted then. But something else. Something darker.

He *wanted* them to cry. He moistened his lips at the sight of their tears.

De Marchand's hand reappeared from beneath the desk, and he templed his fingers, resting the index tips against his lips. The sleeves of his black headmaster robes puddled at his elbows where they rested on the imposing desk. It was a desk shadowed by many such men, passed like a scepter and crown to each new lord of their château.

Lord of what, exactly? Alexandra barely suppressed a roll of her eyes. Lord of little girls? How pathetic.

"Come now," he taunted, his French accent weighting his words with a treacle vibrancy. "You're perhaps the cleverest girl we've ever educated here at de Chardonne."

Alexandra imagined generations of clever girls before her better trained—or more willing—to hide their intellect. "You flatter me, sir. But I confess pure ignorance as to why I've been summoned to your study at so dark an hour."

His lids lowered to a sleepy cast, his eyes darkening to a rather hostile brunet. "Always so polite," he murmured, arranging implements on his desk away from his person. A stack of papers trapped beneath a marble paperweight he returned to their leather folder. "So proper and careful." The uncapped fountain pen he set to the far left. "Perfect marks. Perfect comportment." He put his letter opener to the far right, equidistant from the pen. "The perfect student . . . the perfect woman."

"I am not yet a woman." The reminder felt imperative. Though she was to graduate de Chardonne in a matter of days, at seventeen she was the youngest in her year, and would remain so for some months hence. "And I am quite aware of my defects, sir."

Some days she could focus on nothing else.

De Marchand said nothing; his gaze reached for her across the expanse of the desk until Alexandra became so unsettled her stomach curdled against something she couldn't quite identify.

Something unseemly. An unconsecrated anticipation she *should* have feared.

Instead, she settled her notice in his hair, the lambent color of drenched sand at low tide. Darker than gold, lighter than brown. An unassuming color for such an insolent and powerful man.

"Do you think, Lady Alexandra, that if you are perfect during the day, no one will notice what you do in the dark?"

Alexandra's fingers fisted in the folds of her dress, her breath drove into her lungs like a cold rail spike. She valiantly fought the instinct to flee. "I assure you, sir. I'm ignorant as to what you are referring."

Splaying his fingers on the desk, he stood and loomed over her for a terse moment. A spiteful victory danced across his features. He moved to the sideboard next to the window overlooking Lake Geneva. The waxing moon gilded the mountains with silver, and the town below competed with their own metallic golden light. "Clever people have the most exasperating tendency. They spend so much time overestimating themselves, they underestimate everyone else."

A frown weighted Alexandra's mouth and pinched the skin beneath her brows. "Sir, if I've done something to offend someone, I—"

"Would you like some port?" De Marchand spun from the sideboard sporting a diamond-cut crystal decanter and two matching glasses.

The sight of it turned Alexandra's tongue to the consistency of gravel.

She'd pilfered that selfsame decanter from him not two years ago, along with a bottle of port from his extensive collection of wine.

Which meant . . . *he knew.*

He'd discovered the cave.

The Ecole de Chardonne for girls had originally been built into the side of Mont Pèlerin as a clever château-fortress by a Frankish aristocrat in the eleventh century. In its depths, the boiler churned and roared, and during a night of exploration four years prior, Alexandra had chanced upon a labyrinthine walkway which, when bravely followed, became less of a hallway and more of a cave until it abruptly ended at a wall of ivy and thorn bushes.

Here, she and her dearest friends, Francesca Cavendish and Cecelia Teague, had created a haven for their Red Rogues Society. Red, because they all had hair of some variant shade of such. Rogues, because they spent every moment away from their so-called lady's education, to learn all the things not allowed their sex. They read Poe and Dumas, war reports, and lascivious poetry. They taught themselves Latin and algebra. They'd even given each other masculine monikers which they used during their society gatherings and in correspondence. Frank, Cecil, and Alexander.

They'd become too bold over the years, Alexandra realized as she stared at the port decanter gripped in the headmaster's hand. In their quest to discover and enjoy manly pleasures and pastimes denied ladies, they'd taken to occasionally pilfering a thing or two from the few male residents and employees at de Chardonne. Innocuous things, they thought. Things that would never be missed.

Like one of any dozen of decanters the headmaster possessed.

"Port is not a drink one offers a lady," he started. "But I think you've developed a taste for forbidden things, have you not?" An almost giddy satisfaction dripped from de Marchand as he offered her the glass. "A hunger for pleasures only allowed to men."

Dumbstruck, Alexandra could think of nothing else to say or do but accept the wine with white, trembling fingers. She dared not take a sip. She couldn't have swallowed if she tried.

"You assumed no one knew about your little society all these years?" he scoffed gently. "Your trio of redheads. The fat one with all the wealth and no title. The scrawny, impertinent countess."

Indignation flooded her at his valuation of her compatriots, enough to free her tongue. "I don't at all consider that a fair assessment of—"

"And *you*," he said with ungainly, almost accusatory heat. "The flawless balance of both. Slim, but supple. Delicate and desirable."

Alexandra's dinner roiled in her stomach.

De Marchand stepped back behind his desk and pulled open a drawer.

"It isn't appropriate of you to say such things, sir. My father wouldn't appreciate—"

The sight of the pearl-handled shaving razor halted her breathing, and as de Marchand began to produce the contraband she and her friends had acquired over the years, a strangling sensation paralyzed her.

A pair of braces, a top hat, cuff links, shirts, and several other incidentals. They hadn't all been his, and many others had been castoffs.

Even so.

She hated that he'd been to their cave, that he'd defiled their sanctum with his odious presence. She resented him for touching things that, although not hers to begin with, had become treasures.

Treasures the Red Rogues had fully intended to return upon graduating.

"Four years." The number seemed to impress him as he placed the items in a cluster at the edge of his desk in measured, meaningful motions. "You stole from me when you didn't think anyone was watching. You delved into my intimate things. *Forbidden* things."

A slither of oily disgust oozed through her insides, snaking around her guts and tightening them painfully.

His head shook in barely perceptible motions. "We are more alike than you'd imagine, Lady Alexandra. I, too, have a penchant for forbidden things."

Forbidden.

As forbidden as what lurked in his ever-present dark eyes upon her.

His stare had become a chill permanently lodged in her spine. And that chill kept her posture ramrod straight as she stood before him. It readied her limbs for retreat.

"So clever," he repeated. "But not clever enough to have known I watched you."

"I do know you watch me, sir." She'd been aware of it since she'd been too young to recognize just what glimmered in his eyes. A desire not only *forbidden,* but criminal. "More than is seemly. More than is right."

"Let us not dwell on what is right or wrong." He motioned to her stolen goods. "I've watched you enough to find your eyes search for me, as well."

A breath of disbelief escaped her. "Only like a rabbit searches the sky for an eagle."

"You think me a predator, then?"

Indignation scored at her. He wanted her to fear him. "I don't think of you, at all, sir."

His handsomeness rearranged itself in the firelight into something undeniably hideous. He tossed the port back and set the glass next to his reclaimed property.

Alexandra admitted her guilt. She'd been caught out for a thief. And yet, his sins far surpassed hers, she knew that intrinsically, with every part of herself.

"What do I do with the three of you?" He eyed her with exaggerated speculation. "Were I feeling unduly punitive, I would contact the police. Were I feeling cruel, I could expel you."

"No!" Alexandra gasped. As a woman, she'd have a difficult enough time being accepted into a university. If she didn't produce the recommendation she relied upon from de Chardonne, she'd have no chance, whatsoever. "Please, sir. It was only a bit of harmless fun. I apologize for taking your things. We only intended to borrow them. I promise to make reparations if you'll just—"

He stooped to gather something from yet another drawer of his desk, retracting a long, slim strap every girl at de

Chardonne had come to both fear and despise. The sight of it once again choked the words from her throat.

"After tonight, I will be certain to remain in your thoughts every time you intend to misbehave."

Alexandra set her own glass down, her cold, stiff fingers no longer able to carry it as he rounded the desk to tower over her.

Her nostrils flared with hatred, but she bore down on her dread and extended her palms to him. She'd never been struck before, had never done anything to warrant it. But she'd seen the strap applied in the classrooms to unruly girls. She'd noted their stiff movements for weeks.

"It is my fault, Monsieur de Marchand. Punish me, but *please* leave Francesca and Cecelia out of it. I am the instigator. I, alone, deserve this."

"As you say." He stared at her upturned palms, leached of color and trembling like hummingbird wings.

He lifted the strap, and she turned her head in an involuntary wince as she prepared for the strike.

The strike that never came.

Releasing her breath, she dared a glance at him and instantly regretted it.

A notion darkened his visage as he lowered his arm.

"No." He pointed the strap toward the desk. "No, for *you* the punishment will fit the crime."

She glanced at the smooth surface of the desk, uncomprehending. "How do you mean?"

"You've desired these past four years to be treated like the boys at le Radon?" He grasped her elbow, drawing her toward the desk. "Then you will be punished like one."

"I—I don't understand."

His teeth glowed brilliant white, even in the dim firelight. "Bend over."

Alexandra's eyes peeled wide and she took a step back, tugging against his hold. She knew exactly *where* he wanted to strike her.

"No," she whispered, her mind searching for an out. Francesca would know what to do. At the very least, she'd use her influence as a countess to bring the headmaster to heel. Even Cecelia could use her wealth as leverage. No one dared risk losing the income she provided the school.

What clout did Alexandra have?

"My father, the Earl of Bentham, will never stand for this." She planted her heels into the carpet, to no effect. "When he hears of how I've been treated, he'll ruin you."

De Marchand brought his face alarmingly close to hers. "Everyone knows *your* father couldn't ruin a painted whore, let alone a man with my influence."

He didn't give Alexandra time to consider his words as he shoved her against the desk. With a strong hand between her shoulder blades, he pressed her chest against the surface.

She gasped out a cry of pain as the sharp edge bit into her hip bones.

"Spread your arms," he commanded.

So stunned by the pain, so unfamiliar with brutality, Alexandra complied, smoothing her fingers over the cool mahogany. Closing her eyes, she counted the petticoats beneath her heavy skirts.

They'd soften the sting of the strap at least.

With a breath pinned in her lungs, she braced for the first blow.

Instead, she felt the whisper of cold air against the backs of her stockinged knees.

"No." The hoarse objection ripped out of her once again as she reared back and did her best to twist away.

His hand clamped on the back of her neck, slamming her back over the desk with such force, her cheek ground against the grain.

Terror pierced her more than the pain. This was no simple punishment. No retributive fury.

A current of something angrier, *uglier,* pulsed in the atmosphere around them. What had she done to evoke such a malevolent reaction from him? How could she take it back?

"Please." Fighting to remain calm, she struggled to lift her neck. "Let me up. You're hurting me."

"Do you think the boys squirm and plead so prettily?" His question was punctuated with hard consonants, as though he'd spoken them through his teeth.

If she slid her eyes all the way to the side, she could just make out his shadow over her.

"Do you?"

"I—I—" Helplessness stole her words. Relieved her of all reason.

"No, Lady Alexandra, they take their licks." The unwelcome heat of his breath on her cheek should have warned her. But, being uninitiated in the ways of men, she never could have dreamed that his tongue would follow.

The moist path he left across her cheekbone evoked such revulsion, she had no time to react before her arms were tangled in the layers of skirt and petticoat he'd tossed above her waist.

Stunned, she desperately tried to decide what to do. Should she fight him? Should she scream, hoping to rouse one of their teachers from their beds? Would they protect her? Would they expel her? Should she plead for his mercy? Or give in to the tears stinging her eyes and nose and hope they softened his ire? Should she submit to the lashing and be done with it?

"Thin enough to see the treasure beneath," he murmured, confusing her utterly. "I think I'll keep them on."

Her panic-muddled thoughts only just processed that he referred to her white merino drawers when the first blow snapped against her tender rear.

Had he used the strap, she might have remained submissive. For the sake of a deserved punishment. For the protection of her future goals and her close friends.

She'd have *taken her licks* like a man.

But the bruising imprint of his fingers on her backside—the sound of flesh against hers, the pain of it, the absolute degradation—drew a violent response of which she'd not considered herself capable.

He was able to deliver three more punishing blows before her struggles became too wild for him to subdue with one arm.

He used his body, then, to pin her to his desk. Shaped it to hers. Torso to torso, hip to hip.

"Be still," he panted, his serpentine voice thicker than before. "Or I'll not be responsible for what you drive me to do."

"You *will* be responsible," she hissed. "I'll make certain the law holds you responsible."

His dreadful laugh filled the room. "Who do you think they'll believe, Lady Alexandra? The respected headmaster whose family has educated ancient kings, or the spoiled little thief, making outlandish claims to save her reputation?"

His question gave her a moment's pause.

Who, indeed? She was nobility in England. But here, so far from home . . . what power did she wield?

"Let me up." She'd meant it as a demand, but it escaped as a plea. "Do it, or I'll ruin you."

"Not if I ruin you, first," he snarled into her ear, driving her painfully against the desk with his body.

The shape of what she felt against her backside injected new terror into her veins. Greater strength. More conviction.

She became a wild thing, bucking and rearing against his solid strength. Frantic noises she'd intended to contain words broke from her. She'd meant to command him to stop. Then she tried to beg. But to her everlasting vexation, the sounds escaping seemed to only contain different forms of the word "no."

She said it in every language she knew.

She screamed it as he reached between them to grapple with his trousers.

"Fight me all you like," he breathed into her ear as he found the convenient opening in her drawers. "This won't take long."

And it didn't.

Alexandra watched her rhythmic breaths spreading over the lacquered wood of the desk in a fleeting vapor.

They disappeared with every painful inhale.

Perhaps she could just stop breathing.

This won't take long.

It didn't have to.

Time, she thought, was of very little consequence. It only took a moment to lose everything. One's virginity. One's dignity. One's ability to trust. To ever feel safe again.

One's sanity.

One's self.

Her eyes scanned the space before her, noting the inconsequential—the grain in the wood, the books on the shelf, the curtain the color of blood, a glint in the moonlight before her. The vision of Francesca pulling an object from her pocket flashed in her mind

A pearl handle.

The first item they'd ever taken from him.

The reason he now took her innocence from her.

The razor was cool and smooth in her palm, but when had she reached for it?

It could make him stop, she thought. *I must make him stop.*

She twisted suddenly, slashing the sharp blade across his throat.

The sounds he made now were not unlike the grunts and moans from before. And then they were wetter. Softer. Garbled.

He stumbled away from her. Out of her. Into the shadows. His hands clutched at his throat as though he could hold it together. His mouth formed words his windpipe could no longer lend voice to.

Blood disappeared into the collar of his black headmaster's robes.

Her skirts whispered to the ground as she walked away, still clutching the razor in her aching fist. He reached for her, lurched toward her, and fell facefirst on the rug.

Silently, Alexandra closed the door behind her. She floated like a specter through halls of shadows which were interrupted only by the long, crooked crosses where the moon shone through the windowpanes. She climbed the stairs to the tower in which she and the Red Rogues shared a magnificent room.

The noises he'd made echoed inside her head, stole any other sounds, even the sound of her own voice as she whispered her confession.

"I killed him."

The Red Rogues stood panting with exhaustion beneath a silver night sky as they watched Jean-Yves, the groundskeeper at de Chardonne, plant a stunning array of poppies. It was late enough to be early, and even at this hour the flowers all but glowed with sunset hues. He didn't make neat little rows, but artful gathers of blooms, arranged with the perfect balance of natural chaos and controlled synchronicity.

"De Marchand has always been shit," he spat in weighty, guttural French. "Now, at least, he will be useful shit. Fertilizing the gardens." He took off his cap and swiped his balding pate as he glanced up at Alexandra with an expression of sorrow so complete, it threatened her composure. The drooping bags beneath his eyes were heavier than ever. Alexandra watched the wild tufts of hair above his ears flutter in a gentle breeze off the lake. "His behavior has escalated with no reprisal for too long. I've said for so long that de Marchand would forget himself and . . . and no one listened."

Alexandra lowered her lashes. She hadn't yet shed a tear.

Not as Francesca, in her long blue dressing gown and sleek carrot plaits, had tucked the razor into de Marchand's pocket. Nor when stalwart Cecelia, her heart-shaped face pinched with determination, had rolled the body up in the bloodstained carpet and assisted Jean-Yves in hauling it out to the gardens.

Not even as the three of them had begun to cover his gray skin with black earth did a single tear fall.

The Rogues only allowed Alexandra to hold the lantern, which she'd done rather well, she thought. She'd stood like a statue, brandishing the light even when her shoulder had begun to tremble with fatigue. Even when it ached. Then burned.

Even when something viscous and unthinkable had begun to run down her leg.

She'd not moved.

A part of her feared she'd become so cold. So empty.

So *hard* that she'd turn to stone. That they'd not be able to pry the lantern from her fingertips, and when the authorities came, as they surely would, she would advertise just where the body was hidden.

She could condemn them all.

"I will finish here and then I will make certain the study is cleaned." Jean-Yves motioned toward Alexandra, though he addressed Cecelia. "You take her, and you care for her as we discussed. *Comprenez-vous?*"

Cecelia nodded, placing her hand on the man's shoulder.

"We will speak of this tomorrow." He kissed her temple affectionately, then turned back to his work, dismissing the girls.

Alexandra hadn't let go of the lantern until Francesca uncurled her fingers and relieved her of it.

She felt nothing.

Nothing but sensations beneath her feet as they led her back. First, the chilly dew of the grass. Then the slippery tiles of the back kitchens. The lush carpets of the school halls were welcome cushion against her beleaguered soles.

Her beleaguered soul.

And then she was standing in the tower, staring at the coals in the fireplace as her friends silently bustled around her, not realizing that she was naked until the sensation of the lukewarm water on her foot returned her to the moment.

A blaze flared as two filthy nightgowns, dressing robes, and Alexandra's favorite yellow gown, stockings, and underthings fed the fire.

Francesca added a log or two as Cecelia lowered Alexandra into the tub and bathed her gently.

Alexandra stared at her conflagrating undergarments.

De Marchand had never even taken them off. The slit

made for her necessary conveniences were convenient for men, as well. She'd never once considered that. Had anyone considered that? She suddenly wanted to warn every woman alive.

"Are you certain we can trust Jean-Yves?" Francesca finally broke the silence from where she stood in front of the wardrobe, completely naked, snatching at fresh nightgowns and heavy, warm robes. "I don't like that he knows."

Alexandra clinically examined her friend's lean body. De Marchand had been wrong. Francesca was impertinent, but she wasn't scrawny. She'd the sleek, long build of the thoroughbreds she was so fond of riding. Comprised of lean muscle used for speed and agility.

Her wit was just as quick, her tongue as sharp, and her instincts impeccable.

How Alexandra envied her that. Perhaps she'd have been able to escape before—

"Jean-Yves is the only man I've ever trusted," Cecelia insisted, using the back of her wrist to slide her spectacles back up to the bridge of her nose. "He'll keep our secret, of that I have no doubt."

Francesca paused with a pair of new white drawers in her hand. Her cat-green eyes glimmered with equal parts sardonic speculation and gentle curiosity. "Isn't your father still alive? Isn't he a vicar?"

"Yes." Cecelia's plump, ever-placid features darkened.

"And Jean-Yves is the only man you trust?"

"That's what I said." Her sapphire eyes flashed at Francesca as the latter pulled a ruffled nightgown over her head.

"I know he's important to you, Cecil, but we have to consider—"

"Jean-Yves and I have long had an arrangement," Cecelia cut in, picking up a pitcher and easing Alexandra's head back, so as to wash her hair. "I'm taking him with me once we leave to be a part of my household."

"But—"

"We will speak of this *tomorrow.*" Cecelia echoed Jean-Yves's words with more vehemence than Alexandra had ever marked from her. For the first time in their short lives, her tone brooked no argument. Even from Francesca.

My fault.

The burning, aching tears finally arose, branding Alexandra with the same punishing heat as any fire of inquisition. Her friends were quarreling, and it was all because of her. She'd put dear old Jean-Yves in danger, not to mention Cecelia and Francesca.

My fault. My fault. My. Fault.

Those words repeated through her head like rifle shots in a terrible, terrible accelerating rhythm. Like that of flesh against flesh. She couldn't have said how long Cecelia and Francesca bathed her, or how they disposed of the bathwater. She didn't remember them dressing her. Braiding her hair. Nor could she tell when she ended up in bed.

But, eventually, Francesca's commanding voice calling her name permeated the gray fog in which she'd been floating all night. "Alexandra!"

"My fault!" Her inner thoughts manifested in a raw cry even she didn't recognize. "It's all my fault."

"Dear God, no!" Francesca settled in beside her beneath the wide canopy and rested her head on Alexandra's shoulder. "Nothing that happened tonight is your responsibility."

"Y-you're now my accomplices," she agonized, spreading her fingers in front of her. "I shouldn't have brought this to you. It could ruin your entire lives. This shouldn't be a secret you are forced to bear."

Cecelia lay on her other side, drawing up the coverlet

and sharing her warmth and bosomy softness. "We all have secrets, Alexander. Ones that could ruin us."

Alexandra shook her head, staring up at the white canopy, hating the color of purity almost as much as she hated herself. "Not like this. I—I murdered a man."

"Your rapist." Francesca tucked the quilt beneath Alexandra's chin. "We all might have done the same if . . ." She didn't finish her sentence, displaying a rare sensitivity she didn't often possess.

"We all have secrets?" Alexandra turned her head toward Cecelia, her previous words only just permeating her numbness. "I've known you four years now . . . You've never mentioned a secret that could ruin you."

Cecelia sobered, suddenly appearing so much younger than her eighteen years. "I don't want to share, and yet." She hesitated. "I don't want you to feel alone . . ."

Francesca locked eyes with Alexandra, her elfin face a shade of pale Alexandra hadn't considered anyone but a corpse could attain. "We should all share, then we'll have something to carry that will forge an unbreakable bond of trust."

The gesture touched Alexandra utterly. "Tell me," she whispered. Anything to distract her from the horror of what would face her every day for the rest of her life

Cecelia inhaled for an eternity until she finally gathered the courage to speak through a voice made even huskier by emotion. "I'm a bastard. My mother had a lover. She died giving birth to me, you see, and my father . . . the man who raised me . . . has made it clear there isn't a physical possibility that he sired me. He's spent my entire life insisting that my mother died because of her infidelity."

Francesca nodded, heaving a breath made weary by the weight of so much pain. "Oh, darling, is he cruel to you?"

"Unspeakably," Cecelia whispered, blinking away an unwanted memory.

"Do you know your real father?" Alexandra asked, snuggling closer to Cecelia. "Is it this mysterious benefactor who finances your education?"

Cecelia shook her head and shrugged her shoulders, shame tinging her cheeks even more peach. "I wish I knew. I sometimes am certain it is. I've spent so many years at de Chardonne alone. Before I befriended you, Jean-Yves was the only comrade I'd ever known. And only then because I hid so often as a girl in his gardens and pestered him into eventual partiality to me."

"Now I feel like such a dunce," Francesca lamented. "If you trust him, we shall, as well."

"The more people who know a secret, the more in peril it is. It is right that we are all cautious." Cecelia dashed a few errant tears from her peachy-cream skin. "What about you, Frank? Do you have a secret?"

Francesca locked eyes with Alexandra. "I'm an impostor. My name isn't Francesca Cavendish. It's Pippa. Pippa Hargrave."

Their mouths opened, slackened, then nearly unhinged with shock.

Francesca's emerald eyes were made brilliant by the fire, but a dark veracity emanated from her that distracted Alexandra from her pain, if only for a moment.

"I was born to Charles and Hattie Hargrave in Yorkshire where they served as cook and underbutler to William and Theresa Cavendish, the Earl and Countess of Mont Claire. I grew up in paradise along with their children, Fernand and Francesca."

Cecelia's brow wrinkled in a frown. "I thought the Cavendishes all perished in a fire, but for . . ."

"No one died in the fire."

Alexandra blinked, wondering if distress had made her a lackwit. "What? What are you saying?"

Francesca's brilliant gaze dulled as she gazed into a past so tormented, it seemed to make her smaller, as though it could crush her into the dust. "Have you ever heard of a fire starting in a household of nearly one hundred people in the middle of the day, without one soul escaping it alive?"

"The odds of that happening seem quite impossible, unless . . ." As Cecelia let the thread trail away with a wince, she and Alexandra shared a speculative glance.

Francesca's next words validated what they'd feared. "Unless everyone inside was already dead." She plucked at a loose seam in the lining of her robe as she vacantly stared ahead. "Not dead," she amended. "*Butchered.* Men on horses came during tea. At eight years old, I thought it seemed like an army, but I'm convinced now it couldn't have been more than a dozen or so. They slaughtered everyone. The earl and countess, the housekeeper, butler, the groundskeepers, maids, the children . . . my parents."

She took a breathless moment to compose herself. "I ran with Francesca, but they caught her. Wrenched her right from my grasp. I watched as they . . . they . . . She didn't even have time to scream." She put a hand to her throat, and it was easy to guess how Francesca had died.

Alexandra hated that she took solace in the telling. It didn't speak very well of her, that she found comfort in their secrets. In their pain.

Because it meant she wasn't so alone. That she wasn't the only girl in this room who would live with a clandestine shame.

"Oh, Frank." Cecelia added her other warm, soft hand to the pile. "How did you ever survive?"

For a moment, Francesca's features softened. "Declan

Chandler, he found me, and hid us in a crevasse up a chimney. We thought we were safe until the fire started. We waited as long as we could, until we believed the men had ridden away, until the smoke became too thick and we *had* to escape it. Declan spirited me out of the house and we were running for the woods, for safety, when we were spotted by a man who'd stayed behind to make certain all traces of foul play were erased in the fire. That only ashes remained of the dead. Of the grand and happy house that had stood there since the white rose of York hung over the throne of England."

Francesca accepted the handkerchief Cecelia fetched for her, wiped her eyes, and blew her nose in a way that was anything but delicate. "The man followed us into the woods and Declan, always the hero, created a diversion."

"Did he . . . survive?"

Francesca shook her head for a long time, her chin wobbling with grief-stricken sobs she seemed determined to hold back. "I've looked for him everywhere, but there's no sign of Declan Chandler ever having been born. He was an orphan, after all, and if his mother never recorded his birth, then . . . he wouldn't be missed. What if his poor little body was left there in the woods somewhere, or possibly a bog or a lake? I have this nightmare that I'm the only one left alive who even remembers he existed." A few sobs broke through her slender throat, hoarse little sounds raw enough to mirror the pain in Alexandra's heart.

"You loved him," Alexandra realized.

"Pippa loved him," she sniffed. "And he loved Francesca. And Fernand loved Pippa. When it wasn't a bevy of little heartbreaks, it was the most wonderful childhood one could imagine."

They remained silent for a tear-fraught moment, trying to digest the scope of the tragedy before Alexandra finally asked the inevitable. "When did you become Francesca? Or, I suppose I'm asking, *why* did you become her?"

"The Mont Claire title was not entailed to primogeniture. Which meant if any *one* of the Cavendish children survived, male or female, *they* would be the heir to the entire estate. And so, the gypsies who were allowed to live on the estate took me in, dyed my hair red with henna, and the moment all the paperwork was in order, the trustees and clerks bribed, and my 'godparents' established by paper trail, I became Francesca Cavendish. After I was presented to the courts, it was decided I'd be sent to a boarding school out of the country."

"Why did the gypsies go through all that trouble?" Cecelia wondered. "For the Mont Claire money?"

"No," Francesca insisted. "No, money means nothing to gypsies. They did it for the same reason I remain in this farce of a life to this day . . ."

She turned her head toward Alexandra again, and the fire reignited behind her irises.

Alexandra nodded, her throat clogged with emotion. "Revenge."

"Exactly." Francesca kissed Alexandra on the cheek, her gaze a mix of ferocity and an aching kindness. "Alexander. I will always keep the secret of this murder in our past, if you will keep the secret of the murder in my future. For when I find out who is responsible for the death of my family . . ." She didn't finish the thought. She didn't have to.

Alexandra returned the kiss, tasting the mingled salt of their tears.

Francesca looked to where Cecelia dashed moisture from her cheeks. "I'm so sorry for you both." She hiccupped around a delicate sob.

Alexandra's shoulders came off the bed and she clung

to them both. "You two *are* my family," she swore. "I will have no husband or children. No man would have me and . . . and I want none. Never. I never want to be touched again."

"Nor I," Francesca nearly snarled. "Men are vile, demanding, violent cretins. We are best off without them."

"I agree," Cecelia whispered. "I've never known marriage to be a happy institution. Our lives will take us so many places, but we'll always have each other to return to. To holiday with. To rely upon. We are bound by blood now, as tightly as any family."

Alexandra lay back down, spreading her hand on her chest, just above her heart. She placed Francesca's palm over hers, and Cecelia followed suit. "We are eternally bound," she repeated. "By secrets, blood, and pain."

"And by trust, passion, and revenge," Francesca added darkly.

"And by friendship, love, and . . ." Cecelia sniffed, pressing on the hands beneath her, as if she could touch the heart below it. "And hope. For without that, what reason do we have to endure?"

The enormity of the night crashed through Alexandra with all the strength of a rogue wave, threatening to drown her in despair. When her friends would have pulled away, she clung to them. Without another word, they curled around her, creating a nest with their bodies and the darkness.

In that moment, they were the only ones in the whole world.

But they weren't. Morning would come, and everyone would know. Or they wouldn't. The headmaster would be discovered missing. The intensifying burn between her legs might be unimaginably worse. And she was already feeling dirty again. Aching for another bath.

She'd have to learn to hide who she was. Who *he'd* made her.

A murderess.

God. What if she couldn't keep such a dark secret?

Anguish overwhelmed her until Cecelia huddled closer, her lips grazing Alexandra's ear in the dark. "You'll always be haunted by this night," she whispered, tinged with agony no one her age should bear. "You'll forever miss what was taken from you. But your body will heal, Alexander, and you'll get stronger."

Francesca pressed her forehead to her temple, kissing at a tear. "Your heart will learn to beat again. Until that happens, I'll protect you. I promise."

They'd protect each other, Alexandra fervently swore.

Whatever it took.

CHAPTER ONE

Maynemouth, Devonshire, 1890
Ten years later

Alexander,
Accept the invitation to Castle Redmayne.
I'm in danger. I need you.

—Frank

Alexandra Lane had spent the entire train ride from London to Devonshire meticulously pondering those fourteen words for two separate reasons.

The first, she had been unable to stop fretting for Francesca, who tended to give more than the appropriate amount of context. The terse, vague note Alexandra now held was more of a warning than the message contained therein.

The second, she could no longer afford a first-class, private railcar, and had, for the last several tense hours, been forced to share her vestibule face-to-face with a rough-featured, stocky man with shoulders made for labor.

Alone.

He'd attempted polite conversation at first, which she'd rebuffed with equal civility by feigning interest in her correspondence. By now, however, they were both painfully aware she needn't take four stops to read two letters.

It was terribly rude, she knew. Her carpetbag remained clutched in her fist the entire time, except when her hand would wander into its depths to palm the tiny pistol she always carried. The sounds of the other passengers in adjoining vestibules didn't make her feel safer, per se.

But she knew they would hear her scream, and that provided some relief.

For a woman who'd spent a great deal of the last ten years in the company of men, she'd thought these painful moments would have relented by now.

Alas, she'd become a mistress of manipulating a situation so, even if she had to endure the company of men without a female companion, there would be more than one man. In the circles she tended to frequent, people behaved when in company.

It had worked thus far.

Alexandra braced herself against the slowing of the train, breathing a silent prayer of relief that they'd finally arrived. She'd been terrified that if she'd glanced up once, she'd be forced into conversation with her unwanted companion.

Rain wept against the coach window, and the shadows of the tears painted macabre little serpents on the conflicting documents in her hands. One, a wedding invitation. The other, Francesca's alarming note.

A month past, she'd have wagered her entire inheritance against Francesca Cavendish's being the first of the Red Rogues to capitulate to the bonds of matrimony.

A month past, she'd assumed she'd had an inheritance to wager.

Their little society had seemed destined to live up to the promise they'd once made as young, disenchanted girls to never marry.

Until the invitation to an engagement masquerade—given by the Duke of Redmayne—had arrived the same day of her friend's cryptic and startling note.

The invitation had been equally as ambiguous, stating that the future duchess of Redmayne would be unveiled, as it were, at the ball. Included in Alexandra's particular envelope was a request for her to attend as a bridesmaid.

The subsequent plea for help from Francesca—Frank—had arrived in a tiny envelope with the Red Rogue seal they'd commissioned some years prior.

Alexandra hadn't even known Francesca had returned from her romps about the Continent. Last she'd heard, the countess had been in Morocco, doing reconnaissance of some sort. Nothing in her letters had mentioned a suitor. Not a serious one, in any case. Certainly not a duke.

Francesca had a talent for mischief and a tendency to interpret danger as mere adventure.

So, what could possibly frighten her fearless friend?

Marriage, obviously, Alexandra thought with a smirk. A risky venture, to be sure.

And dangerous.

Alexandra smoothed her traveling skirts, whose smart tweed became more worn and forlorn with each passing year.

She should have taken better care of it. She shouldn't have taken for granted that her father would always be able to buy her another.

The train trundled up to the Maynemouth platform with a series of lurches, sending the man's briefcase tumbling from the seat beside him. It landed at her feet before sliding half beneath her skirts.

"Sorry, madam," he said in heavily accented Continental English as he leaned toward her lap, reaching for the briefcase below her. "I'll just—"

Alexandra surged to her feet, staggering toward the vestibule door. She burst into the narrow hall, stabilizing herself against the dark wood wainscoting as she passed the more judicious travelers who waited until the train came to a complete stop before disembarking.

Could she have acted more absurd?

Yes. And she had, a multitude of times.

She clung to a rail by the door as the train came to a halt, and leaped into the Devon seastorm the moment the porter opened the door.

She'd forget this interaction, she reminded herself as she sought cover beneath the overhang to wait for her luggage. She always did. Embarrassment was nothing compared to safety.

A half hour later, Alexandra nervously chewed her lip as she stood on the platform, lost in a billow of engine steam and sea mist, ready to debark to the infamous Castle Redmayne.

If Cecelia ever arrived.

The coach was supposed to have met her a quarter hour past, but Alexandra might have known her sweet, disorderly friend would be tardy. As good as the woman was with numbers, a concept as simple as time confounded her. Thus, Cecelia forever functioned a half hour behind the rest of the world.

"You got a chaperone, miss?" The endearingly young, knobby-jointed porter with what appeared to be a penciled-on mustache eyed her impertinently. Smythe, his gleaming name badge christened him. "I got to be about me work, see, but I don't like to be leaving you alone. We're running like rats wot with all the toffs arriving for the grand wedding. And . . . no offense meant, miss, but me mother's sick, and I'd rather not lose out on the gratuity by standing still."

By standing next to an impoverished spinster, he didn't say.

He didn't have to.

"Of course." Alexandra didn't bother to explain that she happened to be one of the bridesmaids in the aforementioned grand wedding. Nor did she inform him of her status as one of the "toffs" to which he referred. It would have been well within her privilege as the daughter of an earl to demand he address her as "my lady" rather than "miss."

Instead, she gathered a precious ha'penny from the carpetbag she'd acquired in Cairo, and pressed it into the young man's glove. "Someone will be along to collect me shortly. Thank you."

She enjoyed a bit of relief when the porter scurried away in search of peerage. Indeed, there were plenty more to be found disembarking the train.

She could attest to that, as she'd been avoiding as many as she could.

In case they'd seen her in second class.

In case they'd heard of her family's recently reduced circumstances, and felt the need to remark upon their spinster daughter who was now too old, and too clever, to catch a husband.

If they only knew the truth. What would they say then?

It had been heavy carrying one devastating shame around for a decade. She'd underestimated what the weight of a second scandal would do to her.

It would all be over soon, she supposed. The news of her family's financial ruin wouldn't stay secret for long. And when what was left of her money ran out, her long-ago transgression would be revealed as a direct result.

Because if one couldn't pay one's bills, one certainly couldn't pay one's blackmailer.

Better that Francesca marry now and have the designation of duchess when the scandal broke.

And Cecelia, *dear* kind Cecelia, didn't have the responsibility of a title, nor did she have the protection of one. Her reputation meant little to her, mostly because she was a rather obscure woman in all but her immediate academic circle.

But reputation was nothing next to the hangman's noose . . . and they all might be in danger of that.

Pressing her hand against a pitch of dread in her stomach, Alexandra hid herself behind her meager hill of luggage. A hill because, by comparison, the piles of trunks, hat cases, and garment bags currently being carted from the train were veritable mountains rising from the mists.

The Earl and Countess Bevelstoke hurried past, tucked tightly into their furs and cloaks as an army of servants and porters—Smythe, included—conducted their things in the direction of an ostentatious coach.

Lord and Lady Bevelstoke had once been counted among her parents' most intimate society.

Until lately.

Luckily, the train belched another whoosh of steam, further concealing her from their view.

"Alexandra? Lady Alexandra Lane? Can that possibly be you?"

Alexandra flinched at the sound of her name, but broke into a genuine smile at whom she found behind her.

"Julia? Julia Throckmorton?" she greeted.

They embraced with the exuberance of long-parted friends, and stepped apart to examine what the years had done to each other. They'd been kinder to Julia than to her, as her old school chum was bedecked in more pearls and sapphires than a traveling kit warranted.

"How long has it been?" Alexandra asked.

Julia tucked an errant golden ringlet into her stylish cap, pursing her lips together. "Six years, at least," she recalled. "Our last drink at the café in Boston the summer my husband took us on the grand tour of New England. Then it was de Chardonne before that. Can you believe it's been ten years?"

"I cannot," she answered honestly. It felt like only yesterday, and yet another lifetime ago. "Where is Lord Throckmorton? You're both here for the wedding, I presume?"

Julia's bright eyes dimmed along with her smile. "Of course, you haven't heard. You were in Greece two years ago when my husband passed."

Alexandra gripped her hand. "Oh, Julia, I'm so sorry. I hadn't heard, and when I'm in the field, I never read the papers. I'm hopeless at correspondence. Forgive me for not writing."

"Don't think of it." Julia's smile was tighter when it returned. "I know you've enough on your mind as it is, poor dear." She patted Alexandra's hand in a manner almost condescending, as though reminding Alexandra of her diminished circumstances without being gauche enough to lend them voice.

Oh, yes, this was why Julia, generally considered a friend, had never been inducted into the Red Rogues. It wasn't the lack of the red hue in her hair, it was her propensity to be a bit priggish. Not that she had a reason to feel superior, she'd been married off to Lord Walther Throckmorton, the Viscount Leighton. A man twenty years her senior and at least double that in weight due to his excessive drinking.

"Can you imagine, a dowager at my age? Though Lord Throckmorton left me a vulgar fortune," Julia whispered, increasing the vulgarity by mentioning it. "And now I'm enjoying jaunting about all of Christendom with Lord and Lady Bevelstoke."

"How lovely for you." Alexandra hoped she sounded sincere.

If Julia noticed, she didn't mention. "How mysterious this Duke of Redmayne is. I've heard he's beastly. Have you any idea to whom he's engaged?"

"I couldn't possibly say." Alexandra sighed, already tiring of the gossip. Although she had to admit she'd enjoy Julia's astonishment when Francesca was revealed as the bride.

They'd never got on.

"Lady Throckmorton," Lady Bevelstoke called over the increasing storm from the coach. "We really should go, we've *important* society waiting upon our arrival."

Alexandra didn't miss the slight emphasis she'd placed upon the word.

"Let's do catch up." Julia kissed her on both cheeks and burrowed further into her furs as a footman held an umbrella over her all the way to the coach. *"Au revoir."*

The slap of the whip sent the Bevelstoke carriage axles grinding toward one of the oldest, and perhaps grandest, fortresses still standing on British soil.

Castle Redmayne.

Alexandra scanned the storm, wondering if the castle, or the sea, was visible from here on a clear day. The weather was both peculiar and ominous. Evening darkness loomed much earlier than usual. The raucous clouds so heavy, they appeared black in some places. The storm was lively with lightning, and yet an ethereal fog clung to the ground, refusing to be dispelled by the rain. Displaced by the knees of scurrying travelers, it swirled and eddied, lending an elegance to the bustle.

The small village of Maynemouth hunkered nearby. Charming streets lined with businesses built tight to the rails. The attractive crofts, cottages, and stately homes gleamed farther up the hill, so the clamor of the train and the bustle of industry didn't disturb their infamous Southern tranquility.

A bitter sudden gust drove little needles of rain sideways. As Alexandra and her things had been abandoned at the edge of the awning, the storm and the runoff combined their efforts with the wind to soak her threadbare travel kit clean through.

Do hurry, Cecelia, she urged, opening her umbrella against the onslaught of rain, which disappeared as quickly as it had assaulted her.

Lightning separated the clouds above, forking down toward the train with a brilliant, chaotic snap.

For a magical breath, all occupants of the station appeared frozen in time, respectfully awaiting the thunder before they resumed their business.

Obligingly, a rumble preceded a boom above so brash, Alexandra was convinced that if the awning didn't conceal the sky, they'd have all borne witness to a collision of the clouds violent enough to render such a roar.

Now that most of the passengers had disembarked for their destinations, a bevy of soggy merchantmen and their workers broke against the train like a wave at low tide. Boxcar doors were thrown open on rusted rails and uncouth voices shouted orders and curses in time to the dance of lifting and lowering merchandise to the ground below the passenger platform.

A ramp was lifted onto a livestock car, and a cadre of workers coaxed four skittish thoroughbred horses down the incline by their leads and out to an awaiting coach.

One voice rose above the tumult, commanding the same rapt attention from rough-hewn men as the thunder.

Alexandra squinted across the platform admiring the horseflesh and hoping to identify which man belonged to the distinctly masculine voice. There'd been a resonance to it. Something sonorous and commanding. It plucked the same vibrations within her as ancient cathedral bells.

"He's too unsettled," the voice called from the cavern of the boxcar as two lead ropes were tossed from the gloom. "You two there—keep the tension on the rope until I can get his blinders on."

With the gentry gone—other than Alexandra—Smythe slithered between the remaining travelers, darting toward the livestock car as though a mighty wonder was inside.

What commanded such curiosity? The beast, or the man?

Smythe snatched the rope and cautiously tugged until it ran out of slack. His resolution almost made up for his lack of stature as he wrapped the rope several times around his forearm and wrist before locking it in his grip.

Alexandra stood too far off to warn him of his folly, and dearly hoped that someone else might be observant enough to do so.

No such luck.

A sturdy footman bent to grasp the rope on the opposite side of the plank, but before he could secure it, another streak of lightning blinded them all.

An inhuman scream rent the storm before the largest stallion Alexandra had ever seen leaped from inside the car in a graceful arc, clearing the ramp altogether.

The moment his hooves met the earth, he leaped and

bucked with alarming grace and speed. Pandemonium erupted as the dark bay reared on his hind legs, striking out at whoever was unlucky enough to be in his path.

Several men went down. It all happened so quickly, she couldn't tell if they'd fallen, been kicked, or merely dove out of the way.

Another figure appeared in the doorway of the railcar, a towering man to match the thunderous voice commanding everyone to get back.

At the sound of the man's bellow, the stallion stopped its flailing, and simply bolted. Not toward the trainyard or the road, but toward the still-emptying passenger platform not fifteen strides away. Smythe gave a yelp as he was yanked into the air, and an audible crack might have been his shoulder dislocating.

If he was lucky.

Alexandra glanced behind her to ascertain if any passengers were left, spying an elderly couple frantically helping each other toward the cloakroom. Beyond them, a bleary-eyed mother struggled to heave a carpetbag and push a pram. A girl of perhaps five clutched at her skirts, pointing to the advancing stallion with a screech. The mother turned to admonish the girl, but her words died as she spotted the steed. She froze for a precious, petrified moment before dropping her bag and doing what she could to wrestle both children out of the way.

Turning back, Alexandra gaped at how much closer the stallion had galloped in a matter of seconds.

Poor Smythe! Snagged in the rope he'd wound around his arm, he was dragged like a sack of grain through the mud. His head barely avoided the horse's churning hooves. He worked vigorously to unwind himself, but she couldn't tell if he made headway.

Alexandra searched the vicinity for help for one more frantic breath. No man could be found on the platform, conductor, constable, workman, or otherwise.

Why did she bother looking? When had a man ever come to her aid?

The septuagenarian couple had almost shuffled to the relative safety of the cloakroom, but the mother had no chance.

An idea occurred to Alexandra as a crack of thunder spurred the creature on.

Sweat bloomed inside her gloves.

Time slowed as the bay stallion gathered his muscles for the small leap from the ground onto the platform.

The metal of horseshoes clattered like hammers against the planks. He shot past Alexandra and aimed his one-ton body toward the terrified mother and the few panicking passengers beyond.

Alexandra dropped her umbrella and leaped toward one of the long ropes trailing behind the beast.

Seizing it in her gloved hands, she set her feet and leaned her hips back, putting all her weight into yanking the horse's lead around.

The stallion's head jerked to the side, and with a recalcitrant neigh, his monstrous body followed.

There was no time to think.

Until the whites disappeared from the stallion's eyes, she had to keep him off balance. She darted toward him, tucking her body next to his long middle as she tugged his lead forcefully around with her, compelling him to turn in a continuous circle.

Belatedly, she noticed the other lead rope was empty. The stallion's jump somehow scraped Smythe from his lead.

A quick glance found the young porter in the mud, unmoving.

The beast snorted and tossed his head, but after a few circles, his stamping turned to prancing, which she considered a victory.

It occurred to her with a sense of growing alarm that she hadn't the slightest idea what to do next. The man with the compelling baritone had mentioned blinders. On the next rotation, she snatched up her open black umbrella, and somehow managed to lower it over both their heads, narrowing their entire scope of the world to that of each other.

Alexandra kept her eyes locked with the breathtaking creature, the vapors of her breath keeping time with the deep pants of his flaring nostrils.

"There you are," she crooned, maintaining their circles, but slowing the pace. "I'm not fond of thunderstorms either, all told. Or crowds of rowdy men. Is it any great wonder you've misbehaved?"

The beast snorted his displeasure.

"I agree. You have every right to be cross," she commiserated. "You didn't ask to be dragged here in a cramped and cold train. What you need is a dry paddock, some fresh hay, and warm mash to wait out the storm. Doesn't that sound lovely?"

As pleasant as her one-sided conversation may have appeared, Alexandra wished someone, *anyone,* would relieve her of the beast. Now that the mother and children were safe, a sudden weakness in *her* knees threatened an imminent collapse. If she stopped, she'd surely melt into a puddle of quaking nerves.

Both she and the creature tensed when another flash of lightning blinked around them, but the umbrella kept him steady as they continued their haphazard merry-go-round.

She breathed out a sigh, and resumed murmuring nonsensical pleasantries to the stallion. Dim sounds from outside permeated their odd little universe. The chaos of the men below the platform. The crying of an infant. The intensifying patter of rain against the shingled roof.

Heavy boots taking measured steps up the platform stairs.

"Young miss, can you follow the sound of my voice?"

A shiver of chills danced up her spine that had nothing to do with her soaked garments or the sideways rain. Not fear, exactly. Awareness. Every single hair on her body tuned to the direction of that voice.

Young miss? She was neither young nor a miss.

Could she follow him? If Saint Patrick had had a voice like that, he'd not have had to drive the snakes from Ireland. They'd have trailed him willingly.

Followed him to their doom.

Because his was certainly not the voice of a saint, nor anything belonging to the heavenly hosts. The cavernous timbre contained too many shadows. But not the eerie, repellent kind.

The kind that enticed. Tempted. The sort of shadows which shielded criminal deeds and concealed desires.

The most dangerous shadows of all.

Ones she'd learned to avoid in the most violent way possible.

She realized she hadn't answered his question. "I—I can't."

"It's all right. I'll come to you and take his other lead. But I'll need you to give me the umbrella."

He'd assumed her hesitation was caused by the unpredictable horse, and in truth it should be. Were she any other woman, with any other past, two thousand pounds of horseflesh would, indeed, be more petrifying than two hundred pounds of man.

The truth of it was, she'd rather take her chances with

an unruly equine beast, than to approach the man who belonged to the fury contained in the depths of that voice.

A fury imperceptible to most anyone, but not her.

She'd never again be caught unawares. For ten years since, she'd trained herself to listen. To find the thread of vibrations beneath societal niceties and appropriate fallacies.

And beneath *his* gentle direction lurked an unfathomable bleakness . . . and a banked ferocity that might singe through her soaked clothing and burn the flesh below.

She was about to reply when the train let out one last shrill from its whistle and a simultaneous release of steam from beneath.

The stallion leaped sideways, away from the white clouds billowing up from the mist. His shoulder knocked Alexandra from her feet and into a post.

The weight of the beast lifted immediately as he bucked away, taking her breath with him.

She crumpled into the steam and fog, her mouth open in a silent cry. Her lungs screamed, but her ribs refused to relent as she gulped for air.

She lay on her side, besieged by pain and panic and an encroaching darkness. Wishing, struggling, *praying* for a breath. She felt lost in the mist, worried that she'd sink beneath it forever and simply disappear.

Black spots danced in her vision. Or was it black boots and dark hooves?

Sweltering curses rose above terrified neighs.

Creature pitted against creature. Beast against beast.

Eventually, the man won. *Of course* he won.

Man was ever the better beast.

CHAPTER TWO

Alexandra didn't breathe. Hooves clopped away. Disappeared. Boots stomped their own thunder into the planks beneath her ear.

Faint strings of rapid, angry conversation permeated the fog.

"Find me the sod . . . secure him in the railcar . . . painful execution." That voice.

"Impossible . . . grace . . . was back in London . . ." Another voice. Harried. Afraid.

"What fucking imbecile . . . whistle in the middle of such a crisis . . ."

". . . the conductor cooling . . . couldn't see her . . . the storm . . . terrible . . . grace."

Impossible grace. Terrible grace? Consciousness threatened to desert Alexandra as she tried to make sense of the broken conversation.

Grace was often both impossible or terrible.

But it wasn't meant to be, was it?

Grace was salvation. Divine forgiveness. Would she be granted either?

Likely not.

"Someone will hang for this!" the now familiar voice bellowed, much closer than before.

"Y-yes, you're—"

"*Where* is she?" Fury scalded every word with brimstone heat.

I'm here on the ground, she thought. *Or am I lost?*

Better to remain beneath the notice of his fury. Better for everyone. Perhaps if she just gave herself to the mist, if she disappeared, all the scandal and sorrow would follow her into the darkness. It wouldn't touch her loyal friends, nor would it besmirch what little was left of her family name.

Perhaps this was the solution she'd been searching for.

A heroic death.

As she entertained the terrible thought, black boots appeared from the mist, just before tremendous knees landed beside her.

It was the weight of two strong, careful hands roaming her person that finally sent a full breath screaming into her lungs.

"No!" she shrieked.

Or, rather, croaked inaudibly.

"Don't move." Rough palms snagged the shoulders and bodice of her herringbone tweed traveling kit as she helplessly drew greedy breaths into her chest. "Not until I know if anything's been broken." He exerted gentle pressure on her ribs and, though it was tender, no pain greeted his touch.

Only terror.

And . . . something else.

Alexandra couldn't struggle. Her limbs didn't seem to understand their purpose.

It was her nightmare come to life.

How many times had she battled the dark? A faceless man holding her down, his hands roving her body as her limbs refused to obey her.

Electric shivers coursed through disobedient nerves, returning her strength as unexpectedly as the lightning. She tried to shrink from him, to roll over, and to lash out all at once. The resulting spasm more resembled a seizure than a retreat.

"Someone get a doctor!" he barked, muttering beneath his breath, "And a bloody undertaker."

"No need." Her words came more easily now, lent sound by her slowly returning breath. "I'll live."

She jerked her ankle from his grip, but he caught it and pressed it back to the ground. "The undertaker is for the conductor after I murder him—I thought I told you not to move."

"Nothing's broken." She kicked her leg as though his hand were a bug she intended to shake off her skirts. "I don't need a doctor. Kindly unhand my ankle."

To her astonishment, he complied, returning to bend over her. Loom over her, more like, a swarthy, sinister shock of a man rising from the mists.

The rain had soaked through his shirtsleeves—which must have been white at one time or another—rendering it iridescent, if not obsolete.

Beneath, he'd the chiseled-marble build of a Greek hero, and the features of a Greek tragedy. Shoulders and arms to impress Atlas. A torso to rival the statue of Ares she'd once admired in Hadrian's Villa.

And all the unhallowed malice Hades could summon.

Such scars.

It would be easy to imagine the gods, ever unduly punitive to a mortal who dare challenge their strength or beauty, had sent a creature to rake demonic claws across features so flawless.

"Can you breathe normally?" he demanded. "How do you feel?" The questions might have been gentle if they'd hailed from a chest with a less barbaric depth.

"I feel . . . erm . . ." How *did* she feel? What did she feel? "I feel as though I've been crushed by a horse." She wheezed a vague attempt at levity. "But I can breathe fine and am more bruised than broken."

"You are lucky," he clipped, grasping her hand. "I think you shaved twenty years off my life in twenty seconds."

"What do you think you are doing?" She tried to snatch her hand away, but he held fast, relieving her of her traveling gloves.

"Searching for rope burns." He spread her fingers wide with rough thumbs, examining her upturned palms. "Your gloves were but scraps of nothing."

"I am unharmed," she protested, trying to ignore how warm his skin felt against hers, despite the rain. How small and pale her hands appeared when cupped in his rough, square paws.

How fiendishly strong his fingers were. How helpless she'd be against that strength.

She yanked on his grip with unnecessary violence, tightening her hands into fists and hiding them in her skirts. "As—as I stated before, I'll live."

"So it would seem." A wet chill replaced the warmth his hands had provided, matching the frigid note in his voice.

Alexandra forced herself to look into eyes as electric blue as the lightning, a crystalline clearness almost void of color, and no less sinister for the features into which they'd been set. The scars had something to do with that, certainly.

The shortest of the wounds branched from the dark hairline at his temple and interrupted his eyebrow. Had his dark hair, slicked back by rain, not concealed the wound, she wagered she could follow it high into his scalp. The longest fissure blazed across a sharp cheekbone into a well-kept beard, appearing again as a merciless gash through his lush lips.

Lush? Great Caesar and his glory, had she struck her head?

Alexandra blinked once. And again. Unsuccessfully attempting to tear her gaze from his mouth. Lips so soft simply didn't *belong* on a face so brutish as his. The incongruity both perplexed and compelled her.

"Are you able to stand?" His tone turned as wintry as the storm.

He'd caught her staring.

Alexandra snapped her eyes shut in mortification. He probably assumed she'd been gawking rather than admiring.

Not that she *had* been admiring.

She *hadn't*—wasn't—wouldn't *dream* of—

His hands manacled her arms, but before she could draw a breath of protest they were both on their feet. He released her the moment they were upright.

Alexandra reeled, her world pitching as much from the brief physical contact as the abrupt change of posture. She reached for the post to steady herself, and instead found a disc of hot muscle stretched beneath cool, wet linen. His chest twitched beneath her palm, as if the touch had surprised him as mightily as it did her.

She snatched her hand back into the cradle of her own

chest. The warmth of his flesh again lingered, she noted with no little alarm.

"F-forgive me, I'm a little unsteady."

"Are you certain you don't need a doctor?" He stepped forward, concern etching his scars deeper as his arms reached out to provide a buffer should she fall.

Alexandra shifted out of his reach most ungracefully. "No!" She put up a hand to stop him, fully aware how useless it was to try. No world existed in which her feeble strength could be pitted against his in her favor. "No, I—I am quite unharmed. See? No need to concern yourself further."

Lord, she couldn't look at him again. He was simply too big. Too—male. Despite his cultured accent, he didn't appear at all civilized. Indeed, he could have belonged to the scores of rowdy and robust men her professors had hired to protect them in unknown countries.

Men she'd spent a decade doing her best to avoid.

A silent and solemn stare made most anyone uncomfortable enough to flee her presence. It'd worked on everyone from desert marauders to determined matrons with notions of a convenient marriage for their sons. She'd wielded it with some expertise for years now.

So, why couldn't she make herself lift her eyes from the mist? Why did the warmth of his skin linger in such a strange fashion? Why did her lungs still refuse to fully inflate?

Perhaps she *did* need a doctor.

"I'm trying to decide if you're incredibly brave or exceptionally stupid." His imperious tone broke her stupor.

Her eyes snapped to his, her fears shoved behind indignation. "I beg your pardon?"

"What were you thinking trying to control a beast of

Mercury's proportions? You saw what he did to that idiot porter and the lad is half again your size!" His frown deepened the interruption of the scar on his lip.

"I was *thinking* poor Smythe might be killed if someone didn't do something." Remembering the boy, she turned to where a few men helped him limp away. Smythe's thin face was one heart-squeezing grimace of pain as he cradled his arm to his chest. Half of his penciled mustache had washed off in the mud, leaving his aching youth exposed.

"Is he going to be all right?" She took an unconscious step toward the procession.

"There's a sawbones not a stone's throw from the railyard. He'll set the boy's shoulder and send him home with morphine. Do you know him?"

She shook her head, disconcerted to discover the notice she and her companion had garnered from the remaining passengers, workmen, and railway employees. "We'd only just met when he carried my bags, but what does that matter? I still didn't want to see him hurt . . . or worse."

The man gave her his back, bending to retrieve both her gloves and his. Alexandra resolutely averted her gaze from the trousers stretching across his backside. Had she ever in her life noticed such a thing? Forcing a swallow, she took the opportunity to investigate the condition of her own suit. Mud and whatever other unmentionable slicks of dark grime now soiled her smart white blouse and beige jacket beyond repair. Her skirt had fared better, but only just.

"Better him than you."

His low words froze her hand midair, leaving her coiffure uninvestigated. "I'm sorry?"

He said nothing, extending his hand to offer the soiled corpses of her gloves. A muscle tic appeared at his hard jaw, causing his third scar, mostly concealed by the black beard, to pulse in time to his ire.

"Thank you, sir."

Azure beams of inquisition roamed her from beneath satirical brows. "Though your actions were unduly reckless, that was well done of you. Where did you learn to handle horses?"

The admiration warming his words prickled irritating awareness across her skin. "A camel herder on the Arabian Peninsula once demonstrated to me that very trick on his own beast. I hadn't any idea it worked on horses before today."

He blinked several times before echoing, "A camel herder . . ."

She nodded, the memory animating her. "His tribe could often pack their entire household on a camel's back. Imagine how devastating such a display of beastly temper would have been in his case."

"Devastating." He repeated slower this time, intently regarding her for a pregnant moment.

"Of course, *his* animals were much more properly trained." She shot a pointed glance to the horse cart, where the beast, Mercury, was now blinded and hobbled between the four mares.

The man's lips—why couldn't she stop glancing at them?—did the opposite of what she'd expected. He wasn't smiling. But he wasn't *not* smiling, either.

Those lips parted, then paused.

She likewise hesitated, sensing an as yet unidentified awareness hovering over them like a curious bee. The buzz of silence grew louder the more still they stood.

Should she make some sort of introduction? They'd already broken the rules of civility by exchanging so many words without a presentation by a third party. However, judging by his broadcloth trousers and mud-stained shirt-sleeves, he wasn't a man who lived by civil rule. Nor by that of nobility. Indeed, he was indolent about his attire. As though he couldn't be bothered to have dressed properly to go into town.

He finally broke the silence. "It is . . . fortunate you're unharmed, Miss . . ."

"Lane. Alexandra Lane." Her first inclination was to curtsy, but she ultimately decided to do what she'd done with most men of his social standing from students and factory workers in America, to stone masons and professors in Cairo. She offered her sullied hand for a congenial shake. The working class tended to like that sort of greeting nowadays.

He regarded it as though she'd shoved a rank fish beneath his nose.

Alexandra faltered. Just who was he to put on airs? No gentleman, certainly. For what gentleman would wear his hair longer than his collar? Or work in public without a vest? Or grow anything more unruly than a trim mustache, scars or no scars?

Right as she'd decided to retract her offer, she found her hand once again enveloped in warm solid steel.

He shook twice, the calluses on his palms catching on her skin as his hand slid away. Little shocks rasped at her, as though every insubstantial ridge on his fingertip was electrified with sensation.

"May I inquire as to your destination, Miss Lane? Or is it Mrs.?" Something smoothed the gravel from his voice, as though he'd poured honey over the shards of stone.

"D-doctor," she blurted.

The muscles about his neck tensed, as he went instantly alert. "I thought you said you didn't need a doctor."

"No, it's *Doctor* Lane."

His chin rose a few notches. "Women aren't allowed to practice as physicians in England."

As if she weren't aware. "I earned my degree some time ago at the Sorbonne, if you must know."

"Some time ago?" The words seemed to amuse him. "How many *ages* have passed, I wonder?"

"That's of little consequence," she said crisply, painfully aware her freckles and pert nose still made her appear a few years younger than twenty and eight. "But if you *must* know, I am a doctor of history. An archeologist, all told, my field of expertise being that of ancient civilizations."

"Thus . . . the camels." He reached out, trailing a finger down the collar of her traveling suit. "And the tweed."

She jerked away. "You are too familiar, sir."

His hand remained suspended midair for the briefest of moments before returning to his side.

"My apologies." He seemed neither impressed nor censorious. Nor did his apology contain much in the way of penitence. But she had the sense she'd surprised him just as readily as he had shocked her. "As recompense for your troubles on behalf of my beast, I'd be delighted to conduct you to your destination in my coach-and-four. Or are you waiting on someone, *Doctor* Lane?"

The undue emphasis on the word grated at her. She glanced again toward the dusty work cart to which the four new equine arrivals were tied. Its shoddy if sturdy construction so incongruous with the handsome and stately coaches awaiting or conducting well-bred wedding guests.

Coach-and-four? Oh please. Of all the cheek.

She lifted her chin. "Cecil is tardy but will be along shortly."

That's right, she thought. *Best you move along.* The last thing she needed was to be alone with a man so drenched he might as well have been half naked and dripping with as much virility as he did rainwater.

She had a feeling even the little pistol she kept in her handbag wouldn't stop a man of his size should he take it into his head to—

"Just as well." He jerked his gloves back over his hands, turning the scarred side of his face away from her. "I need to take this beast to Castle Redmayne, where he'll be taught to behave like a gentleman."

Not by this lout, surely.

"Castle Redmayne? You look after the beasts there?"

His lip twitched once more, and Alexandra had the errant suspicion a dimple lurked beneath his beard.

"That I do. I've a great many responsibilities there."

"Well, don't let me keep you from them." Alexandra turned to the road, making a great show of scanning for her conveyance. Her gaze kept blinking back to him, though, just to make sure he'd not surreptitiously moved closer.

At her dismissal, his eyes went flat, and she thought he might have readied himself to deliver a flippant retort before a little body thrust herself between them.

Alexandra found herself the prisoner of a five-year-old's exuberant gratitude.

"Mummy says to thank you," she crowed, clutching at Alexandra's knees through soiled skirts. "You saved us."

"Oh, yes, miss!" huffed the woman as she hurried over, her baby clutched to her breast. "I've never seen the like in me life. You're so brave, miss. I can't thank you enough." The infant was unexpectedly shoved into Alexandra's arms. A soft, familiar ache settled with the little bundle against Alexandra's chest just beneath where the baby rested.

After the mother's interruption, more bystanders and

railway agents rushed forward with hearty exclamations, showering her with praise and expressions of concern.

Alexandra caught the sight of *his* retreating shoulders as he sauntered toward the cart. As though sensing her gaze upon him, he paused, and glanced over his shoulder.

Even from a distance, the blue of his eyes was striking. Preternaturally so. From so far away, they could almost be white.

He nodded, and so did she, realizing that she still didn't know his name.

"You've been saved by the devil, miss." The mother regarded him from behind wary eyes. "The Terror of Torcliff."

"The whom?"

"Oh, aye." The woman leaned in conspiratorially. "They say he's been slashed by a werewolf."

Alexandra had to work very hard not to wrinkle her nose. "That sounds rather . . ." *Preposterous. Absurd. Unbelievable.* "Rather unlikely, doesn't it?"

The woman gave a shrug, stroking the cheek of the baby in Alexandra's arms. How well it fit there. How tiny and lovely it was. "All's I know is, since *he* came back to Castle Redmayne, the mists have been strange."

That seized Alexandra's attention away from the gurgling infant. "Strange how?"

"Just like this here!" She expanded her arms to encompass the station, only just showing signs of recovery from the ordeal. "An animal knows when a devil is about, me Gran always said. No wonder the horse spooked. Danger lives in these vapors. Devils and demons and the like."

"Surely you don't believe he's a demon." Alexandra wasn't a superstitious woman, but a chill snaked its way through her, lifting every hair on her body.

The woman shrugged. "Misfortune haunts every black

soul who lives in Castle Redmayne. Drives them to all manner of lunacy." She jerked her chin toward where Alexandra's savior had disappeared. "And the Terror of Torcliff has known more than his share. The devil's touched him twice, they say."

Alexandra thought of his hands on her. Of the strange sensations they elicited.

"The Terror of Torcliff," she whispered. A devil best left alone.

CHAPTER THREE

Piers dragged a towel across his hair and down the ruined side of his face, wiping away chilling rivulets of rain as he leaned against the stable door. All the while, his thoughts lingered on the feminine curves his hands had negotiated only an hour or so prior. On the most arresting figure of an extraordinary woman.

He'd wrested the blasted stallion into his stall and made certain the animal was given hot mash and a dry blanket.

Not that the blighter deserved it.

Alexandra Lane. He grunted out a steaming breath, testing the syllables in his mind as he had a hundred times in the last hundred minutes.

Alexandra Lane. Sounded more like an address than a bedeviling female.

One would think, when searching for bone breaks or wounds, that the curve of a hip or the length of a thigh beneath all those skirts wouldn't make any sort of lasting impression. Especially not to a man so familiar with the female form as he.

And yet.

His hand twitched each time he recalled the weight of her own palm against his. He could exactly recollect the flare of her waist. The quirk of her lip. The delicate structure of her, not at all shaped by a corset.

Just sensible tweed and womanly flesh.

Alexandra Lane. A confounding dichotomy of iniquity and innocence.

She'd conversed with camel keepers and successfully acquired a doctorate at the Sorbonne.

One touch from him, though, and the lady threatened conniptions.

Not a lady, he corrected himself.

A doctor.

The bloody woman had gone to war with his new stallion and *won.* She'd possibly saved several lives, and had nearly been crushed to death. The moment she'd caught her breath, she'd forgotten to be upset about any of it.

Fearless.

But she'd snatched her hand from *his* as though he'd burned her. She'd been unable to even look at him until he'd rankled her.

Because he'd terrified her.

To be fair, he alarmed and disgusted everyone he met, especially before they accustomed themselves to his fairly new and startlingly dreadful appearance. And yet, something about his interaction with the doctor struck an unfamiliar note. A note that lodged in his head like a song that, when finished, would simply start again until it drove one mad.

He'd frightened her. But . . .

She'd shrunk from him, obviously. Evaded his touch. His gaze. But when goaded, she'd met him head-on with clear eyes and condemnation. Going so far as to engage him in conversation.

He'd spoken more words to Alexandra Lane than he had to anyone in more than a year.

In their moments together, he'd not detected a trace of true disgust. Fear, but not revulsion.

In fact, he'd imagined for a brief moment that he'd read admiration in her whisky eyes. The kind of feminine appreciation his looks had entitled him to his entire life before *the incident.*

Which made absolutely no fucking sense.

In his experience, people often reviled what they feared, or vice versa. So, if she wasn't repulsed by him, why fear him?

Had he been mistaken? Had he read admiration where none existed?

Perhaps his physical reaction to her had somehow interfered with his powers of observation, and his speculation was nothing but fanciful tripe.

A latent yearning for a captivating woman to return his desire.

Because it had been ages. Or, at least, what seemed like ages.

Glancing up toward the turrets of Castle Redmayne with frank detestation, he tossed the cloth aside with undue violence.

It would be ages more. Possibly never.

Tugging his damp shirt from his trousers, he whipped it down his shoulders, away from the chill bumps blooming on his skin. God's blood, it was cold. Cold as gray stone and the merciless sea.

This place. This fucking castle had always been thus, he imagined. Cold. Empty. Miserable. From the moment the Viking, Magnus Redmayne, had mercilessly claimed Torcliff and the surrounding land, up until the current fucking useless lord, it seemed that nothing at all could make this place hospitable.

Piers glared out into the unrelenting storm across the vast castle estates and down to the treacherous red cliffs. Maynemouth Moor, where fifes and fishermen had once lived, had lately been renovated into charming cottages and even boasted a seaside resort.

Where is Dr. Lane resting her head tonight? he idly wondered. In some cozy stone bungalow with an equally erudite man, no doubt. Cecil, did she mention his name was?

Lucky bugger.

They probably pored over maps together, speaking animatedly about curious dig sites, and cursed tombs.

Cecil. He spat on the ground. What a name. Probably wore spectacles and a smart mustache. Likely had a hunchback from bending over texts, soft, scholarly hands and— Piers stroked his beard—and a weak chin. At least he hoped the punter was possessed of a weak chin. Or weak arms, at least.

Piers pictured them in one of the little homes on the moor hunkered over a well-worn desk using bloody, damned—he didn't know what—magnifying glasses and cartographer tools or some such.

Cecil would make a terrible pun. She'd lift her delicate chin and laugh with her entire body, her eyes sparkling with tears of merriment. They'd take dinner. And drinks. Sherry or brandy.

Piers's lip curled at the thought, tightening his scar. A painful reminder why a woman like that would rather have academic Cecil over a hard-hearted huntsman like him.

He kept all the beasts at the accursed Castle Redmayne.

So, what was it about this storm that made him envisage another destiny? What if he'd been born another man?

Suddenly that cottage on the cliffs became something else. The man at the table wasn't good old Cecil.

Dr. Lane greeted Piers, instead, with enthusiastic kisses and a lively story about a runaway horse. Before unpacking the maps and magnifying glasses, he'd light the golden lanterns and check her properly for bruises. Peel away her soiled kit and bathe the chill from her bones. He'd stretch her out upon a rickety brass bed that made unholy noises and proceed to welcome her home properly.

After, he'd feed her from his hands and watch her features beam with enthusiasm as she discussed fucking Borneo or wherever she'd returned from.

Maybe, in this pleasant fiction, they'd take their restless spirits and find meaning and fulfillment reading the bones of the dead.

And why not? Let Cecil keep the beasts at Castle Redmayne.

A sheet of brilliant lightning blanketed the sky, reflecting off the turbulent ocean below the cliffs and wiping away the image he'd so preposterously invoked of a life he could never have.

Christ. When did he develop a penchant for revolting sentimentality?

Piers stared into the dark storm long enough for his entire torso to go numb, watching as one by one the cottages at Maynemouth Moor tucked in for the night.

Best he never saw Alexandra Lane again. The strange longings she evoked were both unsettling and bloody dispiriting. He'd a long and terrible retribution to attend to, and then there were the beasts to consider.

Both within and without the castle.

Though maybe he'd keep her in that cottage on the cliff, locked in his mind.

And when he had a moment to himself, he'd visit her there.

Alexandra combed her fingers through her hair one last time, deciding the fire had dried it well enough.

She glanced around Cecelia's chamber, gilded with golds and greens and delicate crystal, and thought about the history that haunted these stone walls. Francesca would be lucky to be part of the story this keep would tell, not that she'd care. The countess—soon-to-be duchess— would be more interested in the size of the stables than the state of the tapestries.

Castle Redmayne might have been a drafty old keep, but it was in excellent repair and boasted fireplaces large enough to burn a heretic or two should the need arise.

Pressing her hands to her heated cheeks, Alexandra considered sloughing off her robe to cool down. Her attention snagged on the large ancient shutters resting upon iron hinges which kept the storm at bay. Or would have, once upon a time, before a recent clever duke had sturdy windows installed within the old casements.

She'd rather it be cool inside, so she could keep her layers of clothing on.

She always felt more comfortable in layers.

"I'm going to open a window to let in a bit of fresh air," Alexandra called to Cecelia, who was finishing her nighttime ablutions in the washroom.

"Capital idea, old fellow!" Cecelia called back, quite clearly cleaning her teeth from the garbled sound of her words.

Alexandra smiled as she padded to the window and undid the latch. Once the great wooden panels had been secured against the wall, she turned the delicate handle to the window glass, and pushed it open.

Poor Cecelia had been racked with guilt over her tardiness, she'd exclaimed a thousand apologies, painfully aware that had she been on time with the carriage, Alexandra might not have had her encounter with the stallion.

Nor with the—

Alexandra's mouth fell open.

Nor with the *stablemaster*.

The very one who stood across the gently sloping grounds, outlined in lantern light as he leaned against the wide-open stable doors in a pose most pensive.

The Terror of Torcliff.

She instinctively shifted out of his view, but it became apparent that his focus was not the castle at all but the village past the moors or the black swath of sea beyond.

Of course he was still at the stables. The new horses would have to be padded down for the night and the great stallion checked for wounds caused by his misadventure.

The man's features were concealed by the distance, the darkness, and the storm, but Alexandra knew immediately it was *him*. In all her travels, she couldn't remember meeting a man with his proportions.

Perhaps in effigy, or immortalized in stone or marble, but not in reality.

When she had seen him that afternoon, his dark hair had been slicked back by rainwater, but now it hung about his eyes in jagged tufts, as though he'd mussed it in a futile attempt to keep it dry in such weather.

What did he search for in the distance? Alexandra glanced over to the lovely little village and to the edges of the moor, the golden glow of the town ending in an abrupt horizon at the cliffs. It was an unparalleled vista, but her eyes found their way back to the outline of the man. Had he moved? Could he see her?

Likely not. The light was dim in Cecelia's rooms, and the windows of the round tower in which they were housed faced more toward the sea than the stables. Had she not been leaning out to open the windowpane, she'd have missed him altogether.

With a few swift and impatient movements, the man jerked his shirt from the waist of his trousers and ripped it from his shoulders and down his arms before discarding it.

Alexandra clapped her hand over her mouth. Then her eyes. Then her mouth again.

Even from across the lawn, the light silhouetted him so clearly, she could make out the distinctive latissimus dorsi flaring with strength across his back. His shoulders—deltoids—rounded and sloped to his neck in a broad, beautiful sweep.

Arrested by the sight, Alexandra didn't blink until her eyes burned.

Why would he disrobe? To shapeshift, perhaps?

The odd and errant thought shamed and irritated her. Really, what a ludicrous notion. A werewolf indeed. She'd spent a great deal of her life in the company of mummys' curses, resident demons and devils, superstitions, and gods. She understood the science behind them.

Or the lack thereof.

That such a misconception should reside in her own enlightened empire elicited a sigh for the whole of humanity.

She had seen more than her share of bare masculine torsos. Laborers in Cairo. Tribesmen in sub-Saharan Africa. Even a native on display in America once.

Never had she paid them the least bit of mind. In fact, she'd avoided noticing anything about the male physique beyond their bones.

The dead could do no damage.

The dead . . . had none of what made a man dangerous. The things that had lent them life had turned to dust. Strength, blood, muscle, flesh.

Sex.

All of it disintegrated, leaving only a story.

But . . . a man like the one who stood before her detained her notice against her will. Against her fear and her better judgment.

He was built to defy the gods. It seemed impossible that someday he'd be nothing but a pile of bones.

Really, who needed all that superfluous muscle?

A man who rode and trained beasts three times his weight, she supposed.

A hunter.

Alexandra squeezed her eyes shut, banishing all speculative thoughts from her unruly mind. Probably the idiot man wrestled a bear or something equally ridiculous. He was the kind likely drawn to chaos and depraved conduct.

Better that she not look. Better she not *enjoy* what she looked at. Because he was the kind of man who could easily steal from her what she'd fought for years to regain.

Her dignity. Her sanity.

Her body.

"What a magnificent view." Cecelia's unexpected voice so close to her ear would have startled a scream from her had her breath not been locked in her chest.

"Yes," Alexandra wheezed, finding her composure. "Yes, the vista of the sea is incomparable, wouldn't you agree?"

"I wasn't at all referring to the landscape." Cecelia

rubbed her spectacles on the sleeve of her gown and re-placed them on the bridge of her nose, blinking down in the direction of the stables. "They certainly do breed a different kind of man out here in the bucolic south, don't they?"

"I'm certain I hadn't noticed." Alexandra turned from the casement.

She glanced back at Cecelia just in time to catch her friend's pitying look. She quickly hid it beneath a dimpled smile just a touch brighter than the moment warranted.

For such a statuesque woman, Cecelia floated when she walked, her dressing gown of shimmering scarlet silk whispering against her feet. "What do you suppose is keeping Frank? I'm dying to see her."

Alexandra glanced at the door. "I couldn't begin to imagine. Her fiancé, perhaps?"

"Fiancé . . ." Cecelia's expression of concern deepened. "Doesn't it feel strange that Frank has never mentioned a betrothal to a duke all this time?"

The thought had occurred to Alexandra more than once. "Perhaps she didn't know?"

"Perhaps . . ." Cecelia lowered herself to the edge of a chair opposite the fire, her hair catching the exact color of the dancing flames. "I'm not inclined to think poorly of her but . . . do you think she simply didn't say? Because of the vow we took never to marry?"

Alexandra considered it, then shook her head. "That doesn't sound like Francesca. Of all of us, she's the one least likely to hold her tongue."

"True, but we've all become rather deft at keeping secrets."

My fault. The weight under which Alexandra constantly lived compounded with a new heavy stone of guilt. It buckled her knees, collapsing her into the chair opposite Cecelia.

Because their secret was in danger of being a secret no longer, and soon she would have to relay that to her accomplices. She'd been keeping the wolves at bay for ten long years, and now . . .

Cecelia continued, blissfully unaware of her thoughts. "If Francesca doesn't want to marry this Redmayne, why not simply call off the betrothal instead of throwing a masquerade and only *then* imploring our help? She's trapped somehow. I can feel it."

Guilt needled Alexandra once more; she had been too lost in her own difficulties of late. She clung to Cecelia's hand like it was a mooring line in a sea storm. "If she's in danger, we'll do whatever it takes to get her out of it, won't we?" she said with a forced confidence she didn't exactly feel.

"Always. We've conquered bigger demons than that of the Duke of Redmayne." Ever the shrewd examiner, Cecelia studied her through her spectacles "Alexander, are you all right?"

Are you all right?

It was a question people asked of women who'd survived what she had. Even after all these years. *Are you all right?*

The answer was categorically . . . No.

She'd not been all right for longer than a decade. She'd been recovered. Repurposed. She'd been content, if not happy. And accomplished, if not all right.

In truth, ten years had softened the edges of the pain. Had allowed for more sleep and fewer nightmares. Had lessened the trembling and shame and had increased the number of days between the flashes of memory that left her sobbing and scouring her skin in scalding water. Along with a million other allowances and distractions and efforts she made to cultivate a life of purpose and passion, she'd still tended to her loneliness as fervently as she had her friendship with the two extraordinary women she loved most in this world.

Because loneliness was safer than love.

In all, ten years had made her less of a liar every time she smiled and replied to the question with, "Yes, I'm quite all right."

But tonight, she couldn't give that answer. Because she wasn't even approaching all right. And when her friends heard what she had to disclose, they wouldn't be either. Perhaps now was the time to tell her.

"Cecelia, I'm—"

The door burst open and a streak of red and black fluttered in before it slammed again.

Francesca had never been one for knocking.

"Sweet Christ, am I glad to see you two." She panted as though she'd run a league.

The burst of energy had driven both Alexandra and Cecelia to their feet, and they rushed to embrace her as she held her arms wide in silent supplication of their support.

"What's happened, Frank?" they asked in tandem.

Francesca's emerald eyes glinted with solemnity not at all typical of her character. "I need you to help me find proof that the Duke of Redmayne's family murdered my parents," she revealed in a clandestine whisper. "Because if any of them find out who I really am, I might be next."

CHAPTER FOUR

Alexandra gaped at Francesca in dumbfounded silence.

The Countess of Mont Claire had always been a stranger to gravitas, so to see her porcelain skin stretched so tightly over her tense expression was alarming. She'd been possessed of a lean build since girlhood, but her strong cheekbones cut an even more dramatic angle and the cleft in her chin was more pronounced. Alexandra worried she'd not been eating.

As she clutched at the collar of her black silk robe, Francesca's countenance whitened to iridescent, setting her russet hair ablaze. "I don't know what to do."

"We should sit down for this." Cecelia took one of her hands, and Alexandra the other, pulling the distressed woman to the gold velvet settee across from the fire. "Would you like tea?"

"I tell you my life may be in danger, and you offer me tea?" Francesca regarded them as though they'd lost their minds.

Unperturbed, Cecelia made certain they were settled before gliding back toward the sideboard and preparing three cups. "Am I to take it that you decline?" She delicately poured the liquid over the tea strainer in each, before reaching for the sugar cubes.

Francesca huffed, then muttered, "Three cubes."

Cecelia had already plopped three into the first cup, two into Alexandra's and one into hers. The preparation had been the same for almost fifteen years, now.

She returned to distribute the saucers before settling herself in a graceful flourish, arranging her spectacles just so. "All right. Now let's do hear what calamity you've found yourself embroiled in."

Once Francesca found herself on the settee in the company of her trusted friends, she lost the bluster in her sails. She curled around her cup of tea like a vagrant would a fire on a winter's night.

"I'm not even certain where to start." She exhaled wearily. "I haven't allowed myself a moment's sleep the entire three days I've been at Castle Redmayne."

"Why are we here, Frank?" Alexandra asked over a careful sip of the amber liquid. "How is it possible you're getting married? And to someone you suspect of murder?"

Francesca's hand began to tremble, and she set her saucer down, untouched. "I didn't know of the betrothal contract until Redmayne summoned me."

"Summoned you?" Alexandra couldn't imagine strong-willed Francesca ever answering anything close to a summons.

"I would have declined," she admitted. "But I needed a reason to find a way into the castle. How else am I to ascertain if his family was responsible?"

"What makes you think they were?" Cecelia gulped down her cup of tea and poured another.

"Because, when I read the betrothal contract, I found something I couldn't ignore . . ."

"Which is?" Alexandra tucked her slippers beneath her, worrying the inside of her lip with her teeth.

"The date the contract was signed, was the very day prior to the massacre at Mont Claire," Francesca revealed.

Ever skeptical, Alexandra asked, "Have you any other evidence against them? The timing is suspicious but wouldn't bear water in court."

Francesca shook her head and let out a heavy, exhausted breath. "Every night, I've been scouring the castle, poring over various documents and historical texts, even the diaries and ledgers of the late Duke of Redmayne, and I'd found very little. But then I realized I'd been investigating the wrong Redmayne."

"Your betrothed, you mean?" Cecelia puzzled, conducting some hasty maths in her head. "He would have been all of . . . twelve when your family was killed."

Francesca became more animated, leaning forward to declare, "The mother, Gwyneth. She has a son from a previous marriage, one who was adopted by Redmayne, but could never be his ducal heir. Gwyneth's first husband was a Scotsman and, as it turns out, in line to inherit the Mont Claire title. I need to not only find out *how* close he was to inherit, but I'd also need to ascertain malicious intent on her part."

"Or on the part of the son." Alexandra placed a chilling puzzle piece in place. "Where is he now? And *who* is he? I suddenly wish I paid more attention to the *haute ton*."

Francesca leaned forward conspiratorially. "He sits on the Queen's Bench as Justice of the High Court."

Cecelia gasped. "You mean—"

"Yes. The High Court justice rumored to be the empire's next Lord Chancellor. Sir Cassius Ramsay."

"I've heard of His Worship." Cecelia made a face and set her tea down as if it had put her off. "He's said to be all fire and brimstone. Forbidding, merciless, and utterly moralistic."

Francesca shuddered. "Sounds horrifying."

Cecelia nodded her agreement. "The Vicar Teague plans to vote for him, if that's any indication."

It was all they needed.

"It certainly would help Ramsay's chances at a chancellorship with the traditionalists if he were to inherit an earldom," Alexandra ventured.

"It certainly would." Francesca's eyes sparkled with spite.

"Which gives him ample motive," Cecelia said.

Alexandra went to the sideboard and poured them all a spot of brandy, thinking that the news of the night certainly called for something stronger than tea.

And the worst was yet to come. She'd yet to reveal her blackmailer.

Francesca appeared both doubtful and indecisive as she mulled over her problem. "At the time of the massacre, Ramsay would have been seventeen. Almost eighteen. Old enough to commit a murder, but I wouldn't dare say old enough to instigate such a concentrated effort."

"The question remains, why, after all this time, would you be summoned to wed his younger brother? Does Redmayne really want to marry you? Or did Ramsay orchestrate the entire thing to lure you here in order to cut the last branch from the Cavendish family tree?"

"There really is no way of knowing until we find evidence." Cecelia brooded as she finished the plait in her hair. "It was right of you to call us here."

"And find it, we shall." Alexandra handed the ladies their brandies and touched the rim of her glass to theirs.

"You shan't be alone until we've uncoiled the mystery and discovered the culprit."

"Have you entirely eliminated the theory that the Duke of Redmayne simply fancies you and would like you to be his duchess?" Cecelia asked.

Alexandra gave her a fond smile. Cecelia's logic often battled with her innate sense of goodness and romantic naïveté. It was so beyond her to be anything but kind and honest that she forever fought the notion that others could be capable of brutality.

A grimace preceded Francesca's own distinctive eye roll. "That man is as fond of me as he would be of a rash on his arse, which is another reason I suspect his motives for marriage. Why wait until I'm a verified spinster before calling me to heel?"

It was an excellent question, Alexandra had to admit. "What is he like?"

Francesca stuck out her tongue. "He's not at all like a gentleman of his status should be. More concerned with hunting and horses and hounds than being a duke."

"I should think you'd like that," Cecelia said. "You love hunting and horses. And . . . probably hounds. Who doesn't like hounds? Is he handsome?"

Francesca shrugged, taking a generous swallow of her brandy. "He might have been once but now he's just a brutish old boor. Big, dark, and hairy. I hardly see him but he's dressed like a barbarian, rushing from one venture to another." Francesca made a face. "You'll meet him tomorrow, and see for yourselves how incredibly ill-suited we are. Were we to marry, our life would be years and years of senseless battles, him trying to put me in my place, and me trying to murder him in his sleep. I'm telling you, I won't do it."

"You won't have to," Alexandra soothed. "We'll help you out of this mess, one way or another."

"Our first order of business is to find a way into the duchess's locked rooms," Cecelia said. "Hopefully before the masquerade in two days' time. It's better if this is all sorted out before your betrothal to Redmayne becomes public."

"I agree." Alexandra expelled a troubled breath. "But how?"

"Tomorrow morning, Redmayne and I meet in his study with the solicitors," Francesca said. "I've gleaned that Redmayne keeps the key there in a box. I can pilfer it then and we can sneak away to the family wing during the masquerade."

"It seems too great a risk to take it right in front of his nose," Alexandra protested.

"You forget I've been a gypsy as well as a lady. I perfected sleight of hand much faster than I did French." Francesca held up Alexandra's bracelet with a victorious smile.

"I had no idea you were so skilled!" Cecelia clapped delighted hands as Alexandra set her teacup down so Francesca could fasten the small gold chain back on.

Cecelia yawned, stretching her voluptuous body in one lithe motion. Alexandra became certain all the men Cecelia studied with must struggle to keep their minds on mathematical figures, when her figure was on display.

"I'd almost hoped you'd fallen in love. Despite our vow," Cecelia confessed. "I find I should have liked to be Aunt Cecelia." She pursed her lips in a sly smile. "Or Uncle Cecil."

"Not to a Redmayne git, you wouldn't," Francesca snorted. "They're all inelegant Viking brutes with more strength than sense."

"Yes, but we'd teach them to be proper little heathens, wouldn't we?" Cecelia's eyes danced with mischief.

"Can you imagine? Me with a brood?" A shudder appeared to slide all the way down Francesca's spine. "I'd much rather remain a spinster until death, I'll thank you to remember."

Her friend's laughter spilled warmth over Alexandra's unsettled soul, the effect much like a languid bath.

Tomorrow, she promised herself. They could only handle one murderous crisis at a time. Tomorrow she'd reveal her own treacherous secret, and hope the women remembered this moment, because "until death" might just be sooner than they all thought.

To soothe the pervasive restlessness in his blood, Piers escaped the hoard of guests the next morning and unleashed Mercury on the Maynemouth Moors. He set off from the stables at a slow canter, warming Merc's muscles for a hard ride. If he turned right, he'd follow the lowland moors to the village. And so he pointed the stallion's head left, climbing and descending the soft slopes along the cliffs over toward the ruins of the old Redmayne fortress at Torcliff's edge. It was only a mile or so across gentle hills, and from there he could unleash Mercury's full speed over Dawlish Moor.

If he skirted the forest, he'd avoid the hunting party that had left before dawn, many of them still a bit knackered from the night before.

Mercury kicked dew from the vibrant clover and thick, mossy grasses beneath him, pumping his powerful neck as he cantered higher along the sea cliffs toward Torcliff's edge. The skeleton of the medieval Redmayne fortress slowly crumbled over a black cliff edifice into a hungry sea.

The ruin of a time when these shores were invaded, by forces of strong, greedy men.

Until one family was powerful enough to stop them and waves of marauders and enemies broke upon Redmayne strength.

As Piers galloped closer, he noted movement among the white and gray stones. Curious, he dismounted to investigate, climbing the old steps to the fortress tower, which claimed no ceiling but the sky.

Who would wander up this far at such an early hour? Not the hunters, surely. They'd stick to the forests on the other side of Tormund's Bluff, opposite the sea.

Puzzling patterns of colorful skirts twirled into the old courtyard as a trio of ladies, their chins all tilted to the sky, frolicked like a tumble of exuberant schoolgirls.

A feminine exclamation struck a chord of enthusiastic recognition in Piers that traveled all the way down to his sex. "Look at this place! It's a thousand years if it's a day. I'm itching to dig into the walls, to see what secrets are buried here."

Alexandra Lane.

The sight of her took the rhythm from his step, and he nearly tripped on a barnacle-crusted stone.

The sound of her unselfconscious laugh pilfered the breath from his lungs.

And when she'd noticed his approach, something hot and guilty in her garnet eyes stole a full beat from his heart.

What a little thief she turned out to be.

Awareness pulsed through the brined air between them.

She sank into the safety of her compatriots, rousing them from their investigation of a nest residing in a crumbling embrasure.

He'd not recognized Lady Francesca Cavendish until he'd joined them in the old courtyard, which was now little more than a meadow.

"Your Grace," the countess greeted in surprise. "I thought our appointment wasn't for another hour or so."

"Ladies." He bowed.

Alexandra's auburn brows drew together with an expression both astonished and troubled. "Your . . . Grace?"

Their gazes shifted in unison. They'd both noted the glint of metal from behind the old portcullis. The movement of a forearm. The unmistakable click of a hammer.

"Get down!" he bellowed.

Alexandra hurled her body toward the other two women, knocking them back just as a pistol blast joined the din of the hunting rifles in the distance.

Most of the guests awake at this hour were shooting pheasant in the forest beyond the grounds.

A brilliant time for a murder.

All three women had appeared to avoid injury. They scrambled to their feet and ran for what had once been the medieval armory, now a crumbling wall covered in ivy.

Piers launched himself at the gunman, breaking his firing arm before the volley had finished echoing through the stones.

The subsequent violence was, admittedly, self-indulgent, but Piers couldn't stop his fists from slamming into the face of the assailant again and again.

And once more.

As the skin of his knuckles split against a stranger's jaw, Piers tried to think of a more satisfying sensation than the impact of flesh and the crunch of bone beneath his fists.

Nothing came to mind.

There was fucking, he supposed. But he could think of no lover, mistress, nor whore who provided the kind of unadulterated release as did delivering a well-deserved beating.

Not these days, anyhow.

Power. In this arena, the physical one, he wielded it. He studied it. He *became* power. Primal and potent. It no longer had to be something he danced with. Something he was shackled to. Something to run to the farthest corners of Blighty to escape.

Strength gathered in his sinews and flowed through the arrangement of his motion. It bulged in the cords and ropes of muscle he'd built maneuvering through countries where the environs were just as lethal as the locals and the lions.

And almost as lethal as he.

Almost.

Beneath the gray stone grandeur of Castle Redmayne, it had been easy to forget that *this* was a power available to him.

Until the fucking warthog of a man beneath his blows had given him the perfect excuse to unleash it.

"There's another on the hill!" someone warned.

Piers hauled the man around to use as a human shield, ducking to reclaim the pistol his victim had dropped in the moss. He sighted the figure on the hill, drew a bead, and fired.

The man dropped, taking two more bullets to the torso before he hit the ground.

Piers threw the sack of blood and rubbish on the stones of the ruins and pressed the burning end of the pistol against the assailant's head, ignoring his cry of pain. "Tell me what you're doing here before I send you to hell," he demanded from between clenched teeth. An unholy fury thrummed beneath his skin, setting it ablaze.

A few garbled noises bubbled around blood and spittle escaping the blighter's open mouth.

"It appears you've broken his jaw too inexorably for him to confess at the moment." The clear, unperturbed voice of Lady Francesca pulled him around once more. "Though we are lucky you stumbled upon us, if that is, in fact, what you did."

At first, Piers thought it was the haze of red, which often accompanied violence, that touched the three women before him with such unparalleled brilliance.

He checked to make certain. Yes, the stones beneath his boots were gray, the moss clinging to them alternately umber and olive and russet. The ocean winds ruffled waves of verdant grass in the distance, and the sky stretched blue above them.

No, the scarlet hue of blood rage had receded. These women were simply . . . vibrant.

Vibrant redheads to the last one.

Piers blinked past Lady Francesca to Alexandra. His gaze slipped over her supple body, remembering every place his hands had been only yesterday.

Her fists curled tightly at the sides of her slim, midnight-blue skirts, and she gawked at him from eyes so owlish, he could see the whites all the way around the pupils. She wore some sort of stunning female equivalent to a man's suit, complete with a silk cravat trimmed with lace, a high-necked blouse, and a fitted vest.

Inexplicably, he ached to rip away the starched, scholarly layers. To ascertain injury, if nothing else.

Her breasts rose and fell at double the rate of her companions', and her eyes flashed gold in the dappled sunlight.

Piers told himself his cock was at attention because violence was sometimes just as physically arousing as vice.

He told himself that twice, before attempting to speak.

"Are you hurt?" he asked.

Her features were ashen, her lips devoid of the lush color he'd so admired before.

Francesca gave him her usual tight-lipped smile. "We're no worse for wear, Your Grace, I assure you."

He had to remember that his question should have been directed at all of them.

At the Countess of Mont Claire, in particular.

"Francesca?" Alexandra whispered the unfinished question to Lady Francesca, but her eyes never left his bleeding knuckles, which had begun to smart like the very devil.

"Oh yes." Francesca stepped closer, examining the roughshod figure writhing on the ground before she leveled an inscrutable cat-eyed gaze on him. "Ladies, allow me to introduce His Grace, Piers Gedrick Atherton, the Duke of Redmayne, and my fiancé."

CHAPTER FIVE

Piers's eyes narrowed as something meaningful passed between the three women he didn't quite understand and liked even less.

"Your Grace." Francesca continued her introductions as though they weren't speaking over a man he'd only just beaten within an inch of his life. "These are my bridesmaids, Miss Cecelia Teague, of London, and Lady Alexandra Lane, daughter of the Earl of Bentham."

"Pleased to meet Your Grace." Miss Teague spread her lavender skirts and executed an elegant curtsy. Her spectacles hid maybe the most brilliant blue eyes he'd ever come across. The brilliance, he marked, had just as much to do with what shone from behind her gaze, as the hue of it.

A jab from Miss Teague's elbow broke Alexandra from a rather worrisome stupor, and she did something with her knees so ridiculous, Piers couldn't have found a curtsy in it if he'd a magnifying glass.

His absurd bubble of amusement had to be the aftermath of violence still singing through his blood.

"Remarkably swift thinking back there, *Doctor* Lane." He looked down at her with his most imperious expression. "Or should I say, *Lady* Alexandra?"

Lady Francesca glanced between them. She crossed her arms over nonexistent bosoms wrapped in a pink so garish, it almost hurt to gaze upon. On any other woman, the color would have been hideous. On her, it was oddly fetching.

"It appears you two have already been introduced." She narrowed her eyes at Alexandra, though Piers detected no true malice in the look.

"Well—I—no?" Lady Alexandra gasped.

"Is that a question?" Francesca smirked. "You could have mentioned it *last night.*" She pronounced the *t*'s with undue emphasis.

As Lady Alexandra's alluring mouth opened and closed soundlessly for several seconds, Miss Teague crept toward their attacker, who'd given up writhing for limp twitches and guttural moans.

"I say, he seems to be in a great deal of pain. Shouldn't we get him some help?"

Francesca turned to her. "Honestly, Cecelia, he attempted to murder one of us not moments ago. Do let him suffer for a bit longer. I should think he brought it upon himself."

A bold and officious woman in every facet, that was his wife-to-be.

God, they were going to make each other miserable. Not that he disagreed with her on any particular point, it was simply that this was a trait they shared, and with both of them stomping about Castle Redmayne demanding their own way, who would keep the peace?

Assuming she wouldn't notice his inability to keep his eyes off her closest friend.

"I'll need to ascertain which of you the bullet was intended for." Piers dragged his gaze from Lady Alexandra to glare down at the man on the ground between them. "Is he familiar to any of you?"

Both Lady Alexandra and Cecelia stared at the gunman, shook their heads in the negative, then turned to look at Francesca, who blanched.

"I've never seen him before in my life," she announced, almost too innocently. "Though we should probably all take a gander at the man up the hill, just to be certain."

"Good thinking, dear," Cecelia agreed amicably. "Should we take the long way toward the tree line, and then follow it until we can ascertain that there is no one else? It'll make us less of a target, won't it?"

"Indeed." Francesca picked up her skirts and stepped over the moaning man as nonchalantly as one would a pile of manure. "Excellent suggestion."

Piers curled his hands into fists, the masculine equivalent of pinching himself. No, he wasn't dreaming, so . . .

Just who *were* these ladies? Where were the tears and histrionics? Couldn't they have at least afforded him a modicum of feminine display for his—he wasn't too modest to say—rather heroic behavior?

Cecelia followed in his betrothed's wake, performing a little dainty hop over the incapacitated man that did something to her enormous breasts he'd have to be completely blind not to notice. "Do you think we should contact the authorities before or after the ambu—"

"I wasn't aware he was a duke!" Alexandra blurted.

They all paused, turning to look at her.

She stood frozen to the exact spot she had been in since they'd ventured out from behind the stone wall. Rapid blinks and darting eyes revealed a woman still too shocked to have caught up to the moment. "I—I would have mentioned, had I known. *He's* the stablemaster I told you about with the runaway stallion. That one." She pointed at Merc, docilely grazing nearby. "That one right there."

Cecelia made an interested noise. "He's the one we spied on last night? Of course! I should have known from the shoulders."

Piers's head snapped up. *The one they what?*

The thought of Alexandra watching as he'd wrenched off his shirt did little to soothe the battle heat in his blood.

Had she liked what parts of him she'd seen?

"Yes!" she affirmed.

Yes?

"Yes, he's the one! He said—" Alexandra turned to him, a frenzied accusation in her gaze. "*You* said you kept the beasts at Castle Redmayne."

"And so I do." He nudged the man with his boot. "Wasn't it Alexander the Great who wrote, 'Every man has a wild beast within him'?"

"It was Frederick the Great," Lady Alexandra corrected without seeming to notice that she'd done so. "And, as apropos as that quote may be, it still doesn't—"

"Speak of the devil," Francesca cut in. "Don't look now, but 'the beasts' are returning, and are about to stumble upon a fresh kill."

A crowd of inveterate revelers in wool jackets and jodhpurs, with shotguns draped over their arms, tromped through the grass on the ridge not one hundred yards from where Piers had shot the rifleman down.

"What the bloody hell are they doing this far east?" Piers muttered, ducking behind a wall. "They can't see any of us together."

"Oh dear," Cecelia worried. "Perhaps we should head

them off and redirect them to a different path toward the castle?"

Piers nodded, staring down at the mess he'd made of himself. His vest was stained with the man's blood, and his bleeding knuckles were beginning to swell. "There's a deer path that will lead you past a swan pond and the gardens. They'll have to turn left immediately, and double back through the edge of the woods to find it."

"Any other assassins would be daft to shoot into a hunting party," Cecelia reasoned. "They'd never escape without leaking like a sieve."

"Right. Too many witnesses with guns. Do let's go." Francesca lifted her skirts and all but sprinted up the hill with gazellelike agility.

Cecelia took an alarmed step toward her friend. "Don't you want to join Francesca, Alex? I can easily stay here *alone* with the duke and help His Grace lift the brigand onto the horse."

"You'll do no *such* thing," he growled. *Lift the man onto the horse? What rubbish.*

"Oh, it's no bother. I might never be a dainty woman." She held shapely arms and broad shoulders out for his review. "But I can carry my share of a body when called upon to do so."

Lady Alexandra made a distressed sound.

"I'll ruin the handsome side of my face before I allow a lady to assist in such odious work." Piers looked from the countess's determined stomp up the hill to the petrified doctor behind him and back to the Valkyrie offering to help with the heavy lifting. He'd met his share of peculiar women, but this trio simply beat them all.

And he was marrying one of them.

The two women stared at each other for a meaningful moment. "I can't face those people," Alexandra said finally.

"You go. Send someone to find us should we not return *directly.*"

With one more hesitant glance, Cecelia followed Francesca, who'd already made it more than halfway up the hill.

Piers and Alexandra stayed silently concealed within the ruins until they were certain the party had dropped out of sight below the ridge of Tormund's Bluff.

"Are you all right?" He reached to smooth away a curl that had escaped her chignon and caught on her mouth.

She jerked her chin to avoid his touch, tucking the bit of hair behind her ear with trembling fingers. "I'm quite well, all things considered. Shall we get on our way?"

Piers dropped his hand. Of course she was upset. He'd made her feel like a fool for not recognizing the groom in her own friend's wedding.

Oh, and one mustn't forget the part where she'd nearly escaped a bullet.

The gunman lost consciousness, and Piers belatedly wondered if he hadn't beaten the man to death.

He hoped not. At least not before he extracted some information first. His hands itched to strike the man again.

And worse.

"Stay hidden until I have him secured," he ordered.

Setting the gun on what was left of a hip-high wall, he fetched Merc and led the stallion to the unconscious plonker. The man was shorter than he, as most men were, but heavy-handed and rotund. Piers crouched down and verified that the gunman still breathed before he rifled through his pockets. He found nothing but a slip of paper, which he unfolded.

Falt Ruadh

Suspicion twisted in his gut. *This* had been no random act of violence. Not a robbery nor a ravishment.

This had been a hit.

The note was hastily scrawled in a language he was only familiar with because of his Scottish half brother.

Falt Ruadh

Scots Gaelic for "red hair."

Red Hair. Uncommonly, all three of the women were possessed of some shade of the description. Lady Francesca's a brilliant, fiery crimson. Cecelia's a coppery gold. And Lady Alexandra's a russet mahogany that took on the colors of the sunset when the daylight shone on it as it did now.

Hers was the least vibrant color, and yet the most captivating.

Christ. He berated himself as he lifted the blighter's arm over his shoulder and hefted the bulk of him with his back.

What sort of man lusted for his fiancée's bridesmaid?

He heaved the bastard over Merc's saddle, and had to steady the animal when it danced sideways.

Better not answer that just now, he told himself as he retrieved a length of rope from the saddlebags. He used that and one rein to secure the gunman to the saddle by both feet and the arm that wasn't broken. The knots weren't pretty, but they'd hold.

Alexandra recovered the pistol from the wall and checked the cylinder for the remaining bullets.

Two shots left, if he counted correctly.

Piers reached out, palm open, expecting her to gladly surrender the weapon to more capable hands.

He should have known better.

She closed the chamber and lowered the pistol, though her thumb rested on the hammer. "I'll carry this, if you don't mind."

"I *do* mind." He motioned to the sack of shite he'd

trussed to the saddle. "He's perfectly secure. You're in no danger from him."

"I'll carry it all the same," she said resolutely.

He scowled. "Tell me you at least know how to use the blasted thing should the need arise."

She didn't react to his gruff tone and motioned for him to proceed. "Well enough. I practiced on snakes in Alexandria."

Snakes in Alexandria. He snorted as he turned his back and led Mercury toward the path with one rein. *Of course she did.*

They walked along the cliff in silence for a long moment, as the waves crashed against the rocks below.

She maintained a wider distance than propriety dictated, keeping the gun next to her opposite hip.

Out of his reach.

She slid a nervous glance at him. "What was on the paper you found?"

Piers reached in his pocket, and extended the note to her. She scanned it quickly before returning it, her pale features remaining carefully impassive.

"I don't know what it means."

He could tell that it pained her to admit this.

"It's Gaelic for 'red hair.'"

He watched her for a reaction. Her expression remained smooth, tranquil even. But he was a man who'd been in the presence of animals for most of his life.

Even if her countenance didn't convey fear, he read it in every tense line of her body. The distance she established. Her propensity to startle. The quickened rhythm of her breaths and the hoarse trembling barely concealed in her carefully modulated voice.

"Can you think of a reason someone would wish any of you harm?" he queried.

At this, she leveled him an anxious, searching gaze. "Can you?"

"I certainly intend to find out," he muttered.

Her free hand crept to the cravat at her throat. She tugged and fidgeted with it as if to struggle for a few nervous swallows of air. That didn't seem to help, so she pressed a glove to her cheek, then to her forehead, then dropped it back to her side to bury it in her skirts.

Despite the bracing breeze still carrying the scent of last night's storm, a sheen of perspiration bloomed at her hairline. She had surpassed anxious and was leaving frightened behind her in the race toward true terror.

A strange and unprecedented urge welled within him, unsettling him almost as much as the sight of the pistol had.

The yearning was ludicrous—he wanted nothing more than to take her hands in his and smooth away her trembling. He wanted to . . . *hold* her, to offer comfort that he, himself, had never received.

He shook away the notion, landing on a constructive approach.

Misdirection.

"What snakes did you shoot?" he asked. "Some sort of cobra, no doubt."

"Snakes?" It took several seconds for the glaze of confusion to clear from her eyes before she answered. "N-no, there weren't as many cobras in Egypt as one is led to believe. Where our company camped near the lighthouse of Alexandria, we were mostly plagued with horned vipers. Th-they'd, um . . ." She took a shaking breath, lifting the gun hand to toy with her hair only to discover she still held it. Guiltily, she lowered it to point at the ground.

Piers let out the breath he'd caught, using all his self-control not to snatch it from her.

"They were prevalent, these devil vipers?" he prodded, sensing she'd lost her place in the conversation.

"Yes." She refused to lift her eyes. "Yes, and they matched the startling white of the sand, and so it was almost impossible to see them until it was too late."

"I imagine you became quite the markswoman during your tenure there." He said this just as much for his benefit as for hers, as she'd seemed to again forget about the weapon clutched in her hand.

"Actually, no, I didn't have much use for my pistol once I adopted Anubis."

"A dog?"

"A cat."

He pulled up short, causing Merc to toss his head. "I'll admit to not being the best pupil as a boy, but isn't Anubis a god with a dog's head?"

"Yes. But Anubis somehow looked like the statues of him . . . and acted like a dog."

"How so?"

A twitch at the corner of her tight mouth compromised her frown. "She'd pounce on them, seizing the snakes behind their head and shaking the stuffing out of them. I know cats are predators. But I swear I've never seen the like."

"She?" Piers echoed. "Where is this wondrous cat now? I should like to take a holiday to visit her."

A fond half-smile softened her lips, though her voice contained a melancholy note when she said, "I left her with a little orphan girl named Akasha in Egypt."

"What for? We've plenty of snakes in England she could happily slaughter."

"I thought Anubis would get rather cold here."

Piers gestured to the lazy summer grasses and the

warmth of the afternoon tempered by sea breezes. "Plenty of felines seem to do well despite our climate."

"Well, certainly, but they're English cats, aren't they? Anubis didn't have any fur."

Piers gave a melodramatic gasp. "A naked cat? I've never heard of such a thing." He had, of course, but he'd begun to pull her away from the cavern of fear she'd been edging on only a moment ago.

"They're called sphinx cats," she said in the voice of a professor at a lectern. "They're incredibly rare and are considered to be most holy."

He clicked his tongue and chuffed. "You're putting me on."

"I'd never dream of it, Your Grace." She finally brought herself to blink up at him, offering a shy, if shaky smile.

Somehow the sun shone brighter on the surface of the sea, and the wind caressed skin becoming more sensitive and heated by the moment.

Could one smile do such a thing?

"You misrepresented yourself at the train station." Her tone was too mild for a reproach, and Piers wondered if she required conversation to divert herself from the fact that she was accompanied by a bloodstained duke and an assassin.

"Did I, *Doctor* Lane?" He injected uncharacteristic levity into his reply.

"But I *am* a doctor."

"And also, it would seem, the daughter of an earl."

She made an unrepentant gesture. "I didn't want to dangle my nobility in front of a lowly stable hand, especially when he'd come to my rescue."

"And I gather that Miss Cecelia Teague was your dashing escort Cecil?"

Something in the chagrin painted over her features informed him that she'd taken his point. "I was a woman traveling without a chaperone, who didn't wish to give her information to a strange man. What's your excuse for your uncourtly behavior?"

What he didn't say was that he'd not wanted her to treat him like a duke. He'd enjoyed their banter. He'd been impressed by her uncommon—well—commonness.

He'd appreciated that she'd treated him, a scarred stablemaster, with more deference than she did now that she knew he was a man of power, wealth, and influence.

Piers said none of that, he merely lifted a shoulder. "At first, I thought you knew."

"How could I possibly?"

"Everyone in the empire has heard of the Terror of Torcliff."

"Yes . . . Yes, I heard them call you that." She stiffened. "Why ever would they?"

"It's a recent moniker, all told." He gestured to the scar interrupting his lip. "According to local lore, I've been scratched by a werebeast—or a demon depending on whom you're asking—and I've become the monstrous scarred duke who haunts the halls of the accursed Castle Redmayne, eating small children for lunch and virgins for dinner. I'm rather famous."

He'd meant to be comical, but she stepped even farther away, her smile disappearing and taking the sunshine with it. "Perhaps you're not as well-known as you think. I'd never heard of you before yesterday."

"To be fair, it sounds as though you've spent a great deal of time out of the country and away from the *ton*."

"True." She acquiesced his point with a nod, and bent to pluck a tall blade of foxtail grass, worrying it with the fingers of one hand. "I've never been much for *ton* gossip."

No, she wouldn't be, would she? Piers gazed down at her for longer than was appropriate, able to do so because she'd become unduly absorbed with tying one-handed knots into the blade of grass.

As educated and well traveled as she was, she harbored an unspoiled air of innocent naïveté not often found in a woman of her age. Her eyes were the color of dark honey and shy as a fawn's. Her shoulders curled forward slightly, not in an unladylike slouch, but enough to protect a tender heart.

The rest of her . . . well, her limbs were wound tight as a hare's, ready to spring into the safety of the closest hedge should the need arise.

How had such a helpless lamb survived the perils of Cairo or Alexandria?

"Do you?"

It took him a moment to register that she addressed him, and not the blade of grass. "Do I what?"

"Do you eat virgins for dinner?"

He made a rude noise. "Good God, no, virgins are terrible fare at the supper table . . . Though mayhap I've indulged in a nibble of one or two for dessert. The villagers keep throwing them at me, and it does one good to treat oneself now and again."

He directed his most winsome smile at her, ready to bask in her enjoyment of his levity.

She actually grimaced, turning her neck to stare uncomfortably out at the sea.

His grin died a slow and painful death. "It might surprise you to learn women once found me charming."

At this, her head made another owlish swivel to meet his rueful gaze.

"That was, of course, before I became an unholy terror." He motioned to his ruined features. "Perhaps I was just so devastatingly handsome they thought to humor me. Lord save us all now that I have to rely on my underdeveloped sense of humor and apparently nonexistent wit."

"Oh!" She reached out to him, her face soft with guilt, dropping the knotted grass.

He readied himself for the pleasure of her touch, but her hand paused just before they made any contact.

"Oh no, Your Grace, no, please. *Please* don't think my lack of . . . response has anything to do with . . . with your." She gestured toward his beard. "I just . . . I'm not . . . erm . . ." Her words appeared to block her throat as she searched for a way to soothe his offense

"You're not easily amused. I understand." He overacted a magnanimous stature as he fought a smile. "Your high standards do you credit, my lady."

He enjoyed the swift return of her color, as mortification replaced mortal fear. "That's not it at all, Your Grace, I am quite easily amused . . . I promise . . ."

"More fool I, then, if it is so easily done, and I failed so utterly."

She stepped closer, visibly vexed. "Please. It isn't you at all. And I vow that your scars are not terrible, *or* terrifying. They're rather dashing—charming. You're charming, I meant to say—I—I'm just not . . ."

"You're not yourself." Something told him he'd gone too far, and her discomfiture was circling back to uneasiness and fear. "You've had a fright, Lady Alexandra. I only meant to tease you away from it."

The worry drained from her expression, and her brows drew together as though she couldn't decide whether to be relieved or cross with him.

"I've spent most of my life in the company of men," he explained further. "And I'll admit I've little to no practice in conversations with the fairer sex. And, I was absolutely lying when I claimed ladies ever found me charming."

"Didn't they, though? I should think they found you quite . . . erm . . . at least more than passing . . . that is . . . I'm sure they found you . . ." She swallowed audibly.

One of these days, she might actually be able to finish a sentence in his presence. "They found me obscenely wealthy, as well titled as a nonroyal can be, and—as most aspiring noble wives will tell you is an extremely desirable trait for a husband—I am most often abroad."

"Certainly you won't be now . . . now that you are to be a husband."

Instead of answering, he made a great show of checking on the limp prisoner and patting Mercury's neck. The footpath meandered closer to the cliffs before forking either toward the village, or back to Castle Redmayne, and he wished he could think of some other reason to avoid the question until their return.

"I don't know. After Francesca and I perform our duties as Duke and Duchess of Redmayne and the Atherton line is secure, I might venture back out into the world. For now, it seems, I must see to my legacy."

It was her turn to stare for a protracted moment. "You're like no duke I've ever met."

Piers was becoming accustomed to the way she blurted irreverent thoughts before considering their meaning.

"And you're unlike any lady of my acquaintance," he volleyed.

"I—I didn't at all mean that as a slight."

"And I was paying you the highest compliment."

She ignored that, glancing away again. "I only meant to say, you're more at home in the saddle or the stable than in any salon. You and Francesca will have that in common, at least."

Ah yes, Francesca. He made a noncommittal sound, hoping that would end their discussion of his future bride.

"Do you love her?"

He scowled. No such luck. "It is not necessary for Lady Francesca and I to have anything in common but our names and our children."

"That's a rather . . . mercenary view to have of marriage."

"I'm a rather mercenary sort of fellow."

She chewed her lip. "Do you even like her?"

He coughed to hide a bark of laughter. Francesca Cavendish was a sparkling ruby in a lake of pearls. She was bold, brilliant, and beautiful.

And he could barely stand the extraneous energy of her presence for longer than an hour before he wanted to tie her to something to keep her from moving. He didn't like her. And yet, he didn't dislike her. Come to think of it, what was his opinion of the woman? He'd met her all of twice. "I admire her . . . tenacious spirit."

"You mean to say, you don't even like her?" she accused, cutting through his veneer. "Then why marry her?"

"Why not marry her?" He shrugged. "We're betrothed after all. Rarely do persons of our class like their spouses. I don't have to like my wife to do my duty by her. Lady Francesca is a fair woman, she'll bear me strong sons and beautiful daughters." Or she would, if he could bring his cock to attention around her.

Thus far . . . it'd not even twitched in Francesca's direction.

"The betrothal is good for our families. My father—"

Mercury whinnied, leaping forward and crashing into Piers, who then stumbled into Alexandra, knocking her off balance.

Piers was barely able to seize her and draw her into his body, twisting as they tumbled to the ground. He grunted as his shoulders and back took the brunt of the impact, then relaxed into a roll to soften the fall.

He planted his arms on either side of her shoulders, stopping them before they pitched off the cliff. He imprisoned them there in a tangle of limbs and panting breaths, lowering his body to shield her should Merc be close by.

He spotted the sodding stallion a few paces away, prancing around a criminal bumblebee.

It was a good thing, he decided, that Lady Alexandra had not given him the pistol, he'd have shot the animal between the eyes right then and there and dragged the gunman home himself.

His thoughts stalled at the intimate press of uncorseted breasts against his chest. Her thighs shaped to his, strong and sinuous beneath her modest skirts.

He tensed as arousal shot into his body with all the awe-inspiring power of last night's lightning. It blazed through veins unprepared for the visceral rush, flooding his cock with such an aching need, he swallowed a groan against the exquisite pain of it.

She was built to be beneath him.

His body screamed for him to move. To settle his hips into the cradle of her thighs and press his intimate flesh against hers.

Her lips, he noted, were parted in the most inviting way. The soft little puffs of her breath a sweet-scented breeze against his beard.

His tongue found the indent of the scar in his lip. He hadn't kissed a woman since . . .

The metallic click of her pistol broke the moment.

"Get. Off."

Piers froze. The glint in her eyes, the set of her jaw. He'd seen that desperation before. In the eyes of his cornered prey, right before they attacked.

In that moment, he was certain if he made one wrong move, she'd shoot him in the chest, toss his corpse into the ocean, and be home in time for tea.

She scrambled to her feet the moment he rolled to his side, and it wasn't his imagination that she kept the pistol cocked as she backed away from him. "I'll make my way to Castle Redmayne from here."

"I'd prefer to see you safely—"

"Don't be absurd," she spat. Her lovely features arranged themselves into a mask of disdain. "What would people say if I were to approach Castle Redmayne unchaperoned, and then you announced a betrothal to someone else tomorrow? I'd be ruined, and so would the wedding."

On a normal day, Piers would have thought her a bit melodramatic, but he recognized that an assassin slumbered—hopefully—not paces away upon the back of an unruly horse. She'd narrowly missed being shot. Falling off a cliff.

And, if he were honest, being kissed by her friend's fiancé.

What a bastard he was.

"Very well, Lady Alexandra, I will watch you home from a safe distance and follow when you are within the keep."

She met his honeyed acquiescence with vinegar. "You may call me Dr. Lane," she insisted, wagging the pistol at him like the finger of a scolding schoolmarm.

Piers put up his hands as a gesture of surrender.

"And . . . and . . . thank you." This was said with more vehemence than politeness as she turned on her heel and stalked away with a starched-kneed march that would have made a brigadier general proud.

Piers reclined in the indent their bodies had made in the soft grass. Watching her leave did exactly nothing for the state of his nethers. It certainly wouldn't do to return to the stables with a bleeding brigand *and* a cockstand.

Alexandra Lane.

Her name would haunt him for the rest of his miserable life.

CHAPTER SIX

"If you don't hold still, I'm going to stab you," Alexandra warned, hand poised overhead, her weapons of choice a selection of ruby pins.

"I'm almost finished," Francesca promised. She lifted her knee and pressed it into Cecelia's hip, causing Cecelia to emit a little cry of surprise.

Francesca gave Cecelia's corset strings one final, two-handed tug, and cinched them off with all the alacrity of a sailor mooring a ship to the dock.

As was their habit, they'd eschewed lady's maids for the evening in favor of unbridled conversation.

Cecelia ran a hand down her newly compressed figure, splaying her fingers over a waistline several inches smaller. "It's so tight, I'll have to speak in a whisper all evening."

"Should we loosen it a little?" Alexandra suggested.

"No." Cecelia's lips parted in a triumphant smile. "That means it's perfect."

"Besides, we can't undo my concentrated efforts." Francesca would have wandered off had Alexandra not seized her shoulder and thrust the ruby pins home, completing the magnificent coiffure.

"Really, Cecil, you've a lovely figure." In lieu of a corset, Alexandra rolled the wide panels of silk over her chemise, flattening her breasts to her ribs. "I don't think you need to accentuate it so dramatically that you're miserable all evening."

Alexandra didn't miss the subversive glances her friends gave her wrap when they thought she wasn't looking. They refrained from commenting, as they understood this had been a practice of hers for years, one meant to divert the male eye as often as possible.

"If I cannot breathe, I shall be deterred from the refreshment table." Cecelia settled the cage of her bustle to her generous hips and checked her reflection in the mirror before gathering her petticoats. "Besides, I want to look especially good for this occasion."

"I don't see why." Francesca accepted Alexandra's assistance with pulling her crimson skirt over her head while avoiding her hair. "If all goes as planned, this won't be an engagement masquerade, but the unmasking of a massacre plot."

"Should we find anything condemning in the duchess's rooms, do you have immediate plans to unveil it publicly?" Alexandra queried. "Tonight?"

"Absolutely."

The vehemence of Francesca's reply drew the corners of Alexandra's mouth down. "Are you certain that's wise?" She pictured the duke's features, scarred and weatherbeaten and absolutely furious as his family was deposed and dishonored in his ancient keep.

Something about that scenario tugged at her heart just as much as it terrified her.

It shouldn't bother her so much, most especially if

Redmayne was complicit in evil. But what if he wasn't? Should a man be crucified for the sins of his family?

She thought of the charming, self-effacing man who'd strolled with her along the cliffs. His wit such a contrast to his bearing. To look at him, one could imagine the Terror of Torcliff. And not because of his scars, but because of the violence of which he was capable. Because of the predatory way he moved. As though he owned the very land he trod upon.

Which, come to think of it, he did.

"The more quickly any Redmayne or Ramsay involvement is exposed, the less likely we are to have a repeat of yesterday," Francesca said sensibly as she turned her back to Cecelia, who abandoned her hair to fasten Francesca's crimson bodice. "If we were to reveal the truth, we would be much safer than if we were to enact our own private revenge."

"In light of recent events, I'm inclined to agree." Cecelia nodded, her voluminous curls, caught in violet ribbons and pearl combs, threatening to come tumbling from their confines at any moment. The effect was marvelous, as one might catch oneself wanting to pluck out a comb or pin in order to make it do just that. "Should anything happen to us subsequent to the reveal, the finger of guilt would automatically point to Redmayne or Ramsay."

"Precisely." Francesca, in turn, fastened and flounced Cecelia's teal gown, settling the train over the bustle in a fall of shimmering silks. "And since it was confirmed that the gunman was after me, it's more imperative than ever that we act quickly."

The morning prior, Alexandra had found her friends instantly upon her breathless arrival at the keep. She'd informed them of the paper the duke had found in the gunman's pocket and a great deal about her interactions with Red-mayne.

She'd studiously left out the physical parts of their in-teraction, though she didn't want to examine why. It had only been a tumble, hadn't it? So why couldn't she bring herself to speak of it?

Because he'd been on top of her? Because, for a mo-ment, she'd looked up at his bold features weathered by the foreign sun and fearsome scars, and she'd seen some-thing she'd recognized.

A weariness. No. A *wariness.*

Something familiar reflected from eyes as blue as the sky and fierce as the sea. Something tired and wounded.

When the tip of his tongue had tested the scar interrupt-ing his lip, the uncertainty of the motion had elicited something tender within her. An emotion warmer than pity, softer than curiosity. It had tugged at her and, for a miraculous moment, she'd forgotten to be afraid.

A strange awareness had flooded her. A shocking sense of something she distantly identified as . . . shelter? Safety? His body above her was solid and heavy. It didn't seem ludicrous to imagine that he was invulnerable, a bulwark against all that would do her harm.

And for a moment she'd felt as though she could have remained beneath the temple of his strength forever. Safe. Protected.

Until his eyes had found her parted lips. And the warm, yielding muscle above her had become hard as iron, and the uncertainty had heated to . . .

She didn't want to think the word. Men didn't *desire* her anymore. She made certain of that. No, Redmayne had re-acted like any man might do with a woman beneath them.

Any woman.

Mortification still needled at her when she thought of her response. She'd threatened him with a pistol. If she wasn't mistaken, to do so with a duke might be considered criminal.

She'd been beyond caring. Helpless terror had lanced through her with such violence, her options had been to escape or pitch herself off a cliff.

She'd die—no—she would have *murdered* him before considering the alternative.

Alexandra pulled the unfussy silver gown up over her hips and slipped her arms into the long, gossamer sleeves. She eschewed a bustle or corset, or anything else that might garner her favorable male attentions.

To avoid *unfavorable* attentions of the female variety, she acquiesced to fashion with artful gathers of material for her train, and the tight silk wrap that, on her trim figure, imitated a corset without accentuating her curves. Even if she sparkled with diamonds and gleamed with muslin, she'd be covered from throat to toe.

"Don't you find it passing strange that the Duke of Redmayne was in the ruins yesterday morning at the same time we decided to take our exercise?" she remarked.

"I found it exceedingly strange." Francesca pulled her skirts up past her thighs, revealing surprisingly muscular legs as she fiddled with the ribbons securing her stockings.

"Did you see his face as he beat our aggressor?" Alexandra couldn't forget the mask of demonic rage as the duke had driven fists the size of pike hammers to devastating effect.

She was unused to such displays of brute strength.

"He's certainly no stranger to violence," Cecelia concluded. "That's something we mustn't forget. but also, his wrath was unleashed in protection of us, or . . . at least of his fiancée."

"To think that one of you could have been shot yesterday." Francesca's voice wavered with aberrant sentimentality. "It's a tragedy beyond imagining. One I'll do anything to avoid."

Gathering her courage, Alexandra smoothed at a bejeweled tassel in her friend's twinkling gown. "All three of us were exploring the ruins, Frank, we can't be absolutely certain the attempt was on your life, alone."

Francesca tossed her head and let out an undignified snort. "Who else?"

"Itmighthavebeenme." The words fled on a whoosh of unsteady breath, pent for days and dying to escape.

Her friends gaped at her, their faces identical—if lovely—masks of unadulterated astonishment.

"How is that possible?" Cecelia cried.

"What are you talking about?" Francesca demanded.

Alexandra swallowed profusely, suddenly reticent to heap another mound of trouble on to shoulders already weighted with so much. But the attempt on their lives yesterday illustrated the direness of their situation.

There was no time left for secrets. She knew that now.

"Someone knows," she whispered.

None of them moved. None of them breathed. Her words transported them to a place they desperately avoided.

Except in their nightmares.

Every crystal lantern, glinting silver hairbrush, and glowing mirror disappeared into the darkness of a horrific night ten long years prior. The glisten of their gowns became the grime of the garden. The red ringlets of their hair became the blood they would scrub from their skin once the deed was done.

"Alexander?" Cecelia's husky, usually soothing voice quivered with uncertainty. "What, exactly, are you saying?"

It took Alexandra longer than she wanted to clear a tight ache from her throat. She clung to her friends' hands, terrified that they'd pull away from her. That she'd be left in this dark memory alone. "Someone knows what we did. What *I* did back at de Chardonne."

"How?" Francesca breathed. "If it wasn't one of us, it had to be Jean-Yves."

"It can't be!" Cecelia cried. "Jean-Yves lives with me and could want for nothing in the world! I even brought him along to Castle Redmayne as my manservant. Alexander, you can't believe—"

"I don't know." Alexandra shook her head, standing to collect herself and gather something from her trunk, wrapped in a handkerchief. She returned to the settee and sank onto it, feeling almost as numb as she had the night it happened. "Perhaps someone watched us as we buried him in the gardens. They've known where he's been all this time, and I've been paying them for their silence every month since the Sorbonne."

A dumbfounded silence greeted her confession as the enormity of their situation sank into the two women who'd been blessed with a decade of ignorance.

Cecelia recovered first, swiping her spectacles from her face to pinch the bridge of her nose. "You mean, you've paid him . . ." She performed a hasty calculation in her head. "One hundred and twenty-six times, and never mentioned it to either of us?"

"I've been trying to protect you!" Alexandra rushed to stem the tide of emotion attempting to carry her away. To stall the condemnation surely forthcoming from her friends. "As long as I've paid, our secret has been safe . . . but . . . but the thing is . . . My father has recently revealed that the estate has been floundering for quite some time.

He called me back from Cairo to announce that we are bankrupt. I haven't been able to make my payments for two months. And only last week, on the very same day I received your invitation, this was delivered to my doorstep."

With trembling fingers, Alexandra unwrapped the handkerchief, unveiling the pearl-handled razor she'd used to open Headmaster de Marchand's throat.

The one they'd buried in his pocket.

"Oh, Alexander," Francesca said gravely.

"I know." Alexandra dashed a tear from her cheek before it could finish its trail down her chin. "I am so ashamed of the danger I've put you in. I wish you'd just hate me as much as I hate myself. I deserve it."

Heedless of her dress or even of Francesca between them, Cecelia lunged forward and scooped both women into her. "We only hate that you've carried this terrible thing with you for so long without our help."

Alexandra's tears fell in earnest. "I don't know what to do." The bereft confession tore out a piece of her soul. She always knew everything. Could handle anything. But this . . . this was beyond her scope.

The dinner gong vibrated throughout the house, driving them apart.

Cecelia pulled back and took a centering breath, her quick mind working behind eyes bright with emotion. "Here's exactly what we'll do." She stood, pacing to help her think. "We'll go down to dinner and make certain it is known we enjoyed ourselves immensely. We'll be absolutely dazzling, won't we, ladies?"

Alexandra and Francesca nodded.

"Once the dancing begins, we'll excuse ourselves at five-minute intervals and rendezvous at the blue sitting room at the top of the east wing stairs just as we'd planned.

We'll use the key that Francesca pilfered—well done, you—and search the duchess's study. Alexander, you'll stand watch and divert anyone who might happen by."

Alexandra splayed her fingers on her lap. "What if we come up empty-handed?"

"We're not thinking like that." Cecelia quieted her with the lift of a single black glove. "We *must*." She marched to the door and laid her hand on the knob. "Afterward, we'll meet back here and plan our next move before Redmayne reveals Francesca as his betrothed at midnight."

"What about Alexander?" Francesca asked.

"Alexander has borne the financial brunt of this blackmail for much too long. We have enough in our accounts to cover the cost until we can figure out a long-term solution."

"I forbid it!" Driven to her feet by outrage, Alexandra hurried to Cecelia. "I can't let you do that. I'm the one who *should* pay for what happened to de Marchand. I'm the one who kil—"

Cecelia opened the door, cutting off the words no one had ever actually spoken.

Alexandra found herself enfolded in Cecelia's arms as she whispered in her ear. "Any one of us would have done what you did. Let us help you."

Francesca rested her hand on Alexandra's shoulder. "All of us have secrets, you remember. We're in this together."

Touched, Alexandra nodded, her heart still railing against it.

Cecelia turned to Francesca, her features beset by gravitas. "If we find evidence that exonerates Redmayne, you might want to consider going through with the wedding."

"Why in the devil would I do that?" Francesca protested. "I'd rather be stretched on the rack than *actually* marry him."

"Because . . . should Alexander's blackmailer become

spiteful, or the money not get there in time, the protection of the Terror of Torcliff as your husband could save all our necks from the gallows."

Piers stood back from the balustrade above Castle Redmayne's ballroom and observed the swirls and eddies of nobility below him as they waltzed in time to "The Blue Danube."

The candles flickered in black iron chandeliers cast by a blacksmith some centuries ago. Dancing shadows drifted over bejeweled masks, lending the revelers an almost macabre appearance. An overabundance of diamonds and gems caught the candlelight, draped and dangling from elegant throats and wrists. Piers unfocused his gaze, divining constellations in their lustrous gleam.

God's blood, how he disliked these people. And none of them cared for him.

He was born a powerful man, so when he called them, they came.

It took all his will to appear unperturbed. Unaffected.

Yearning for the open plains of Africa or the dense jungles of the Amazon seized him. At least in such places, where plants and insects were just as deadly as the vipers and predators, he knew his place. He easily identified his enemies. He understood his power.

He'd earned it by right of strength and ferocity.

Here was a different terrain, one every bit as chaotic and treacherous as any he'd conquered abroad.

But these beasts were not so simple. Their hunting grounds, unfamiliar. He'd done nothing but slide into the world with the correct pedigree, and everyone below him either loved him or loathed him for it.

None of it made sense. The creatures swathed in finery spoke out of both sides of their mouths. When lions would roar and charge, they purred, then gutted you once you'd let down your guard.

He'd found among the animal kingdoms something he'd not realized he'd been searching for. An honesty, a simplicity, the like of which he'd never encountered in the human domain.

Such complicated creatures humanity had become. Swathed in the artifice of civilization . . .

A black bit of taffeta and muslin broke into his view, and Piers had to bite back a snarl.

Rose Brightwell. A dark beauty with a black heart and the charms of a snake. He'd been in her thrall for so long. Long enough to forget she was Rose Brightwell no longer.

Now she claimed Atherton as her surname, which was what she'd wanted all along, wasn't it?

Only his name. His title. Nothing else.

And he'd be damned before she became a duchess.

"Did ye love her?" The brogue was as deep and rich as the Scotch he'd just swallowed.

Piers tensed. Only one man had perfected the ability to approach him without detection. And no matter how Piers honed his instinct as both a hunter and possible target, he'd never bested his half brother, Sir Cassius Ramsay, in the art of subterfuge.

Even when they stood side by side, as they did now, no one would assume they were family. Ramsay was archangel gold to Piers's demon darkness. He'd not a lambent hair out of place, nor a whisker unshaved. As ever, Ramsay was perfectly starched, steadfast, and in Piers's opinion, rather stuffy.

"Your Worship," he muttered.

"Yer Grace." They always greeted each other like this, formally, with barely concealed comradery, and half-hearted contempt.

Theirs was a complicated affection.

"Did ye love Rose?" Ramsay repeated, joining him to gaze down at the colorful chaos below them.

"I must have," Piers mused. "Else why would I hate her so bitterly now?"

Ramsay made a noncommittal sound, and sipped from a champagne glass that, in hands the size of his, appeared to be from a little girl's play set.

It would be the only drink he allowed himself. His one concession that he attended a grand ball instead of the gallows. Even his mask was dreary, an unadorned black silk band with slits for the eyes, tied in the back like some sort of highwayman. A paragon of self-containment, that was the Honorable Lord Chief Justice of the High Court Sir Cassius Ramsay.

"I imagine all this is for her," Ramsay said, pointedly *not* looking at Rose Brightwell.

"All of what?" Piers wished his mask didn't conceal his scowl.

His brother nodded toward the room at large. "All this pomp and drama and mystery. The unveiling of yer future duchess, et cetera. It's quite unlike ye."

What was it about an observant insight that made a man yearn for a drink? "I've a new reputation to uphold, or hadn't you heard?" he said flippantly. "Doesn't *this* seem worthy of the Terror of Torcliff?"

Ramsay snorted. "These people are as absurd as the moniker they've christened ye with."

"On that, dear brother, we can agree." Piers glanced at Ramsay through narrowed eyes, conducting an assessment of his own. "Yet you slither among *these people* as though they were your own. You should have been a duke, not I."

"The thought has crossed my mind." Ramsay lifted a wide shoulder in an insouciant shrug. "Necessity dictates

I navigate their world. But only so that I may mitigate their barbarity."

Piers smothered his surprise at the note of disdain his brother had allowed into his voice. He'd always assumed Ramsay enjoyed the way he'd infiltrated the *ton*. Not by way of birth, but by a prestige and presence, not to mention wealth, that they couldn't ignore.

As an erstwhile duke, Piers had never looked up to his elder brother in any way but literally, as the bastard was all of three inches taller and outweighed him by a spare half-stone.

Perhaps Ramsay *should* have been the duke; he'd the temperament for it. All steely resolve and unimpeachable morals.

Or, should he have been the huntsman? He'd the stature for it. The ferocity. The iron will and apparent fortitude for suffering. His Scottish father had given him the rough-hewn build of his Highland ancestors, and their mother had imparted all the British imperious pretension his great, loutish body could convey.

"If I'm honest, I'm surprised you came," Piers murmured. "It's not even an election year. Why should both of us have to suffer through something so tedious?"

"I'm as breathless as the rest of the empire to meet yer bride." Ramsay slid him a droll look from blue eyes identical to his. "Besides, I should be seen with strong family ties." He clapped Piers on the back with a solid hand, and Piers wondered if he did it for his benefit, or for that of the *ton*. Their eyes were like a thousand tiny lances pricking him with dubious regard.

"Which family?" Piers sneered. "Your disfigured, ne'er-do-well younger brother, or our cousin who allowed himself to be seduced by my former fiancée while I was on my deathbed?"

The ghost of a wry smile haunted his brother's lips before vanishing, and Piers tried to remember the last time he'd ever seen Ramsay smile.

Maybe never, come to think of it.

"I'm sorry she turned out to be like our mother." Ramsay drank again, his features turning to stone as he gazed out toward the woman Piers had been avoiding all night.

"Case." The nickname fell from Piers's lips as easily as it had when they were boys. "I'm fairly certain someone attempted to murder my fiancée yesterday."

That earned him the full brunt of Lord Ramsay's regard. Was it any wonder criminals and nobles, alike, trembled before him? It wasn't just his size, stature, and power that intimidated, it was the force of his disdain. The Caesar-like, tyrannical dominion he wielded.

"Fairly. Certain." As usual, he plucked the most important words from the exchange.

"I chanced upon her and her bridesmaids exploring the ruins yesterday morning, and barely arrived in time to interrupt two gunmen."

"Christ's blood." His brother tensed, alert as a hound on point. "Why did I not hear of this? Was anyone shot?"

"Only the gunmen. One is dead, and the other hovering quite close." A dark satisfaction rose within him at the thought. "I was hoping you'd look into it. Use your vast connections to suss out any reason someone would want my fiancée dead."

"Piers, chances are that person is here tonight," Ramsay cautioned. "Ye should have yer woman and her companions protected at all times."

"I can see all three women at this very moment, though I must be careful lest the observant, hungry crowd make any correct assumptions before the reveal." He smirked. "I'll admit I enjoy their suspicions and suppositions."

A put-upon sigh was his brother's reply. "Ye ken, I'll need to know the identity of yer bride and her companions sooner than later, if ye want my help."

"I'll narrow it down to three, but I'll not gesture."

Ramsay stepped closer to the balustrade. "Who are they?" he muttered, his lips moving imperceptibly.

"Lady Francesca Cavendish." Piers found her scarlet skirts immediately, as red tended to be her color of preference. "She's dancing with the dandy young Viscount Crossland at the moment. Then there's Miss Cecelia Teague, in the peacock mask. She's over by the refreshment table."

"I can see why she'd entice ye," Ramsay commented, taking another sip as he thoroughly inspected the intrepid Miss Teague.

"I told you not to stare." Pierce nudged him.

Ramsay blinked, breaking from some sort of trance. "Of course, who else?"

"The third is Lady Alexandra Lane, over by the door to the grounds." Piers's eyes ached for the sight of her.

But what if he never looked away?

"The wallflower trying to melt into the fern?" Ramsay asked.

Losing the battle with himself, Piers found her without difficulty.

Her features were softened by distance and dim lighting, but he could feel the absorption with which she studied the fourteenth-century falchions some ancestor of his had mounted on the wall in lieu of portraiture.

Her greatest nemesis: a row of topiary potted beneath the display.

She rose to her tiptoes, doing her best to examine the handles cruelly hanging just beyond her scope. She leaned so far forward, she lost her balance and nearly toppled into the branches before correcting herself with a few wild flings of her arms.

Instinctively, Piers took a step forward, only relaxing when she swatted at her skirts and scanned the ballroom to ascertain how many people had witnessed her misstep.

No one had noticed. Now that he'd allowed himself to look at her, to inspect her around her peers, he realized that she cultivated her own invisibility.

The ladies clustered in his ballroom like vibrant gemstones glittering in their jewel-toned silks and lace frippery; the good Dr. Lane draped herself in a soft shimmering silver.

A woman at such a soiree generally eschewed high-necked daydresses for dangerously low-cut bodices. She was encouraged to bare as much of her shoulders and arms as was possible whilse maintaining a nod to propriety with lace or something equally iridescent.

Lady Alexandra, however, had swathed herself in modest moonbeams from neck to wrist, her gown draping about the bodice in Grecian gathers to both accentuate and obscure her bosom.

Every other figure on shameless display somehow became redundant and uninteresting. The only vision he wanted, frustratingly concealed.

His fear had been validated. He couldn't physically bring himself to look away, not even to save her from mortification.

He knew the moment her gaze found his, even from across such a distance. Every hair on his body vibrated with awareness of it. She ducked behind the topiary in an equally ungraceful motion and Piers found himself fighting an enchanted smile.

"Ye're marrying the Countess of Mont Claire, obviously." His brother's correct deduction broke Piers of his enchantment.

"How, pray, is that so obvious?"

"Because Miss Teague, while a . . ." He paused as he examined the woman for longer than was necessary. "A desirable candidate, is a commoner, and Lady Alexandra's family is not only recently destitute, but she's socially irrelevant and an infamous eccentric. The countess is the only appropriate choice of the three."

"Is that so?" Piers scowled, disliking the defensive knot in his gut where Lady Alexandra was concerned.

"Yes. Lady Francesca is the last of the Cavendish line. To marry her would fulfill yer father's wishes toward her and is well done of ye." The gentle approval in Ramsay's tone reminded Piers of their mutual affection for his dearly departed father.

"If I remember correctly, Lady Francesca's family died under rather horrific circumstances." Piers watched the lithe, vivacious woman fight for the lead of the waltz with her overwhelmed companion.

"A suspicious fire," Ramsay confirmed gravely. "No one ever found the culprit."

"Do you suppose that could be connected to the shooting today? Do you have any idea if the Cavendish family still has enemies?"

"Not that I've heard of." Ramsay gave another half-hearted shrug before he tilted his head in puzzlement. "Why do ye think I'd know?"

"Because you make it your business to know everything about these people. Because their secrets grant you your power. And—" Piers took the note from his pocket, the one with his brother's native language scrawled upon it.

Ramsay glanced at it before grasping his bicep in a vise

grip. "Piers, I ken this is my language, but ye can't think I had anything to do with—"

"It never crossed my mind." He narrowed his eyes at his brother, the years and pain between them yawning like a chasm upon which they stood on opposite sides. "Strange, that it should cross yours."

Ramsay released him, visibly vexed for such a self-contained man. "All three of these women have hair some shade of red."

"Therein lies the problem."

Ramsay pocketed the paper and they both watched as Lady Francesca broke from her dance partner as the waltz ended, slipping through the crowd and down the eastern hall. "It would be easier to do if ye'd not rendered the assassins uninterrogatable."

"One of them might pull through." Piers made a helpless gesture. "And eventually he'll be able to move his jaw again."

His brother shook his head. "I'll try to have an answer for ye before the wedding. In the meantime, keep yer fiancée and her companions out of trouble."

Piers was interrupted from a reply as the dowager Duchess of Kent, a great friend of his father's, engaged him with congratulations and a not-so-subtle interrogation regarding his impending nuptials.

He paid as close attention as he could to the woman, his notice drawn again and again to the corner Alexandra Lane had disappeared around.

When Francesca didn't return after five minutes, he worried that he should follow her. Could she be in danger, even here at the castle? Would anyone dare to accost her under the nose of the Terror of Torcliff?

He found Miss Teague as she politely returned an empty cup of punch to a footman with a cheery smile before drifting toward the same hallway down which his fiancée had disappeared.

Odd. Was she searching for Francesca, as well? He'd assessed Miss Teague to be a canny creature. Should he follow?

Excusing himself from the growing circle of dowagers and matrons flocking to him like a conspiracy of sharp-beaked ravens, he searched once again for Alexandra.

There. She'd finally peeked out from around the corner in which she'd ensconced herself, and was hurrying across the ballroom with no little alacrity.

They were up to something.

Piers made his excuses, and swept down the stairs, intent upon finding out just where the three intrepid redheads were going.

And what trouble they were certain to find.

CHAPTER SEVEN

"Did you find anything?" Alexandra whispered through the small crack in the door.

"It's easier to search if we don't have to answer that question every five seconds," came Francesca's hissed reply.

"Just . . . *do* hurry," she urged. "I don't know how much longer our luck will hold." Alexandra peered down the long stone hall. The shadows of restored tapestries hung in neat rows like windows to another time.

A darker time.

The east wing layout of Castle Redmayne was all wrong for such a caper. Gargantuan windows set into alcoves lined one side of the hallways, and treasures and objets d'art cast unruly shadows onto grand chamber doorways. The shadows occasionally shifted, threatening to snap her nerves strung as tightly as the violin strings currently serenading the ballroom with Strauss.

The melody filtered up from two flights below, and

Alexandra couldn't decide if it added to the tranquility of the temperate night, or to the eeriness of it.

She decided she was a terrible watchman—watchwoman? Was there such a thing?—as she found it difficult to keep her eyes from the unnerving suit of armor in the alcove opposite her. Hadn't the helmet been faced the other way last time she'd marked it?

"Oh, I've found her diary," Cecelia exclaimed, doing her best to keep her excitement contained within a whisper.

"And I a family Bible containing the Scottish line of the Ramsays," said Francesca.

"Do read quickly," Alexandra hissed back, wishing she could school the note of desperation out of her plea.

The lack of rejoinder from inside the chamber suggested they were doing just that.

Alexandra itched at raw skin beneath her mask of silver silk and white dove feathers, bedecked with tiny crystals, aching to rip it away.

She'd always hated these sorts of soirees. Masquerades in particular. What was it about a mask that granted an entire room of supposed nobility the permission to behave like debauched tavern revelers?

They couldn't possibly imagine that there was any true sort of anonymity.

And yet, men's hands grew bolder, venturing where they'd dare not otherwise. Women drank more, flirted shamelessly, even encouraged lascivious behavior.

To what end? Copulation? What woman would desire a man to do such things to her? To treat her so disgracefully?

To hurt her so terribly?

When Redmayne had entered the grand ballroom, she'd understood a little better why he'd select a masquerade for his first reintroduction to society. His black satyr mask covered all but his mouth and the very point of his beard, hiding all but the scar on his lip. It seemed he'd decided to embrace his new tenure as the Terror of Torcliff.

She couldn't help but admire his courage.

Her fingers tightened on the door latch, remembering.

Until tonight, she'd thought him comprised of all weathered angles and animalistic sinew. But tonight he wore more black than was fashionable and the effect had been stunning. All that unbridled power, now contained in a suit coat, threatened to burst forth at any moment. She'd been astonished to discover the thought compelled her more than it had repelled her.

Eschewing the convenience of gaslights, he'd had hundreds of candles lit for the occasion, casting a medieval glow over the revelers. They blazed in the chandeliers, and flickered from priceless crystal and silver candelabra on tables laden with delicacies and delectables. Clever little cups at the base of the candles caught any drips of hot wax.

A fortune in candles. Because a fortune he possessed.

He'd drifted through the twirling eddies of waltzing couples with feline grace, like a dark ghost who expected no one to notice him.

Or perhaps a lion who'd known the crowds of lesser creatures would part for him.

And they did. They all did. How could they not? He stood head and shoulders above most, his titanic size surpassed only by his enigmatic potency. The guests not only parted for him, they danced around him as though he were an ancient pagan god in demand of worship.

It made a great deal more sense that some of the more superstitious ancients believed certain men could be made into gods. Or that they'd been sired by one.

Conversely, she supposed, perhaps it made sense that the modern mind, influenced by penny dreadfuls, made a shapeshifting devil of him, instead. England had long since agreed upon one God, but in this unhallowed world, there were still demons aplenty. And since he had such mysterious wounds, and the build of a beast, it wasn't much of a leap for minds prone to such whimsical imaginings.

The candlelight had glinted off the dark layers of his hair, still too long and unruly to be strictly proper.

Alexandra had done her best to disappear behind a potted tree in the corner of the ballroom. Not a wallflower. Wallflowers sat where they hoped to be observed, aching to be danced with. To be romanced.

She'd fashioned herself a moth in a field of butterflies, and the effect seemed to be working.

A few times, she fancied she'd caught the gleam of a blue gaze in her direction from the slits in his hellish mask.

She knew better than to fancy that Redmayne had searched for her, but she'd caught her breath all the same.

Alexandra didn't like him in a mask. It covered his exotic cheekbones, and the hint of the playful dimple beneath his close-cropped beard.

Behind his sinister disguise, no one could read the boyish sparkle in his gaze. They might not notice the suggestive dissonance of his full mouth against such a marble-hard jaw.

Then they'd misjudge him even more fiercely thus, wouldn't they?

For in his dark attire and macabre mask, one could truly imagine he was the Terror of Torcliff, stalking the shadows for his next victim. Something helpless, something delicate and decadent. Like the virgins he claimed to dine upon.

She'd heard the assembly whisper about him, as he'd stood at the balustrade with Lord Ramsay. A terribly hostile-looking man as dissimilar in looks to Redmayne as he was in reputation.

Their jaws had a similar set, she supposed. Their mouths the same lush cruelty.

And their eyes, she'd noted. A wintry blue. The color of the sky after an angry storm.

"Look at this." Francesca's murmur rose in volume, breaking her reverie. "I've found where the Cavendish and Ramsay lines intersect."

"What does it say?" Alexandra whispered, opening the door a little wider to overhear.

"Drat." The book slammed shut, and Alexandra could picture the irritation tightening Francesca's mouth. "Sir Cassius Ramsay is something like eleventh in line to the earldom. He'd have to murder half the *haute ton* to bloody get his hands on the Mont Claire title."

"His mother . . ." Cecelia tsked. "What an awful woman. Her diaries seem to be mostly lurid and disgusting accounts of her vast affairs. She delighted in cuckholding her husband. I should not like to read further, but here, the year your family was killed, she mentions nothing of the massacre. In fact, she's lamenting that her sons are on the Continent, which places them solidly out of the country and—"

"Wait a minute." Francesca's voice became agitated. "I've seen this name before. During my previous investigation."

"Which name?" Cecelia's skirts rustled closer to Francesca's voice.

"Kenway. Lord Kenway. He's only second in the line of succession after me—"

The shadows shifted once again, drawing Alexandra's notice from the conversation. She slammed the door shut, trapping her friends inside. Squinting into the distance of the hall, she held her breath, certain she'd caught sight of a figure sliding into the darkness between the windows.

Just as she was about to open the door again, the character emerged into the silver shafts of moonlight cascading from the window nearest her. The sight of his satyr's mask sent her heart diving toward her stomach in a sickening, desperate attempt to escape.

"Your Grace!" she gasped, secret and troubling parts of her clenching at his stealthy approach, even as her hand searched for her concealed weapon.

"Doctor," he greeted her blithely, though she detected something ominous beneath the calm façade.

Fidgeting with her mask, she kept her voice loud enough for her friends trapped inside the chamber to overhear. "What are you doing here, Your Grace?"

"What am *I* doing here?" He signaled casually to the moonlit hall. "In my wing of the house? The wing I kept dark to dissuade any trespassers?"

She emitted a shrill sound that was meant to be a laugh but fell absurdly short. "Oh, is that where we are? I didn't realize . . . I was just—"

"Snooping?"

"Exploring." She gulped. She knew as well as he did there wasn't much difference between the two.

"Well, you won't find anything of interest in there." He gestured to her hand still wrapped around the door latch. "That was my late mother's chamber."

She released the latch as though it had burned her. "Oh? I never met your mother."

"Consider yourself fortunate."

There was that banked fury again. The one forever lurking beneath the rasp of masculinity. At his rather distressing reply, Alexandra had to attempt three swallows around a dry, paralyzed tongue before she could speak again.

Her job was to distract him. To draw him away from the door so her friends could escape. And all she wanted to do was to lift the hem of her skirts and flee down the hall back toward the stairs.

Only one thing stopped her from doing just that. The knowledge that he'd catch her, this predator. She'd not make it past the first window before he pounced on her.

And God only knew what would happen next, once his instincts had been roused.

"You have such an impressive collection here." She adopted an overbright tone, tripping toward the suit of armor gleaming in the moonlight. "Is this sixteenth-century Italian?" She fiddled with a pauldron that had tilted off kilter.

"Fifteenth-century Burgundian, actually." He drifted closer to her. Close enough for the scent of whisky, leather oil, and bergamot to entice her to breathe deeply. "But why did I get the feeling you already knew that?"

The pauldron suddenly came off in her hand.

"Merde," she cursed. Partly because of the mistake, and partly because he was right.

He reached around her, the hard disc of chest brushing her shoulder. She flinched away, and would have dropped the heavy metal armor had he not already grasped it.

If he noticed, he said nothing. "Cursing in French is so much less offensive, isn't it?" he stated casually. "Though I rarely find it as satisfying." He returned the pauldron to its original place, taking care to see it straightened, she noted.

"Have you seen Lady Francesca?"

The sound of her friend's name on his lips knotted a small frown between her brows which she refused to examine. "Not for quite a moment, Your Grace."

"Really? When I noted that you'd left together, I was certain I'd find a conclave of you drumming up some sort of mischief."

She stepped to the side of him and around, so she was no longer cornered in the alcove. "We most distinctly did not leave together." They'd made sure of it. Five-minute intervals to the moment. Well, ten for Cecelia.

He made a sound deep within his throat that could have been disbelief "My mistake. You wouldn't happen to know where she is? I'd speak to her one last time before the reveal."

Panic choked her, and she willed herself to remain calm.

Did he know? Was he toying with her like a cat was wont to do with a helpless bird? Did he hear them earlier and was merely allowing her to bury the three of them in a grave of lies?

Don't bolt, she admonished herself. *Stay calm.* "Francesca?" That came out as a word, right? Not a squeak? "Where she is? At *this* moment?" She took one tiny backward step down the hall toward the beckoning light at the top of the stairs. "I—I could not say where she is, though I would wager she's a bundle of nerves. Situations such as the one we find ourselves in tend to make one anxious, don't they?"

"Evidently." He glanced around, his mask taking on an almost lifelike cast, half in moonbeams, half in darkness. "Your friend never struck me as the sort to give in to bouts of nerves."

She retreated one step more. "Yes, well . . . it's impossible to decipher anyone's true nature, is it not? The most charming smile could be cloaking a devious evil, and the bravest countenance can disguise a coward. We all wear something of a mask, don't we?"

"Indeed." The bleak note in his reply struck her. "What are you hiding behind yours, I wonder?" He reached out to smooth an errant dove feather.

Alexandra summoned every bit of her will to remain still. "Me? Oh, oodles of secrets, upon my word."

"Care to share any of them?" He took a step closer, and she a simultaneous one in retreat. Why must he be so bedeviling? Why did his mere presence send her pulse fluttering like a bird trying to escape?

"Isn't it the nature of secrets not to share?" she challenged.

"You make an excellent point. I'll leave you to your secrets and ask you to share something else."

A kiss? she wondered. Alarms in her head warred with a strange and discomfiting clench in her belly.

"A drink." He motioned to two closed doors across from a high veranda overlooking Torcliff and beyond to where the dark sea met the sparkling horizon. Long sheer drapes fluttered in the breeze like specters in gauzy white robes. Angels or ghosts, depending on one's perspective.

Alexandra hesitated. The door to which he'd directed her was two doors farther from escape.

And yet, Cecelia and Francesca needed to stay hidden.

"Come and share one drink with me, Lady Alexandra," he pressed. "We can discuss my future wife, since the two of you are so close."

She found it was the last thing she wanted to discuss with him.

"You really must call me Dr. Lane," she said almost tartly.

At this he merely shrugged and lifted one side of his mask with a lopsided sneer. "It's my castle, I'll call you whatever I like."

"And you prefer Lady Alexandra?"

"I find that I do." He said this as though it had significance.

"Have you made any progress with our attackers from yesterday morning?" She latched on to a change of subject.

His gloves made a sharp sound as his hands curled into fists, and Alexandra worried about how much pain his knuckles must be in after the beating he'd delivered.

"The one I shot is at the morgue, the other in hospital." His tone denoted more pride than disappointment. "But as soon as he wakes, the authorities will allow me to be present for his interrogation."

"Wonderful," she said with a relief she didn't at all feel.

Approaching a room, Redmayne opened the door, and swept his arm gallantly for her to enter first.

She paused in the doorway, all the blood draining from her face.

Forcing her limbs to move, she gave a weak cry and leaped away, retreating to the far side of the hall.

Chapter Eight

Alexandra somehow knew that beneath his mask, Redmayne regarded her as though she'd lost her mind.

For a moment, she had.

Because she could not cross the threshold into *that* room.

"Not the study." She shook her head vehemently, a tremor overtaking her limbs. If she saw his desk, she'd go mad.

"Why ever not?" He peered into what was surely, to him, an innocuous room. "Did you see a spider?"

A spider. "Yes!" she said. No better excuse for hysterics. "Yes, I—think it was a spider."

"Well, show it me. If I can save you from two grown gunmen, surely I can vanquish an eight-legged interloper."

"I—I'd rather not get close." She backed farther away, unable to compel her body to cease until a wisp of a curtain caressed the backs of her arms. "Might we tarry outside to the veranda?" At least there, someone could hear her scream.

"Certainly. I prefer the outdoors to a stuffy room filled with books." He examined the doorway for errant arachnids. "And to drink?" he asked idly. "Wine? Sherry? Brandy? Port?"

"*No* port," she announced, rather more insistently than she'd meant to.

At this, he produced an imaginary notebook from his pocket and equally invisible pencil, which he moistened on his tongue. "Emphatic dislike of port," he pretended to note. "Fear of spiders, studies, and stablemasters, but not snakes, stallions, or scandalously unclad felines." He looked up as though to consult her. "Anything else?"

Something about the dramatic patient expectancy behind his demon mask struck her as absurdly comical and threatened to disarm the clamor of the bells inside her head.

"We've not the time, nor you the imaginary lead to dictate the alphabet of my neuroses," she lamented wryly.

"Very well then." He flipped his invented notebook closed and repocketed it. "Whisky or wine?"

"Whisky, if you please," she decided, and hoped for a large, medicinal dose.

"A gentleman's drink. I should have known." Careful to avoid any hiding spiders, he disappeared into the study, leaving the door ajar.

"You've dropped your pencil," she called after him, unable to help herself. He'd not returned that imaginary object to his pocket.

"Let the servants try to find it," he volleyed back, his voice warm and beguiling. "It'll give them something to do."

Despite herself, she indulged in the nervous laugh he elicited.

He returned with two generous pours of whisky in elegant glasses and didn't hand one to her until they'd drifted past the curtains onto the balcony.

Alexandra took a brooding sip, chagrined that they could still see most of the hallway through the uncommonly large windows.

She brought the whisky to her lips, drinking deeply. A part of her wondered if the flavor of caramel and salt caressing her tongue was part of the whisky, or the man who'd handed it to her.

"You are worrying about your friend, I think . . . what with her being coerced into marriage to a brute like me."

Alexandra paused mid-sip. She'd not been worried about that at all, she'd been thinking that it felt rather strange and intimate to put her mouth where his fingers had just been.

"I would . . . be a liar, Your Grace, if I said I did not fear for Francesca's future happiness."

He watched her with undue interest as she savored the velvet burn of the blend as it slid down her throat and trailed a path of light and fire all the way to her belly.

"Such a careful, clever woman, you are," he murmured, turning to consult the moon hanging close as a lantern on such a clear summer's night. "You are a school friend of Francesca's?"

"Yes."

"Tell me about school. De Chardonne, was it?"

It was the last thing she ever wanted to discuss. "Not much to tell, really. Between a lady's useless curriculum and regimen, we mostly romped about the lake and read books we weren't supposed to, thinking it made us proper heathens."

And buried the odd murder victim.

"I'm familiar with the place," he remarked. "A mill for eligible young noblewomen to launch into the marriage market. How extraordinary, that none of you wedded until now."

"We promised not to."

"Why?"

She detected no censure in his voice. Only curiosity.

Because I was raped. Because Cecelia's father was cruel and Francesca watched men in masks slaughter everyone she loved. What draw had the opposite sex after all that? Besides, were they to marry, their lives, their dreams, and their money would no longer be their own. Because—until now—no one was willing to pay the price for the protection a husband could provide.

None of them had needed to.

"For reasons, innumerable," she muttered.

He made a droll sound. "No doubt. Well, I'm not ignorant of the fact that the countess would rather kiss a toad every night than my malformed lips. I suppose she'll have to let the duchess stipend and subsequent heir bonuses ease the misery of being a casualty of my vengeance."

"Duchess stipend?" Alexandra lowered her whisky glass to rest on the marble ledge of the veranda.

"It's an antiquated practice, I know, but her indulgent father insisted upon it." He smirked. "A lurid sum of money, even by my standards."

Alexandra clutched the railing. He must have known he was being terribly uncouth to speak of it. And yet, none of their interactions had resembled anything close to propriety.

Why start now?

A duchess stipend . . . A lurid amount of money.

A soft thud and a strange click from the direction of the duchess's rooms drew both their notice, and Alexandra had to make a desperate move to keep him from investigating.

Panicking, she spouted the first thing that had come to mind. "What happened to your face?"

To her relief and chagrin, it worked. He turned back to level her with the kind of examination one tended to save for whatever was being crushed beneath a microscope.

"Oh, I've offended you, haven't I?" Why was she forever doing that? Blurting out the most ridiculous things.

The duke reached up and slid his mask away, revealing his scars. "You mean you don't believe I'm a werewolf?" he asked, his eyes glinting a dark azure challenge in the night. "Or a demon?"

She could believe both of those things.

God's bones but there was something . . . inhuman about him. Something at once bestial and ethereal. Primal and preternatural. Elegant and enigmatic.

How could such a paradox of a man exist?

And why did he bedevil her so?

"I don't believe in curses or demons," she reiterated. "Are not men monstrous enough?"

For a moment he said nothing, and then, "A jaguar came upon our company in the night whilst on a hunt in Peru. It swiped at me, I shot at it. We wounded each other. Not a very exciting story."

Alexandra took a drink, trying to imagine the pain of such a predator's claws flaying open one's face. He was lucky to have kept both eyes.

He was lucky to be alive.

"The wounds refused to heal," he continued. "And then I came down with such a terrible fever, no one expected me to survive. I even sent a good-bye letter to my fiancée."

"To Francesca?"

"No, no, I'd forgotten Francesca existed. For the first ten years after her family's death, it was barely agreed upon that she'd survived that fire. And once her survival had been established, our fathers were both dead, and she was naught but a girl I'd never met on a faraway shore. No, until very recently, I'd fancied myself in love with another." He drank deeply, finishing his whisky in two swallows. "I thought to spare both Francesca and myself from an unhappy match by declaring the silly contract void years ago. Your friend seemed eager enough to do the same."

"What changed your mind?"

"I returned three months to the day after I'd written the farewell letter, to find my fiancée married to my cousin, the next in line to the Redmayne duchy." He stared at the bottom of his glass, as though lamenting its emptiness.

"That's . . . why you resurrected the contract with Francesca?" The pieces of the puzzle began to fit neatly together. Francesca's summons truly had nothing to do with her past, and everything to do with his.

Redmayne nodded, guilt playing a thief with his gaze. "Your friend overcame the reputation of death as miraculously as I did. Noble marriages have been built on less. To be honest, any lady of lineage would do. I don't want a particular woman. I want what only a woman—a wife—can provide me."

"An heir," Alexandra whispered.

"Two or three, if possible. Just to make certain that devious bitch never becomes a duchess."

Alexandra frowned. "Seems like a rather spiteful reason to sire a child."

"Spite is the only reason I have left." He sent a heart-stopping glance toward his mother's chamber door. Alexandra only breathed again when she verified that it remained closed and the shadows still. "My legacy has been built on spite and violence. Why not honor my savage Viking lineage, as well?"

The spark of an idea began to itch at Alexandra's mind. One that both enticed and terrified her.

"Did you kill him?" she asked.

"No, if he wants such a faithless woman as Rose, he can have her."

It took her a foggy moment to realize he'd mistaken her meaning. "I meant the jaguar, not your cousin. After you recovered, did you hunt him?"

A muscle bunched next to his jaw. "Oh, yes. It took me a deuced eternity to find him. But find him, I did."

"Did you kill him?" she repeated, feeling as though a cataclysmic decision hung upon his answer.

"No." He answered upon a long sigh. "I had him in my sights. Up in a tree. He was thin and mangy; due to his wound, he'd probably not been able to hunt for a while. But he'd blood on his mouth from a fresh kill and recent meal. We stared at each other for ages. Neither of us moving. My finger lingered over the trigger." He caressed an imaginary gun as he stared out to the sea. Alexandra imagined he was not here in Devonshire at all, but back in that jungle in Peru. He blinked and the spell was broken.

"I found I'd lost all taste for the hunt. I no longer wanted to pit myself against predators. Not of the animal variety, anyhow."

"You let him live," she marveled.

"And he let me leave. I suspect we'd both had enough of the entire business."

"That wasn't spiteful, it was compassionate," she said, her decision made. "And he was the one who condemned you to be the Terror of Torcliff."

He turned to her, looming closer. Larger. "Don't," he whispered.

"Don't what?"

"Don't try to make me a good man."

"I wouldn't dream of it, Your Grace." When she should have retreated, she didn't. Instead, she finished her whisky as well, enjoying the warm languor spreading from her middle to her blood.

"Good." He became very still, watching as she licked the last of the honeyed liquor from her lips. The cool of the night suddenly disappeared, the air turned heavy with salt, and moisture, and . . . something more illicit. Possibly dangerous. "Have you ever really been kissed, Alexandra Lane?"

She blinked. And froze. However, the usual paralyzing terror that would have cinched around her bones at such a predicament . . . didn't. Fear was more of a faint shimmer through veins made sluggish with whisky.

It was accompanied by another, more curious emotion. Not excitement, but something adjacent to it.

Why did he want to know? What did he hope her answer would be? Indeed, what should she say?

The truth, of course. A lie would not serve her here, and besides, she'd too many of those on her conscience to bother with a flippant fib in the dark.

"N-no." She wished her voice were stronger. That she'd had a different, more worldly experience to share. But alas, she'd never allowed a man close enough to kiss her. As far as she was concerned, men had long ago ceased wanting to.

"I thought not," he murmured, setting his glass next to hers on the banister.

Alexandra forced another swallow. "How—I mean—why thought you not?"

And why was she suddenly speaking nonsense?

A faint hint of arrogance brushed at his lips. "Men like me can just tell."

Her heart kicked against her lungs, evoking shorter, shallower breaths. "Men like you?"

"Hunters." The vibration of the word spread down her spine and unfurled in the most alarming places. "Your lips, innocent as they are, beg to be kissed whenever I am near. Your tongue moistens them. Your teeth worry at them. And when I stare, as I am doing now, they soften and part, like an invitation . . ."

Stunned, Alexandra curled her lips around her teeth as if to hide them from him. Had he really gleaned all that from her mouth? Had her lips truly betrayed her so?

He paused, glancing up. "Your eyes are always afraid, though. I think it's because you can sense I want to kiss you, too."

"Y-you do?"

He nodded, his own lips melting into a soft smile at the abject astonishment in her question. "Since the moment we met on the train platform, I've dreamt of kissing you in more than a dozen ways."

The sound she emitted was somewhere between a cough and a gasp. Were there more than a dozen ways to kiss? How many more?

"We . . . we shouldn't be speaking of such things, Your Grace." She turned away from him, suddenly trembling at the edge of an abyss, ready to leap into madness.

He drew close, never once touching her. But the heat and strength of him stretched beyond his physical being, threading through the night toward her, endangering her composure. Her resolve.

"It's wrong, I know it," he murmured, his voice containing an agony that tugged at her racing heart. "I'm to announce my engagement to your friend this very night, and all I can think of is what you'd taste like. I'm more of a monster than any scars or scandals I claim. But I've not kissed a woman since before the jaguar. I've not particularly wanted to until your lips drove me to distraction."

Unable to hear any more, she whirled around. "Would you marry me?"

The idea had sparked like a fever, an idea that could fix everything. An idea that would release them all from the clutches of their sins.

All it would cost was her soul.

"What?" The question drove him backward.

A strangled sound emitted from the room containing her friends, but he didn't seem to notice it.

Maybe it was the moon, the whisky, or the chance for redemption that steadied her. That gave her a voice through the throes of torturous tremors threatening to steal her knees from beneath her. But she was somehow able to repeat the question with much more conviction the second time.

"If I let you kiss me, Your Grace, would you accept *me* as your willing bride, rather than Francesca?"

His mouth fell open, deepening the crease of the scar there. "What are you on about, woman?"

This time, it was she who advanced upon his retreat. "You said it yourself. You don't much care for Francesca. Nor she for you. You've admitted to wanting to kiss me, and so it stands to reason you might want to do more. To do . . . everything."

"It . . . stands to reason?" he echoed.

Surrendering what was left of her pride, she said, "I find that I'm in need of a wealthy husband, as my family is bankrupt and at the mercy of their debtors. My father is . . . he's not well. And so I hope you will consider my offer, as the daughter of an earl, an alternative to your present course of action."

He turned away from her, but not before she caught the compress of his lips into a tight line. "It was the duchess stipend, then, that enticed you to make this most generous offer?" A hint of derision threaded into his words.

Alexandra had to clear nerves from her throat to answer. "I'll not lie to you, sir, it was."

Wasn't it?

"Nothing *else*?" he pressed darkly.

"Nothing else, I assure you." She hurried to put him at ease. "I'm not after the title of duchess, the prestige, nor do I have any false expectations of love or affection. This would purely be a business arrangement, much like you had with Francesca's father. Funds in exchange for heirs. My family is notably fertile, and—"

"What about Francesca?" His hands tightened into fists as he pressed them into the banister, leaning all his weight out toward the darkness, as though prepared to jump. "You would do this to your friend?"

"I do this *for* her." Alexandra took one more step forward. "You admitted yesterday morning that you don't like her. And you only just mentioned that she'd rather kiss a toad than marry you. What kind of future is that for either of you?"

His chin touched his shoulder. "Has she said this to you?"

Alexandra flinched at his hard monotone. What if she'd read this entire situation all wrong? What if he had wanted Francesca more than he'd let on? "Not exactly in those words . . ."

Tension threaded into the muscles beneath his suit coat, further straining the seams. "What words did she use, *exactly*?"

"Well, I don't want to be rude . . ." she hedged.

"I think we're beyond propriety."

She had to admit he'd a salient point.

"Francesca mentioned the rack as a favorable alternative to marriage." At his gruff sound she hurried to amend. "Though I'm certain that would apply to *any* marriage. Not to you, specifically."

He crossed his arms over his impressive chest, turning to lean a hip against the banister as he regarded her with eyes the color of the frigid winter sky. The very night held its breath alongside her. The breeze died, the curtains fell still, and her racing heart seized within her chest.

Finally, he spoke in tones only amplified by moonlight. "My lady, you've managed to transfix and trouble me all at once."

"I'm sorry." It was the first thing she could think of to say, and she was surprised that it touched his mouth with amusement.

"I'm inclined—no—I'm utterly tempted to accept your proposal. But I hope I do not offend you by saying I do not know enough of your character to take you by your word."

"No offense taken," she answered honestly. "Neither of us has a good measure of the other to assume any trust."

"Then let me suggest an amendment to your proposition."

"An amendment?" For the first time since they'd met, he truly sounded like a duke. All airs and graces.

"I will be at the top of the stairs in the grand ballroom at midnight, as per the original design. I will call everyone to attention and invite my future fiancée to join me for our inaugural dance." He pushed away from the banister and closed the distance between them in languorous strides. "You will be standing next to Francesca at the foot of the stairs, and whichever one of you ascends to take my hand, she shall have it in marriage. I will then know that the *other* gives her blessing."

It pleased her that, despite his desire, he did not wish to take what Francesca might not wish to forfeit. Despite his protestations to the contrary, it was easy, in that moment, to fashion him a good man.

"That is more than passing fair." She stuck out her hand, exactly as she'd done at the train station. "I believe we've struck a bargain."

This time, he didn't hesitate to take her hand, but instead of shaking it, he drew her toward him.

She resisted. "What are you doing?"

"Why, I'm collecting my kiss." He leaned lower, his eyes fixed upon her lips.

She pressed her trembling hand against his chest. "But you do not yet know if we are engaged to be married."

"Kiss me, Dr. Lane. As my future bride, or with a last touch of grace before I pledge myself to another, give me this kiss to remember you by?" The bulk of him hovered above her hand. Giving no quarter, but gaining no ground.

He could have. So easily. It would have been nothing for him to thrust her arm aside and invade her space. Her mouth.

Her body.

But he didn't. He remained where he was, a tide of seductive grace and masculine desire controlled only by the feeble blockade of her quaking palm.

"If I decline?" she whispered.

He looked down at her hand, covering it with his own before he lifted it to his lips, pressing the ghost of a kiss to her knuckles. "You'd send me away a bleak and forlorn man."

His back was to the moon, casting his features in shadow. She yearned to ascertain if his gaze was as playful as his voice had been. "If I sent you away . . . you'd go?"

She sensed rather than saw his frown. "If that is your wish, I will trouble you no more."

"One kiss. Nothing more?"

"One kiss." His head tilted, and the moon shone on his wound. His tongue touched the ridge of the scar, as though he hoped it might have disappeared. "One taste. That's all I ask . . ."

"Ask?" He was *asking* for a kiss? Which meant she could deny him.

She readily understood that in order to grant him the heirs she'd promised, she'd have to do a great deal more than kiss him. Her head swam, as if a fog had rolled in from the sea. Thinking beyond the powerful shadow in front of her became as difficult as swimming against the tide.

She couldn't think of that now, or she'd do something ridiculous.

Like run.

"All right." She couldn't decide where to put her hand, so she gently rested it on his shoulder. "Just one k—"

His mouth was upon hers before she could think, before she could react, or respond, or change her mind.

She'd expected to tolerate his kiss like a maiden subjected to an acute torture. She squeezed her eyes shut, drawing her lips tight against her teeth.

But his kiss wasn't torturous at all. Merely a brush at first. With no more pressure than a hummingbird used to land on a lilac bush.

A confusion of sensations paralyzed her. How could she feel both panicked and protected? Both delicate and desirable? His shoulder beneath her palm was tense. Unyielding. But he didn't grasp at her, or draw her in, or press her close.

He didn't touch her with any part of his body but his lips.

His mouth was infinitely gentle as it did little better than hover above hers in the merest caress of a kiss. A soft warmth suffused her, one she expected had nothing to do with the whisky. It drove the cold fingers of dread to release her lungs and rescued her heart from its panicked stampede.

Only when she allowed herself to exhale did he press his mouth fully to hers, coaxing it to soften in sweet, aching drags. She felt the impression of his scar. Sensed his hesitation as it caught against her lower lip. And in that moment, she felt the need to encourage him more urgently than she required reassurance.

She lifted her hand from his shoulder to shape it over his jaw. The hair there was wondrously soft, and she tested it with questing fingers as she turned her mouth to press against the tight stratum where his scar interrupted his lip.

At this, he went impossibly still. His own breath catching as he awaited her next move.

She didn't have one to make. She enjoyed the feel of the bristles above the fullness of his lips. The square rigidity of his jaw and the angle at which it filled her palm. His profile was so male. So abstractly dissimilar to her own oval features.

His breath faintly smelled of whisky, and she thought she might taste it as she breathed it in. Just as her insides melted into a liquid puddle, his tongue slid along the seam of her mouth.

Alexandra reared away from him, breaking their kiss. She pressed her fingers to her lips, as if she could keep the sensation trapped there. Attempting to reject the bile rising in her throat. Pushing away the memory of another man's tongue.

Running along her face as he pinned her down . . .

"Forgive me." Redmayne's voice was colored with an

indulgent fondness she'd not expected to exist among the darker shades of desire. "You're so fascinating. So intelligent and straightforward, I forget that you're also— untried."

"I'm—"

"Until midnight, Lady Alexandra." He pressed his lips once more to her knuckles before releasing her. "I'll leave you here to consult with your friends and make your decisions." He cast a pointed glance at his mother's room before collecting his mask. He only paused for the space of a breath in front of his mother's chamber before donning the mask and disappearing around the corner.

Alexandra gaped after him in sheer amazement, her fingers still pressed to her mouth.

He'd known. He'd known they were there the entire time.

Alexandra lurched over to the door and placed her hand on the latch. Her arm was nearly wrenched from its socket as Francesca yanked it open and barreled into her.

"Alexander, no!" Francesca gasped, shaking her none too gently. "What could you be thinking? Have you gone mad?" She pressed her hand to Alexandra's cheek, then her forehead, shifting the mask out of place as she checked for a fever.

Cecelia swatted at her hands, the peacock feathers in her mask glinting vibrantly in the moonlight.

They reminded Alexandra of his dramatic eyes.

He'd kissed her. Only once. He'd taken no more, even when she'd pulled away.

"Let me do this," Alexandra said resolutely. "My mind is made up, Frank. Marriage to Redmayne solves nearly all our problems."

"Oh, *horseshit*," Francesca cursed. "This is tantamount to you falling on your sword for the sake of—"

"I can't have any more attempts on your lives because of me!" Alexandra wailed. "If I lose one of you because of what I've done—"

Cecelia stopped her with a hand on her arm. "I thought we were under the impression that yesterday was an attempt on Francesca's life."

"Are we? Whoever is blackmailing me has made it painfully clear that if I couldn't pay in funds, and soon, they'd take everything else from me. Including those I love." A familiar ache tightened her throat, and fear unsettled her stomach, replacing the warmth left by a singular kiss. "Even if the shot *was* aimed at Francesca yesterday morning, it could have been a warning to me. We simply don't know."

"Alexander." Francesca struggled to retain her composure. "I know we're both in a great deal of trouble at the moment, but that is no reason to marry a *man*." She said the word as though it tasted foul. "When has the addition of anyone of the opposite sex ever *improved* one of our situations?"

"Now wait a moment," Cecelia said defensively. "Jean-Yves has been a great help to me for several years. I take him with me everywhere."

"He doesn't count. He's too old to be any trouble," Francesca snarked.

Cecelia ceded the point, redirecting her regard. "One of you needs to climb those stairs tonight and accept the duke's proposal . . ." She rubbed at the back of her neck, breaking away to pace a little. "I can't think of an outcome where marriage to Redmayne would be anything but a disaster for either of you."

"It's half ten," Francesca said. "We could run. We could catch a midnight train in Torquay or Exeter, and be back to London before dawn."

"You know that's impossible, Frank." Alexandra emphatically shook her head. "Tell me now, though I know the answer, are you desperate to become the next Duchess of Redmayne?"

"You would ask that of me? When you very well know I am not."

Alexandra stiffened her spine, gathering her strength. "Then I shall meet him at the foot of the stairs tonight. Redmayne seems to me an honorable man. The idea of his strength and skill used in my defense is more than a little appealing, should assassins beset us in the future."

"Does that mean you'll tell him everything?" Cecelia's features twisted with doubt. "It appears that he and Ramsay are on good terms and the Scotsman might just be grim and ruthless enough to enjoy a good hanging . . . or three."

"I would never dream of it," Alexandra vowed. "But until the three of us figure out what to do next, the duchess stipend will buy us as much time as we need. It would be of some comfort to rely upon Redmayne to protect me both physically and financially."

Francesca shoved her mask of raven feathers and rubies aside to spear her with a dumbfounded stare. "But . . . but . . . you'll have to trade your body, *your life,* for that protection. It's not worth it, Alexander. We'll find another way."

"Is it not the way of woman to lie beneath her husband in exchange for his protection and sustenance? How would I be different than any other wife for thousands of years?"

"Alexander, we all know why you're different. Why this is a greater sacrifice than anyone could expect you to make." Cecelia placed a staying hand on her arm. "We've already promised to help with what money we have. To marry would be madness. You don't know what he'll expect of you. What it'll be like to—"

"I know more than any of us what it'll be like. What to expect in the marriage bed." Alexandra silenced her friends with a direct gaze, fiercely keeping the fear from stealing her conviction. "It can't be any worse than what has already happened."

"You can't be sure of that," Cecelia whispered, a singular dread tinging her words.

"Nevertheless, I won't allow Frank to take his hand." Alexander pulled away from them, needing a breath. "Francesca, you found the proof you needed to exonerate his family from the crimes against yours. If I marry Redmayne, then you remain free to seek your justice."

A shadow of doubt darkened Francesca's features before she visibly shoved it away. "No. We'll find another way. If we have to suss out this blackmailer and put him in the ground like we did de Marchand, we'll do it rather than sacrificing you on the altar of—"

"It's crushing me, Frank." Alexander rushed her friend, gripping her tightly as a wave of emotion threatened to wash her away into the void. "The guilt, the shame, the memories, the fear. I lose inches from my height because of this weight on my shoulders. I lose bits of my soul each time I'm contacted. Each time I pay with my father's money. I can't bear it anymore."

Tears sullied the inside of her mask, and she ripped it free. "When I received that razor in the post, I could have ended my own life with it. Did you know that? The only thing that stopped me was that once I was gone, there was no one to protect you. I can barely leave the house for fear someone's watching me. Or that my family or my freedom will be taken from me. Not to mention the danger to the two of you. I do not dread Piers Gedrick Atherton's bed so much as I do swinging beside you and Cecelia on a rope. Do I make myself clear?"

Cecelia and Francesca both held her, bearing her weight.

"Besides the razor, what other evidence of our involvement could anyone possibly have?" Cecelia asked reasonably.

"The carpet? What's left of the body? Who knows what sort of correspondence de Marchand made about me. Or us. What if he kept a diary, chronicling what he wanted to do to girls? Or made stock of what we pilfered from him? Who knows what kind of evidence damns us? We were so young, there's no way we could have considered all the ways in which we could have been caught. I lie awake at night and think of every possibility, and if I lose any more sleep over this, I'll go well and truly mad."

She pulled her head back from Francesca's shoulders, doing what she could to compose herself. "And so . . . to spare me this, I'll submit to whatever indignity Redmayne can devise upon my person."

Her friends said nothing in the dark for a very long time.

Cecelia shook her head, worrying at her lip.

Francesca's shallow breaths heaved against hers as her sharp mind aggressively sought another way.

"Besides," Alexandra amended. "I think . . . I think I want children."

"You think?" Francesca released her.

"*I do.* I do want children. I always have. And we all know there's only one way to go about getting them." The idea lent her watery smile a genuine tilt. "As it turns out, Redmayne has a need for an heir and a spare. Our ends, at least, are not at odds with each other. Whereas yours, Francesca . . ." She let the end of the sentence die away.

Francesca's expression was a paradox of elation and

misgiving. "What sort of friend would I be if I allowed you to do this?"

Alexandra took Francesca's scarlet-clad hands in her silver ones, enjoying the rasp of silk against silk. "The best sort. The sort who trusts me when I say I need this."

"The sort who would bury him in his own gardens if he hurts you," Cecelia offered.

"Yes, and this time"—Francesca's voice hardened to cold marble—"there would be no witnesses."

CHAPTER NINE

"My lords and ladies, it is my extreme pleasure to present to you the future Duchess of Redmayne."

Piers stood at the top of the grand ballroom staircase. Or rather, staircases, as two of them split from the platform of the opulent second-floor tier to deposit descenders on opposite sides of the ballroom, leaving the revelers in the middle undisturbed.

He extended his hand toward the crimson carpets of that staircase, at the bottom of which the Countess of Mont Claire and Lady Alexandra Lane gripped each other's hands like sailors about to walk the plank.

They'd come to an agreement, but neither of them readily moved.

Piers allowed the glittering guests to assume the pause was for dramatic effect. Hundreds of the *haute ton* stood below him, miraculously silent as they held their collective breath. It was as though, with his declaration, he'd frozen time.

A gasp ripped through the room.

Someone had begun her climb. Someone would take his hand, and with it, his freedom.

Piers couldn't bring himself to look. His heartbeat spiked, the sound akin to the night drums of the Liberia Jabo in his ears. It drowned out the murmurs of the crowd as ladies bent their heads behind their fans of silk and lace to discuss their snide astonishment.

And still he did not look.

Fuck. He forced a swallow past a cravat suddenly cinched as tight as a noose. He should have accepted *her* proposal there in the dark.

Decency be damned.

He should have swept her away with him, and stormed into the grand ballroom with her in tow, staking his claim immediately.

For, after what little intimacy she'd granted him, how could he kiss another?

Why would he want to?

Once a man tasted ambrosia, the idea of any other sustenance curbed the appetite.

Christ, she'd been sweet. Her amber gaze, accentuated by dove feathers and clouded with uncertainty, had nearly unstitched him. How had he never noticed the heat, the variation of hue, the abject brilliance and beauty of brown eyes before?

All that red hair accompanied a banked fire in her gaze. Not the spark of wit, like Miss Teague's, or an inferno of personality, such as Lady Francesca's.

Something warmer. Something ultimately more desirable.

How he yearned to fan the coals of heat he'd detected into a flame of desire. He longed to awaken within her something he could sense had lain dormant for so long. Perhaps her entire lifetime. Something no other man had ever stumbled upon.

Had anyone even searched? Or dared to brave the layers of her prickly intellect, her dowdy garments, and furrowed frowns to find the sensuous potential within the prim spinster?

Apparently not. All that exquisite softness had gone unnoticed.

Untouched.

Unkissed.

Until him. For a man who'd forged the most remote mountains in order to be the first to plant his flag upon its peak, he couldn't remember an expedition that'd ended with such unmitigated pleasure.

So why had he walked away?

Because the soft, accepting press of her lips against his scar had threatened to undo him. Because passion had overcome caution, and his hunger had driven him to taste her.

Because he'd frightened her, again, and her vehement retreat from his kiss had reminded him that he was no longer merely the Duke of Redmayne.

He was also the Terror of Torcliff.

An unsightly, ungainly brute with nothing but a title and a fortune to recommend him.

She'd said as much, hadn't she?

Rose had been after his title, and Alexandra was now in need of his fortune.

At least Lady Alexandra had been decent enough not to pretend otherwise. She'd made no overtures of affection. She'd applied no tactics of seduction.

And yet, he was in danger of becoming thoroughly seduced by her.

Perhaps it was better that Francesca climbed the stairs and took his hand. Theirs, at least, would be an uncomplicated misery. One free of the perils of longing.

The Countess of Mont Claire would never be in danger of having power over him.

Power he'd never again surrender to another woman.

Never.

A silken glove slid against his, and he knew it was *her* before he ever turned to verify. He'd pressed those exact dainty fingers to his lips. He'd enjoyed the feel of them against his chest.

His heart took one last jolting leap, and then, to his utter surprise, it settled into a rhythm of relief.

Her scent was becoming pleasantly familiar. A mix of orange blossoms and something earthier. Like fresh-cut grass or a spring garden. Faint, gentle, unobtrusive.

Just like her.

Alexandra Lane.

He turned to her, showing her proudly to their stunned audience. "I give you Lady Alexandra Lane, soon to be Her Grace, Alexandra Atherton, the Duchess of Redmayne."

He lifted her glove once more, allowing the tiny diamond bracelet on her wrist to dazzle him as he pressed another slow kiss to her knuckles.

Applause erupted from the gallery, and she gripped his hand with astonishing strength, as though he, alone, could keep her from being overrun by the raucous noise of their felicitations.

The orchestra struck up a lively Russian waltz in their honor, and over it all, Piers could hear the little explosions of her rapid breaths as she offered the room at large a tremulous smile.

"Should we take this dance?" he suggested.

He imagined she'd have given him the same look if he'd asked her to set herself on fire with any one of the thousand candles in the room. "Do—do we have to?"

Laughter washed over him with abrupt resonance, and he knew their audience would assume she'd said something witty or flirtatious. They might even assume this was a love match.

For why else would the Duke of Redmayne pick an unknown spinster daughter of an impoverished earl? With all the glitter, glamour, lace, and frippery bedecking some of the youngest, loveliest, and most eligible women in the empire. Why the educated bluestocking in an unadorned silver gown?

Had she even had a season? It was something he'd forgotten to ask. Something he'd never considered.

Why her?

If they only knew. Perhaps some of them did. Perhaps they could also identify what mesmerized him so completely. They'd be fools not to.

She was a soft, silver moonbeam in a room full of glowing golden candles.

And all the more radiant for it.

He leaned in close, his lips hovering above her ear as he breathed her in. "Forgive me, darling, but I'm afraid this waltz is in our honor. No one will be able to enjoy themselves until we open it."

"I was afraid of that, too."

Her odd reply drew another smile from him. He tried to remember the last time he'd smiled this much without artifice.

Had he ever?

He was pleased to note that every bit of poise and elegance she'd learned at de Chardonne was evident in the way she glided down the staircase with him. At the landing, her friends each grasped her hand in a show of excitement. Or congratulations.

But there was a desperation in their hold upon each other. A promise passed between glances that he neither liked nor understood.

What had transpired between them upstairs?

What had they been doing in his mother's rooms? He'd initially guessed they'd been idly exploring the future duchess's new holdings.

Had they been about something more deceptive? Something more deserving of her guilty behavior above stairs?

In the end, did it matter? Not really. In a month he'd have a bride, and she a fortune, and each of them would be satisfied.

No, he realized. No, he'd not be *satisfied* until he'd taken her to bed. He'd not be contented until he'd unwrapped the layers and uncovered the enigma that was Alexandra Lane. He'd determine if the sweetness he sampled from her mouth was amplified within the other recesses of her body. He'd thoroughly explore each uncharted curve of her, discover every freckle, every sensitive, secret place with his profane mouth.

He'd learn the exotic flavors belonging only to her.

And then, when he'd taught her what it meant to be an endeavor of his, and she was left spent and sweat slicked with the pleasure of it . . .

Only then would he claim her.

Then would he plant his flag, so to speak.

Suddenly a month felt like an eternity.

Piers didn't miss the way she stiffened as he pulled her toward him, sliding his hand around her ribs to prepare for their dance.

She quickly dispelled his worry that she might have forgotten how as, the moment he'd given her the cue, she followed his lead with practiced elegance.

As he suspected, their synchronization was flawless. Precise. Piers had never been fond of dancing, but he'd taken to it as easily as he'd taken to all things physical. In fact, he'd often picked his lovers directly from his dance card.

He'd noticed early in life that if one found an easy rhythm with a woman whilst dancing, the same was almost always true for fucking.

At the thought of that particular pastime, he looked down at the woman who felt as though she were made to fit within the circle of his arms.

As was appropriate, she kept her head tilted away, her gaze fixed elsewhere.

Actually, her eyes seemed unable to focus on anything as he twirled her about the ballroom in flawless cadence to the orchestra.

He spotted familiar faces in the crowd as they coiled past. A few Cambridge mates. An adventurer or two, most of whom had ceased to brave the wilds with him when he'd insisted on exploring deeper than caravans, comforts, and servants would dare to venture.

Those men, those so-called friends never once called upon him during his year of recovery.

His brother, Lord Ramsay, as always a stone-faced pillar of respectable contempt.

His cousin, Lord Patrick Atherton, Viscount Carlisle, and the raven-haired Rose beside him, narrow-eyed beneath a delicate ebony mask.

How strange that Rose wore the colors of mourning.

Piers lowered his head, his lips grazing the warm shell of his intended's ear. "Are you enjoying this, my lady?"

Because, to his continual astonishment, he was.

She turned her head sharply toward him at the touch, discovering too late that the motion brought their faces dangerously close. "I—er—which part?" she breathed, her tremulous whisper barely audible over the music.

He nudged his chin toward the extravagant ballroom as couples began to join them, though many merely watched, enthralled. "The part where you're alternately the most envied woman in the room, and the most pitied."

At that, she tilted her head to look up at him, a puzzled frown tilting her lush mouth. "Pitied?"

"While I am an obscenely wealthy duke, let us not forget what I look like beneath this," he mocked. "You're marrying a monster."

Her lashes fluttered beneath her own mask, which concealed nothing but flawless skin kissed by the sun with adorable freckles. "You are mistaken, Your Grace, I could never bring myself to marry a monster." She said this with such solemnity, such conviction, that a curious obstruction lodged in his throat. He had to clear it before replying.

"Either way, they're all looking at you."

"Don't say that!" She would have faltered if he'd not caught her and smoothed the ruffle with an extra twirl. Piers found the misstep more than passing curious as he stared down at the soft curve of her cheek just barely visible beneath white feathers.

"Why ever not? Don't ladies always take a rather mercenary pleasure in the jealousy of others? Don't you yearn to be the object of admiration?"

"Not this lady," she muttered. "I prefer isolation to admiration, truth be told."

"Because . . . you are shy?"

His question caught her off guard, and she took more than a passing moment to reply. "Am I shy?" She must have been addressing the inquiry to herself, because she provided the answer. "I suppose I am. But even if I weren't, I'd not care for this . . ." She nodded to the grandeur of the ballroom. "Because it's all empty, isn't it?"

"Empty?" he scoffed. "I find it rather overcrowded."

"Your castle may be full of people, Your Grace, but it's empty of authenticity."

Without meaning to, Piers clutched her closer. Could she be real? Did he hold in his arms the rarest of creatures? A woman of substance. Of integrity? One who tended more carefully to the capacity of her heart than to her coiffure? One who thrived on intellect and honor and genuine interaction rather than the empty endorsements of her peers?

He'd begun to despair that such a person ever truly existed.

Her beauty certainly appeared effortless. Her blushes authentic. Her grace artless.

Her kisses . . . innocent. Untried and unpracticed.

Was it truly possible that he'd found his heart's desire on a train platform, covered in tweed and mud?

"I wish they'd stop staring." A fretful note touched her voice, making it almost childlike. "When is this dance going to be over?"

A protective instinct he'd not known he possessed encouraged him to press her closer into the defensive shell of his body. "Relax against me," he urged upon sensing her hesitation.

"I don't think I know how." Her breath was quickening again, the pulse in her neck visibly rapid.

"Do try." He gazed down at her, the picture of the adoring groom. Indeed, his fond smile was more genuine than he could remember in a long time as he did what he could to soothe her.

"Don't let them see your fear," he cautioned. "They're like hyenas in the wild. They'll surround you and laugh whilst they rip you apart, all the while fighting over the shreds of what's left of you."

At this, she quivered but relented, drawing tighter against him, deciding for the moment that he was the lesser of two evils. "I—I don't think I'll make a very good duchess." She gave a forlorn sigh. "Perhaps you'll want to change your mind."

Never, he thought with more conviction than he'd expected.

He released her from his grip to hold his arm above her head, twirling her beneath it until their arms were stretched as far away from each other as they could.

Her eyes widened, as she realized that if he let her go, her momentum would tip her over.

Unworried, Piers enjoyed her skirt as it twirled and swayed against the floor like a fountain of liquid silver.

He demonstrated his strength, his control, as he tugged her back to fit scandalously against him, without missing one step.

Once again, the room erupted into enthusiastic applause.

He might have noticed it, if he'd not been so enthralled by the press of her body against his own. Gods but did he intend on enjoying every single one of her curves.

"I won't let them have you," he whispered against her ear. "You belong only to me."

CHAPTER TEN

Alexandra squinted down at her notepaper, trying to ignore the fact that she stood in a duke's bedroom about to make one of the most ludicrous decisions of her life.

Perhaps she'd brought entirely too many notes for a proper seduction.

She worried at her lip as she stared down at the rows of her neat, precise scrawl, the product of painstaking research from hundreds of texts. Resources ranging from epistolic to medical, scientific to fiction.

Alongside her academic pursuits, she'd devoured all writing she could find on anatomy, physiology, biology, mating habits of ancient and contemporary cultures, ritual, conception, childbearing, and the odd romantic novel. The most pertinent ones she'd read over and over in her desperate search to understand men. Or herself. Or the act.

To understand what had happened to her.

Now that she'd completed the research theory phase, she needed to move to the next step.

And quickly. Before she lost her nerve.

At the ball, once the initial fervor after Redmayne's declaration had died down, Alexandra had accepted felicitations from what had seemed to her every person in attendance.

But one. His former fiancée, Lady Rose Atherton, Viscountess Carlisle. The petulant woman had disappeared, and Alexandra couldn't say that she was sorry.

There'd been toasts, another dance, and not a little hovering from Frank and Cecil.

Alexandra had detected the entire scope of artifice in her interactions with the *ton,* from gentle curiosity to outright hostility. Who was she to become the next Duchess of Redmayne? A spinster and a bluestocking? Where were her parents? What was her pedigree? How had she and Redmayne courted?

Redmayne had been her bulwark. His arm, corded with strength beneath his fine suit, remained firmly attached to hers, sometimes quite literally holding her up as she stuttered and stumbled through social dictates she'd taken for granted as a young and well-adjusted girl of noble birth.

She'd been among scholars and skeletons for too long.

He had been the perfect paradox of charm and menace, his interactions ending either with delighted pleasantries or a victim struggling to recover from his caustic rejoinders.

He'd been quick to jump to her defense when necessary, and Alexandra couldn't have been more grateful.

Just as soon as she could politely do so, she'd escaped to her rooms, snatching her notebook as another idea had taken her hostage.

Their wedding would take place in a month's time. Which gave her thirty nights to lie awake and dread the wedding night, building nightmarish scenarios in her mind until it drove her mad and she leaped from the tower rather than go through with it.

Most distasteful duties, she'd discovered, were worse in the anticipation than the application. Also, if she could control the . . . the *situation* as much as possible, perhaps she could endure it more readily. If the worst of it was behind her, she could maybe stop obsessing about it.

With this in mind, she'd slipped through the dark back to the east wing and let herself into Redmayne's chamber. And here she sat, awaiting him like an executioner at dawn.

She had used her tiptoes to perch on the tall, cavernous bed situated on a raised stone dais in the center of the room. It was odd, surely, not to have a headboard against a wall. But the duke's chambers were situated in a round, grand tower at the top of resplendent spiral stairs. Besides, the proximity to the fireplace was lovely during winters or sea storms, and the two enormous windows afforded a breathtaking view of the sea beyond Maynemouth Moor.

From here, one could use the moonlight to spot the very tip of the fortress ruins peeking over the crest of Tormund's Bluff.

Alexandra contemplated the view as she idly picked at the tassels of the cord restraining the cobalt velvet curtains to the bedposts. She was a Red Rogue in a blue room. Blue, like his eyes. Like the blood in their veins that made this marriage feasible.

She clutched her list, stamping down the instinct to flee.

Her thoughts were doing the thing again. Where they became too loud, too fast, and disjointed. Where every shadow hid a dragon and every sound contained unseen dangers.

Her heart paused every third beat, then kicked against

her ribs most disconcertingly. Her stomach rolled and her limbs were as steady as a moored dinghy in a hurricane.

But she could do this. She *must* do this.

She simply needed to focus. To think through the entire act so she could shed this unholy trepidation and finally sleep.

He'd kissed her and it had been . . . almost entirely lovely. Until his tongue had attempted to invade her mouth, and the soft bloom of warmth his kiss cultivated had been doused by the icy shards of her memory.

Should they avoid that again, it might be all right.

And if not . . .

Well, there was plenty here to keep her mind occupied while he . . . did the deed. She could . . . date the tapestries on the walls by inspecting their weft and weave. Or she could categorize any one of a dozen artifacts artfully strewn about tables, the fireplace mantel, bookcases, or the escritoire.

If all else failed, she could close her eyes and think of England.

Alexandra did her level best to find a seductive position. Perhaps one she'd seen in the *Venus of Urbino,* a woman reclining on her side, her knee bent to accentuate the curve of her hip.

Or maybe standing against the bedpost, hands behind her? She discarded that one immediately as a supplicant pose.

She flopped to her back, maybe if she—

Footsteps approached from the hall, and her throat seized on a gasp as she sat up.

When the latch turned and Redmayne's wide shoulders filled the arch of his doorway, Alexandra exploded into a series of loud, uncontrollable coughs.

He was at her side in a few long strides, his scars pinching as his brow wrinkled with concern, then alarm. "What's happened?" he demanded. "Did you ingest anything?"

Alexandra attempted to speak through the spasms, which only served to make it worse. She seized his wrist as he made a frantic search of her vicinity and pulled him back toward the bed.

Her coughing resolved itself with a mighty sneeze.

He stared at her as though she'd just exorcised the devil. "What the hell is going on?"

Blinking up at him from watery eyes, she croaked, "No need to worry. I was choking."

"On what, in God's name?"

On her own fear. "On . . . myself. You startled me."

"*I* startled *you*?"

His brows fell impossibly lower, and only then did Alexandra notice that he'd not only relieved himself of his mask, but of his cravat, tiepin, and jacket as well. His shirt fell open to the divot in his neck. She remembered what he'd been like in the storm. Wild and wet, the dark whirls of hair covering the swells of muscle on his chest visible beneath the shirt the rain had plastered to his torso.

"Alexandra." His voice lowered in pitch. "What are you doing here?"

She stood on the round dais next to the bed still clutching him, finding that her fingers couldn't even encircle his dense wrist. Though he stood a step beneath her on the dais, she still had to drag her eyes upward to meet his. What she found in those azure depths made her swallow hard and release him.

Her mission, she observed, shouldn't at all be difficult to achieve if his gaze already contained such things.

"I've come to seduce you," she announced.

His furrowed brows climbed toward his hairline in surprise. "Seduce me?"

It was her turn to frown. "You're making a habit of repeating what I say as though it's extraordinary or astonishing."

"You're making a habit of saying extraordinarily astonishing things," he volleyed back. "I'm often uncertain I've heard you correctly."

"Oh, well, you have."

"Excellent." Looking exceedingly pleased, he tugged his shirt from his trousers.

"Wait!" She held out a hand to stop him. "Don't you want to know why I've decided to seduce you?"

He paused, eyeing her like Cecelia did the pastries she never denied herself. "Is it too much to hope that you were so overcome by my masculine appeal and erotic prowess that you couldn't stand to live another moment without the pleasure of my touch?"

Alexandra gaped at him, rendered momentarily speechless.

His lips twisted wryly. "You're worried you won't like the marriage bed; no doubt you've heard horror stories, and, being ignorant of the act, you're here to conduct some sort of scientific assessment of our physical compatibility before we take our vows."

Just as she'd recovered, this second observation had precisely the same effect upon her.

Because his guess was closer to the truth than she could bear.

"Well," she breathed. "Well, I—I'm not ignorant of the act, you see. I've read several anatomical texts and have done multitudinous research."

"Multitudinous, you say?"

There he went, echoing her again. "My research indicates

that females do—might—enjoy the act of congress. If it's performed correctly. Under the right variables, I mean."

He stepped on to the dais, crowding her backward toward the bed. "My research has indicated that as well," he murmured.

"What research?" She took one look at his self-satisfied smirk and frowned. "Oh." Alexandra couldn't tell if it relieved her or bothered her that he'd pleasured a woman before. Some stomach-curling amalgamation of both.

It was probably a good thing. He seemed as though he knew what to do.

He leaned in, reminding her of the substantial width and breadth of him. Their proximity to the bed forced her to inhale a deep, calming breath.

She could do this.

His nearness both overwhelmed and enthralled her. Here stood a dangerous man, an untamed creature, made more so by his wounds and his size and the ever-present wary tension in his wide shoulders.

He surveyed the world with disdain. With distaste. She'd noted it at the ball as she'd watched him on his platform, looking down at those below him like a king.

Like a god.

But when he gazed at her, as he did now, a warmth ignited in his eyes, turning them from winter skies to summer heat. The hard brackets beside his mouth softened.

And that dimple. It was almost unfair. She couldn't help but be charmed by it.

"It is getting more difficult to wait patiently," he rumbled, clasping his arms behind him.

"For?"

"For my seduction, of course." He smiled before her notepad on the sapphire coverlet snagged his attention.

Alexandra leaped for it before he could reach it, hugging the pad to her chest.

"Something you should learn about me as a husband." He chuckled, interest sparking in his gaze. "If I know I'm not meant to see something, it makes me all the more determined to do so."

Alexandra cleared nerves from her throat. If he'd sailed the Amazon and hacked through the Himalayas, she could likewise be brave.

She could do this.

Peeling the notebook from her chest, she looked down at the neat writing, taking comfort in a well-researched list. "Before I—we start. I have some conditions."

His dimple deepened until she couldn't look anymore. "Sexual conditions?"

That word. It made it more difficult to breathe. "Yes."

"Very well." He sat on the bed, indolently reclining on his hands. The very picture of patience and leisure. The lines of strength in his long body stood out, even when contained in his clothing. She could trace the cords of his shoulders and arms, the distinct lines of his thighs beneath his black trousers. A lion at rest. "Let's hear these conditions."

"Oh, um . . ." Alexandra stalled. In truth, she hadn't expected him to capitulate so quickly. She took the pencil from the clip and tapped it next to the first line. "It is reasonable to kiss me, but not with your tongue."

His scars, she noted, made his face more expressive. They moved with the muscle beneath his jaw, or when his eyes crinkled with bemusement as they did now. "Am I allowed to inquire as to why not?"

"Of course." That only seemed reasonable. She itched at her scalp with the pencil, as she searched for an explanation.

She hadn't thought to expound. His mind was an inquiring one, it was one of the things that drew her to him. "I'm . . . not prepared for that intimacy," she said simply, hoping vague would do. "Not yet."

He stroked his beard in a thoughtful gesture. "You're prepared for me to make love to you, but not for a kiss with my tongue?"

"Precisely," she lied. She was prepared for none of it, but could only endure so much. "That's the whole of it. And, whilst we are on the subject of tongues, I'd also like to avoid cunnilingus."

He shot up straight. No longer a lion at rest, but at attention. *"What?"*

"Cunnilingus," she repeated carefully, consulting her notes. "It's an oral sex act performed on a female's genital—"

"I know what it bloody is," he blustered. "I'm trying to figure out why in God's name you wouldn't want me to."

She blinked at him, frantically composing a reason that made any sort of sense. Judging from the rather graphic explanation of the act, she'd assumed any man would be rather relieved not to perform it. The female sex organ seemed to be a confusing and complicated structure for pleasure. From what she could tell, most men were likely to find the entrance, use that for its intended purpose, and then be done with the whole business.

"I just don't." She knew her reasons were all incredibly ambiguous, but in her present state. Alone. With a man. And a bed. About to do what she was about to do . . . well, her brain refused to perform the proper functions.

Thank Jupiter she'd written everything down.

Agitated, she stepped down from the dais, putting space between them, and made an investigation of a lovely velvet chair near the fireplace. Though she couldn't look at him for a moment, she could feel his eyes tracking her every move. "In fact, if you could refrain from licking me anywhere, I'd be obliged."

"As a gentleman, it's my duty to be obliging, though I'd like you to note my hearty objection on your list."

Alexandra looked at him askance.

Where she'd expected to find ire in his reply, something else threatened.

Laughter.

However, when she searched him for any sign of mocking, she found his features disturbingly enigmatic.

He stood, as though sensing she wasn't, quite yet, as ready for the bed as she'd claimed.

"I'll keep my tongue inside my own mouth." He gave a bereaved sigh. "Though you needn't return the favor."

At the implication in his eyes, her mouth, made dry as the Sahara by nerves, flooded with moisture. She'd read about such things, but it never had occurred to her until this moment that *she* might taste *him*.

That he'd want her to. That kisses need not be contained to the mouth.

Did he want that? Did he expect that as part of the seduction?

Her mouth on him. Her tongue on his skin?

Did she want to?

"Your other conditions?" He stepped off the dais, stalking closer.

To avoid watching the graceful way his body moved—and because doing so had strangely stolen every other thought from her head—she consulted her notes, finding her spot. "I'd prefer . . . that we take our . . . that we disrobe."

"That would be my preference also." He was closer, disturbingly so, and she couldn't manage to stop staring at her white-creased fingers as they gripped her pad with an almost violent desperation.

"Good. Good. We agree on that." She made an affirmative mark next to the note. "Then, perhaps we could face each other? I am aware of other positions but I must insist—"

"For the first time, I agree that's best."

Her head snapped up. "For every time."

At this, his lips quirked in a self-satisfied smile and Alexandra found her anxiety replaced by annoyance. "You'll change your mind," he predicted.

He didn't know. She had to remind herself. He didn't realize what she was doing. What these conditions avoided.

What her first time had been like.

"I *won't* change my mind," she insisted.

Something in her voice must have brooked no response, though his expression was equally skeptical and amenable. "You've given this entirely too much thought."

"I had to," she breathed. "That is how I . . . it's what I do."

She'd have backed away from his careful approach if his features hadn't softened into something so tender and fond, it rooted her feet to the ground.

"So I am beginning to gather." He kept his hands clasped behind him, a gesture both unthreatening and self-possessed as he made a great show of peeking at her list. "How many more of these conditions are there? I'm worried I won't be allowed to touch you by the time you're through."

"Just one," she whispered, distracted by the scent of him. By the way the soft fire gilded skin already darkened by the sun.

"Thank God."

"Perhaps we—" She had to swallow once again. Could she be hungry? Had she eaten anything at dinner? She couldn't remember. But something about his scent, that particular blend of clove, brandywine, and leather affected her in the same manner as would a succulent meal. She even felt it in her stomach.

And lower.

"Perhaps what?" he prompted mildly.

Gathering her courage, she glanced away. Staring at her list and seeing nothing. "Perhaps when you're . . . when we're . . . conducting the act, you could move slowly? Gently? So as to cause less trauma to the cervical tissues—"

"Good God, Doctor, put that away," he begged, his shoulders trembling with barely suppressed mirth. "I have to say this must be the most peculiar seduction in history."

Was it? She didn't have to ask as she watched his lips twitch as he valiantly fought his laughter.

She'd bungled it.

Deflating, she tried to puzzle out how to salvage the evening. "Which part did you find most peculiar?"

"Well, for starters, I've never heard tell of a woman demanding a man not use his tongue."

That hadn't been what she'd expected. "Really?"

He let his hands drop to his sides, and for a moment, she thought he might reach for her. Instead, he said, "Darling, it's the part of the anatomy most requested by ladies, all told."

"More often than the . . ." Unable to say the word, she pointed in the general direction of his hips, trying not to notice that the appendage in question had become noticeably larger.

"Categorically."

She made a face. "Why? It's so . . . wet and slippery."

"That's rather the point." He chuckled, the color in his cheeks a little higher than she'd previously seen.

Was he . . . blushing? Did men do that?

"I can't imagine how—"

"We can readdress that later." He held his hand up as though he could take no more, finally reaching for her. His finger slid beneath her chin, tilting it up. His face was a bemusing mask of ferocity and tenderness. "Don't fret. You've seduced me, utterly."

"I did?"

"And you need not fear what we're about to do. Only a beast wouldn't be gentle with you," he whispered earnestly. "Especially the first time."

To her horror, tears ached in the back of her throat. "Didn't you say all men are beasts?"

"Of course we are." His knuckle caressed her cheek. "It's why we need a beauty like you to temper us. To tame us. To teach us how to appreciate something delicate."

"Oh." She couldn't think of a single thing to say to that as her heart fluttered behind her ribs like a trapped sparrow.

"Now," he said. "Do you have anything else, or may I kiss you yet?" His head lowered, this time not intending to wait for an answer.

"Wait!" She reared away, placing the chair between them. "Don't you think we should remove our clothing before physical contact?"

The dimple returned. "Might I suggest an alternative?"

"Of course," she breathed. "Whatever it takes to make you more comfortable. It's your seduction after all."

He chuckled again at that. "Often during lovemaking, the lovers undress each other. Whilst kissing. Is that anywhere on your list?"

Lovers. A noun. A person having a sexual or romantic relationship with someone, often outside marriage.

That's what he was about to be. Her lover.

Not her rapist.

"How many lovers have you had?" The question escaped before it had fully formed in her mind.

He choked. Coughed. Then groped about for an answer.

"I don't need a precise number," she hurried to amend. In fact, she unconditionally didn't want one. Why had she even asked? "I was just trying to ascertain if it were enough for you to be considered well educated on the practice."

"I am, I assure you," he finally managed. "Let us leave it there."

"Very well." Alexandra stepped out from behind the barrier of the chair feeling somewhat akin to Joan of Arc or Ann Boleyn. Brave. Unsure. And . . . something else. A little curious?

Better to face the gallows now than to dread them for a month. Best to get this over with.

He was a kind man. One with demonstrated protective instincts, gentlemanly conduct, and—as yet unconfirmed—sexual skill. She could enjoy the kisses. She could endure the rest.

He took the list from her trembling fingers, an affectionate fondness tilting his lips. "I almost want to check this for anything else, but I'm afraid to."

There had been more. So much more she didn't write down. She'd wanted to ask him not to pull her hair. To request that the moon not shine. To inquire as to how violent his passions were.

She wanted to ask him, very bluntly, not to hurt her.

But then, because he was an instinctively observant man, he'd know what happened to her. He'd guess why she was *so peculiar,* as he'd put it.

And she didn't want him to know. Because then he'd ask who, and when, and how.

She could confess none of that. Not ever.

"It's natural to be nervous," he continued, lacing a finger through one of the curls spilling over her shoulder. He watched her with those keen, perceptive eyes. "You don't have to, if you've changed your mind. As difficult as it would be, I could wait until after the wedding."

Yes, she did. She *did* have to. The anticipation gutted her with every hour that passed.

"I need to do this," she told him. "I came to you."

"So you did," he murmured. "And before one of us leaves this room, you'll come for me."

"Wha—?"

He stopped her question with impatient lips. Impatient yet gentle lips.

This, she thought as a foreign, electric sensation poured through her. This intimate thing. This melding of mouths and breath and skin. She'd been unprepared for it before. It had tangled her up inside, amalgamating fear and enjoyment into a complicated and overwhelming array.

But this time. This time . . .

It was just a kiss.

Just a kiss, she thought, like the desert was just sand. Or the ocean was just water. Kissing Piers Gedrick Atherton was like standing at the mouth of the Nile and realizing the scope of it was beyond comprehension. That the beauty matched the peril, and in the awe-inspiring danger existed its own strange appeal.

He could break her.

He could protect her.

She feared him.

She needed him.

She wanted . . . *this.*

This sweet, languorous kiss. She wished it to go on forever. She felt the kiss in every part of her. In the places she ignored. It threatened the loneliness she'd so carefully cultivated. It stirred parts of her mind she'd kept dormant. The parts that had nothing to do with intellect and analysis. The darker places where she kept her young, fanciful desires hidden under shame and regret.

Perhaps shadows weren't so bad, she thought as he brought both his hands to rest at the sides of her jaw. If creatures like him, both wary and kind, drew her into the dark and kissed her like this.

Little sparks and sparkles of light shimmered through her, lighting her up from the inside.

She could do this.

She could kiss him back.

Alexandra reached for him, placing her hands against his chest as she'd done before. This time, not as a barrier, but as a caress.

The sound he made vibrated through her. Through him. A soft growl of encouragement she felt in her lips, her throat, in the hands against his chest. He rumbled like a great cat, purring to be stroked.

His lips pressed further, his kisses taking on a hungry edge. He opened his mouth against hers, his warm breath flavored with something sweet, something seductive. His tongue hovered, but it never touched her.

He kept his word. How much did it cost him?

Her lips parted beneath his encouraging pressure, parted and closed again in a voluptuous rhythm with his. Their mouths danced, driven by a primitive instinct she'd never known she possessed. Compelled by instinct, she stepped into him, and only then did he enfold her in his arms.

She stiffened, but just for a moment before he distracted her with a nibble on her lip that thrilled through her.

Beneath the buttery soft material of his shirt, his body was hard as iron. And warm. So very warm, latticed with dizzying power she sensed rather than experienced.

He'd never used it against her. Not once.

She thought she'd feel shackled, captured, helpless in a man's arms.

Yet here, surrounded by the scent of him, the strength of him, she felt . . . sheltered rather than shackled. Cosseted instead of captured.

And helpless, yes. Helpless against a beguiling, restless anticipation she couldn't begin to understand.

A hunger. Yes, a hunger. To touch, to taste.

Her tongue ventured past his lips before she even realized what she was doing, rendering her the worst sort of hypocrite.

His breath hitched, and his great body seized, then shuddered.

She pulled back, and his head followed her briefly, retaining the seal of their mouths for as long as possible before she broke contact. "Did I—I shouldn't—my tongue—I'm sorry."

He rested his forehead against hers, his breath labored as though he'd run a league. "You can use your tongue however you want." He leaned in for more.

She dodged his mouth. "But it's not fair, when you can't use yours. Because . . . that hasn't changed. I'm sorry."

"I forgive you." He released a breathy chuckle, pulling her more tightly against him. "I'll forgive you anything." He pressed a kiss to her temple. Her cheek. Her jaw. "Now let me carry you to bed."

She stilled, her silent war tearing her apart. She liked what he was doing. Liked the scratch and tickle of his soft beard against her neck and the contrast of his smooth lips.

Liked his tendency to warn her before he was about to do something.

She liked . . . him.

Didn't want him to stop.

Nor did she want what he was going to do next. She detested it. He'd become a revolting, thrusting, straining animal.

A true beast.

Gods, how she wished she didn't have to see him like that.

I can do this, she reminded herself.

"Yes. Take me to—" She gasped as she found herself swept into his arms. He reached the bed in a few giant strides and set her next to it.

Time raced after that. Faster than her dazed thoughts could process. He kissed her again, drugging her with his potent concoction of scent, strength, and restrained need. His arms closed around her as before, and in a few jerking motions, her dress loosened.

His questing hands drifted into the unlaced bodice. Slowly, deliberately, they drew up her stiff spine, encountering the wrap she'd contained her torso in.

"What's this?" he asked against her mouth.

"I don't like corsets," she explained.

"Mmm," he acknowledged, his lips already ravishing hers again before they took a similar path as they had once before. Down her jaw, toward her neck, nuzzling beneath the loosened collar to find the delicate skin of her throat.

"I—I hope you don't find that too scandalous," she fretted.

"Exceedingly scandalous." He nibbled at her ear with questing lips, and she forgot her name for a moment.

"It'll take longer to undo, as it's wrapped several times,"

she explained in a husky voice she didn't recognize as her own. "I suppose you don't have to take that part off."

"Oh, but I do." He slid her bodice down a little, exposing her shoulders to his lips.

Panic flared, but she forced herself to focus on keeping her quivering knees intact. She gripped him as he dragged his lips over her shoulder.

The beard helped. It swept over untouched skin eliciting an eruption of delicious shivers, chasing away the ones caused by her fear.

She could do this. The mantra had grown stronger this time.

Emboldened, she drew her hands down the vast expanse of his chest. His skin pulsed hot beneath his shirt, enticing her to explore.

The sounds he made fascinated her, little hitches of breath and moans released as soft vibrations. She wanted to—

"I wouldn't believe it if I didn't see it for myself." A snide female voice permeated the clamor of her thoughts and the rush of blood in her ears. "The beast and the bluestocking."

Alexandra stiffened as his fingers curled around her arms, stopping just short of painful.

His breath quickened, but when he pulled away from her, his eyes had become remote again. Frigid. His features, once melted to tender, fond warmth, now hardened to cold steel.

"Rose," he growled before turning around to face the dark beauty standing in the shadows of a bookcase swung wide on well-oiled, invisible hinges.

Alexandra clutched her bodice to her as the Viscountess Carlisle raked her with a calculating estimation and quickly dismissed her in favor of Redmayne. Her newfound confidence drained from her as quickly as the blood drained from her extremities.

What had the woman seen? What had she heard?

Why was she here?

The heat leached from her limbs, scalded her cheeks with a vicious blush when she realized the woman stood in front of a secret passage from, presumably, her rooms to Redmayne's.

Passages she'd quite obviously used before to gain entrance to his bedchamber.

"He's changed since his return, I assure you," Rose purred, touching her hair with the tip of a gloved finger. "More than just his features, I imagine. We should compare him sometime, the body I'm intimately familiar with, compared to the one he has now." She raked him with a lascivious glare that lit a fire of antipathy in Alexandra's belly. "I'm certain you're getting the better bargain."

CHAPTER ELEVEN

Piers had never been violent with a woman. Had never before been so utterly tempted. The inferno in his blood, ignited by the innocent ardor of his lovely intended, flared to a volcanic temper at the appearance of his former betrothed.

How dare she? How *dare* she invoke the pall of suspicion into Alexandra's eyes. How dare she make use of the passages he'd made available to her when their relationship had been definite and their passion had been new.

Containing the rage seething beneath his skin, Piers slid Alexandra's bodice back in place and pulled her in against him to reach around and adjust the laces he'd loosened.

Alexandra's breaths lifted her shoulders against his chest in small, rapid bursts, as she fought a valiant battle to retain her poise. He'd thought he hated Rose before, but now the bitter emotion that welled within him was amplified a thousandfold.

Damn her scheming hide.

"I need you to go," he managed through clenched teeth.

A grim determination compressed Alexandra's soft mouth into a hard line as she seemed to gather courage from him. "Yes, it's best you leave," she addressed Rose stiffly.

Piers was proud of her, shy little bird that she was, but she'd mistaken his meaning.

He cupped her face in both his palms, her skin hot with mortification. "No, darling, I need *you* to go."

Her neck tensed, and her amber gaze sharpened. "Me?"

"Yes." He kissed lips now stiff with distress before he could bring himself to look at Rose, who glared at them with raptorlike interest. "I don't want you to have to see this."

Her chin moved against his hand in a short nod, and when he looked at her, the uncertainty in her eyes nearly broke his heart. Christ, but she was beautiful, her peach lips glowing red from his kisses, the skin around her mouth lightly abraded by his beard.

Her lashes swept down, and she worried her lip, as appeared to be her habit when she had a question she didn't want to ask.

"I'll come find you, once my business here is finished," he promised, pressing his lips against her forehead.

Mutely, she nodded, trailing her skirt of moonbeams as she glided out of his chamber with her spine held perfectly erect.

"Alexandra Lane?" the viscountess scoffed, relieving herself of her black gloves by pulling at her fingers one by one. "Really, Piers, how utterly you've shocked us all. If you're marrying to make me jealous, you might have picked someone younger. Or at least wealthier."

Piers's fury struck him momentarily speechless. Were she a man, he'd have thrashed her soundly and thrown her out. "You will keep her name off your venomous tongue. Do I make myself clear?"

He took distinct relish when she hesitated, a spark of fear igniting at the bite in his words. She masked it instantly, wandering into his chamber.

Revulsion slithered through him. How had he ever thought her beautiful? The most desirable woman the *ton* had to offer? Her dark, exotic almond eyes had held him in their thrall. She'd enticed him with long, insolent gazes and silent, sensual promises.

She'd a fine-tipped elfin prettiness, coy and mysterious, all bashful lashes and sharp features.

Now, all he could find were her flaws. Her imperfect teeth. The beauty mark below her eye that would become an unsightly mole with age.

Her faithless soul.

She had the temerity to perch on the edge of one of the chairs across from the fireplace, her every motion posed and calculated.

She wanted to remind him that he'd fucked her on that chair.

He wished to God he hadn't.

She'd always loved to goad him. To push him beyond his limits of patience and control. To find his dark places and banked fires and fuel them with her subtle manipulations. Oh, he remembered how she liked him feral. Like an animal. She wanted bruises and marks, and fast, hard fucking.

She wanted him angry.

The purple skin stretched tight over his bruised knuckles as he reined in his temper and addressed her with a chilly calm belying the inferno raging within him. "I'd be tempted to brick over that passage," he said casually. "But since you'll not receive further invitations to Castle Redmayne, such action won't be deemed necessary."

"I've come to make peace, Piers," she said as though he'd not spoken.

He silenced her with a sharp gesture. "*You* will address me as Your Grace, or not at all."

The jut of her chin was the only indication his imperious command had affected her.

What a perfect little actress she still was.

"Surely what the peasants and patricians in this part of the world have taken to whispering about you isn't true." She smoothed her hands down her skirts, molding them to her thin legs as she flicked a glance at the door Alexandra had vacated. "That you've developed a taste for virgins?"

"I've a taste for the woman I'd make my *duchess*."

Another hit. She'd been unable to conceal her wince.

"It's almost cruel to thrust that mantle upon her. That woman is a mouse. She may be the daughter of an earl, but it was plain tonight that she'd neither the wish nor the proficiency to fill such a responsibility."

"And that is one of the many things my intended and I have in common." Somehow, discussing Alexandra with Rose already felt like a betrayal.

Standing, Rose swayed toward him with careful, measured steps. Her pale shoulders thrust back, her breasts clad in barely there black proudly displayed. "I know you're angry with me, but I've never had the chance to defend myself. Don't you think I'm owed that? Don't you wonder why I did what I did?"

"You married the heir to my title little more than a month after you received my letter informing you I would *likely* die," he said drolly. "Your reasons would be obvious to a blind man."

"That isn't fair." She pouted. "Patrick and I both loved

you—love you—it was our grief that drove us into each other's arms."

He speared her with his most imperious glare. "A shame it didn't keep you there."

"You've always been beastly." She lifted her hand to shape it to his scarred jaw, but he jerked his neck away, capturing her wrist. "And now you look like one." Her tone became acerbic. "You're many things, *Your Grace,* but you're not stupid. Everyone knows the Lane family is destitute. She's marrying your fortune. How does that make her any different than what you accuse me of being?"

He flung her hand away, hating the truth. Detesting that she knew it.

Rose's eyes narrowed, her fingers turned to claws. "Has she convinced you that she wants you? That timid wench? Do you really think she can look past what you've become and desire who you are? You didn't see her face, as you kissed her shoulders. You didn't mark the revulsion. The fear. She doesn't want you, she'll suffer beneath you so she can spend your money."

In desperation, she threw her arms about him, pressing her body against his as she breathed a husky whisper into his ear. "I've never stopped loving you. Desiring you. Your scars make me want you more. They show what you've always been to me. A magnificent beast. You're the Terror of Torcliff, you deserve a lover who can slake every monstrous desire."

She was all prickly jewels and tight, corseted posture, and as she crushed her curves to his body, the last of the heat Alexandra had ignited was doused by ice.

His hands had long forgotten the shape of her.

And now longed for the shape of another.

Was there any truth to what Rose claimed? Was Alexandra's reticence less timidity and more revulsion? Were her ridiculous conditions so she could stand to be touched by him?

"You're here to seduce me, Rose?" He said her name like it was a curse. "Is it my monstrous body you want?"

Her eyes watered. "I'm here because I saw you tonight and I died from wanting. I'm here because all I ever wanted was to stand on the tiered balustrade with you. My place was beside you. *Is* beside you. That is what you promised me, don't you remember?"

His lip curled into a sneer, his face tightening into something he was certain was as ugly as the feelings she evoked. "I promised you my heart, you fell in love with the rest."

"Your promise was empty!" she cried. "Your mother made certain your heart was as cold as hers. You chased me like one of your animals. And once ensnared, I became another pretty thing to mount on your wall. You pledged your love to me but fled your duty again and again. For two *years,* I waited for you to return from every corner of the earth, happy with your trinkets and your passion. But don't ever think for *one second* I caught a glimpse of your heart, because you never let me see it. I'm not convinced you have one."

Piers thrust her away. "Had you loved me, you'd have mourned me. Had you mourned me, I'd have returned to you. I'd have been your beast. Your animal. I thank that jaguar every night for the monster he made me, because it revealed what a monster *you* are."

"You can't mean that." She stumbled back, her hands out in supplication. "We're family now, Piers, at least let us—"

"Get. Out." She'd drained what little he'd left of his self-possession.

Reluctantly, she turned to leave, her ebony train dragging

like an inky trail behind her. She paused at the book-case, looked back at him. "You'll tire of her," she pre-dicted. "And when you do, I'll welcome back the beast."

The bookcase slid shut behind her, and Piers wrenched at the lever, rendering it useless.

He never intended to have a clandestine lover.

He was not his mother. He was not like Rose.

Once he'd married, he'd never stray.

Alexandra Lane would be his one and only lover.

He was her beast now.

May God have mercy on her soul.

It had taken no little doing to calm Francesca and Cecelia down. They'd returned from the ball to find Alexandra missing and had worked themselves into a frenzy of worry by the time she'd slipped through the door.

She should have thought to leave them a note, but in her hurry, she'd taken her pad with her and quite forgot.

Three fingers of whisky had eased Alexandra's shak-ing hands and released the coil of tension from her chest enough to recount the evening's events. As she did so, her friends' eyes widened in identical, almost comical incre-ments until they resembled two redheaded owls staring at her in disbelief.

"You're so brave." Cecelia sighed rather dreamily. She had divested herself of her gown and corset the moment Alexandra had been confirmed safe and stood in the middle of her discarded attire donning her nightgown. "I would have been terrified of him."

Alexandra frowned at the defensive knot in her stom-ach. "Why would *you* have been?"

"He's just so big, isn't he? And ever so fearsome." She paused, her brows knitted with concern. "What was kiss-ing him like? Was he . . . gentle with you? Considerate?"

Alexandra had trouble conjuring the word for what she and Redmayne had shared. "He was . . . pleasant." She realized the inadequacy of the word the moment she'd said it.

Kissing Redmayne had been pleasant, surely, but it was too tame a word. What could she use, instead?

Agreeable? Enjoyable?

Pleasurable.

That was it. Kissing Redmayne had been a pleasure. She could have kissed him all night. She could have kissed him forever.

"He put me well at ease," Alexandra explained. "I don't believe we should have stopped if Rose hadn't interrupted us."

"Rose Brightwell has always been a horrid bitch," Francesca swore as she yanked ruby pins from her coiffure. "Remember when I roomed with her at de Chardonne in the early days? She made everyone so miserable. What Redmayne saw in her I couldn't begin to imagine."

"She's Rose Atherton now." Alexandra draped herself on the chaise, too exhausted by the entire ordeal to even disrobe. "And she's really quite beautiful." If one liked perfect, exotic women with elegant features and a figure straight from a lady's catalogue.

A sick suspicion curled within her. As she and Redmayne had kissed, as their intimacy progressed, he'd pulled her against him, and she'd felt his . . . his lust. His sex. Turgid and hard against her belly.

He'd been about to peel away her dress. She'd been about to explore his topography. Minutes later they might have been on the bed.

And then Rose had driven her away. No, Redmayne had *sent* her away.

What were they doing now? Alexandra wondered. Were they fighting? Was Rose apologizing? Or . . .

"Do you think lust is transferable?" As she was wont to do, Alexandra gave the thought voice before it had fully formed.

Cecelia froze in the middle of cinching her robe. "You're not wondering if Redmayne and Rose are—"

"That's exactly what I'm wondering." Alexandra sighed miserably. "We'd . . . progressed in our intimacies enough for him to . . . respond physically. Now that he has another beautiful woman in his room, do you think that they might be . . . ?" She covered her eyes with her fingers, wishing she could blind her imagination as well.

"I don't think that's how it works, dear." The cushion next to her depressed as Cecelia joined her on the couch, placing a hand on her arm to pull her hands away from her eyes. "Besides, Redmayne has made it obvious he's furious with his cousin and Rose. I daresay he detests them."

"Certainly, but isn't there a fine line between love and hate?" Alexandra gave voice to the devil's advocate whispering in her ear.

Francesca leaned forward intently. "The real question is, why does it matter so much to you?"

Alexandra hesitated, pressing her fingertips to lips still tingling with sensation from his vital, gentle kisses. Why *did* it matter? She wasn't jealous, was she? Of a woman she loathed and a man she didn't love? Lord, she'd only known him two days. Only encountered him a handful of times.

And now they were to be married. He would be her husband.

Given her circumstances, her past, any woman might welcome a mistress into their situation to avoid a distasteful act.

And yet . . .

"I wouldn't surrender a shawl I was passing fond of to Rose," she muttered bitterly. "Let alone a husband."

"I'll drink to that," Francesca agreed.

Cecelia lifted her glass. "Hear. Hear."

A sharp knock surprised Alexandra into gulping her whisky rather than sipping it. She set the glass down on the table, her eyes watering at the burn.

I'll come find you.

"It's for me." She stood, making certain her friends were out of sight of the door before she went to it. She pressed her hand to her belly as though to contain the riot of moths within.

He'd come. And it had only been minutes.

But, as she was well aware, the act could only take minutes, and one needn't disrobe.

Gathering her courage, she opened the door.

Redmayne's eyes touched her everywhere, absorbing her features from the dimly lit alcove.

He'd donned his waistcoat and tamed his hair but left his necktie off. There was no way to tell whether or not he'd only just finished an interlude of a physical nature.

"You are not alone." His voice pulsed with the familiar fury.

Perhaps she'd also identified its source. Rose.

"I'm not alone," she confirmed.

"Might I speak to you?" He gestured to the empty bartizan alcove. It would afford them a modicum of privacy, at least.

"Of course."

He didn't step back to make room for her, and the moment the door closed behind her, Alexandra found herself enfolded against a solid wall of heated steel.

Once, she might have panicked. Or struggled. He didn't

warn her, and she'd not prepared herself for the physical contact.

But as he gathered her against him, one of his large hands pressing against her back and the other cupping her head, she found that her limbs didn't seize with the familiar instinct to thrash or flee.

A strong, rhythmic thump against her cheek held her in thrall. His heart raced, pounded, and the sound of it hypnotized her, lulled her into a sense of contentment

He held her closer than he had before. With less deference and more desperation, as though he'd been half afraid he'd find her gone.

Breathing deeply, Alexandra searched for a foreign or female scent but found nothing but his distinctive, alluring essence.

She smiled at this. Rose had been drenched in a floral French perfume. Surely if they'd embraced—if they'd been intimate—he'd reek of her.

Indulging in a sigh of relief, Alexandra relaxed against him. She even slid her hands around his ribs to his back, attempting to encircle the great, big whole of him and found it almost impossible.

She burned to know what had happened, but she sensed he needed this. Needed her for another silent moment.

Silence she could give him. Silence she had in spades.

What a thing it was to be held. An odd and oddly ubiquitous, intrinsically *human* thing. A thing, she realized, she'd not experienced for ten years. And never by a man.

Until now. Until him.

She'd uncovered a grave in Pompeii where the bones of a man and a woman had been intertwined in just such an embrace. Alexandra had stared at them for incalculable hours, bereft at the idea of separating them. Wondering at what had driven them together like this, and if they'd clung to each other in life as they had in death.

And why.

This, she thought once more. This was why. A body, a heart, needed another nearby. An embrace fed an elemental physical need she'd never known she'd lacked until an abundance had been available.

And here was the physiological proof. His heart slowed against her ear, adopting a more reasonable rhythm. Incrementally, his muscles melted from steel to iron, his arms relaxing until his hands idly explored the length of her spine.

"Do you fear me, Alexandra Lane?" She heard the words as a resonant vibration in his chest.

His perceptivity was beginning to be problematic. "I do. I have," she admitted carefully.

He hesitated, his chest hitching on a breath. "Does it frighten you to have to—look at me?"

"No," she assured him. "No more than it frightens you to look in the mirror."

"I don't look in the mirror," he rumbled.

Alexandra leaned back to see him, though his arms tightened at her waist as if he wasn't ready to let her go.

"Why?" she asked gently. "Is it difficult to face who you are?"

He gazed down at her, his features stony and tense. The left side of his aspect turned slightly to her, as though daring her to face the parts of him she should fear. "I don't always see the man I am, I see the man I could have become. He is difficult to look at."

Despite herself, she reached up and shaped her palms to his jaw. "You're going to think me silly, but when we met I fancied that ancient gods had done this to you out of jealousy for your mortal perfection." She grazed shy fingers through his beard, tracing the angry marks.

He tensed. Twitched, but he didn't move.

"I'm sorry for your pain," she continued earnestly. "But these are a part of you now, and this encounter altered you for the better." She lifted onto her tiptoes, and nudged his head down, pressing her lips to the fissure on his cheek. "Both inside and out," she amended. "I think you're quite handsome. And, beyond that, I think you are good."

Something lit in his eyes that sparked an answering ache in her heart. Half disbelief, half yearning. "Then why fear me?" he puzzled. "Because of what happened at the ruins? Because I killed a man?"

Alexandra didn't say a word as her lashes swept down to cover her expression. She was the last person who could condemn him for that.

"Was that the first . . . person you've ever killed?" she queried, wishing she could tell him that they shared this kinship. Wondering if his hands were stained with the blood of others.

The length of his breath answered her before his words ever did. "No. I've been attacked before. In Argentina we hunted too closely to an American company's gold mine. We'd a brutal encounter, I couldn't tell you the body count. And, there have been other times, but I can promise you I've never taken a life that hasn't been in defense of my own. Or that of another."

They were silent in the dark for a few breaths before he pressed, "Can you forgive me that?"

"There's nothing to forgive." She ventured a look at him. "I know there are reasons to kill."

Redmayne pulled her back into him, relief and regret lowering the timbre of his voice to a soothing depth. "Even so, I'm sorry you witnessed the savagery of which I am capable. I want you to know I've never in my life used my strength against a woman."

Alexandra relaxed into the dark, pleasant circle of his arms, groping for words. "What did—how did Rose—?"

"Marry me."

Puzzled, she pulled back enough to look up at him. "I thought our engagement had already been established."

The smile he gave her was full of infinite tenderness before he dropped his head to trail his lips against her temple. Her cheekbone. The corner of her mouth. His lips didn't take hers, instead they indolently explored the soft, sensitive place where her neck met her jaw, his hands brushing her hair over her shoulders to give him better access.

"Tomorrow," he whispered against her ear. "Not in a month's time in some stuffy cathedral in London. Tomorrow in the old rectory."

Alexandra's heart assumed the frantic pace his had only just abandoned as she stepped away from his embrace. She needed to think, and she couldn't while his mouth was doing . . . *that* to her ear.

"Why tomorrow?" she asked.

His eyes were two shards of ice in his swarthy face. "There is a ship that sails for Normandy tomorrow evening. We could spend our wedding night at sea and wake up away from these people. From this castle. From the men who attacked yesterday. Away from a bedroom where I—" He broke off, but Alexandra knew the end of that sentence.

Where he'd been with Rose.

"A French university has been unearthing ruins in Normandy for the last several months; my father used to fund them years ago, trying to verify Magnus Redmayne's connection with William the Conqueror. Patrick revived the project when he thought he'd become a duke."

He let out an intemperate breath at the mention of his cousin. "Even upon my return, I didn't have the heart to shut the operation down, and I recently received word that the archeology students might have discovered where Magnus Redmayne's father is thought to be interred. They're calling in an expert to assist with the final excavation."

As he caught a tendril of hair at her nape, his features tightened with a yearning for something she identified instantly.

Escape.

"I don't share my father's obsession with the past," he continued. "But I would hazard that you do, Dr. Lane. Would you like to see the place for our honeymoon? Poke about the dig sites?"

His enthusiasm to abscond was infectious, and Alexandra found herself on the edge of convinced. She'd rather swim the length of the Channel than walk down the aisle at Westminster Abbey or wherever one would marry a duke of his standing. And it moved her that he'd select a honeymoon spot tailored to her interests.

"What about the licenses, the banns, and the priest? My family hasn't even been notified."

"Would they be terribly upset if you eloped?" He touched his nose to hers in an affectionate gesture.

She gave that a good deal of thought. "Not with a duke," she concluded.

His smile was at once wry and bitter, an admittedly unsettling sight on features as satyrlike as his. "In that case, I happen to be a duke, and related to a very influential politician." He released her. "Leave the details to me."

Feeling more than a little dazed, Alexandra nodded. "Do you want to . . . resume what we were about before Rose—erm."

He took her face in his hands once again and pressed a searing, searching kiss to her lips. "More than anything. But I want to have you as my wife. Away from here. Away from *her.*"

Alexandra found she vehemently agreed. "Tomorrow then," she mumbled in disbelief.

"To think, I found a treasure like you on a train platform." He kissed her swiftly and released her. "Be ready in the morning."

She watched him go until he was nothing but a hulking shadow in the distance before turning back to her room and facing the two women pretending they hadn't been eavesdropping.

"Tomorrow, then," she echoed, unable to shake herself from a daze. "I'm getting married tomorrow."

CHAPTER TWELVE

Alexandra only remembered flashes of her wedding day, but she'd recall her wedding night the whole of her life.

So much of that morning had been lost in a frenzy of preparation. She, Cecelia, and Francesca had arisen early, and by some miracle had cobbled together a wedding dress from a pearlescent evening gown of Francesca's that was so tight, she was forced to acquiesce to a corset rather than make alterations.

Cecelia sent Jean-Yves to the gardens and presented her with a breathtaking crown of white chrysanthemums in lieu of a veil an hour before the ceremony.

An announcement had been made at breakfast, of all places, that whoever desired to attend the wedding could do so in the rectory at precisely two o'clock.

At a quarter past noon, a gentle knock on the door drove Alexandra to her feet. She'd flung the door wide, expecting a visit from Redmayne, hoping for last-minute assurances.

"Oh. Hello."

Manners dictated she school the disappointment from her expression when she found a grim-faced stranger rather than her intended. He was possessed of dark hair, a fair complexion, and a large build, but something about the eyes and the cruel set of his mouth struck Alexandra as familiar.

"Can I help you, sir?" she asked politely, his presence infusing her with instant unease.

"Lady Alexandra Lane?" he inquired, his accent as clipped and starched as his collar.

"Yes."

"Allow me to introduce myself." He bowed at the waist. "I am Lord Patrick Atherton, Viscount Carlisle, at your service."

The familiarity at once made sense. Patrick Atherton. The duke's disloyal cousin.

Rose's husband.

Cecelia and Francesca drew up behind her, doing their best to match as bridal attendants in gowns of vastly varying shades of violet.

Since Alexandra couldn't bring herself to address Rose's husband, she was forever grateful for Cecelia's interjection. "What service can you mean, Lord Carlisle?"

His eyes, a darker copy of Redmayne's, lingered on Alexandra in an insulting manner even as he replied with never-failing politeness. "His Grace is aware you haven't family in attendance to give you away for your nuptials, and so the duty falls to me, as his closest family member."

"I thought Sir Ramsay, his brother, was his closest family member," Francesca said frankly.

Lord Carlisle's features remained remarkably passive, though Alexandra detected a tightening about the mouth. "He is conducting the ceremony, my lady," he said before dismissing Francesca altogether. "Now if you'd accompany me, Lady Alexandra, I shall take you to the rectory." He offered a stiff elbow, lifting his eyebrows with expectation.

Why would Redmayne send his detested cousin to escort her down the aisle? As a taunt, perhaps? A reminder that Lord Carlisle had very little chance of ever becoming a duke now that Redmayne was marrying and likely to bear children?

For a moment, she had almost forgotten Piers had precipitated their marriage as a vengeance against Lord and Lady Carlisle. Or, perhaps she'd begun to make more of their swift connection than he.

Because this gesture on his part was anything but gentlemanly.

Which reminded her of how truly little she knew of Redmayne. To say nothing of his intrinsic self. His less-than-heroic qualities. His flaws and failings. Suddenly, his warnings began to cycle through her thoughts, barraging her into silence before Redmayne's rather impatient cousin.

I'm a rather mercenary sort of fellow.
Spite is the only reason I have left.
Don't try to make me a good man.

Swallowing a surge of nerves, she managed to reply. "T-tell His Grace that I appreciate his thoughtfulness. I'm sorry that you've taken the trouble, Lord Carlisle, but I have an old family friend in attendance who will be performing that service. I thank you for your pains." She closed the door on his bewilderment without awaiting a response.

Something about the interaction, about the entire situation, set her teeth on edge and left an oily feeling in her belly, as though she'd swallowed a bad scallop.

The feeling persisted as Lord Bevelstoke, eager to regain the acquaintance of her family now that she was to become a duchess, conducted her down the aisle of the overcrowded rectory.

The ceremony had been quick, or eternal; she couldn't really recall anything but the stifling heat and how out of place her fiancé—husband—appeared in a church with his pagan beauty contained in an obscenely expensive suit.

All eyes were on him.

There'd been a chaste kiss. Nothing like the ones he'd bestowed on her the evening before. Bells tolled as Redmayne hurried her back down the aisle. Flower petals were thrown when they burst from the rectory. She'd eaten none of the celebratory food, and couldn't have named a quarter of the people who wished her well. She clung to each of her friends as they left, receiving encouragements she couldn't hear before she was whisked into the most luxurious coach imaginable.

When they reached the docks, Redmayne had evacuated the coach before the wheels had even stilled, explaining that he'd last-minute arrangements to look after.

Alexandra had sat in a dreamlike daze as frenzied porters had unloaded their trunks, and then her, from the coach.

Somehow, she'd made it to their lavish stateroom. *Staterooms,* she'd corrected, as she wandered through the luxuriously appointed sitting room to the bedroom, her fingers tracing over a plethora of velvets, mahogany, and leather. She appreciated the open windows through which a briny summer breeze swirled about their cabin, tinkling the crystal on the lamps.

Constance, a shy and efficient lady's maid, had been selected for her from Redmayne's staff. However, after Alexandra had been dressed in one of her well-worn nightgowns with an anemic froth of white lace at the sleeves, she had sent the maid away, preferring to brush out her hair on her own.

She'd been brushing for a long time, now. Too long. Long enough for the sun to have completely disappeared. Long enough for her hair to have spun into a vibrant mahogany mass, gleaming and soft, and her fingers to ache from how tightly she gripped the handle.

Apprehension warred with anticipation in a tumultuous tumble of emotion. Did every bride feel some variation of this?

Even the innocent ones?

How was she going to endure tonight? Perhaps she could do what she'd done before and step outside of her body. Stand at the window and wait for it all to be over.

At least the act didn't take long, she recalled. They could get to it as quickly as possible, and then it would be over. Done.

She violently wished for the hundredth time that they'd not been interrupted the previous night. When she'd had more courage. When she'd been less exhausted and more fortified with whisky.

A drink. Now *there* was a capital idea.

She stood and left the bedroom in search of a decanter or a bell pull when the key turned in the lock, rooting both her feet to the middle of the floor.

The door revealed Redmayne with a creak of hinges.

A delicate thrill followed the pang of dread. His black wedding suit was still immaculate, but the sea wind had disheveled his consistently unruly hair. A sable forelock hung over his scar, and Alexandra's fingers suddenly ached to smooth it away.

He closed the door to the stateroom and locked it, turning to allow his gaze to wander over her with an indolent appreciation.

"I sometimes forget . . ." he murmured as though to himself.

Alexandra swallowed layers of nerves before she could speak. "Forget what?"

"How beautiful you are." He undid his cravat as he traveled the length of the sitting room. "Then I see you and realize that memory cannot compare to reality. I'm left as breathless as the first time we met."

Alexandra's breath abandoned her, as well. Stolen by his proximity. By the potency of his masculinity and the possibilities of what the next hours might hold.

By his lovely words.

She turned from him, retreating with measured steps back toward the bedroom. "The first time you saw me?" She gasped out what was supposed to be a casual laugh that wouldn't have fooled a deaf man. "Covered in tweed and mud?"

In three strides he was behind her. His fingers smoothing through the gleaming mass of her unbound hair, following its length to the small of her back. "You are more beautiful covered in tweed and mud than any woman swathed in silk and diamonds."

Alexandra withdrew once more, belatedly realizing that the farther away she drifted from the man, the closer she came to the bed.

Neither option seemed safe. And yet, both were inevitable.

"You don't have to say those things to me," she breathed. "I needn't be wooed. Perhaps we could just begin—"

"Oh come, Doctor, you're a woman of science. Surely you can appreciate a statement of empirical fact." He followed her, drew up behind her once again, and slid his arms around her middle.

Beneath that fitted, cultured attire, a torso rippled with unthinkable strength. Muscle corrugated his entire frame with unmitigated power.

And all that power was behind her. *Behind her.* Securing his arms beneath her breasts and pulling her against his body. Any time he wanted he could push her toward the bed. Bend her over and—

"I am not flattering you," he murmured into her ear. "Your beauty is undeniable, and evidenced by my pervasive desire for you."

He brought their bodies flush, his ribs against her shoulder blades and the hard, pulsing intimate length of him pressing against her back—

Alexandra twisted and leaped out of his grasp. *Air.* She needed air. She raced over to the bedroom window and threw it open, gulping in large breaths of the cool summer breeze.

He'd let her go, she told herself, trying to rein in her runaway pulse. She'd pulled away and he'd let her go. This was significant, something she could clutch onto during the ordeal that was to be her wedding night.

He didn't know. How could he realize what agony he'd created by approaching her from behind?

He couldn't know. And she couldn't tell him.

God, what he must think of her.

Drawing in one last, trembling breath, Alexandra whirled to face him. She blinked around the golden stateroom, bedecked with beveled crystal and mahogany, polished to an impossible gleaming finish.

And empty of the mystified duke she'd expected to find.

"I thought you might be in need of this." His voice rumbled from the doorway to the main quarters. Redmayne

strode toward her, lips tilted faintly, a healthy dose of caramel liquid glinting from a glass in each hand.

Alexandra could have cried as she took the whisky from
him, the little points of cut crystal a welcome abrasion
against her trembling palm.

She finished the entire thing in three desperate swallows, releasing a few breaths of fire before attempting an
explanation. "Forgive me . . . I . . ."

"You're nervous." Indulgently, he relieved her of her
glass and replaced it with his own, encouraging her to take
another sip, which she did. Slower this time, and with more
relish.

He strode to the end table next to the bed and made a
show of opening each drawer.

Curiosity overcame her. "What are you doing?"

"I'm searching for a notepad," he explained, flashing
her a charming half-smile. "I've the feeling a list might
lend you courage. A schedule, maybe? Or did you have
your seduction notes nearby? I shouldn't mind picking that
up where we left off."

The very fact that he'd evoked a smile in such a moment also brought her dangerously close to tears.

When had she become such a wretched mess?

Alexandra set the glass on the nightstand. "Do you remember the conditions?"

She noted he didn't smile as much with his lips as he
did with his eyes. They wrinkled at the corners, his cheeks
tightening with mirth.

Perhaps smiling caused him physical pain?

"Let me see . . ." He ticked them off on his fingers. "I'm
not allowed to use my tongue. We're to be completely nude.
We're to face each other—" He paused, eyeing her pensively. "Oh dear, I've broken a rule." At this his lips split
in a crooked devilish smirk, disavowing her previous

notion. "We never did discuss a punishment for just such an occasion. Something appropriately dastardly, no doubt."

Alexandra couldn't tell if it was the whisky or the un-settling appearance of his wicked smile, but something warm glowed in her middle, threatening to melt the icy daggers of fear. "You forgot one."

That warmth was mirrored in his eyes as he reached for her, his hand grazing the curve of her cheek, the rasp of his calluses catching her downy skin. "No, I didn't." He stepped closer, bringing his other hand to hold her face, cradling it in his palms as though she were made of glass. "My appearance, my manners, and my voice may be harsh, Alexandra, but I promise you my hands will never be any-thing but gentle with you."

Moved beyond words, Alexandra slid her fingers into his open suit coat and encircled his lean, hard waist. She couldn't say if he pulled her close, or if she stepped in, but she found herself delving into his embrace once again, lux-uriating in the scent of him. Warm and rich and undoubt-edly male.

It encouraged her, she thought, that she could not only endure his nearness, his touch, but that she could enjoy it. That she could see herself becoming not just accustomed to him, but also forming an attachment.

Was that such a terrible thing? To like one's husband?

"You may have read everything there was to read about what we're about to do," he murmured, finding a spot on her temple with his lips he seemed fond of kissing. "So, it isn't any wonder you're dreading it."

She drew back, tucking a thread of hair behind her ear. "It isn't?"

He caught her hand, lifting it to his mouth. "Did your books teach you about desire? About sensation? Could they adequately explain how the lightest of touches, the whisper of a kiss, can be felt throughout your entire body?" His breath scalded her skin as he turned her palm up and pressed reverent lips to her fingers, letting them feather across his mouth with an expectant patience.

His eyes fluttered closed when she traced the seam of his scar, the healed skin a shiny, smooth dissection from the velvety feel of his lips.

Mesmerized, Alexandra did her best to remember just what she'd read about . . . about anything. Ever. She couldn't. Her entire being was focused on his mouth. "I—I don't recall that passage," she breathed.

His beard scraped against her fingertips as he moved his attentions to her palm. He slid the lace of her nightgown back, discovering the delicate skin of her wrist, nibbling at the iridescent vein he found, then smoothing a kiss over it. "You must know, Doctor, that there is so much more to be learned in application, than can ever be taught in a lecture hall or read from a book."

"T-true." Something melted in her knees, turning the bone to liquid. Her breasts were suddenly tender, the tips rigid and sensitive against the worn cotton of her night rail.

He released her hand, and it dropped against his chest, her wrist limp and fingers trembling.

"What did your texts teach you about temptation, anticipation, longing, rapture, or bliss?" he queried. One hand skimmed her spine, the other investigating the modest, spun-lace collar held together by a trail of pearl buttons.

She struggled through a swirling fog of a thousand, thousand emotions, sensations, and reactions to reply to him. "N-nothing."

His eyes crinkled with a masculine arrogance, tempered with a glint of an emotion so genuine, so incredibly foreign, Alexandra couldn't identify it if she tried.

He leaned in, his lips pausing before they brushed hers. "Let me teach you about pleasure," he said against her mouth, nudging her nose with his in an oddly affectionate gesture. "And I'll do my best to spare you pain."

Alexandra shared hot, whisky-scented breath with him for an eternal moment. She expected him to take her mouth. To press those warm, aching kisses against her as he'd done before. But he stood impossibly still, his lips so close a moth's wing wouldn't have survived between them, his great body quivering beneath her hands. His ribs bunched and grooved like those of a thoroughbred before the start of a race.

Did she have the courage to unleash his desire? All the straining lust and male need she sensed boiling beneath his herculean restraint?

She had to.

Besides, he seemed so certain. So absolutely sure that he could bring her pleasure.

He already had, hadn't he? With gentle kisses and patient caresses, he'd already dissolved some of her frigid distance. He'd already taught her something about need.

And perhaps desire.

Because she wanted to kiss him again.

"Yes, husband," she exhaled. "Yes."

His first kiss was just a whisper. A chaste press of his warm, dry lips against hers. He did that for a moment, putting her at ease, vanquishing her defenses. It was only after her blood ceased its riotous pulsing that Alexandra noticed his lips were behaving so eminently civilized, while his hands, however, were anything but.

Her nightgown slipped down one of her bare shoulders before she realized with no little alarm that he'd expertly undone the entire placket of buttons.

"Can we douse the lights?" she asked.

His gaze lingered at the line of her collar. Had his expression graced features any less savagely masculine than his, she'd have called it a pout. "I want to see you."

Alexandra chewed her lip. She had to go through with this, but she had no idea how she'd react. What if terror seized her? What if she wept?

What if the sight of his aroused . . . *sex* overwhelmed her, and she fainted? It would be better, easier, if she only had a few senses activated at a time.

"I—I don't . . . I'm not ready."

A shadow darkened his gaze before he carefully wiped it away. He released her to reach for the lamp, his hand slipping over his beard, to brush his scars, before he plunged the room in darkness.

To reward him for his patience, Alexandra undid the rest of the buttons on her nightgown, allowing it to slide from her shoulders into a puddle beneath her.

How strange that she felt better like this. Naked. Exposed.

All right, she thought, anxious to begin. To be done.

For better or worse.

She reached for him, finding his shoulder first. Wordlessly, she dragged her fingers over the fine fabric of his black suit until she found the lapels.

He made to reach for her, but she slid the jacket from his shoulders, imprisoning his arms to his sides until he shucked the garment altogether. Next, he assisted her in gathering his shirt from his waist, the buttons plinking against the carpet evidence of his haste.

Shivering, she found his shape as her eyes began to adjust to the darkness. She caught his forearms as he was searching, and held them, caressing down to his wrists.

It was easier like this, she thought. Grateful that he

allowed her to control where she placed his hands, to decide where and when he touched her.

She shivered to her bones, despite the balmy summer night, as she placed his palms on her bare waist.

He distracted her mouth with long drags of his lips as his thumbs stroked the thin, satiny undercurve of her breasts. A moan vibrated against her as he cupped them, testing their weight in his palms.

"You hide these," he chided softly. "Beneath that wrap of yours."

"I—I'm sorry."

"Don't apologize. I'm simply acknowledging another delightful discovery." He rested the distended nipple between the seam of his fingers, exerting gentle pressure.

The sensation of her cool, naked breast against the heat of his palm stunned her, overwhelmed her, and she flinched away.

No one had touched her there before. But the hungry looks they'd elicited in men had repulsed her.

So she'd wrapped them, hiding them from view.

"I'm sorry." He reached for his drink once more, granting her a reprieve with which to catch her breath.

They were silent in the dark for a moment until he pressed, "Why do you conceal your shape?"

Alexandra crossed her arms, unsure of why she felt defensive. "In my line of work, I need economy of movement. I don't want my wardrobe to be another cage. I can't be mired in a world of muslin, unable to properly move or breathe. Nor can I be chained in gold and jewels, draped like a display. It isn't practical."

"And you value practicality over what is socially acceptable." The gentle curiosity in his voice disarmed her.

"I do," she said. "All our lives, we're told we mustn't, we shouldn't, we can't. I don't like those words. I never have."

"Nor have I." His voice was reverential as he abandoned his drink.

"I-it's part of why I didn't want a husband. Because I thought he would use those words against me. But I . . . I don't think, that is to say, I hope you're not that sort of man . . . that sort of husband."

"I don't want us to be impediments to each other, Alexandra." He reached for her once more, his body throwing off waves of heat. "I'll not be a forbidding husband, if you'll not be a faithless wife."

Swallowing hard, Alexandra pressed her palm against his bare chest. Somewhere left of center, over the unrestrained tempo of his heart.

"It is not in my capacity to stray," she said. "I can never imagine wanting another man."

She could have never imagined wanting this one. Of doing what they were about to do without a great deal of suffering, And yet, she had to admit, the swells and contours of his chest were a magnificent blend of smooth skin and rough hair. The abrasion against her palm was rather lovely. She drew her hand down, counting the depressions of his ribs, marveling at the width of his trunk.

The touch interrupted his breath, then he released a foul word. "You're always one step ahead of me, woman."

"I am?"

"Not for long." His mouth descended with more urgency than before. His lips coaxing hers to open, their breath mingling in the darkness.

She braced for his touch, for his hands to travel down her hips and lower. So when he spanned her rib cage with a gentle exploration, she tensed, her nerves stretching taut. "Do you want me to lie on the bed?" she asked.

"Eventually."

She didn't guess what he was about when he bent down,

until the heat of his mouth replaced that of his hand over her nipple. A gasp escaped her as a cry when he compressed his lips, tugging gently on the aching bud.

"You can't!" Her fingers clawed into his hair, wrenching his neck away.

"Can't I?" His voice matched the night around them. Darker, even. Laced with a savage carnality. "I didn't use my tongue."

Every part of her was trembling now, thoroughly overstimulated by what he'd just done. By how it affected her.

There.

Between her tightly clenched thighs, something had stirred.

At her silence, he gathered her to him. "It's all so much for you," he crooned. "So new. They tell women to be afraid of their own need. To be ashamed of it. But I can't have that. Do not allow what you feel, what you want, to frighten you."

How could he know just how deeply shame and fear dominated her life?

She allowed him to draw her to the bed as he inquired, "Is there aught you're curious about? Anything you want to ask me?"

"I just . . . I'd rather get it done."

She felt rather than saw his smile. "Anticipation can be cruel," he acknowledged.

Passively, she let him nudge her onto the bed, and stretch her on her back over the silk coverlet. Her breath trembled in and out of her, her ribs struggling to contain lungs that threatened to seize at any moment.

Alexandra expected him to crawl over her, between her legs, to insert himself inside her.

Instead, he joined her on the bed with his trousers still on, lying beside her raised on one elbow. "I need to make you ready," he murmured, tucking her hair behind her ear and leaning down to bury his face against the curve of her neck. "Then we will 'get it done' as you so poetically put it."

"Ready?" The word was a breathy whisper as his lips nudged at the sensitive flesh of her earlobe and his hand caressed over her breast to drift along the silken skin over her ribs, and the quivering expanse of her belly.

Alexandra squeezed her eyes shut, her jaw locking. Any moment he would touch her. He would claim her.

She *wasn't* ready. She didn't—

The little drag of his teeth against her earlobe shocked her away from her thoughts and shot an electric sensation *there*.

She clenched her thighs together, her intimate muscles pulsing around emptiness.

Confused, distraught, she reached to him for comfort, and he lifted himself so her arms could encircle him, so she could clutch at the curious columns of muscle bracketing his spine. "I don't know if I can—" She hated that her voice sounded so young. Hated that she was so utterly at his mercy. "What do I do?"

He paused, his fingers splayed just below her belly button, and rested his head in his other hand. "You do nothing, darling," he crooned. "I want you to let go of all control. Just lie back and let me teach you. And in doing so, I will learn you, as well." He nuzzled at her, his beard grazing her cheek, his lips seeking hers in the dark.

He found them as his hand brushed over the sealed seam of her thighs, nudging them open.

She didn't resist him. Was afraid to. If she never denied him, he'd never technically have the opportunity to coerce her into anything. To force her.

Once her legs had parted enough, he curled his knee

between them, resting the weight of his muscled thigh against her open one.

The hair on his body was softer than she'd imagined, less crisp on his legs than on his chest. Why she noted that, she couldn't tell. Perhaps because she was doing her utmost to catalogue pleasant things.

Perhaps because she was trying to ignore that place. The one now exposed to the ever-cooling night air.

He didn't allow that for long.

His fingers slipped through the little tuft of hair there, his chest emitting an animal sound as he found the smooth, swollen flesh inside.

Alexandra's throat slammed closed. Her eyes squeezed shut. Her jaw clenched and her lips compressed beneath his kisses. She clung to him, her hands clawing into fists.

Instead of pulling away, he folded over her, allowing her to tuck her head beneath his chin and tremble her way through this.

His fingers found pliant, silken skin and he danced around it in the softest circling strokes until Alexandra recaptured her breath. Her heart still pounded. The muscles in her limbs refused to unknot, but . . . it didn't hurt. She didn't fight the queasy revulsion as she'd expected to.

In fact, his movement over her most intimate place incited a strange, almost . . . rosy sensation. One which poured and crept over her skin in a languid, heated blush.

Without her permission, her legs parted wider and his appreciative husky moan washed her in warmth.

He drew a quick finger lower, carefully laving through the slippery substance he found there. Just as Alexandra gasped, her protestation died on a strangled breath as he parted the ruffles of flesh protecting the silken peak and he grazed it with a featherlike stroke.

Alexandra's entire world blurred. She lost control of her

limbs as they seized with shivers, but not of the usual sort. A needle of foreign, frightening pleasure lanced her with such force, her body locked with it. She was suddenly afraid if she moved, if she breathed, whatever he'd just done would never happen again.

But it did. His fingers explored the pliant ridges of her sex and teased around the now-throbbing peak. Slipped and slid over it, beneath it, discovering her mercilessly as he emitted a carnal encouragement at each unbidden jerk and gasp.

Some of the dark, erotic sounds, she realized, were too high-pitched to be coming from him, but surely she'd never made such noises.

Beneath the clever ministrations of his fingers, something inside her core melted, twisted with exquisite, rapturous heat. His fingers were so incredibly wet, gliding over every tender recess, leaving sweet trails of pleasure in their wake. Teasing her, driving her to the brink of. Of . . .

Something.

Alexandra's hips lifted from the bed, as a visceral jolt seized her. "Piers?" she gasped.

"Let it come, darling," he breathed. "Don't fight it. Embrace it." All his movement centered on the throbbing peak then, awakening from her body an unholy delight.

"I . . . I . . ." It tumbled over her like a rogue wave, seizing her limbs and dragging her away from herself, from shore, from any solid ground. She lost herself in the wondrous, terrifying power of it as he coerced her into throbbing, thrashing, delicious spasms of incomprehensible pleasure. Just like beneath the water, every sound was both amplified and muffled. Every movement dreamy and slow. She surged against ecstatic pulses of bliss until they reached a fevered pitch, and her body twisted to escape them.

Her husband kept her thigh captive with his own as he pulled her head above the water, so she could breathe. His stroking fingers slipped away from her bud, lower, to explore the cascade of moisture he'd elicited.

Alexandra could do nothing but lie there, limp and misted with sweat. Marveling silently as she tried to remember how to move her limbs. Tried to decide if she ever wanted to.

All this time, her body had been capable of such bliss. All she'd needed was a man tender and skilled enough to find it.

He played with her still, gliding through slick flesh until he circled the tender opening with his fingertip, emitting another savage growl. "God, you're . . ." His finger paused, tested, and probed with increasing urgency. "You're so . . ." He breached her, only slightly, then further.

Alexandra gasped. Froze. Expecting it to hurt, expecting any number of terrible things.

Instead a gentle, aching pleasure goaded her intimate flesh to make way for him, until he'd sunk in to the knuckle.

She spent a moment wallowing in relief until she heard his low curse. Felt the strange sensation of his finger inside her.

"Fucking hell," he bit out.

And then he was gone. Not just his hand, but all of him, leaving her alone on the bed.

CHAPTER THIRTEEN

Piers didn't dare speak as he blindly riffled about in his trunks at the foot of the bed.

"W-what's wrong?"

He ignored her question. Disregarding the soft note of uncertainty laced beneath the lingering throaty tones of a passionate afterglow.

Where in the fuck had his valet packed his . . . ?—Oh, there it was, thank God.

He seized the box containing his cheroot and grappled it open. Cursing his unsteady fingers, he lit it and dragged in a burning breath.

He caught the outline of her beyond the glowing bead at the end of his smoke.

She'd risen to her elbow, dragging the coverlet over her, as though she needed modesty in a nearly black room.

Christ, but she was flawless. She really was.

As he took his next smoke, he inhaled the intimate scent of her lingering on his fingers.

His mouth flooded with moisture.

His veins flooded with murder.

Piers did his best to keep the tumultuous heat from his voice when he could finally unclench his jaw enough to say, "I've been tricked a few times in my day. By some of the best in the world. But you. *You* put every double-crossing con man and swindler to absolute shame."

Her silent astonishment became a tangible thing reaching out to him in the dark.

Even now, he ached to soothe her. To ease her distress. The protective instinct she'd aroused within him was so powerful that even the surge of his fury couldn't fully contain it.

"I—I don't understand." Her voice wavered with perceptible confusion.

"You claimed you'd never even been kissed?" he exploded.

"I haven't!" she insisted. "*Hadn't.* Not until—"

"Well, you've certainly been fucked," he snarled. He stalked to the doorway, needing more distance from her body, which called to him still. "It's hard to imagine how you'd manage one without the other."

He waited. Her silence screaming across the darkness, creating a cavern between them where only a few paces truly existed.

Where were her maidenly protestations? Couldn't she at *least* deny it?

His mother always had.

Every time she'd been caught in a compromising position in a darkened corner with one of his father's so-called *friends* at a soiree. Every time she'd abandoned them for weeks on end, galivanting with a younger man, a more handsome one, giving only the most imperceptible of concessions to decorum.

She would, at the very least, adamantly repudiate all involvement.

Of course, everyone had still been aware that the unparalleled beauty Lady Gwyneth Atherton, Duchess of Redmayne, was a faithless whore. Women held their husbands closer when she'd walked into a room. They'd kissed both her cheeks then whispered malice the moment her back was turned.

And worse, everyone had likewise understood that her husband, Piers's father, had been pathetically besotted with her. That when the money had run out, or the passion, or the novelty, she'd abandon her current lover and sweep back home to Castle Redmayne reeking of gin and unmentionably shameless things.

As a boy, Piers would rejoice upon her return, he'd missed her so. He'd been inured to the whispers, but not to his lovely mother's doting. She'd present him with a gift, her azure eyes sparkling as he opened it. She'd lean down to embrace him, expecting his adoration, his forgiveness, which he both quickly provided.

His kind father would be so delighted to see her, so overwrought with joy at holding her . . . and then her inexorable melancholy would set in, and the cycle would begin again.

Until one day, when Piers was sixteen, Gwyneth had gone to Italy with some dashing count fifteen years her junior, and had stayed away nearly a month longer than usual.

Upon her return, his father had ordered a feast prepared. They'd all celebrated and enjoyed the spectacular wine she'd brought back with her. It'd been a lively, lovely evening.

Piers had found his father the next morning, hanging

by the neck off the very balustrade from which he'd announced his engagement to Alexandra.

His mother had met her next lover at the funeral.

Still, even in the face of accusation, Gwyneth Atherton had adamantly controverted her frivolous dalliances. Had maintained that the gossips were particularly jealous of her wealth and status. Or that a man she'd denied had started malicious rumors.

Lies. Always lies.

Rose had been such a breath of fresh air when contrasted to his mother's honeyed tongue. She'd been brash, bold, and brutally direct. He didn't care for a woman's supposed purity or virtue. In fact, his former fiancée hadn't been a virgin, either, but she'd announced it to him right away. Admitted she was also a slave to her passions, and had desired none so much as him.

He'd fallen for her impish ways and her challenging honesty. He'd believed her when she'd spoken of love, of marriage—when she'd claimed his title meant nothing to her—because she told uncomfortable truths. He'd assumed her the antithesis of his mother.

How wrong he'd been. For they'd both been liars.

One had merely denied her actions, the other justified them.

The years had taught Piers not to care so deeply, and not to forgive so willingly. His eyes had been opened to every calculated gesture of the feminine sort. Or so he'd thought. He'd become hardened to the coy machinations of sycophantic damsels in need of a husband.

Or wanting a duke.

It was why he'd chosen Francesca.

Partly, yes, to honor the wishes of a departed father, and partly because she hadn't particularly wanted him. Theirs would have been a comfortably contemptible life. He'd never have expected affection from her. Only children.

He'd vowed so long ago that his interactions with women would forever be biological and acquisitive. Until a sweet, seemingly innocent archeologist had, once again, taught him the abject agony of hope. She'd charmed him, captivated him so thoroughly with her artless, beguiling naïveté.

What he wouldn't give to be Ramsay in that moment, all cool composure and stone-faced dispassion.

But then, passion had always been his downfall, hadn't it? Since Piers was a boy, he'd chased his appetites with a rampant enthusiasm bordering on recklessness. He didn't consider the consequences, because they rarely applied to him.

Nothing was ever denied him. Not just by the status of his birth, but by the force of his will. He wanted what he wanted. He did what must be done to get it.

He possessed an incessant need to conquer everything. To climb the tallest mountain, to explore the deepest trench. To forge the longest river. To pit his own strength and skill against the most lethal of apex predators.

And for what?

What did it mean to him? What sort of man had it made him? Why did he care?

Why did he care so fucking much about everything and everyone?

This weakness of his had earned him nothing but wounds. Deep, unhealed sores wrought by the elegantly sharpened claws of nature's absolute craftiest creature.

Frailty, thy name is woman.

God, but his wife was an entirely excellent sort of fraud. A consummate actress. An ingenious observer of men.

She'd known just what to do, exactly what to say, how to touch the only tender, masculine parts of him he'd managed to salvage. How to reach past the barriers he'd erected around his heart and play upon the chivalric tendencies he'd always been prone to.

Even now, as her silence condemned her, he found himself praying she'd say something perfect. He willed her to explain away the swirling abyss of suspicions tainting his every tumultuous thought.

He itched to light a lamp. To gauge her reactions and assess her expressions.

What good would it do? He'd been pitifully hopeless at that thus far.

Besides, if he looked at her now, naked and lovely, her lips and hair glossy and lush . . .

He might throttle her.

Or make love to her, despite everything.

What a foolhardy fuck he was, to play white knight to her damsel in distress.

The fire of his temper had begun to fade in the quiet dark, smothered by cool fingers of ice. With each silent moment that passed, a frigid wall made of memory and misgiving barricaded his ribs, turning his very core into a monument of glacial bitterness.

He drew in a breath of velvet smoke, imagining he exhaled all his growing devotion for her. Three days, he'd only known her three days, how had he become so beguiled in such a short time?

Would he never learn?

"You've nothing to say for yourself? No explanations, no excuses? I should think a brilliant woman as fond of lists as you are would have a contingency plan for just this occasion. Did you think me such a lackwit that I'd not notice?"

"That's not it . . ." She let her words trail into the dark once more.

"Then tell me *why*," he demanded. "Why you felt you needed to lie to me in the first place."

"I didn't lie," she stated carefully. "I never claimed to be a virgin. You inferred that on your own."

"But you claimed not to—" He broke off, pinching at his temple against a stabbing ache.

She was right. By God, she'd been right. He'd asked her if she'd ever *really* been kissed, and she'd denied it.

"Really" was such a broad term, wasn't it? Open to so much interpretation.

So why mislead him? Why act like the innocent ingenue when she'd had a previous lover? A terrible suspicion curled in his gut, cording his muscles taut with disgust.

"Have you gotten yourself into trouble?" It'd happened to him before, when a mistress of his had become pregnant. He'd been all of twenty and three, awaiting his bastard child with almost rampant anticipation.

A child who'd appeared early, apparently sired by an Asian lover.

Bloody hell, was it happening again? "Did you mark my need of an heir, and grasp at the opportunity to make another man's child a duke?"

Had that been her reason all along? Why her behavior had been so strange? He thought of her blurted marriage proposal, her artless seduction, her offer to resume even after they'd been interrupted by Rose.

Had her intention been to get him inside her no matter the circumstances?

"I'd never!" she cried. "Please. It's not that—" She broke off, swallowing a note of hysteria before asking, "What are you going to do?"

The anxiety in her voice tugged at him, which brought his rage surging back.

"I'm not going to annul the marriage, if that's what you're asking. Not until I can be sure one way or the other. Despite how I look, I'm not a monster, you know." His voice belied his claim, as it could have belonged to the coldest demon in hell. "The terms of our agreement haven't changed. Funds in exchange for heirs. Isn't that how you so charmingly put it?" Because, damn his soul, he still wanted her. Still burned for her. Despite the bleak poison curdling what was left of his heart, his body insistently throbbed for the ambrosia he'd found between her thighs.

As was her bedeviling way, she'd aroused more desire in the dark than an entire household of painted French courtesans lit by golden lanterns.

"Then . . . should we . . . resume?" She sounded as though the prospect of a night in his arms held as much joy for her as a night spent in the iron maiden.

Had she always felt thus? Revolted by him? Perhaps Rose had been brutally honest back at Castle Redmayne. Perhaps she'd seen what he did not.

He frightened and disgusted the woman who'd done her level best to seduce him. But, come to think of it, her repugnance had been evident in their every interaction. Hell, she'd nearly shot him at Torcliff. Her ridiculous lists. Her visceral reaction tonight when he'd established intimacy . . .

Fucking hell. She'd asked him to douse the bloody lights. What validation did he need beyond that? She couldn't bring herself to look at him.

How had he been so blind?

Because genuine feeling had glimmered in her eyes when she'd cupped his face and called him handsome in the darkness of her doorway.

He'd believed her.

And, just like that, he was no longer angry at her. Only at himself. Had there ever lived such an absolute dupe?

"How long until your monthly courses?" he asked on an exhausted sigh.

"I—I'm sorry . . . Pardon?"

"I'm not unsympathetic to the woman's plight." He summoned into his voice an unperturbed tranquility. "I do not insist on being the first man who's fucked you, but I do insist on being the unquestioned father of your child."

"I'm *not* with child," she vowed. "Please. I can't explain, but I can swear to you that—"

He wanted no more empty promises. No more lies. No more secrets. *No. More.* "I'll ask you only once again." A foreign, acerbic vehemence crept into his tone, one that had sent warlords and beasts alike scurrying away in fear. "When are you scheduled to bleed next?"

"Ten days." Her voice had become so small, that something withered inside of him, as well.

"Ten days," he clipped. "Very well. When it arrives—*if* it arrives—I'll come for you after." He snapped up his jacket and shirt and stormed out into the night.

Chapter Fourteen

It'd taken Alexandra an alarming portion of the next morning to search the entire first- and second-class decks for her missing husband.

Where could a duke hide on a ship?

And what would happen once she found him?

She should have dressed and gone to him last night instead of awaiting his return, sobbing quietly until exhaustion claimed her.

His valet had awoken her upon discreetly sliding into their rooms to obtain some of his things.

As Alexandra hunted, she berated herself. For such an educated woman, she could certainly be a magnificent dunce. How had she overlooked such a tiny detail as her missing virginity? She'd read about a hymen in certain texts and had known she no longer possessed one. However, it'd never once crossed her mind that a man would notice.

That he'd be so furious.

That he'd draw certain conclusions.

It had never crossed her mind because she simply would never have considered such a deception. Despite her terrible secrets, she'd never been a devious woman. She was a scientist, after all. She dealt in facts and data. Fictions and fibs never served her but the one.

The one keeping her neck from a noose.

What sort of woman would try to pass off her bastard as a duke's heir? As any man's child, really. To do something so shameful was abjectly unforgivable.

Alexandra put a hand to her belly, where unease mixed with relief. There were situations where a woman could be so desperate, so destitute, she'd be driven to that sort of deceit. The world was a cruel place, even crueler to the helpless.

"Thank God," she whispered for perhaps the hundredth time. Thank God de Marchand hadn't sired a child that night. Because, as much as she ached for one now, the evidence so long ago would have been damning.

So, what should she do about today's disaster?

She'd absolutely choked when faced with her husband's fury last night.

It wasn't that she'd forgotten his banked rage, it was just that Redmayne seemed to discard it in her presence. As though *he'd* forgotten it when she was nearby. He'd treated her with such tender deference. Like she was a treasure he'd uncovered. Something precious.

That was the case no longer, and his rage was currently directed at *her*.

Exhaustion and despair drove her to the railing of the first-class promenade deck where she did her best to breathe in a few balancing inhales. Stark taupe cliffs lined the shore of Normandy, capped with grasses so lush and green, they reminded her of Devonshire. As a Channel crossing could be concluded in mere hours from Dover to

Calais in these large steamships, one from Maynemouth to Le Havre was conducted overnight.

In no time, they'd dock and disembark.

Alexandra was desperate to smooth things over with Redmayne before then.

She'd only have to find him first.

"Duchesse?" The aged Frankish male voice startled her from her reverie, and Alexandra turned to find a short but stout man standing at the rail with her. Beneath his golden traveling hat, his kind chocolate eyes, bracketed by an attractive web of fine lines, threatened to dissolve her composure into a puddle of liquid tears. The man had a timeless quality about his middle age, and the Rogues used to speculate about just how old he might be. A well-worn forty-five or an aged sixty? It was still impossible to tell. He'd barely aged a day in ten years. He'd traded his dirt-smudged gardner's kit for a smart morning suit more appropriate to his position.

"Jean-Yves," Alexandra gasped in surprise. "Whatever are you doing on the ship? Is Cecelia with you?" Surely, she'd have more sense than to accompany her, uninvited, to her honeymoon?

"Duchesse, est-ce que vous allez bien?" He ignored her question, placing a careful hand on her elbow, exerting the same pressure as one would on a piece of blown glass.

That question again. *Are you all right?*

He asked because he'd been there. He'd seen her that night with blood on her gown and her innocence shattered into a million pieces.

He'd helped her cover her crime. To piece her life together. And for that, Alexandra would always be thankful.

"I'm very well," she answered him in French, accepting the hastily folded letter he held out to her. "It's good to see you."

Alexandra avoided his alert, worried gaze as she broke the Red Rogue wax seal and opened the letter. Why she should feel awkward around him, she couldn't say, but his presence brought too many memories to the surface.

Because he always watched her with the same soft pity as he had since that night in the garden. To him, she was always that helpless girl.

The one she'd tried so hard to leave behind.

Alexander,

I sincerely beg your forgiveness of my presumption, but with all that's transpired we simply couldn't bear to think of you alone and so far away. I've sent dear Jean-Yves to keep watch over you from a discreet distance. I didn't tell you because I know you'd refuse, but it was the only way to keep Frank from booking passage on the ship and making a nuisance of herself on your honeymoon. Jean-Yves will be staying at the Hotel Fond du Val along with the others from the dig, and he is at your disposal.

Sir Ramsay has been investigating the gunmen. I'm told he's not convinced of the intended victim as of yet. Though Frank insists it's her, I cannot shake this impending premonition she's utterly mistaken.

Do be careful out there, darling Alexander. Stay close to Redmayne, I feel that he'll keep you safe.

I hope your travels are wondrous and your honeymoon full of unexpected pleasures.

All my love,
Your devoted Cecil

Tears of longing sprang to Alexandra's eyes as she read the letter again, and once more. Dear, devoted Cecelia, voluptuous and vigorous and ruthlessly brilliant.

Possessed of the gentlest heart in the empire.

She ran a finger over the bottom of the page where an overlarge inkblot belied Cecelia's contemplation before the words "unexpected pleasures."

Her friend had been worried about her wedding night but, ever the supposed vicar's daughter, was too circumspect to say so.

Unexpected pleasures. Those words could certainly be used in conjunction with her wedding night.

Among others.

"Duchesse," Jean-Yves prodded. "You are distraught? Your husband, does he hurt you?"

Alexandra grasped his hand and gave it a reassuring squeeze. "You may report to your mistress that I am very well," she said. "My husband has not hurt me in the least."

Rather, it seemed, she was the one to cause him pain. Enough pain to spill over into anger.

"I must go find him," she explained.

"Of course." Pleased, Jean-Yves bowed over her knuckles. "I will be nearby."

Releasing him with a grateful smile, Alexandra ventured toward the stairs that would take her down to the second-class decks, and perhaps below to where great loads of cargo were being wheeled out in preparation for incomprehensibly large cranes to load them onto the docks.

"Your Grace!" a dim feminine voice called. "Duchess!"

She'd been so distraught by the events of last night, so plagued by nightmares, and dejected at waking up in an empty bed, that she didn't mark the call as addressing her.

A hand seized her elbow, and she whirled to find Julia Throckmorton, resplendent in a crisp white sailing kit, holding on to her magnificent hat as the wind tried to rip it away from her luxurious curls.

"You little minx!" she crowed as she threw her arms

about Alexandra, crushing her breath from her lungs before releasing her abruptly. She motioned to her companions, Lord and Lady Bevelstoke, with wild, excited gestures as she spoke almost too rapidly to follow. "There she stood on the train platform in absolute *rags* and let me speculate for *hours* as to the identity of the new duchess and gave not a single clue it was her all along!" Julia elbowed her meaningfully. "How cruel you are to an old and dear friend."

Alexandra made a pathetic attempt at a winsome smile. Is that what they were, old and dear friends? Or was that how Julia wanted to shape reality now that Alexandra had become a duchess? They'd not conversed for hours on the train platform. It would be kind to speculate that they'd chatted for minutes.

Lord Bevelstoke, a man of superfluous wrinkles and distracting chin waddle for a man in his mere fifties, had made his blustery apologies right before he'd been called upon to walk her down the aisle.

Lady Bevelstoke, however, stepped forward to render her kisses on the cheek as though she were approaching royalty. "How fare your Lord and Lady Bentham, Your Grace?" she asked in her tight, tiny voice. Alexandra had used to quip unkindly with her brother, Andrew, that the woman resembled her precious Pekingese in more than just her looks, but her voice and temperament as well. "I shall call upon your parents upon my return to Hampshire first thing."

Alexandra offered them a polite nod, feeling as though another attempt to smile at these people would crack her face like ancient pottery. "I'm certain they'd appreciate that, Lady Bevelstoke. If you'll excuse me, I—"

Julia cut off her anxious attempt at a polite escape. "Off to your honeymoon, I see. Where are you going? I'm desperate to know. Oh, I've guessed it. It's obvious you've not had your wedding trousseau yet. Is Redmayne taking you to that genius seamstress in Rouen? She'd give one of her fingers to drape you, as you could make sackcloth and ashes look couture. You're such a beauty. That's where we're headed before our Continental tour, her shop in Rouen. I could lend you one of my appointments! We've added Italy to our schedule, and I needed extra gowns, isn't that right?"

Her head spinning from the speed of Julia's conversation, Alexandra glanced down at her simple day dress. It was one of her favorites. A light frock the color of the Egyptian desert at sunset, with sturdy braided cord at the bodice and hem to weight it against the sand and wind. It just barely occurred to her that most of her clothing was more suitable for an archeologist than an aristocrat.

"Actually." She nudged her chin up a notch. "The duke is conducting me to an archeological dig in Normandy. Redmayne ancestors are thought to be buried there."

At least, she *hoped* that was still the plan, if he hadn't thrown himself overboard in the night rather than honeymoon with her.

"Just where *is* that mysterious husband of yours?" Julia queried, making a great show of looking around the deck. "I tried and tried to meet you at the masque and the wedding, but the two of you were surrounded by scads of people. With Francesca and Cecelia glued to your side, I couldn't get close."

Alexandra found it overwhelming that Julia tended to discuss two or three subjects at once, so she decided to answer her first question.

"His Grace has gone for . . . coffee," she lied. "I'm to meet with him soon to disembark."

Julia threaded her arm through Alexandra's. "Let's take a turn about the decks until then, shall we?" Her voice was a suggestion, but the arm locking Alexandra to her side gave no room for a polite extraction. "Pardon us schoolmates for a moment, won't you, Lord and Lady Bevelstoke?"

The Bevelstokes fell over themselves with solicitous exclamations as Julia led Alexandra across the wide deck and past large and lovely windows toward the aft.

"If you're going to dig in Seasons-sur-Mer, then you must know Dr. Thomas Forsythe," Julia exclaimed. "He's in second class somewhere, headed to the selfsame dig to excavate some godawful thing."

The name distracted Alexandra momentarily from her distress. "I do know Dr. Forsythe from Cairo." They'd been friendly some years ago.

"I spied him at the hotel in Maynemouth only yesterday." Julia leaned in conspiratorially. "He's a perfect specimen, isn't he? I've always had a weakness for those vital, poetic intellectuals. I'm intent upon making him my lover just as soon as we're introduced."

"Julia!" Aghast, Alexandra blinked around, worried someone had overheard.

"Oh, don't be a prude!" Julia admonished, shaking her arm before directing them to the steps leading toward the lower decks. "What happened to the Alexandra I went to school with? Always reading forbidden novels, drinking spirits, and attending clandestine meetings with Francesca and Cecelia in the middle of the night in trousers. We're married women now, we can have such conversations."

Once they'd emerged from the stairs to the shelter deck, an elegant couple bowed to Alexandra and offered their felicitations. She'd couldn't for the life of her recollect their names or rank, but she did the best she could to be gracious.

She really was going to make a terrible duchess.

Julia lowered her voice as the couple moved on. "Speaking of matrimony, how fared your wedding night?" She made a sound of pure rapture. "Bedded by the Terror of Torcliff? You should hear the talk among the *ton*. Was that the first time, or have you been lovers for ages?"

Stunned, Alexandra gaped at her. "It was . . . I . . . What talk?"

Julia slid her a glance full of mischief. "Oh, you must know that before his—um—disfigurement Redmayne was quite the rogue. Bedded every pretty thing with a title above a baroness until he met Rose. Every *available* pretty thing, I should say, as he never took married ladies as lovers. More's the pity." Her face twisted as though she'd licked a thousand lemons. "What a misfortune you have Rose as a nemesis now, and a relation. She was such a beast at school.

"Anyway." She moved back to more salacious subjects. "Everyone's been speculating as to why Redmayne has been living as an absolute *monk* since he's been home. And now we know, don't we? He's been in love all this time. We all thought it was his vanity, I mean his scars are so ghastly. Don't they frighten you, or do you merely turn off the lights when he's—you know?" She lifted her eyebrows.

Dumbfounded and distressed, Alexandra groped for an answer. For a lie. She'd asked him to douse the lights . . . but it had nothing to do with his scars.

And everything to do with hers.

Tired of waiting for an answer, Julia stopped and jerked her to a halt so abruptly, Alexandra felt her bones clack together. "You're not . . . in a family way, are you? You can tell me, I'll keep your confidence. But I'll warn you that is the speculation around the *ton,* that the reason for the astoundingly odd and accelerated circumstances for the wedding was because of a little future duke or lady on the way."

Alexandra's lips pressed together, acknowledging that anything she said to this woman had absolutely no chance of remaining a confidence. She was likewise forced to admit she didn't know what to expect with this marriage, but it certainly hadn't been that everyone would assume she was pregnant.

"I assure you, I am *not* in the family way."

"Oh, look! There is His Grace now, and he's chatting with Dr. Forsythe, what an *excellent* coincidence. Come, come!" Julia yanked her toward the portside railing, where Alexandra noted the two men stood, broad backs to the commotion.

The beaches drew nearer, as did long wharves stretching from the lovely port city of Le Havre to accommodate the incoming ships. The men leaned indolently on the rail, watching the cliffs loom in the distance, their rumbled masculine conversation interrupted only by careful sips from their hot tin cups of coffee.

Though every line of his body and deportment bespoke innate power, Redmayne's attire showed little of his breeding. He'd donned a midnight-blue suit that brought out the brilliant darkness of his hair and the cobalt sheen in the unruly layers imparted by the relentless summer sun reflecting from the sea.

As Redmayne conversed with Forsythe, his manner was polite, engaged, but a hard glint never smoothed out of his gaze. An ever-present alert tension kept the bulk of his shoulders rigid. It was as though he always prepared to spring into action, toward or away from danger.

He never seemed quite civilized, did he? Not even in his wedding suit, come to think of it. He'd the large-boned, barbaric build of the marauding ancestors they were about to examine, and something about that innate savagery caused a strange, not altogether unpleasant flutter under Alexandra's ribs.

The world beneath her feet felt as though it would give way at any moment, and not because the engines chugged to a halt as the ship prepared to drop anchor.

It was her husband who threatened to tip her world over. The sight of him. The proximity to him.

Memories of the previous night flooded her with an indecent awareness. She ogled as though truly seeing him for the first time, dissecting the parts of him she'd never noticed before.

His lips. Well, she had noticed them, hadn't she? All along they'd held a particular allure. Capable of imparting the harshest, cruelest words as well as the most delirious, dizzying kisses and heart-melting sentiments. She suddenly longed for them to curl with amusement the way they did when he fought a smile.

His hands. His strong, clever hands were roughened unlike any other aristocrat she'd known. His calluses had abraded her skin with delicate rasps, eliciting goose pimples and shivers of pleasure.

Pleasure. Those hands had taught her the truest meaning of the word. As promised, he'd become her erudite instructor in the ways of her own carnal delight. Her sex had always been a challenge for her. Something to ignore, to avoid. Somehow, he'd layered an astonishing bliss over the memory of pain that had owned that area of her person for so long.

And she knew he'd so much more to teach her, so much more she could learn from him.

She absurdly wanted to thank him.

If he'd ever deign to speak with her again.

"Look who I've found, Your Grace," Julia announced boldly, presenting her to her husband.

Redmayne spared Alexandra a wintry glance. "You cannot find what was not missing."

All the words spoken and unspoken between them hovered in the sea air until they fell at their feet like shards of shattered glass.

Among the mess, Alexandra's confidence might have been found. Along with her heart.

"Gads, can that be young Dr. Alexandra Lane?" A handsome and robust man kicked his hip away from the railing, abandoning his coffee to offer the approaching ladies a proper greeting. His cream linen suit coat flapped out behind him as he lifted his hand to wave before shielding his eyes against the eastern sun.

"Dr. Forsythe! What an absolute pleasure." Alexandra couldn't fight a smile of genuine delight at the sight of his sandy curls and self-effacing smile. She'd only known him a short while in Cairo, but he'd never treated her like a woman. Only an intellectual equal. She'd always appreciated that more than she could express.

"You know better than that." He accepted her gloved hand in both of his and shook it with winsome enthusiasm. "You may call me Thomas, please, just like before."

A dark prickle tuned every hair on Alexandra's body, and she glanced over at her husband in time to catch a black shadow cross his features.

A sharp jerk at her elbow reminded her of her manners. "Thomas, Your Grace, allow me to introduce Lady Julia Throckmorton, a chum from school."

"Delighted." Julia reached out delicate hands, dressed in white lace gloves, to receive her due from both men. "Just what are two cultured gentlemen of your caliber doing on the cargo decks, one must wonder?"

Alexandra's gaze collided with her husband's, and she feared he'd admit that he'd spent their wedding night away from her.

Dr. Forsythe gestured to a few of the crates stacked on wide wooden bases while burly sailors folded ropes at their corners securing them with gleaming steel hooks. "I invited His Grace to inspect some of the sundries I'm accompanying out to the dig," he explained in his lively, cultured accent. "Besides, Redmayne and I found the coffee wasn't strong enough in first class, isn't that right, Your Grace?"

Redmayne said nothing as he tossed the last of his tin back, the taut muscles of his neck working over a swallow in a most distracting manner.

Julia abandoned Alexandra's arm to sidle closer to Dr. Forsythe. "Your brilliant reputation precedes you, Doctor," she simpered. "I find the subject of your work simply enchanting. Promise me you'll tell us all about it."

"Oh, you'll find it quite tedious, I assure you." Forsythe directed a polite smile in Julia's direction before turning back to Alexandra. "But, dear Dr. Lane, you'll be absorbed to learn that they've broken through the ground of an ancient settlement above Le Havre and found a Persian aristocrat buried in the same crypt as what appears to be a Moorish prince and a Viking sailor. I'm aching to take you to the catacombs and show you what we've found. If my suspicions are correct, oceanic trading was taking place far earlier than we've suspected—"

"Dr. *Atherton*." They all turned to stare at the duke as the growled name was familiar to no one, least of all Alexandra.

"Pardon?" Forsythe cocked his head in a rather spaniellike gesture.

"You are addressing Her Grace, Lady Alexandra Atherton, Duchess of Redmayne." He enunciated every word with abject clarity. "You never mentioned, Forsythe, that you're acquainted with my *wife*."

"I didn't realize you'd married, Your Grace. I wasn't aware *she* was your new duchess." As though he realized the danger he was in, Forsythe sputtered artlessly, his vigorous color intensifying to ruddy. He retreated maybe two steps before Alexandra felt compelled to jump to his rescue.

"We're on our honeymoon, Thomas." Alexandra flinched at her overbright tone. "This jaunt to the archeological dig is my new husband's indulgence of my voracious obsession with the past."

"Well." Forsythe recovered his look of surprise rather deftly, reaching out to reclaim his coffee cup. "May I offer my belated felicitations." His congratulations sounded genuine, but his earnest brown eyes were touched with a tinge of melancholy. "I see we are about to dock, and I've a few things to attend to before we disembark. I will bid you good morning, Your Graces, until we meet in Seasons-sur-Mer. I imagine you're staying at Hotel Fond du Val in town?"

Lips compressed into a white line, Redmayne nodded curtly.

Once again, Alexandra rushed to be gracious. "I'm looking forward to seeing the catacombs, Thomas," she said.

"I'll follow you, Doctor," Julia offered solicitously, threading her arm through another elbow that had yet to be offered. "You can tell me all about your Persian Vikings."

Over her golden head, Forsythe and Alexandra shared a wince at Julia's disgraceful grasp of history. His eyes crinkled before he departed with a good-natured wink, Julia attached to him like a barnacle.

Alexandra turned to her husband, who watched Forsythe's retreat with a flinty glare. "Tell me, wife, is *he* a part of your obsession with the past?"

His question evoked a stunned laugh from Alexandra's throat. "Thomas? Decidedly not. I barely recalled his existence until today."

"Thomas?" A dark, skeptical brow lifted before he turned away from her to watch seamen throw great ropes overboard, and dock cranes lower to attach to prodigious crates of cargo.

"Dr. Forsythe is a friendly and respected professional colleague." Alexandra joined him at the railing, not appreciating the undeserved cold shoulder he offered her. "It's not as though he ever had access to my bedchamber by way of secret tunnels. He's never had intimate knowledge of me with which you two could compare notes."

It wasn't in her nature to throw Rose between them, but Alexandra had never been one to suffer the double standards upon which her sex was expected to castigate themselves.

She wasn't about to start now.

"Touché." Redmayne leaned on his elbows, stubbornly keeping his eyes on the distant cliffs past the long golden beaches.

Alexandra studied his strong profile, which concealed the disfigured side of his face. From this vantage, his masculine beauty was startling. The sun heightened the dusky hue of his skin, kissed by many such days beneath its relentless heat. The wind tossed his disobedient hair with abandon, and she longed to reach for it. For him. To cover the cold expanse of his fury and find the warm, tender man he'd so often been with her.

"Piers." She'd not made use of the intimacy of his first

name, and she wished doing so would remind him of the
subtle intimacies she'd hoped they'd share as husband and
wife. "I can promise you, Dr. Forsythe has never been of
any interest to me. He's not my lover, and I had no idea he'd
be here now. Need I remind you it was not I who suggested
this voyage, nor did I make the miraculous arrangements
to do so—"

"You need remind me of nothing," he said grimly. "I am
aware our situation is entirely of my making. We've no
need to discuss it further."

"You say that, but last night—"

"Did you not hear me?" He turned to her, his features
forbidding, eyes glinting with disdain. "I don't wish to discuss last night. Nor are the circumstances of your previous lovers a particular concern of mine." He spat into the
sea, as though he'd a sour taste in his mouth. "I was the
fool to have assumed you were *virgo intacta* in the first
place. You are a worldly, educated woman, quite apparently much in the company of men. Since you are lovelier
than the usual bluestocking, it doesn't at all surprise me
that you were seduced."

"I wasn't—"

"Furthermore," he cut her off. "As you've so judiciously
pointed out, I've had scores of lovers, myself, and objectively have no real moral reason to begrudge a beautiful
spinster her pleasures."

Alexandra squinted up at him. Had he just insulted her
and called her beautiful in the same sentence?

"Unfortunately," he continued drolly. "The fact remains
that *my* heir needs to be born of your body. And, as impertinent as you might find it, I must be certain any issue
of yours belongs to me. Thus, we can forbear each other's
company for ten days or so; I'm certain you won't find that
too much of a chore."

"I wouldn't resent forestalling our intimacies to ease your mind," she said carefully.

"Of course you wouldn't." He swiped up his coffee cup and stared into the grounds at the bottom, as though wishing to divine the future in their depths.

"I confess to being confused by your logic," she admitted.

He slid her a level glance. "How so?"

"Well, if we avoid the marriage bed for now, it'll be proven that I am not with another man's child at this time," she began. "But when I conceive in the future, how can you—or any man, for that matter—be certain that a child belongs to him. There's no way to tell."

"I'd know," he growled.

"You couldn't possibly." Her brow puckered. "It's something that, as a scientist, I've always found odd about our society compared to many of the ancients. A name follows that of the male line, however, one only has categorical proof that a child is the product of a woman's body. No man can be absolutely certain a child is of his line, that his wife hasn't taken a lover, unless he's with her every moment of every—"

With a furious burst of strength, Redmayne hurled his cup overboard. It sailed through the air, reflecting the sunlight with every rotation until it splashed into the water and disappeared.

Alexandra stared at the place it sank, not daring to meet the dangerously glinting eyes now boring a hole into the side of her head even as he bent to grit into her ear, "I'd. *Know.*"

She turned her face, her cheek meeting his, grazing the grains of his beard. She expected him to pull away, but he didn't. The absurd notion to rub against him like a cat rose within her, and she drew her cheek across his.

"I wouldn't," she whispered against him. To any onlooker, they'd appear to be the besotted newlyweds, nuzzling each other beneath the French sun. "Take a lover, that is. I don't betray my vows. I hope you can trust that."

His cynical grunt was hot against her neck, as he rooted into the hollow behind her ear, inhaling against her hair. "There's no reason to trust you," he lamented, his fingers curling around her arms to draw her closer. "And I probably never will."

"Why?" she asked, breathing him in, as well. His exotic scent mixed with the brine of the sea, intoxicating her. What a strange conversation to be having with their mouths, when their bodies reacted to each other's proximity in such a conflicting way. "Why do you doubt I am in earnest?"

"Do you trust *my* word?" he challenged, his mustache tickling at her neck before his lips pressed there. "When you know next to nothing about me?"

She hesitated. He was right. What did she know of him? She'd no idea if he was truly a man to be trusted. Not with her body. Her past. Her secrets.

Her life.

She knew the smell of his sweat was anything but repellent. That she liked to sink her hands beneath the lapels of his jacket just so she could shape her fingers over the breadth of his chest. That for such a big man, he had yet to use his strength against her. Even in anger. And that horses allowed him to be their master. That an extra sense of such beasts could often pick up the measure of a man.

Jean-Yves had a dog whose ears would flatten, and lips would curl, at the presence of Headmaster de Marchand.

It should have been a warning.

But the horses and hounds at Castle Redmayne, they responded to Piers's firm lead because of his alternate gentility with them.

The beasts trusted him.

Shouldn't that count for something?

"Perhaps, my lord, rather than avoiding each other for ten days, we could spend our honeymoon in each other's company?" she suggested.

He stiffened and pulled away.

She missed him instantly.

"That really isn't necessary. What would be the point?"

"Well, if we are to be Duke and Duchess of Redmayne. If we are to raise a child—children—together it might be easier if we are better acquainted. Friendly, even."

He tossed his head in an almost equine manner. "Dukes don't generally have much of a hand in raising their own children."

"No . . ." she acquiesced. "But Redmayne, while very grand, isn't like modern vast estates so it's unlikely you'll be able to avoid them. Or me."

"Not if I install you somewhere else," he muttered.

She decided now wasn't the time to mention that she'd never remain *installed* anywhere. She would go where she pleased. "Is that your design? How will I bear you a bevy of heirs if I'm not accessible to you?"

He paused, his frown deepening to a scowl, as though she'd made a point he'd not considered. "What are you proposing, exactly?"

"Merely an appointed time every day where we share each other's company," she suggested. "A dinner, perhaps. Or a walk of some kind, like the one we took the other afternoon along the cliffs. Minus the assassin, of course."

"You mean the walk when you threatened to shoot me?"

Alexandra bit her lips to suppress a grimace, or a smile. Perhaps both. "I only threatened to shoot you because you were on top of me."

"I'd just saved your life, if you remember."

She did remember being on the precipice of a cliff, in more ways than one.

"It wouldn't do to spend our honeymoon apart," she said, turning from him. "But if that is your wish—"

He seized her arm, pulling her back into their intimate posture, his breath hot against her ear as his body melded to hers. "Do you have any idea, wife, what ten *minutes* in your company does to me?" His whisper was almost like a snarl in its animalistic intensity. "Do you really think I can smell your scent, that I can watch you knowing what lies beneath your shapeless dresses, and keep myself from tasting what is mine?"

Alexandra surreptitiously glanced at the workmen on the deck, all of them doing their utmost to *not* notice them and succeeding superbly.

Too well, in her opinion.

"Now that I've explored your curves, tasted your breasts, and experienced your pleasure, I'll think about nothing else until I have you naked once again, do you understand me? Our time together now is an agony, in more ways than one."

Three days ago, his words would have frightened her beyond imagining.

Three days ago she'd not known what it was like to experience the ruthless patience of his passions. To be the object of his desire and to find that desire ignited in her own dormant soul.

"I don't see why . . . we couldn't make some sort of arrangement," she offered breathlessly.

"Arrangement?" The word sounded indecent from his voice.

"We could . . . trade favors. Without intercourse. It could . . . help us to further our acquaintanceship."

And, if they were lucky, they could teach each other a little about trust.

"I have one condition," he murmured into her ear.

"What's that?"

"You let me use my tongue."

Alexandra's reply was lost in a raucous crack from above. Men shouted. The grind of metal and splinter of wood was deafening.

Redmayne's entire bulk moved in synchronous slow motion, as he seized her, effortlessly lifted her, and surged across the deck with his head ducked over hers.

Had he been a millisecond slower, the thousand-pound crate would have crushed them both.

CHAPTER FIFTEEN

Piers didn't know which suspicion he detested the most, that someone might be trying to kill his wife, or that someone might be trying to fuck her.

It unsettled him greatly that he hadn't been able to take his eyes off Alexandra. Not only because she was the most captivating woman, but because, no matter how many panicked maritime admiralties assured him that the incident on the ship the prior morning had been an accident, he couldn't shake the suspicion that it had been anything but.

How could it be that even though the suspicions in his wary heart threatened to eat him alive, he felt the need to guard his new wife like a precious possession? As disenchanted as he was by their wedding night, as much distance as he'd vowed to maintain, he was unable to leave her side.

Not during their journey north to Seasons-sur-Mer, a little hamlet by the sea from which they could still admire the ancient rooftops of the port city of Le Havre. Not when they'd arrived at Hotel Fond du Val, and not even when she'd accepted Dr. Forsythe's invitation to accompany him on an introductory tour of the dig site and catacombs the prior afternoon.

Piers had to force himself not to lock her in their rooms while he booked immediate passage back to Devonshire.

Where he could secure her in the tower of Castle Redmayne.

Something about the whiff of impending danger made a man want to cosset those closest to him in a fortress.

Until he could be certain she was safe. Until he could be certain she wasn't with child.

So he could plant within her a child of his own.

The idea held a darker appeal than it ever had before. For darker reasons. This morning there'd been a shift, he noted, from his original motivations for siring an heir.

Rose and Patrick were no longer at the forefront of his mind.

This morning, as he watched his wife's head bent toward Dr. Forsythe's as the two passionately argued over the provenance of a bracelet they examined, his motivations had everything to do with possession.

If Alexandra were ripening with child, every man who'd dare to look upon her would know he'd put it there. Would understand she was taken. Claimed.

One would assume that a man with Dr. Forsythe's ostensible intellect would know better than to trifle with the Terror of Torcliff's wife. That he'd be more cautious about concealing his longing. More judicious with his smiles and lingering gazes.

Apparently, Thomas Forsythe wasn't as intelligent as his reputation would lead one to believe.

Piers couldn't blame the doctor. Not when Alexandra shone with such brilliance, even when surrounded by drab tents and the soiled bones of the ancient dead. The incident aboard the ship the prior morning might as well have been forgotten, her fear replaced by a radiant joy as she surveyed the artifacts splayed in organized disarray. Her umber eyes glowed a feral gold, lit by some inner glow ignited by her passionate appetite for the past.

A longing ignited within Piers, as well, one he fervently attempted to ignore.

What if she looked at him with half the joy as she did the iron torque in her hand? What if she stroked his skin, his live warm flesh, with a modicum of the reverence with which she handled the bones of the dead?

What if she smiled at him with the same warm delight glittering up at Dr. Forsythe as they shared their professional insights?

She'd claimed Forsythe had never been her lover. Could he trust her word?

Categorically not.

Piers studied the banked heat in the other man's gaze, the barely leashed hunger of a predator sniffing about his next meal.

There was a chance she told the truth. Because he also believed that poor Dr. Forsythe wouldn't be so entirely, pathetically famished for a woman whose charms he'd already sampled.

Alexandra signaled to the ancient skeletons laid out over neat rows of tables, gesturing with more enthusiasm than she ever had in his presence. "I can see why we are assuming that the Moor, the Persian, and the Viking were all buried here during roughly the same century," she posited. "But then if this was a graveyard, or a crypt, where is the church? In *my* estimation, these men were not buried before A.D. 1000, but Granville Priory was built in the ninth century and is in the town of Le Havre proper. Why not inter these obviously wealthy dead men on holy ground instead of a cryptic catacomb on a cliff so far out of town?"

Forsythe rubbed at the divot in his chin, his eyes twinkling down at her. "That very question is why I've been called back here, Dr. Lane—that is, Your Grace." He spared a glance of chagrin for Piers.

The smarmy fucker didn't fool him for one moment. Forsythe had not made a verbal mistake, but a calculation. Piers was sure of it.

Placing the bracelet next to the porous and scratched wrist bones of the skeleton laid out before them, Forsythe went to the tent's entrance and pulled back the flap to gesture toward the ever-widening entrance to the catacombs. Workers smudged with mud and dust wheeled heaps of earth up planks laid over the five stone steps that led underground.

"The rumor is that the workers and archeology students will be bringing a Byzantine trader up from the catacombs tomorrow or the day after; that is, if they can finish excavating the final crypt, wherein two bodies are still in the final stages of being uncovered. I'd love for you to be there." Remembering himself, Forsythe gave another casual nod toward Piers. "For both of you, of course."

"I wouldn't miss it!" Alexandra accepted enthusiastically. "Byzantium was my obsession at school. I daresay I was fanatical."

"Who wasn't?" Forsythe said with a solicitous chuckle.

"Oh, plenty of people!" she exclaimed. "Those students who were more interested in the Romans and the Greeks, for example."

"Philistines." Feigning disgust, the doctor winked.

"Them, as well!" She laughed.

Forsythe reached across her under the guise of retrieving a map.

Piers noted that she avoided physical contact with her colleague, always keeping proper distance. She never reached for the man. Didn't flirt, coo, or bat her amber lashes. Not only *didn't* she return Forsythe's longing looks, it was as if she didn't take notice of them.

The only shadow over Piers's triumph in that regard was that she didn't pay *him* any more feminine attention than she did Forsythe.

It was the dead men who held her consideration the longest.

And Piers refused to be jealous of a man who'd been departed from this world for nearly a thousand years.

"Ancient Egyptians are distressingly popular these days," she lamented, carefully examining a scrap of woven robe laid out next to the body. "But they aren't the only ancient civilization worth such obsession."

Piers moved closer to the tables, cataloguing the bones of the departed, imagining the matching ones in Forsythe's body equally broken and dismantled.

By his bare hands.

He'd never learned much about exhuming corpses, but he certainly knew how to make them.

Alexandra turned to Piers, distracting him from his black impulses with an attractive idea brightening her expression to ecstatic. "Do you really think your Redmayne ancestor might be among those buried here?" she postulated. "Perhaps even that Viking over there? Wouldn't that be something?" She clenched her fists in front of her like a child who'd been offered a surprise gift.

The brilliance of her smile turned Piers's soul all the way over, imparting a cool balm to his bitterness and exposing his shadows to the light.

In moments when she looked at him as she did now, he forgot all his reasons for being suspicious of her. He forgot what he looked like. Who he was. What she might want from him.

But not what he wanted from her.

Which—goddammit—was more than just her incomparable body.

Unsettled by the strength of his desire, he glanced away, inspecting the skeleton of the Viking on the far table. "This man was buried with a blue sigil." He pointed to the scrap of heraldry laid out beside him along with the splinters of a blue shield. "Redmayne's colors were always crimson, for obvious reasons."

"An excellent observation." The condescension in Forsythe's tone set Piers's teeth on edge. "Though I don't think your father was too far off when he suspected that the Redmaynes launched with William the Bastard from these shores. William Malet built his fortifications here, and he was instrumental in winning the Battle of Hastings alongside William the Bastard-turned-Conqueror.

"Malet wrote about red-haired Norsemen rather extensively, a father and a son. One died on these shores, the other, Magnus, built your Castle Redmayne. Or at least the fortress turned ruin. I'd love to talk with you about an excavation on your grounds someday."

"What a capital idea!" Alexandra agreed, turning a hopeful gaze to Piers.

The polite thing to do would be to extend an invitation to Forsythe, but it would be a cold day in hell before he allowed Forsythe anywhere near Castle Redmayne.

Piers emitted a noncommittal grunt, letting those gathered interpret it however they would.

His stare locked with Forsythe's; a current of understanding passed between them. They disliked each other equally.

Too absorbed by her specimens to notice the undercurrent of masculine tension, Alexandra stepped around the Persian's table to examine the Moorish skeleton and the neat piles of pots, baskets, and finery next to him. "If the Redmayne elder was so instrumental in helping William the Conqueror unite the empire, why would they possibly bury him in an unmarked pauper's grave on a hill outside of town?"

Forsythe moved to join her, but Piers placed himself next to his wife, forcing the other man to take his place opposite the Moor's examination table. He picked up a ring of crude yet masterful workmanship and examined it, enjoying Forsythe's anxious intake of breath.

"Forgive my uneducated opinion," he said dryly. "But very few of these men appear to have been paupers."

"You're right, of course," Forsythe reluctantly agreed. "While they're often wealthy traders from distant lands, I initially assumed that this place had been sanctioned for the burial of foreigners. However, there are outsiders interred at the priory on holy ground."

"I've got it!" Alexandra reached out and gripped Piers's bicep, her fingers becoming claws as she shook his arm, unable to contain her enthusiasm. "Pagans!" she exclaimed.

"By Jove," Forsythe breathed.

"These men, the Viking, the Moor, and the Persian, they were none of them Christian, and therefore not considered fit for burial at the priory." She turned to Piers, whose entire being focused on the feel of her hand gripping his arm.

There it was. The sparkle in her eye. The unmitigated gleam of intellectual brilliance and girlish glee. A thoroughly heady concoction that settled an ache somewhere south of his gut.

"Your ancestors, the Redmaynes, were they Christian or pagan?" she asked.

Piers struggled to consider as he stared down at his wife. Could he really make it ten days without bedding her?

"Magnus Redmayne, the son, built Trinity Priory on Redmayne land almost immediately after the fortress," he recalled. "However, by all accounts, he insisted upon a traditional Viking burial."

"He was burned on a barge at sea?" Her face shone with an almost romantic rapture and some of the queer chill Piers had been holding in his heart thawed.

"That he was." He flashed her a teasing smile, aware the effect was somewhat lost due to his deformity. "In the old days, it is said, their wives were burned with them, so the women could accompany their husbands to Valhalla."

"What tripe." Alexandra rolled her eyes. "I'm certainly glad of our more modern sensibilities." Her eyes narrowed, then rounded as something struck her. "Don't tell me Magnus Redmayne's wife was burned with him?"

Piers chuckled, finding her outrage adorable. He caught at a ringlet that escaped from beneath her sensible hat. "No, my bride, she lived to a ripe old age with her three unruly sons, always favored by the new English court."

"Oh. Well . . . good." Appeased, she tilted a lopsided smile up at him.

The atmosphere between them shifted, warmed. Piers read in her eyes unspoken and uncertain apologies.

Was he going to remain angry with her? She'd been obscure, but had she been dishonest?

Was she deceitful now?

The look she gave him whispered of earnest emotion; half hope, half despair. All day she'd seemed as though something cataclysmic perched on her tongue, ready to spring forth and further decimate the fragile bond they'd forged.

Without meaning to, Piers leaned down toward her. Closer. The fresh scent of linens and citrus enveloped him; he silently willed her to whisper it to him. To put them both out of their misery.

What are you hiding? he wondered. What secrets lie behind those pools of whisky and honey?

With a polite clearing of the throat, Forsythe announced himself, breaking the moment. "I'll just . . . go and garner updates from the workmen on how the excavation of the catacombs is coming along since I was here last." He tipped his hat uncomfortably and left them alone with the dead.

Piers looked down at the silken lock curled in his finger. *Falt Ruadh.* Such lovely red hair. Such a unique and lovely wife.

What if she was taken from him?

The concern that had been churning beneath his skin all day boiled to the surface. How could he be so elementally troubled by the loss of something—someone—he'd only known, only desired, for four days?

Why couldn't he shake the feeling that someone was trying to take her from him?

"Was it you?" he wondered, not realizing he'd spoken aloud until her lips pursed in puzzlement.

"To what do you refer?" she queried, all wide-eyed innocence and incomprehension

But that couldn't be. He'd only just witnessed firsthand her unique intelligence. He'd trailed after her all day like a sentinel, observing her in her element.

His wife, it seemed, was never more alive than when surrounded by the dead.

Something had his hackles up like a wolf scenting danger in the forest. Too many strange and dangerous things had occurred since they'd met. Mercury's escape. The gunmen in the ruins. The incident on the ship.

"Falt Ruadh," he murmured. "Can you think of any reason anyone would have to harm you?"

"I—couldn't tell you." She didn't look guilty, but neither did her denial seem particularly convincing.

The canvas made a thick sound as a burly worker punched it open, storming inside. "Your Graces!" he exclaimed, the outline of his eyes extraordinarily white against the grime covering the rest of him. "They've found his sigil! They've found the tomb of Redmayne in the catacombs!"

With a exclamation of pure delight, Alexandra drove herself into his arms.

Stunned, Piers looked down at her, struck by the realization that this might have been the first time she'd ever initiated such physical contact.

He folded his arms over her, disconcerted by how well—how easily—she fit within them.

"Let us go have a look, shall we?" he suggested, and was unable to finish the sentence before she was all but dragging him bodily out of the tent.

Chapter Sixteen

Hours later, Alexandra gawked at the stranger in the mirror.

It wasn't the expensive foreign gown, exactly, that caused her not to recognize herself. She couldn't even say it had anything to do with her conceding to the corset, or the appallingly and—she supposed—fashionably low neckline that revealed much more of her décolletage than she was accustomed to.

It was a little bit of everything. Insubstantial changes had turned her into an absolute foreigner. Where she'd often considered her eyes a dull brown, she found a glisten of amber fire within them. A gleam of something indefinable and undeniably feminine. Her lips seemed fuller, somehow, flushed with a peach that matched the high color in her cheeks. Could it be possible that whatever new feelings her husband had begun to evoke now shone on her countenance?

Was joy beautiful? Because today had been joyful, hadn't it?

Transcendent, all things considered.

Even her hair glinted with a brighter sheen, coiled in a simple but flattering braided knot that shimmered in every form of light.

When they'd parted at the end of their day at the catacombs, Alexandra and Redmayne had each been covered in a fine layer of cobwebs, stone dust, and a patina of cheerful exuberance.

Her husband had seemed much his prior charming self, and willing enough to let them retain some of their previous amicability.

He'd barely been an arm's length away from her the entire day, a looming—some might say hovering—tower of virile muscle and grim caution. Something about the intensity, the *insistency,* of his proximity had both alarmed and appeased her. The words he'd spoken when they'd been alone had evoked whispers of warmth within her that didn't want to abate.

Her body shimmered with awareness—and not a little caution—when he was so close. And yet, she felt absolutely protected beneath the shadow of the Terror of Torcliff. As though any of the danger they'd faced in Devonshire couldn't touch her here.

He'd even displayed some interest in the catacombs as they'd surveyed the walled-off entrance to the final tomb. His eyes had glowed with pleasure as he'd verified the Redmayne sigil decorating the worn red banner over the entrance.

Tonight had been subsequently decreed a celebration. Of the serendipitous find. Of their nuptials. Of wine and food and summer evenings by the sea.

Tomorrow, the work on the Redmayne tomb would begin in earnest.

Julia Throckmorton had decided to spend a few nights in Seasons-sur-Mer to further her pursuit of Dr. Forsythe.

It had taken her all of five minutes to declare Alexandra's wardrobe hopeless, and she'd thrust upon her this emerald silk gown bedecked with bronze beads at the sleeves, hem, and neckline.

Alexandra had been given no recourse but to accept the woman's insistent kindness.

Before she'd left her room, Alexandra had pinched herself soundly, admonishing herself for a fanciful fool. She was clean and presentable and attired as a duchess should be attired. What else mattered when it all came down to it?

She floated down the hall toward the grand hotel's open ballroom, following a path lit by crystal wall sconces and faded striped paper.

Ever interested in her setting's history, Alexandra had learned that the Hotel Fond du Val had been a majestic resort before the Napoleonic wars, and had sunk into disrepair, though it was lovingly and patiently being restored by a new owner. The accommodations were clean and spacious, if not opulent, and Alexandra found herself utterly charmed by the touch of rustic in a missing crystal or two of the chandeliers, or the dull creaks of the undervarnished floors.

Because of this, the rooms which had once housed Philippe de France, the beloved brother of Louis XIV, could now be let to everyone from gentility to humble archeologists to merchants from the city on a seaside holiday.

She paused at the top of the stairs, smoothing her gown for the thousandth time. Beset by nerves, she consulted the faded golden carpets beneath her feet before gathering her courage to look up and find her husband.

She forced a shaky breath into her constricted lungs, grateful for the fragrance of the summer sea air wafting through windows flung wide. In the northwestern corner of the grand room, several white linen-covered tables were set apart by topiary and serviced by perfectly attired footmen offering an informal dinner.

A dark wood bar stretched out below the stairs, behind which a small, harried man struggled to fill glasses that drained faster than he could pour.

Alexandra hadn't hesitated on the steps to be noticed, though she became painfully aware of the increasing number of eyes upon her. It was the sight of her husband that had rooted her to the ground and had her grasping at the finely wrought mahogany railing for support.

Redmayne stood at the bar conversing with a gathering of gentlemen, sipping occasionally from a glass of red wine.

He was an oak among aspens. A mountain among men.

When would she ever get used to the sight of him in formal attire?

So often, he was to her the man she'd met on the platform. Indolently dressed in a casual workman's kit, throat exposed and dusky muscles hinted at beneath thin, white shirtsleeves.

How did she prefer him? The hunter, predatory and insolent? Or the duke, charismatic, sleek, and cunning?

Either way he'd the same effect on her mind, which endlessly churned with thoughts, ideas, anxieties, and plans, and seemed to sputter to a crashing halt in his vicinity.

His effect on her was most unnatural. Distressing, even.

If only his hair wouldn't gleam like ebony pitch beneath the lamplight. If only that one unruly forelock, forever trailing out of place in a most distracting manner, would cease calling her hand to smooth it down.

Or perhaps his jaw should be less bold, less square and unabashedly male. His wintry eyes flashing with fewer storms.

Alexandra had stood in one place for so long, her thoughts agitating as loud as factory machinery, that she only just noticed that the lively chatter in the hotel's dining room had hushed to a murmur. The guests' activities and gestures, once as busy as leaves in a sea breeze, died away as the air went still.

Redmayne cast a questioning glance at the quieted crowd, noted the direction of their collective gazes, and found her at the top of the stairs.

Alexandra could hear her own breath rattle about in her chest as he performed a slow, thorough, and very public examination of her.

His expression remained impassive, his eyes shuttered, but the wine in his glass sloshed violently before he abandoned it to the bar and strode toward the stairs with the unmistakable intention of claiming his place at her side.

He conquered rather than climbed the stairs, and Alexandra realized why he'd hidden his gaze. Only depravities lurked there. Wickedness and wanting. She had to look away from the intensity of his regard as he drew nearer.

It was that, or faint.

Her husband stopped two steps below her, took her gloved hand in his and, as was his custom, placed a kiss on her knuckles.

It was as though her gloves were insubstantial. The warmth of his lips suffused her instantly, sending a swarm of hummingbirds alight in her belly.

Her restless eyes lit on Julia by the unlit fireplace, clad in a dress of vibrant violet. Julia frowned up at Dr. Forsythe who, in turn, stared at Alexandra in a manner almost wolfish. Beyond them, she found Jean-Yves lingering at the bar nursing a white wine and watching the spectacle closely. She smiled fondly at him, the almost paterlike pride in his eyes setting her cheeks aglow.

To her chagrin, Redmayne followed the direction of her smile and, having never met Jean-Yves, misinterpreted the object of her delight.

His hand tightened on hers. Not painfully, but, she dared to think, possessively, as he conducted her down the stairs.

Alexandra looked up at him sharply, finding his wintry eyes glaring shards of ice toward Forsythe. He leaned down to her, scandalously close, his breath warm on her ear. "You'll have to tell me, wife, from whom you acquired that dress . . . and for whom you are wearing it."

If only he knew how wrong his suspicions were. If only she knew how to tell him.

I wore it for you.

"My friend Lady Julia Throckmorton lent it me, as I only own the one silvery ballgown and didn't think to pack it for an archeological dig." She slid her arm through his, trying not to note the tense muscles contained beneath the jacket. "I thought it nice, to commemorate the occasion."

"Consider it commemorated," he muttered, steering them toward the quaint dining room.

"Am I to take it that you approve?" A trill of pleasure warmed her breast.

"You are to take it that every man in this room approves, a bit too much for my liking. I thought it was your practice to hide those away." He glanced down at her bosoms, his eyes darkening before he dragged his gaze elsewhere.

His frown deepened to a scowl as he caught a young waiter gaping at her with a slack jaw. The maître d' whipped him in the back of the head with a towel and sent him back to the kitchen with some harsh words in blistering French. That accomplished, he floated toward them on lean legs made for dancing, and flashed a smile made for seduction beneath his precise mustache.

Alexandra liked him immediately.

"Monsieur le duc, madame la duchesse, I have prepared your table as instructed, if you would please follow me." He bowed one too many times and led them to an intimate corner table on a dais that could very easily have fit a party of four, but boasted two elegant settings beside which a silver five-pointed candelabra glowed.

The corner was constructed of more windows than walls, and even in the darkness of the evening, whitecaps of raucous waves and golden beaches were illuminated by a waxing moon.

"I shall direct you tonight to consider the superb duck confit, coq au vin, or swordfish à la niçoise." The maître d' filled glasses of wine to the perfect line without even looking, never breaking solicitous eye contact with Redmayne. If he was affected by the scars, one would never know. "I will allow you to peruse the menu and will return at your convenience." He bowed and slipped away with little fuss, hovering nearby like a pleasant summer cloud.

"I'm considering pilfering him for our household," Redmayne remarked. "It is a skilled servant who knows when he is needed, and a masterful one who knows when to disappear."

Their household? Alexandra bit back a pleased smile.

"It surprises me, my lord, that you requested a table alone," she observed. "This fete is technically in your honor, and that of your ancestor. I should think a long table would have been more appropriate, so you could converse with others."

He made a face. "I've spent all day conversing with other people, and when those musicians over there start to play, no doubt we'll be expected to grant dances as we are a duke and duchess. However, I wanted to have—" He looked at her, started to say something, and then changed his mind. "A meal, at least, all to myself."

For some ridiculous reason, his surliness evoked a soft, teasing laugh from her chest. "How magnanimous you were with your august person, Your Grace," she teased, enjoying the flicker of shadow cast in his scars by the candles. "It never before seemed to tax you so, to walk amongst the common plebeians."

He gave a derisive snort before lifting his wineglass and drinking deeply. "I find it no burden to be among stone workers, academics, and groundskeepers. However, it taxed me greatly to interact with the intrepid Dr. Forsythe and not grind his face into the nearest lodestone."

An unexpected laugh burst from her just as she'd taken a hearty sip of her own burgundy, and she had to press her glove to her lips in order to force a swallow.

"I don't at all see how that's funny," he grumped.

Alexandra returned her wine to the table, and pressed her lips together to stifle her mirth. "It's only that I find your jealousy of Thom—Dr. Forsythe—unnecessary."

"You think me jealous?" He gaped at her with incredulity. "Of some noodle-armed nancy you met in a library somewhere? Don't make me laugh."

He didn't appear anywhere close to laughter, but Alexandra thought it imprudent to mention.

"You're being unkind," she reprimanded around a smile she was helpless but to convey. "You've noticed Dr. Forsythe is no weakling, my lord. Furthermore, many women find intelligence every bit as diverting as Vitruvian musculature and rampant, virile masculinity."

He leaned forward, placing his elbows in such a way that his biceps and shoulders strained against his jacket in a most distracting manner. "Rampant, virile masculinity?"

The ghost of amusement haunted his lips, warming his husky baritone. "Are you referring to anyone in particular?"

Alexandra's cheeks heated. "I wasn't necessarily referring to you," she lied. "Though I'll tell you what isn't attractive—arrogance."

He made a dark sound of derision in his throat. "There are many forms of intelligence, as I'm sure you're aware. Some can be found in books, others are more . . . elemental. Environmental. Observational, even."

"Tracking panthers through a jungle, for example?" she suggested around another sip of wine. "Or keeping beasts, bending them to your will?"

"Well, it would have been immodest for me to say." He gestured to the maître d'. "*Arrogant* even, but since you brought it up I'll mention that I also received high marks at Oxford in my day."

"Forsythe is a Cambridge man."

"Bloody figures," he muttered.

"I confess I've never understood the rivalry between the two institutions." She sighed. "Not when everyone accepts the Sorbonne as the superior establishment."

He gaped in mock outrage. "You consider yourself so clever, do you?"

"We Sorbonne alumni don't have to consider anything. We already know," she challenged.

"Who's arrogant now?" He smirked. "Although you ended up with me as a husband," he added wryly. "Some would call not only your intelligence into question, but your sanity, as well."

Alexandra noted a shadow beneath the levity in his tone, and momentarily wondered if he'd ever shared her feelings of unworthiness.

"Others would ascribe my marriage to you as my greatest achievement, despite the fact that I'm only one of a handful of female archeologists in history."

"What is *your* assessment of the predicament you find yourself in, Doctor?" An ebony brow rose over his abruptly alert regard.

Now there was a dangerous question. One she was unprepared to answer. "Would you like to know what I think?" She idly drew light circles around the rim of her wineglass, not realizing what she was doing until his eyes drifted to the pad of her finger.

"My breath is bated," he replied.

"I think . . ." She thought that this conversation in this setting with this man was perhaps the most exciting masculine interaction she'd had in some time. She'd *thought* she'd never be able to flirt with a man, let alone her husband. She *thought* that in the candlelight Redmayne was perhaps the most compelling, handsomest man she'd had the pleasure of knowing. Indeed, she thought about kissing him again. And more. She thought all manner of things she dared not say as her heart trilled against her ribs at the prospect of vocalizing any of her unruly speculations.

"I *think* . . . you dislike Dr. Forsythe so heartily because the two of you are so alike, and that tends to rankle a person," she deflected.

His eyes narrowed. "Do tell."

She shrugged, strangely enjoying the glint of danger in his eyes. He was like a caged panther, daring her to provoke him, and something about this wild night by the sea stirred a recklessness inside of her. She reveled in the feeling of this audacious part of her called forth by the wicked, boyish twinkle in his eye contrasting with his ever-sinister features. "In truth," she said, "and I'll thank you not to quote me on this, Dr. Forsythe is little better than an adequate scientist. But because of his other skill sets, he is often much sought after, especially in the more exotic camps in unstable locales."

"What skills is he perceived to possess?" Redmayne asked with droll insouciance.

"He's rather adept at keeping camps secure and protected," she recounted. "And fed, as he is an accomplished hunter in his own right and skilled with all manner of firearms, languages, and even certain exotic combat techniques."

"Is that so?" His eyes slid past her, as the musicians began to tune their instruments.

Alexandra thanked the maître d' when their plates arrived. Redmayne's glower was fixed on some point behind her.

"I would have predicted the two of you to get along splendidly, as you're both such avid outdoorsmen," she said as she tucked into her divine dish.

"We might have done." He picked up his own utensils, holding his knife like a weapon as he speared her with a speaking look. "Were he not trying to seduce you from beneath my nose."

"How many times do I have to tell you, my lord, there is absolutely nothing between Forsythe and me but a fond friendship."

"As many times as I have to tell you you're either blind, obtuse, or lying."

A spurt of irritation chased away any flirtatious feelings. "That doesn't cast me in a particularly pleasant light, does it?"

"You mean to tell me a handsome, accomplished, and, by your own assessment, masculine doctor has never once caught your notice as a desirable romantic entanglement?" he asked.

"I mean to say that until now, no man *alive* caught my notice as a desirable entanglement, romantic or otherwise. Full stop."

He stared at her with a sort of aghast incomprehension, and Alexandra felt compelled to continue, rather than go back over what she'd just said to dissect what he might not understand.

"The only thing Forsythe has over you in my estimation, my lord, other than an avid intellectual curiosity, is the propensity to listen to me when I speak."

He leaned forward, grinding at the succulent duck with distracting flexes of his jaw. His eyes glinted dangerously. "Do you mean to say, wife, that you or Forsythe are more intelligent than I am?"

"Not at all." She took another bite, making him wait for her explanation. "As you said, there are many forms of intellects. You've certainly mastered a great deal of them, but you have to consider that Dr. Forsythe and I might be a bit more well read."

"Well read!" he blustered. "What do you imagine one does in the wilds after the sun goes down? I've read every sort of thing."

Alexandra smiled at the confounded offense collected on his features. Though she hadn't meant any, she felt as though he might need a thorough humbling. "Oh come, Dr. Forsythe and I have dedicated our lives to academia; you can't possibly be asserting that you're as well educated."

"As you say, I couldn't possibly." He regarded her for another long and mercurial moment wherein she couldn't tell if he were angry or amused. "All right, Doctor. I propose a game. A battle of wits, as it were."

"Between you and Forsythe?" she puzzled.

"Hang Forsythe. Between you and me."

Alexandra's fork paused halfway to her mouth. "What are the terms of this battle?" she asked skeptically

"Three quotes." He wiped his mouth with a linen napkin and drank deeply from a bloodred Bordeaux. "Scour your learned mind of all the books you read at the Sorbonne. If I guess the first one, I get to name the place and time of our interlude tonight."

"Interlude?" she breathed.

"You did say we were to continue to trade favors, did you not?"

"Well, yes but—"

His expression was all wickedness and heat. "I'm merely making things interesting. Upping the stakes, as it were."

Alexandra's own eyes narrowed, apprehension twisting with anticipation in her core. "What if you guess the second?"

"Then I get to choose what I do to you." His voice deepened. Darkened. Along with his unmistakable intent.

"Did you change your mind? Do you mean to consummate—"

"I mean to show you, wife, just how much two people can do to each other *without* consummation."

The wine Alexandra gulped did nothing to moisten her dry mouth. She hadn't forgotten what he'd said on the ship earlier before the accident.

You let me use my tongue.

"A-and the third?" she stuttered around lips going numb.

"Well, you'd best make that a very obscure quote, indeed." He leaned back, a deep breath filling his deeper chest. "Because if I guess that one, then I'll get to choose what *you* do to *me*."

Alexandra might have choked if she hadn't just swallowed

hard. Setting the empty glass down, she lamented how improper it would be to ask for another. As if she'd summoned him with the thought, the maître d' was there with a decanter and an obliging smile.

Bless him.

If she were lucky, the wine would lend her bravado.

She searched her thoughts for excerpts both apropos and somewhat obscure, while remaining fair.

"'O, beware, my lord, of jealousy,'" she warned, "'it is the green-eyed monster which doth mock. The meat it feeds on . . .'"

He made a wry sound, his eyes shifting as though searching through his memory. "While uncommonly wise, Shakespeare didn't have my faithless mother, nor did he have Rose in his past. Though he had a Rosaline . . ." The uninjured side of his lip lifted rather triumphantly.

Drat. She'd gone too easy. Everyone knew Shakespeare.

Something he'd said tugged at her. "You don't speak of your parents often," she observed. "And when you do mention your mother, it's most unfavorably." She didn't follow her observation with a question, but he replied as though she had.

"My mother was cruel and my father was weak. They made each other miserable. My mother chipped away at his heart—his soul—with broken vows, frivolous flirtations, and callous dalliances until there was nothing left. Until he'd become such an empty husk of a man, he ended his own life."

"I'm sorry. How awful." Alexandra fought to school the pity from her gaze, sensing it had no place in this conversation. But her heart ached for him. For his distraught father.

"It was a long time ago." His tone remained impassive.

Lighthearted, even. But he sawed at his food, stabbing at it as though it'd disrespected him most egregiously.

"They say time heals all wounds, don't they?" She expelled a caustic breath, her own fork idly scraping across the plate. "And I suppose that's true to a point. But there is no mistaking the scars . . ."

She searched his face, his sinister, scarred face, thinking that perhaps his own heart bore the remnants of unseen wounds just as grievous.

Was it any wonder he was so cynical? So distrustful of women. He'd watched his mother destroy a kind and beloved father, and subsequently fell in love with a woman just as faithless as she had been.

"I'd rather not speak of parents and the past." He waved his hand, brushing the distasteful subject aside.

"Now let me see . . ." He considered her for a moment. "I must ponder when and where it pleases me most to kiss you next, as I've won the first prize of three."

"Kiss me where on my person . . . or where geographically?" she asked, pressing her hands to cheeks that were flushed and hot even through the silk of her gloves.

"An excellent question," he purred.

Alexandra glared at him, taking extra time with her next bite as she contemplated her next quote.

"Consider that you might want me to win this, wife." Sin colored the timbre of his voice in decadent, velvet notes, seeming to even darken the candles flickering over their feast.

Did she?

It was a dangerous thing, she was beginning to realize, to underestimate the Terror of Torcliff in any arena, physical or otherwise.

"Tell me," he continued, covering the hand she'd rested

on the table. "Does the thought of being at my mercy entice you?"

Alexandra froze. How could she say yes? The thought of being at his mercy terrified her, as he was a man most famously *without* mercy.

And yet. How could she say no?

Because she'd be that much more a liar.

Locking eyes with his, she said, "'Teach me to feel another's woe, to hide the fault I see, that mercy I to others show, that mercy show to me.'"

His eyes narrowed, darted this way and that, as though grappling with his own memory behind them.

She had him, she thought triumphantly. She'd bested him.

"You are confounded, my lord?" she teased.

"A bit," he confessed, almost sheepishly. "It bemuses me that a scientist should have quoted such a religious poet as Alexander Pope."

Alexandra gaped at her husband. Not sheepish at all! Rather, a wolf in sheep's clothing. She should have known.

And now . . . she would answer for her hubris by allowing him unrestricted access to her body.

To do with as he wished.

CHAPTER SEVENTEEN

Piers tried, and failed, to remember when victory had ever been so delicious.

He'd many to choose from.

Even as he appreciated a bite of his sumptuous dinner, he savored the delectable tinge of peach and pink rising from beneath his wife's bodice to splash over the creamy skin of her chest.

When was the last time he'd enjoyed a conversation so much? When had he been so intellectually challenged, and at the same time, so at ease in someone's company?

Once again, he failed to call such an interaction to mind.

Never had he delighted in something so ubiquitous as a woman's blush. Never had he wanted to collect his prize so desperately as in this moment.

But despite the fact that the table hid his body's reaction to the wicked reward he'd been promised, he hadn't lost enough of his civility to drag his wife from a crowded room in order to ravish her.

Besides, he wasn't ready to be done teasing her. Playing with his prey.

There was, after all, one more question. But at least now, her body was his, if not for the taking, at least for the tasting. He kept a tight grip on his fork, forcing himself to appear unaffected. To maintain their conversation, and to keep up with her quick mind.

"Your selection of quotes makes me wonder about you," he drawled around another bite. "Are you a pious or God-fearing woman?"

For a woman with a tendency to let whatever thought skipped through her mind fall from her mouth, she gave this question a great deal of consideration. With her bow lips pursed in contemplation, she took the opportunity to study the view beyond him rather than his features.

"I do not live in fear of any particular God, and neither do I know which one to believe in," she finally answered gravely. "I've studied so many of them, enough to know that it is more reasonable to live in fear of man than God. Of what man makes of this world. For we are capable of enough evil without a god or a devil to influence us one way or the other."

Piers absorbed her words, studying a bleakness in the depths of her burnt-whisky eyes. What had she seen, he wondered, that put in her the fear of man? He'd picked up rather similar ideals in his lifetime and in his travels. He'd seen too much blood shed in the name of one God or another to ascribe his faith to any of them. Strange, that he would have found a spouse who felt the same. Who'd seen similar corners of the earth and lingered in the shadows of gods more ancient than their Anglican one.

"What about death?" he queried. "Do you fear existential judgment after this life?"

"I used to," she murmured. "I used to worry about it

obsessively. Perhaps it is why I study those who have already passed on. I learn what I can from them. I honor their journey through this world, and hope they have found peace in the next. That . . . I might also find peace." She studied the napkin in her lap. "Sometimes, though, I fear the weight of my sins will pull me into the abyss. I hope if God exists, if we are to stand judgment, that justice is more compassion than vengeance."

Piers studied her, noting the weight of which she spoke curling her shoulders forward in a self-protective posture most ladies wouldn't indulge in public. The sadness emanating from her permeated the fortifications he'd erected around his heart.

"What sins could you possibly have committed—?"

The unmistakable sound of silver tapping against crystal evoked a pall of silence among the attendees as Forsythe called them to attention.

Piers glared over Alexandra's bare, smooth shoulder at him, wishing fervently the crystal would break and slit the man's wrists.

No such miracle occurred.

Alexandra turned in her chair to heed the man, and Piers set his jaw against a maelstrom of churlish resentment.

"Mesdames et messieurs," Forsythe began, lifting his glass as he prepared a toast. "It is with humbled gratitude and fervent anticipation I accepted the commission to become the next foreman of this exciting archeological expedition. So often, as surveyors of the past, we archeologists are called to distant locales where the climates, both political and ecological, are so very inhospitable. It is in such places, one learns to appreciate, to admire and esteem, those closest to him."

Forsythe's gaze slid to Alexandra.

Piers's grip on his knife tightened as suspicion churned the meal he'd enjoyed to bricks of disgust.

"I am fortunate in this particular vocation, in this lovely country, that we can study the ancients of our own vast and violent English history, rather than those of another mystical society," the doctor continued, swinging back to the company at large. "Fortunate, indeed, that the descendant of our Viking specimen is not only among the living, but among us here, tonight." He turned to their table, directing all attention not to Alexandra, but to Piers, himself.

"To His Grace, Piers Gedrick Atherton, the Duke of Redmayne, and his new and incomparable duchess. May your marriage be long and fruitful."

"À votre santé!" the audience toasted, and Alexandra turned to Piers, her smile radiant as she urged him to stand, to accept the applause beginning to swell. When he didn't instantly comply, she stood, obliging him to do so, or to risk disrespecting her in public.

Piers didn't hear their applause as he stood.

He still contemplated the meaning of the word "sin." The sins his wife might have committed in her past. The ones she might commit against him in the future.

The sin he wanted to commit with her here. Now. Iniquities so fiendish, even the devil would blush.

"Would Their Graces indulge us in a waltz to begin the evening?" Forsythe stroked his mustache above a cheeky grin and the assemblage made affirmative noises as the chamber musicians thrummed the first notes of Strauss.

Piers advanced, thinking Forsythe would look a great deal better wearing the champagne rather than drinking it. Such seemingly innocuous words. Appreciate. Admire. Esteem.

But not when it came to his wife.

My wife. The beast within him snarled. *Mine.*

Was he too quick to believe her when she claimed there was not—nor had there been—a relationship between them? Forsythe's look had certainly conveyed more. And for a man who disliked Piers as heartily as he was certain Forsythe did . . . why would he take such pains to show him such public courtesy?

Curious, indeed.

What Piers wouldn't have given to have been able to catch the look Alexandra had given back to Forsythe.

Had it been one of similar meaning?

A small hand slipped into his, as Alexandra stepped out in front of him, a vision of mahogany hair, emerald silk, and metallic gems as she glided past a few tables, the topiary, and the grand fireplace.

She nodded to Forsythe and her vapid friend—Piers forgot her name, Jane?—but then she paid them no further heed as she led Redmayne to the middle of the grand room.

Piers pulled Alexandra close, closer still as he twirled his graceful wife across the marble in a seamless, flawless waltz.

He hoped the *intelligent* Dr. Forsythe made some keen fucking observations. Such as, the perfect fit of her body against his. How synchronous their rhythm was. How, even though Piers was arguably the unsightliest man in the room, he could still get the most beautiful woman in the world to smile up at him, just as she did now.

Light from the chandelier gilded flecks of gold into her eyes.

She smiled despite the dark subjects of their conversation. Even though they'd spoken of God and death, scars and sin, something about the atmosphere of the evening, the gather of the west wind beyond their enchanted golden celebration, and the feel of her glorious shape locked in the circle of his arms gave Piers the fanciful sensation of dancing on a cloud.

Because, yet again, she didn't look away from him. Even when she ought to.

She didn't look at Forsythe. She didn't arch her lovely neck away as propriety dictated. She kept her gaze firmly affixed to his and, for a moment, Piers thought she might possess the acumen to look past the scars on his face, through his eyes to the ones on his soul.

Those were uglier, he feared. Those would drive her away surely, even if his physical deformities did not.

For the first time, Piers's step almost faltered as Forsythe's form spun into view. He'd abandoned his untouched champagne and affably followed his intrepid partner—Judith?—as she dragged him to the floor.

A strange question haunted Piers, one he'd never thought to ask.

He'd been so focused on what this marriage might mean to him, his future, his legacy, his revenge, he'd never stopped to think about what it would mean for his bride.

In his mind, he'd saved her from financial ruin. Because she'd asked him to.

But what of *her* heart? He'd never thought to possess it before. He'd not expected to, as it wasn't something he could equally trade for.

Could it belong to another? Had he, by taking her hand in marriage, also taken any chance at future happiness, as well?

Perhaps that was why she'd been so aloof. So reluctant.

Suspicion surged through him, chasing away the clouds upon which he danced and weighing him deftly to the ground. He gazed into her eyes. Such beautiful eyes, a brown so amber that the shades in her hair set a certain fire to the color. Not red, but close.

If only he didn't read secrets in their depths. If only her thoughts weren't so infuriatingly opaque.

Perhaps she wasn't dishonest with *him* about feelings for Forsythe, but with herself. Sometimes Alexandra was the most logical woman he'd ever met. And other times, she spoke the most utter nonsense. She'd claimed to have no prior romantic entanglements, and no interest in such.

And yet, she'd taken a lover.

She claimed that lover hadn't been Forsythe.

In this moment, so much of him wanted to believe her, even though his shallow, black heart screamed that to do so would be folly.

What if he fell for her? What if he fucked her?

What if she then gave birth in nine months to a golden-haired genius with Forsythe's unctuous features? The very idea had him contemplating walling the bastard in with his ancestor and leaving him to rot.

Piers would hate himself for allowing it. For being as weak against her multitude of charms as his father had been.

He'd hate her for being so deceitful.

He'd hate the child for not being his.

After the life he'd led, a deception of this magnitude would be his undoing.

He couldn't allow this fate. No matter how much his body yearned for her. No matter what sort of spell she weaved with her wit and her wisdom.

He would wait to claim her. He would wait until the machinations of fate were more under his control.

He would not allow himself to fall. It was better that way, for them both.

If he never loved her, he could never hate her.

But that didn't mean he couldn't set about some machinations of his own.

No matter what happened in ten days—eight now—he could still lay siege to her body. He could—he would—pleasure her, and then he'd take what pleasure she could give. If two people such as they couldn't share trust or love, at least they could indulge in this. This connection threaded through the warp and weft of his very fabric, thrumming within him a constant erotic longing.

Oh, he'd have her.

He'd use his hands and mouth and skill to erase the memory of any other man, so that by the time he took her, she'd not only have forgotten the feel of her former lover inside of her.

She'd have forgotten his name.

"Where did you go?" she whispered gently. "You're miles away."

"I was visiting the future," he said casually.

"Oh?" Her brows rose. "And what did you see there, pray?"

"You," he murmured, inhaling her vaguely tropical scent. Sweet and citrus. Intoxicating.

"And what was I doing?" she inquired.

He leaned in as low as he could while maintaining their waltz. "You were screaming my name."

She blanched and would have stumbled had he not such a solid hold upon her. "W-what?"

"You were crying out blasphemies to every god you don't believe in while you came apart in my arms."

Her breath sped against him. Her limbs trembling a little.

Excellent.

"You mustn't say such things. Not here in public." She looked around at the couples who'd joined them in their waltz, offering many of them a shaky smile.

"No one heard me." He chuckled darkly.

"I heard you!" she huffed.

"Yes," he crooned. "And you owe me another quote."

"Now?"

"When else?"

"Um." She searched for words.

Piers sent a triumphant glance at Forsythe, who appeared to be very pointedly *not* watching them.

Her eyes followed his gaze and she frowned.

"I've one for you," she clipped. "'Those wars are unjust which are undertaken without provocation. For only a war waged for revenge or defense can be just.'"

Before he could summon a rejoinder, a dapper middle-aged gentleman tapped him on the shoulder. "*Pardon, monsieur,* but I have never had the opportunity to dance with a *duchesse.*"

"Of course." Piers bowed to the gentleman, and bent to his wife. "You'll meet me on the west veranda at half past the hour."

He placed her hand in the older man's as she sputtered. "But—outside?—you didn't guess—"

"Cicero," he said over his departing shoulder, searching for a dance partner among the local countrywomen.

The next time he touched his wife, it would be in places she wouldn't soon forget.

Chapter Eighteen

He couldn't really mean to share intimacies out of doors, could he?

Alexandra crept through a small entry from a back corridor out onto the west veranda.

She hadn't understood the size and scope of the structure until this vantage. Not only did it wrap around the edifice of the hotel, it boasted several dozen potted trees, ferns, flowers, intricate screens, and furniture from which to enjoy sumptuous sunsets over the ocean.

The sun had set hours ago, and a cold, silvery moon illuminated white waves across which England awaited.

The night breeze feathered over flesh unused to exposure to the elements. Her bare shoulders, the swells of her breasts pressed unnaturally high by the corset, indeed all her skin welcomed the cool kiss of the night.

For the past hour her husband's gaze, heavy with illicit promises, had turned her entire body into a furnace.

She'd barely been able to concentrate on her waltz with Jean-Yves, let alone a civilized, pleasant conversation. By now, half of France likely assumed her the most bumble-headed ninny alive.

But how was one supposed to think clearly with the weight of his gaze teasing little shivers from the fine hairs at the back of her neck?

How was it that a man, not just any man, *her husband,* could affect her in such a manner?

Her slippers barely made a sound as she navigated artful arrangements of furniture in search of him.

She found Redmayne leaning forward against the railing, his face lifted to the moon. Eyes closed and nose flaring as though he enjoyed the fragrance of wisteria, posies, and night-blooming jasmine shamelessly baring themselves beneath a tall wych elm.

He didn't seem to mark her approach, even as she joined him at the railing not more than an arm's length away. She could only make out the scarred side of his face. Even in the dim light, the silver moon drew such savage lines through his beard.

For a protracted moment, Alexandra could do nothing but stare.

Everything about him, from his scars to his soul, held her in an undeniable thrall.

Why hadn't she noted the sartorial elegance beneath his sardonic savagery before now? Certainly, he was a bestial creature, fierce and unruly as his barbaric ancestors. A hunter of beasts. An apex predator. But a nobility lurked in the long, sophisticated lines of his form, as well. Something handsome and almost . . . wholesome in a sort of robust way.

Almost civilized.

Almost.

Therein lay the draw, perhaps. Whatever lurked in his blood, whether the Viking warrior, the fabled were beast, or fearsome demon, it was undeniable that something sinister and sinful rippled beneath the ducal bearing. Something ferocious and ancient that might have earned him a pagan's grave upon a day.

He did not belong in this age of gentility.

Staring at him now made her think of reincarnation. Had his soul graced these shores before? A thousand years prior, such a man launched from these Norman beaches and invaded England, handing a crown of blood to the bastard who would become a conqueror. A king.

And here stood the Redmayne progeny. The product of an old and unbroken legacy chock-full of strong warrior sons.

As Alexandra pressed her hand to her belly, a breath of longing escaped her. His decedents would be hers, as well. In truth, as a scientist, she'd never much given credence to noble bloodlines, even her own. Titles could be granted and taken away. Dynasties rose and fell through the sands of time, some of the greatest families already long forgotten.

So why did it give her such a strange shiver of pleasure at the thought of bearing such a man's child?

That he should choose her to do so.

Not that he *chose* her, she reminded herself. Rather the opposite.

She'd selected him. Out of desperation, at first.

And now unexpectedly—astonishingly—she'd discovered within her a desire for him to choose her back. Or, perhaps . . . she merely wanted to be considered worthy.

Shame had been her companion for so long. So very long. She had to admit it was difficult to hear the whispers about her. To know the *ton* considered her undeserving to stand as consort to such a man. To such a duke. She was too bookish. Too educated. Too old and unsocial.

Everything she'd once made peace with, had been proud of, she now questioned.

She hated that her growing feelings caused her to question herself. Hated even more that he questioned her. Her loyalty. Her word.

That he had good reason to.

What a long road they had to travel, the two of them, toward any kind of marital contentment.

They each had so many scars.

As she stood shoulder to shoulder with her breathtaking husband, she realized what her vanity had been trying to tell her all evening.

She'd looked in the mirror in her bedroom this evening, and had seen a beauty. She'd acknowledged that beauty without once thinking of de Marchand. Without being ashamed of or repulsed by the idea that Redmayne might see her thus.

Because, if she were being honest, she'd found within herself the desire for Redmayne to look at her. To *see* her. She wanted him to find her beautiful. He'd declared so shockingly this morning that he'd a difficult time being in her proximity without wanting her . . .

And, despite everything that had happened between them, and before him, she found within her a longing to encourage his desire. Because beneath the fear his lust evoked, an answering flame had undoubtedly ignited within her. Warming that very part that made her essentially female and tuning it only to him. So much so, that one appreciative gaze from him, one brush of his gloved hand against hers, sent curious little electric thrills through her.

Because she now knew the magic of which those hands were capable. And the gentleness. And restraint.

Because that magic preceded the act that would give her his children.

How very cruel it was to fear and crave something—someone—in equal measure.

Redmayne growled low words into the night, breaking her reverie. The wind carried them in the other direction, but he finally turned and speared her with those hot, damaged eyes.

Blue fire.

Blue flames always burned the hottest, didn't they?

"P-pardon?" she stammered around a constricting throat.

"I said you've ruined me."

Her brow crimped into a frown. "How is that possible? I've done nothing."

He stepped closer, staring down at her as though she were an aberration of the moon, one strong hand clinging to the railing as though it, alone, tethered him to the earth. "You vanquish my will, Alexandra," he accused. "You make me want to forget that it is safer to be cold, and alone."

She drew abreast of him, looking up into his features as they failed to conceal some sort of bitter struggle. "You tempt me to trust you, as well," she admitted. "To make me forget that we are neither of us safe."

"*You* are safe." His steely expression melted into something tender as he reached for her hand, pinching at the fingertips of her glove one by one until he'd loosened it enough to draw it off. That done, he discarded it to the railing and brought her palm to his mouth.

The soft brush of his beard gave way to the hot press of his lips. The sensation was so exquisite, she almost lost his reply. "I married you, and no matter what happens at the end of what remains of the ten days, our marriage will not be undone. It only took seeing you in the arms of other men, even for a dance, for me to realize that no matter what, despite myself, I've claimed you as my own."

"There *is* no child, Piers," she said fervently.

"I wish I could believe you." His fingers tightened around hers, holding them to his face. "*If* there is one, and it's a girl, I'll claim her as my own. If it's a boy, I'll do what I can to give him a life, if not a name. My brother has done remarkably well in a similar situation and—"

"But I'm telling you, there won't be—"

"I'm telling *you* it doesn't matter." He drew her other glove off, before running his rough hands up her chilly arms. "It won't change the fact that I desire you above all others. My vows are ironclad. What happened before we met will not be held against you. I am your faithful husband from now until the end of my days. My fealty and my body, such as it is, belongs to you. You can rely upon that, Alexandra. You are always safe in that."

Her breath fluttered in and out of her as she was overcome by a tide of keen and confounding emotion.

He'd said nothing of love. It wasn't likely they ever would. But such words could threaten even the stoutest of cynics.

He still didn't understand her fear. He could only see it through the lens of his own.

"'Safe' is one of those peculiar words, isn't it?" She shaped her fingers to his jaw, sliding her hand past his ear and threading through the sleek sable locks at his nape. "It often means something different to those who speak it than those who hear it."

"What do you mean?" he asked in a voice that belonged to the night.

"Only that I've never been afraid that you'd dishonor me. I never doubted you'd keep your word." Her fear was a physical one. A female one. One he'd nothing and everything to do with. "I meant it when I said no man but you has ever made me feel . . . made me want . . ." She couldn't finish her sentence as his hand skipped over her shoulders, inching toward her clavicles. His touch was like a balm, smoothing away the scars she'd worn like armor for so many exhausting years. "All I can do is allow for time to prove to you that I can keep my word as well," she finished.

"God help me if you don't," he groaned. "God help us both."

He drew her to him, wrapped himself around her as though to protect her from the night wind and the sea and the moon, and anything that might tear her from his arms. When he took her lips with his it wasn't just a kiss.

But a claiming.

Piers would never tire of her taste. Each time he kissed her had been a revelation of sensation and flavor. Tonight she was wine and honey tinged with brine by the scent of the sea.

His tongue dipped past the seam of her lips and she broke the seal with a gasp, covering her mouth with her fingers.

"I know many couples do not kiss thusly." He grappled his lust down, pulling on a reserve of patience. "But we are husband and wife. There is no desire too scandalous that we are not allowed to indulge. Besides . . . we are in France, after all." He pulled her closer. "When in Rome and all that."

"I . . . just . . ."

Piers smiled into the darkness. "Need I remind you of our game? I won, my lady, the night is mine. I intend to enjoy my good fortune."

Her expression wrinkled with both awareness and alarm. "Should we retire to your bedroom? Or mine?"

He bent back over her, hungry. Famished. Eternally yearning for more of her. "Here will do just fine."

"What if someone sees us?"

"Come into the shadows with me." He drew her toward an alcove, resting his thighs against a waist-high ledge protruding from the brick wall. "No one could possibly see us unless they searched to the very edge of the veranda and we'd hear them coming."

He covered her next words with another searing kiss.

This time when he nudged at her mouth with his tongue, her lips parted after only the briefest hesitation.

Instead of delving into her soft heat as his inflamed body screamed at him to do, he played and coaxed. Darting soft licks against her bottom lip. Tracing her teeth. Sucking her lower lip into his mouth, exerting only the slightest of pressure until the tension leaked out of her in excruciatingly slow increments. Until he sensed his tongue was no longer an intrusion, but an enticement.

Victoriously, he drank in her sigh of surrender. Devoured her little moan of pleasure, supping on her lips with the eternal delight of a starving man at a feast.

Where she'd been passive beneath his ministrations before, she now pulled him closer. Deeper.

Her response devastated him as she allowed her weight to become his, melting against him with boneless pliancy.

Lust drenched him as her body pressed against his turgid cock, shocking him with the sensation. Her thighs molded between his, her breasts contained within the stays of her corset bunched against his chest. The little beads and gems on her bodice pricked his clothing, becoming welcome abrasions. Every tiny sensation of her against him imbued him with primitive arousal.

His heartbeat synchronized with the insistent pulse of his sex, pumping against the layers of their clothes, aching to be free. Or, rather, to be contained.

Inside her.

It took every bit of his strength *not* to crush her to him. To lift her against the wall, wrap her legs around his waist, and sink into her welcoming body.

No. *No.* There was time for that. A *life*time for that. Tonight was for discovery.

His.

Hers.

He'd offered to show her what pleasures could be had beyond fucking, and he meant to do that very thing.

Cupping her face, he dragged his mouth across hers in drugging sweeps. Her little coo of appreciation stirred a primitive grunt in reply. Gods, but everything she did brought him to the edge of wanting. The edge of his control.

She trembled against him, a lithe shiver he echoed in his very bones.

Aware that the night air might chill her, he reversed their position, allowing her to rest on the ledge without breaking the seal of their kiss. He wanted her bared to him. Naked and writhing.

Which was why he'd chosen the veranda.

It was imperative that he go nowhere near a bed with her, or he'd damn the consequences, and damn himself, by making love to his wife.

Here, in the out of doors her breasts and curves, and soft, svelte body, had to remain covered, her coiffure undisturbed.

But that didn't mean they couldn't misbehave.

After discarding his own gloves, he molded his hands to her hips and lifted her the scant inches onto the ledge.

She gasped and tensed, but relaxed deeper into the darkness. She liked it here, he remembered, in the dark.

He tried not to ponder what that meant as his hand bunched at the fabric of her skirts, lifting them until his fingers slid along the silk stockings clinging to her shapely legs.

The fine muscles tensed and quivered as he stroked behind her knee and charted up her thigh, stopping to trace the silk ribbon at the seam.

The image of her on her back, legs in the air, with nothing but these stockings on nearly proved his undoing.

Piers devoured her, heating the kiss in the forge of her mouth until it became liquid and molten. His hand found her drawers and drew up to the apex of her thighs, nudging them apart.

Her heat beckoned from the other side of the thin cotton, and he searched for the long slit in her undergarment that would grant him access to the slick flesh beneath.

In his eagerness to get to it, the search proved fruitless and frustrating. He could find no such opening, and in his building frenzy he slid one arm beneath her pelvis, lifted her, and pulled the garment over her hips and down to her knees.

"Piers!" she gasped against his mouth.

"I like it when you say my name," he growled. "I'll like it even better when you moan it."

"What—what are you doing?"

"I'm going to make you come."

"Come." She whispered the word as though testing it, and the husky, illicit sound of it almost broke his last vestige of restraint. "Like—like you did last night? With your fingers?"

Christ, was she trying to kill him? "Is that what you want?"

She paused, her short, hard breaths breaking against his. In that moment, he would have given his left eye to see her expression. "I would," she said breathlessly. "I want . . ."

Piers swept her drawers from her ankles. He nudged her knees wider, thrusting his hips between them as she buried her face against his throat. Her arms slid around his neck clinging to his back, her fingers clutching at his jacket as though he could save her from falling.

Piers found her artless trust in the gesture rather touching. He nudged her nose with his before pressing an almost chaste kiss to her lips. "I have you," he murmured.

She drove her lips against his mouth, clinging to him with a desperation that seemed to mirror his own. Her hips nudged his hand, the silken hair between her thighs painting a brush of her desire against his palm.

Dear God, she was already wet.

To be cruel, he feathered a few light strokes over the plump lips, tracing the seam of her sex, massaging the mons above.

She squeezed her knees around his hips, her breaths hitching over a closed throat.

To be kind, he furrowed a questing finger into the tender cove until he found the source of her desire. He slid through the elixir with delighted strokes, aching for the moment it would ease the way for his sex.

She whimpered. Trembled. Her clawed fingers clenching and releasing like a kitten in the throes of a good petting.

He stroked the tight entrance to her body, letting the tiny muscles pull at him.

Gods, this was torture. Pure and exquisite.

And if he had to endure it. So would she.

He thrummed his thumb across the throbbing hood of her clitoris, only the once.

Her breathy moan of encouragement nearly took the starch from his knees.

Piers reveled in the muffled sounds of her pleasure as he allowed his fingers to play and discover. They traced the pulsing folds of her swollen sex, returning to leave a glossy trail against her delicate bud. He was deliberate. Relentless. Waiting for her pleasure to climb in torturous increments instead of allowing it to take her.

She would learn tonight, to whom she was mated. The Terror of Torcliff would leave her a puddle of bliss. Ruined. Drenched. Exhausted by pleasure.

Small sounds climbed her throat and he drew back, nudging her face away from its hiding place within his neck to swallow her little mewls. He licked her lips open, tasted her moans, reveled in the dance of her hips against his hand as she began to writhe for him.

Their patience ran out simultaneously. With one soft, continuous circle with his thumb he brought her to the brink. She locked her legs around his with a sound of incredible relief as she came undone. Her thighs clenched in rhythm to the pulses of her pleasure and he had to smother her delectable, inarticulate cries with his lips.

God, her pleasure aroused him. He was hard as a diamond. If she touched him now, he'd be unmanned.

He couldn't have that. He wasn't ready to be finished with his discovery of the delights of her body.

Giving one last shudder against him, she dropped her forehead to his shoulder, letting his straining muscles support her languorous weight.

"You are . . . so incredible . . ." she panted.

A chuckle danced in his throat. "Thank you."

"I was trying . . . to say . . . incredibly wicked."

"You don't know the half of it." He slid from her grasp. "Lean back, darling," he prompted.

"Why?"

She'd been threatening to drive him to his knees all evening, and now, that's exactly where he decided he should be.

"Because." He lifted her hem and slid it over his hair and down his back, creating a tent of her skirts. "I'm not through with you yet."

CHAPTER NINETEEN

His tongue.

Alexandra sagged against the wall, crumpled into her gown like a collapsed soufflé.

Later, she would try to pinpoint the exact moment his tongue no longer offended her. Had it happened incrementally? Or suddenly? She couldn't be sure.

She was certain of his intent. His directive. She understood what he meant to use his tongue for next.

She'd done her utmost not to think of her rapist as her husband had licked into her mouth.

But the comparison had been there.

And the contrast had been in the intention.

De Marchand's purpose was to humiliate. To dominate. To take her innocence and worth and courage until she'd become a supplicant to his cruelty. He'd licked her face, wanting to taste her fear and sample her pain, savoring it like a rare and exotic elixir.

She'd known that, instinctively.

Her husband was dominant, too. Of course he was. How could a man such as him be anything but?

He didn't take from her, though. Not once.

He gave, and gave, and gave until she felt as though she might overflow with the absolute carnality of it.

He did not wield his tongue as a weapon against her. He'd probed at her gently, seeking entrance to her mouth rather than demanding it. He'd made promises with his body, whether intentional or not, that soothed the spasms of fear threatening, always threatening.

He'd turned them into very different spasms altogether.

She'd sensed the building ferocity of his lust until his entire form was sculpted of need and strength and feral sexuality.

And yet, he'd sampled her as though *her* pleasure was his delicacy.

His tongue, strong and sure and slick, hadn't disgusted her in the least.

His tongue had tasted of desire. Had gifted it to her. Had quelled her moans and sparred with her own. It was as though he would not endure the idea that his pleasure, his desire, could be greater than her own.

His tongue . . .

Was inching above the seam of her stocking, and the playfully torturous journey stole away the intellectual capacity for further analysis.

His lips nibbled at the thin, sensitive skin on the inside of her thigh. His beard tickled along the surface, causing her intimate muscles to twitch and compress.

"I'm about to make you rue the moment you suggested I never do this," he rumbled, settling his shoulders between her thighs, nudging them wider.

"You . . . don't have to," she whispered huskily, groping through the miasma of complex emotion and sensation for a semblance of herself. She couldn't think. He did steal that from her. Her ability to form coherent thoughts. It was the only thing he took without asking. "From what I read, it sounded . . . unpleasant . . . for the man . . . for you. And I've never had any great desire for—"

"Put your hand over your mouth, wife." His hot breath stole her words, as well, as it teased at the fine fibers of hair at the apex of her thighs, evoking a whisper of sensation, an echo of arousal beneath the languor of her postpleasure state. "I don't want your cries to draw a crowd."

His powerful shoulders sank forward, spreading her legs further as his mouth gently parted her, his tongue drawing through the pleats of slick flesh until he drank of the abundant moisture he found there.

He swallowed it.

She clamped her hand over her mouth and bit down on the flesh of her finger.

Hard.

He feasted upon her with a tender yet relentless exactitude. He knew her sex better than she did. He understood just when to coax and when to torment. His lips would nibble delicately one moment, then his tongue would swirl and slide the next.

It was as though he'd discovered the secrets to an intricate mechanism engineered only for his mouth. For his personal use.

Multiple times Alexandra was certain she'd lose control of reality. She wanted to grasp at him. To push him away. To pull him closer and tug at his hair. She couldn't process the wickedness of this act. The wet, silken depravity they conducted here in the open night air.

A need welled within her so deeply, she couldn't identify it.

Please. She wanted to beg him. To stop? To never stop?

Please, she silently prayed. Not to a god. Not exactly.

But to a man who might as well be one.

Only a whimper escaped as her hand clamped harder over her lips, the sounds gathering in her throat and screaming to be let free.

Her legs trembled. Quivered. Her buttocks clenched and unclenched as he laid a slick and silent siege to her sex.

Because he took nothing, her body seemed intent upon relinquishing her dignity. Her humanity. Becoming a feral, physical creature. Writhing and mindlessly forcing breaths and gasps and groans through her nose as she valiantly fought the cries and pleas flooding her throat.

He gripped her hips. Ruthlessly pinning her still as he focused wet, rhythmic darts of his tongue across the trembling peak of her clitoris. The sensation of it seized every one of her muscles with such arching force, she'd not realized what his other hand was about to do.

Until his finger sank inside her.

She clamped her other hand over the first, unable to contain her scream. The pleasure locked her muscles. Held her captive in a dizzying, almost terrifying summit.

She ceased to breathe. She may have ceased to *be* as his agile tongue held her a captive of unfathomable sensation.

A part of him was inside of her.

And it was . . . incredible.

It was as though the sea-swept wind carried her away from herself, catapulted her across the cosmos where she could meld with grand, ancient secrets incomprehensible to mortal senses. Perhaps in this pulsating place she could understand the concepts language tried and failed to convey.

Concepts like God and time and love.

When she thought it would break her, the peak crested like the white-tipped waves a scarce league away. It broke upon her again, and again, and once more until the tide passed and retreated, leaving her a dark, smooth surface. Pliant and undone.

He withdrew and kissed her thigh, leaving a slick of moisture behind.

With a naughty gesture, he brushed her petticoats over his beard, wiping away the wet aftermath of her bliss before his dark head appeared in her line of sight. Her vision dimmed by the immensity of what she'd just experienced more than the darkness of the night.

He prowled up her body, which was as limp and boneless as a jellyfish in contrast to the mass of coiled muscle that was his tremendous frame.

Alexandra peeled her hands away from her mouth, setting them on biceps strung so tightly, her grip didn't even compress the iron flesh.

"If every woman tasted like you, a man would hunger for nothing else." His voice held a tightness, a husky, cavernous ferocity it hadn't before. "God, what you do to me. I've never been so—"

A veranda door opened on the far side of the hotel. The light had become faint by the time it reached the corner around which their alcove had been tucked. Anyone would have to walk several paces to discover them, but footsteps creaked on the planks. And the low hum of voices reached them.

A string of low, hard, foul words from Redmayne's mouth blistered Alexandra's ears as he set her to rights.

"Go," he bit out.

She blinked incoherently up at him for a moment. "Aren't you coming with me?"

"No," he growled. "I'm not going anywhere for several *long* minutes."

"Oh." She swallowed, unsure of what to do. Or if her legs would carry her anywhere.

"Go. Inside," he ordered.

"Will you . . . come and find me later?"

He bodily turned her and all but shoved her toward the hotel entrance, and in her stumbling astonishment she missed his reply.

Alexandra smoothed her hair as she dreamily drifted through the shadows back toward the nearest door, not looking in the direction of the conclave of revelers on the far end of the deck.

All she could feel was the slickness between her legs as she walked.

All she could think of was what would happen next once her husband came to find her.

Because he still had a prize yet to claim.

And his desire hadn't been satisfied.

Sweet merciful Christ, was it possible to expire from wanting a woman? Could a man completely go mad with desire? Lose his humanity altogether?

Because Piers was perilously close to just that. Giving in to the beast.

By the time he had nigh limped across his room to his wife's adjoining door, he'd thrown his cuffs, ripped open his jacket, untied his cravat, and shucked his shoes.

He made a pathway of distinct intention before pausing with his hand gripping the door separating them.

Never in his life had he been in such a state. His cock hard and heavy as wrought iron, an insistent, pendulous weight aching for one touch from her. His bollocks drawn unbearably close with a need so pervasive, he could feel the clench of a building release even now.

Every muscle stretched taut over his bones, screaming to surge and grip and thrust and fuck.

Thus, his hesitation.

He'd fuck her tonight. The minute the door was open. The very second her scent reached him. The moment her sweet form came into view.

He'd seize her and bend her over the first smooth surface he could find. He'd toss her skirts over her head and part the globes of her soft ass so he could watch himself spear into the sex he'd made slick and swollen and ready.

Oh, he'd fuck her. He'd fuck her well and plenty.

And when his senses returned to him, he'd berate himself for a fool for the rest of his bloody life.

He didn't want her to be another regret.

He couldn't go in her room, he realized on a tortured groan. In this state, he was more animal than man, and the moment he sensed sexual submission, he'd mount her, he'd rut upon her like a stallion in the frenzy of an all-consuming primal drive to mate.

And she'd offered her body already for the taking.

She wanted him to plant a baby inside of her.

His cock surged at the thought, eliciting a vague nausea deep in his gut.

With a tortured grunt, he palmed himself over his trousers, expelling a strangled noise as textile abraded turgid flesh.

He could do it.

She was his *wife*.

And yet . . . there could already be a child. No matter how prettily she denied it. How ardently he wanted to believe her. He must be certain.

He must.

And so he could not have her. For the sake of his future sanity. For his legacy. For all that was holy. He. Could. Not—

Someone knocked on his wife's door to the hall.

Forsythe?

Unable to stop himself, he tilted his ear to the door.

"I'm told you've retired for the night, Your Grace," Constance, her lady's maid, called into the room. "Would you like me to dress you for bed?"

"No, thank you. I've done it myself and am brushing out my hair. I'll bid you good night now."

"Pleasant dreams, Your Grace."

"You too, Constance."

A soft humming reached him through the door, lilting, preoccupied, and a bit melancholy.

God's blood, what her voice did to him.

Were he not in such a state, he would have entered her rooms and teased her for spoiling the servants. He'd watch her brush her hair, perhaps relieving her of the implement and doing it himself. How intimate it would be, to run his hands over the crackling strands until they gleamed the color of dark, ripe cherries. He'd sweep the hair over one shoulder and kiss her neck, the downy hollow behind her ear, the places he knew flared chill bumps over her entire body. The collar of her prim nightgown would give as he patiently unbuttoned it, sliding down the creamy silk of her shoulder until he could reach inside to palm her heavy breast.

Her red hair would tangle with his fingers as he toyed with her nipple, simultaneously nibbling at her ear.

Falt Ruadh. Someday that hair would curtain his hips.

He bit his lip hard enough to bleed.

Not tonight.

Eight days. Seven tomorrow. Devil take him, he might die before then. Die of blood loss to his head.

He drew his hand down his ruined face, pausing when a distinctive scent roused his senses and infused his veins with raw fire.

There. On his fingers, the faint essence of her sex still lingered. The proof of her pleasure. Her desire. Her capitulation to his need.

Tonight in the dark, a part of him *had* entered her, if only for the briefest of blissful moments . . . and she'd drenched him with her sweetest release.

At once, his cock was no longer in his trousers. He dipped the finger into his mouth, then another, searching for the trace of her flavor. Leaving moisture on his fingers, he brought them down to his pulsing sex, spreading what he could over the steely length of him.

He wanted this to be her hand. Soft and small where his was large and rough.

Or her mouth. Hot and wet and welcoming.

Oh, the things he could do to that mouth.

Safe on the other side of the door, his wife began to hum a different tune. Something husky and foreign. Persian maybe. The vibrations of her voice traveled through his blood until he could feel his body tremble with an answering rhythm.

Unbidden, his hips curled forward, his hand drew over the blunt crown and down the length of his shaft.

He'd wanted to do this while his head was buried between her trembling thighs. To take himself in hand while he reveled in the scent and taste and heat of her.

Remembering what he'd saved from the veranda, he reached into the crease of his jacket beneath his arm and pulled out her undergarment. White linen bedecked in tiny pink and green bows.

He brought it to his nose, drew in a breath, and found the palest hint of her distinct female musk.

God. His mouth flooded at the memory of the taste of her. Had there ever been a woman so sweet? Had there ever been a sex so perfectly formed?

He ached to strip her bare in the afternoon. To throw open the draperies and spread her wide, letting the sun glisten between her parted thighs, illuminating each and every soft, secret, hidden part of her.

Someday, he would.

His cock was as hot as a branding iron in his hand as he pumped his fist down the length once more, and again.

How perfect she would look sinking down upon the full, pulsing veins of his shaft. Those tight, female muscles would resist him at first, but he'd ease his way inside until she held him to the hilt.

His hips thrust into his hand in a disappointing parody of what he truly craved.

He savored the intimate scent of her as he moved his fist harder. Faster. Working the velvet skin of his shaft around the unyielding rod beneath.

As long as he lived he'd crave this succulent female flavor. Hers alone. She was his to dine on as he pleased.

One man didn't deserve such fortunes.

Eight . . . More . . . Days . . .

The climax began as a burn in his spine, spilling down his entire frame like an avalanche. Inevitable. Unstoppable. Overpowering.

As the shocks of release became surges, he made a sound only an animal could have. Bringing her drawers down to his hips, he spilled liquid heat on the snowy-white linen. The sight of it inflamed him further as pulse after pulse was pulled from his very core for such a length of time, he wondered if it would ever cease.

Finally, the grip of his bliss abated, and he folded forward in blind relief, resting his forehead against the door with a thump.

Alexandra's humming died away at the sound, and soft footfalls padded toward the door. "Piers?" A tentative invitation painted his name, and his still-pounding heart accelerated. "Have you returned to . . . would you like to come in?"

Trying to regain a semblance of wit, he reached for the door.

And threw the lock.

"Not tonight, pet," he managed.

She hesitated. "But aren't you . . . you're in need of . . . you still have your third prize to claim, if you are so inclined."

Despite what he'd just done, his cock twitched at the offer.

Piers placed a hand against the cool wood of the door, picturing her doing the same.

Oh, he'd claim his prize. Of course, he would. But not until he could regain some of his lost self-control. Not until the scent and sight of her didn't whip him into an unprecedented, animalistic monster. Until he could be other than this rutting beast he'd only just become, aching to mount her like a prized mare.

Wondering who'd mounted her first.

That thought was enough to push him away from the door. There would always be a barrier between them, wouldn't there? A secret. A past.

Hers. His. Someone else's. It didn't matter.

"Get some rest," he rumbled, battling a hollow ache in his chest.

"If . . . if you're certain." Was it disappointment or relief in her careful voice?

He couldn't tell through the door.

Berating himself, he promised that he could no longer toy with desire without giving in to it completely. He had to wait. Had to keep his hands, his mouth, all the parts of him that hungered for her to himself.

"Good night, Doctor." He injected as much kindness as he could into his voice before he went to the basin to wash, assuming she'd shuffled off to bed.

"Good night, husband," she called softly, pausing once more. "And . . . thank you."

What exactly had she thanked him for? he pondered as he undressed, washed, and settled into his cavernous, lonely bed.

Her pleasure? His company?

Or for leaving her alone?

CHAPTER TWENTY

For four days, Alexandra *almost* forgot she had killed a man.

That she'd been raped by one.

That someone perhaps wished her ill, or worse.

For four *blessed,* busy days, she'd buried her troubled memories in the familiarity of a crypt. She'd toiled alongside her husband to unearth the bones of his celebrated ancestor.

Instead of focusing on her own grave concerns, she spent a great deal of time enjoying her husband's company.

And lamenting the fact that he didn't attempt to drag her into any more dark alcoves. That he hadn't so much as kissed her since that night on the veranda.

Why that bothered her, she couldn't tell, but it did.

It bothered her with increasing frequency and intensity.

He'd teased her, flirted with her. Tormented her, even, with scalding looks and brief, if titillating physical contact. A brush of his hand. A stroke of her hair. A memory of what they'd already shared. A promise of what was to come.

But nothing more.

They dined together. Drank together. Laughed and chatted and socialized. Every moment in his company had been naught but a delight. And, from what she could tell, he enjoyed her company also. Despite his brutal features and intimidating moniker, he'd won over students and servants alike with his unabashed wit and unpretentious nobility. It wasn't just his title that she could take pride in, but the man, as well.

Alexandra woke every morning less and less astonished to find that she felt enthusiastic, impatient even, to dress and hurry downstairs. Not only to begin her work at the catacombs, but to find her husband awaiting her at the bottom of the stairs, offering his elbow to escort her to the site.

She went to bed every night alone with nothing but a kiss on her knuckles as a token of his esteem.

It kept her up at night, the why of it.

She'd asked him about it the night before last. Invited him into her bedroom.

His hand had tightened on hers, but his mouth was no less gentle as he pressed it to her knuckles.

Blue flames had threatened to singe her as he'd replied. "Five days."

This morning, after awakening no less than a hundred times in the night plagued by a restless and terrible feeling, Alexandra capitulated to the idea that she'd get no more sleep and had dressed uncharacteristically early.

Three days now, she'd realized as she all but skipped down the stairs awash with a new, optimistic fervor and a smile in her heart. Three days and the state of her empty womb would be confirmed.

Three days and he'd be one step closer to trusting her. In this respect, at least.

She'd reached the lobby before her husband did, and was called over by the desk clerk.

"A note for you, Your Grace." He extended a small ivory envelope with a solicitous smile.

An envelope identical to the one she'd dreaded nearly every month for the last decade.

It might have been another lovely day, Alexandra mourned as a flush of hot panic ignited little pinprick fires over her skin.

If she'd never killed a man.

She knew the author of the letter before her unsteady fingers grappled it open.

Her sin had followed her to Normandy.

It followed her everywhere, didn't it? Wherever she'd escaped to on the globe, her blackmailer had known. Had found her. And a letter had arrived like a clockwork nightmare.

You'll bring the money to the Redmayne tomb tomorrow night.

Stomach churning, she read the note again and again, scanning it as she always did for something. *Some* clue as to who had written it.

It was never any use. The writing was always different. Very brief. No signature.

Tears blurred the letters and Alexandra squeezed her eyes shut, despair threatening to pull her under.

She might have known. Because she'd let herself relax if only for a moment. She'd taken shelter in the shadow of her oak-sized husband, allowed him to shade her from the oppressive glare of the truth beneath which she'd perspired for so many anxious years.

She'd known that her moments of peace would be

tainted, eventually, but she thought she'd have another month. At least a chance to return to Castle Redmayne and receive her duchess stipend before she had to worry about where to send the money.

Alexandra barely kept herself from crumpling the paper in her fist as her dread heated to a helpless fury. Why must she be the one to suffer, to pay for the loss of her innocence? To be condemned for a torment thrust upon her?

Why did her frantic decision, made in the mind of a traumatized girl, have to follow her throughout her entire life? Would her children be made to pay for de Marchand's death? Her grandchildren?

When would it end?

She turned the envelope over, wondering how many postmarks it would carry this time. Usually the demands would originate from a telegraph office somewhere rather exotic. Morocco, perhaps. Or Berlin. Then it would make its way through a few countries to wherever she was.

She'd followed the trail before, even finding the originating telegraph office, but no one had been able to divulge who'd commissioned the message.

Forever untraceable.

This envelope, however, was completely blank but for her name written in block capitals. The script neither masculine nor feminine.

You'll bring the money to the Redmayne tomb tomorrow night.

Bring. Not post.

Which meant . . .

"I'm sorry," she asked the desk clerk in a voice more unsteady than she would have liked. "May I inquire from where this letter arrived?"

"From here, Your Grace," the clerk answered. "No postmark. It was delivered in person and left in your box last night."

The hand she'd laid flat on the table curled into a fist as she tried to rein in her galloping heart. "By whom?"

"No one can say, unfortunately." His mild expression dimmed to one of sheepish regret. "The night concierge was called away from the desk a few times by a rather demanding guest."

Her hopes began to plummet. "Would it have been left by a night courier maybe?"

He shook his head. "Any courier would have known to wait for a desk clerk, Your Grace, as they wouldn't have known which mail slot belonged to you. We're not in the habit of releasing room numbers of our guests, I can assure you." He hesitated. "Though, I suppose it isn't much of a surprise that you and the duke are staying in our most luxurious suites."

After a sharp intake of breath, she felt a pinprick of light pierce her encroaching despair. She thanked the clerk and wandered toward the fireplace, staring at the note as though she could see through it to the answer on the other side.

Few people knew of her whereabouts in Normandy, and even fewer could confirm that de Marchand was dead.

Two very *specific* souls, staying here in this very hotel, had been at de Chardonne when the incident had occurred. Lady Julia Throckmorton and Jean-Yves. Could Rose be nearby?

Julia had decided to stay in Seasons-sur-Mer for a few days to further her pursuit of Dr. Forsythe. Or was that merely what she claimed? Had she been an enemy this entire time?

Alexandra shook her head, doing her best to reject the notion. It made no sense. She and Julia had always got on famously, and it was well-known the woman had obscene amounts of money. Alexandra's monthly payments would have been a pittance compared to Julia's holdings.

They'd fallen out of touch since de Chardonne, but had never fallen out with each other.

According to her unfailing memory, Julia's bedroom had been on the east side of de Chardonne, which meant the chances of her witnessing them bury de Marchand would be minuscule as the gardens faced the west.

Besides, the idea that Julia was clever enough to have so ingeniously tormented her this entire time was absurd.

Wasn't it?

Still . . . could her motive be cruelty? Could she be hiding her wit beneath blond curls and an artless veneer of vapid triviality?

And what about Jean-Yves? Cecelia's dearest, fatherly companion sent to keep her safe.

He'd buried the man she'd murdered.

He could have taken the razor blade from his pocket when they'd gone. Along with any other bit of evidence he needed.

Was it possible his concern for Alexandra was feigned? That his absolute loyalty to Cecelia was a lie?

Alexandra's chin quivered at the thought. They'd been so certain all this time that he was the last pure and decent man left in their sphere.

To find that the older man's kindness had been contrived would break Alexandra's heart.

But it would kill Cecelia.

Dear, trusting Cecelia who, despite being abandoned, bullied, and blamed for her mother's sins, still managed to find the goodness in everyone. She loved the old man to distraction, doting upon him like a surrogate elderly father.

Even though she "employed" Jean-Yves, the Red Rogues

had visited enough to have seen that, other than the occasional errand, Jean-Yves was more of a companion than a servant. He spent most of his time with his feet up by the fire in his own sitting room while Cecelia read to him. Or gloating as Cecelia let him win at chess. His title as employee was more for his pride than for his keeping, and Cecelia had even shared the amount she'd settled upon him as a salary, which was more than generous.

So, was Cecelia's generosity not enough for him? Were the fine wines and expensive, comfortable shoes he favored purchased with Alexandra's blood money?

A calculating thought helped to smother the flames of her fear. If Alexandra were anything like Francesca, she'd see this as an opportunity.

She was to bring the money to the dig site. Not mail it. Nor wire it.

Bring it. Which meant tomorrow night, she might finally face her tormentor. Perhaps glean some answers. And if a surrogate was sent for her blackmailer, there was still a chance she could use her newfound title, wealth, or influence to sway some information from a hired brigand.

A heavy and terrifying thought snaked through her.

What if this was her final payment? What if she met her doom in Redmayne's crypt?

She swatted at the idea. It made no sense that her blackmailer would wish her harm. If she were dead, the source of the funds dried up, as well.

It made more sense, now that she was a duchess, her tormentor wanted to discuss new terms.

How utterly lamentable, that such a thing would be the lesser of two evils.

Heavy boots approached across the marble floors and Alexandra blinked like a madwoman, hoping to erase all traces of emotion. She'd recognize the sound of that confident stride anywhere.

She summoned a smile from deep in her wounded soul, but it faltered when she met the concern in his gaze.

"Did you receive bad news?" he queried, a note of concern lacing through his comforting baritone. "You've gone a bit green about the gills."

She stared at the paper, moving her eyes as though it contained more lines than only the one. "It's my, um. My parents."

"They're upset about the wedding," he said wryly.

She looked up, blinded for a moment by how the morning light painted a cobalt sheen into the ebony of his hair. Next to his tawny glory, her pallor must appear positively anemic.

"On the contrary," she rushed to appease him. "They're sending along their felicitations."

"You appear to me anything but felicitous."

She let out a nervous laugh that escaped at a higher pitch than she'd thought possible. "I'll grant you they're . . . a bit piqued that they weren't at the wedding, but Father might not have been able to make it anyway, and Andrew is abroad and couldn't have taken the journey on such short notice."

She hated how easily the lies tripped from her tongue.

One dark, scarred brow lowered. "Then . . . why do you look as though someone walked over your grave?"

Because there was a small chance someone wanted to make his ancestor's grave her own.

Tomorrow night.

She lowered her voice to a whisper, painfully aware of their public venue. "I am tremendously abashed to be so indelicate as to inquire about my um . . . my stipend. I would send it to them, if I may, to ease their financial distress."

And she would. Whatever was left of it would go to her parents and her brother. She'd make certain they were taken care of should anything happen to her.

His tense expression relaxed a bit, as though relieved the source of her distress was something as paltry as money. "I'll have my solicitor contact theirs upon our return to Castle Redmayne to set up an allowance for your family."

His flippant benevolence pricked her conscience with a thousand poisoned needles, and the toxins coiled in her gut as she choked on her reply.

"Their need is a little more dire than that, I'm afraid. Might I send it in a post or with a courier? It would save you and your solicitor the trouble," she rushed to offer.

"A courier from France? Are they so in need they cannot wait out the week for us to return home?"

"I'm ashamed to say . . . that might just be the case." Alexandra dropped her head, the shame very, very real. Shame for being deceitful. For casting her own family in a worse light to save her own secrets.

He put his hand beneath her chin, lifting her overwrought gaze to meet his own. "I'll wire my solicitor today, have him courier it to Bentham Park straightaway. They'll have it in two days."

Alexandra never thought it would be possible to feel both tenderness and desperation at once. But here it was warring inside of her with enough enmity to make her ill. "Might we just visit a bank in town? Draw upon funds there?" she suggested hastily. "My father is . . . as I said, he's not well. And my brother doesn't know the extent of our troubles. He would rather the money come from me, I think. It would ease his tattered pride."

The scar in her husband's lip deepened, as it did when he was perplexed or displeased. "I'll lose some in the exchange rate . . ."

"Take it from my next payment. From my trousseau or in lieu of a ring," she blurted. "You can dock it from whatever you like. Indeed, I vow that I will endeavor to see after my own maintenance from here on out. I'm an educated woman, after all, willing to work for my own fortunes. I don't want to be a bother. I don't . . . I don't want you to regret—"

A finger pressed over her lips, silencing her, before lifting to dash at a tear she hadn't realized had escaped. His savage features glowed brilliant in the break of the sun, but what truly astounded her was the temperate compassion with which he regarded her.

"No wife of mine need ever know shame." This was decreed with a steely yet tame sort of affection that stymied her into silence. "So many of the old nobility are in similar dire circumstances these days. What with agriculture giving way beneath industry and tenant farmers abandoning their lands for more profitable factories." He lifted his finger from her lips and smoothed at her trembling chin. "If you promise to lift your spirits, we'll go to the bank in Le Havre tomorrow and I'll draw upon whatever sum you like."

"T-truly?"

"Don't look so surprised," he chuffed. "I'd not deny your family a living, and perhaps in time your beloved brother can learn a bit from Ramsay and me about venture schemes and capital markets. I'll do what I can to build the Bentham title once more. As you help me secure my legacy, so I can help secure Andrew's. It's the least I can do."

A surge of relief, gratitude, and an emotion so powerful Alexandra couldn't begin to define it, drove her against him in a scandalous public display of affection. "What did

I do to deserve such a generous husband?" She let a few more tears fall, these wrought of happiness.

He gave a little bemused chuckle, his big hand drawing little circles of comfort on her back. "Well . . . you must have been very wicked, indeed, to have been sentenced to a life in my company."

"No." She pulled back to look up at him, searching his rather bewildered expression. "No, you are wonderful. Truly, incomprehensibly wonderful. You are quite literally saving the lives of those I love most in this world. I'll do anything I can to repay you."

Piers basked for a moment in her exuberant gratitude. Surely, she was exaggerating the scope of his assistance, but if the result was her arms around him, who was he to say nay?

Besides, he didn't hate the idea of collecting upon her appreciation . . .

He'd missed this. The press of her body against his. The scent of her hair. The gentle weight of her cheek on his chest.

Though they'd spent an inordinate amount of time in each other's company, he'd been careful, *so* careful, not to fan the sparks of his ever-present desire into an inferno that might reduce them both to naught but ash.

Three days.

Three days and he'd spread her naked upon a bed and not let her up until neither of them could move. Then they'd eat, rest, and do it all again.

Three eternal, *infernal* days.

Her rapid breaths against him had begun to slow as she took the comfort his embrace offered her. Not for the first time, Piers found himself thanking the stars that this eccentric, impulsive woman had proposed to him. His marriage, while fraught with danger both physical and emotional, had exceeded his expectations in almost every aspect.

Not that his expectations had been particularly high.

Quite the opposite, in fact.

But the thought of lording over Castle Redmayne with Francesca Cavendish felt as arduous as a prison sentence.

Because marriage to Alexandra had thus far been something like freedom. What other woman would toil alongside him as he excavated stones from a centuries-old catacomb? What man could boast of a wife who was as learned and well traveled as he? Perhaps more so? How many men could entertain the idea of taking their woman on exotic adventures to the far-reaching corners of the globe?

Exotic often meant uncomfortable and dirty, and his wife didn't seem to be put off by either of those conditions.

Was it possible that he'd found in her a companion whose wanderlust matched his own?

Three days and he'd have his answer.

Wait. *Christ.* He was such a dolt. In three days her courses were due to arrive. If they did, would he have to wait five more subsequent days to claim her?

Could he?

He'd never been squeamish about such things.

Was she?

When he'd descended the stairs, he'd been stunned to find her already dressed and waiting. The startling pallor of her cheeks and the mist in her eyes had worried him.

Because over the course of the past four days, he'd begun to suspect that she was being honest . . . At least about her lack of a pregnancy. He'd watched her closely for any signs of such a condition, and had encountered none.

But this morning she'd been so wan and sickly, he wondered if she was struck by the illness that plagued most mothers in the mornings.

Guilt pricked at his relief to find her distress was merely emotional rather than physiological. So much relief, in fact, he didn't at all mind being a little oversolicitous to her inquiries for money.

Not if it brought her color back and soothed her sorrow. It wasn't her fault her father's fortunes had failed. Women had little power over such things, and he could only imagine the helplessness of it, or the intense discomfort of being reduced to beg for money from her husband to spare her family shame.

He'd longed for the return of her smile.

She'd been energetic and enthusiastic in the mornings. Her wit had been sharp and her disposition, for the most part, sunny. For all her blunt and impulsive interactions, she'd displayed fathomless wells of patience with workmen and students, alike. Even her corrections didn't ruffle the most fragile of male egos as her praise and passion for her work were more effusive and openly genuine. She spoke every language, he was certain of that. French, Italian, German, Portuguese, and had even been able to translate an Arabic text that had stymied Forsythe.

That had been a particularly enjoyable moment.

They all had, if he was being honest. Every moment in her company was more pleasant than the last.

He'd relished discovering his past alongside her more than he'd ever imagined. It was like uncovering his own mystery buried with the bones of his ancestor.

Ivar Redmayne had been interred by a people not his own, who'd respected him enough to bury his possessions alongside him. He'd died alone while his son was away at battle, but buried with him were treasures that bespoke a beloved and powerful man.

Trinkets made by a granddaughter. A fur cloak crafted lovingly by his wife, Hildegard, a depiction of her etched into the inside of his shield.

Redmayne men, it would appear, had a penchant for possessive, bordering on *obsessive,* relationships with their women.

Something to keep in mind, when navigating this complex arrangement with his own wife.

Setting her gently but firmly away from him, he kissed her forehead and strode to the concierge to make arrangements for a meeting with a bank in Le Havre for tomorrow.

That done, he'd turned around to find that, once again, Lady Julia Throckmorton had arrested the attentions of his wife.

As usual, the vapid woman chatted animatedly, flailing her hands this way and that. However, Alexandra was less engaged than was her habit. Her delicate features still knotted into a sullen frown she was obviously trying to untangle into some semblance of amiability.

It appeared that Lady Throckmorton had worn out her welcome where his wife was concerned.

Julia, while friendly, could try the patience of a saint, and Piers often found himself marveling that his wife remained unperturbed by her.

Not so, today.

After such distressing family news, the overwrought duchess was stretched to the edge of an invisible tether.

Generally, he agreeably enjoyed the reminiscing banter of the two school chums, but today he would do what he could to ease his wife's social burden until she could collect herself.

"Lady Throckmorton," he greeted. "Are you awaiting your Dr. Forsythe?"

Several guests started when she threw her head back, exposing her neck in an overexuberant giggle. "*My* Dr. Forsythe? Listen to you! I think he left early for the dig. I was on my way to see him now."

"That is where we're headed as well." He tucked Alexandra's arm in his own. "I'll bid you good—"

"Oh, that's wonderful." Lady Throckmorton gestured expansively. "Might I prevail upon your generosity to conduct me there? Dr. Forsythe mentioned that they'd finish transporting the Redmayne bones today, and he seemed thrilled to distraction over the prospect. I promised him I'd be there, but I fear he has left without me."

It wasn't in his nature to pity Forsythe, but he was mightily tempted. It appeared the good doctor was doing his best to avoid the tenacious flirt, and suddenly Piers found he was impatient to conduct her to Forsythe's side.

"You may share our conveyance, of course." He led his brooding wife and the beaming Lady Throckmorton to their carriage and handed them both inside. The catacombs were less than two miles away, short enough to walk, but the day promised to be hot and did its best to melt them in their work clothes. The sooner they got underground, the better.

Since Alexandra seemed incapable of conducting conversation as they trundled over the ancient cobbled streets, Piers rose to the occasion. He'd learned that one only needed to wind Julia Throckmorton like a clockwork toy and then sit back and make appropriate noises until she ran out of breath.

"My wife tells me, my lady, that you have quite the tour of the Continent scheduled after your stay here. What is your itinerary?"

Her expression turned rapturous. "Dress fitting in Rouen, then off to Paris for a fete with the Duc de Longley, and Venice and Milan. After that I have been invited to a soiree in the Alps where two eligible Prussian princes will be in attendance. Then I'll see out the summer at Lake Geneva, where they're having a marvelous grand party for our ten-year reunification at de Chardonne." She turned to Alexandra. "You, Francesca, and Cecelia are planning to attend, aren't you? Especially now that you're married to a duke. How properly sick with envy everyone will be, and it'll give us something else to reminisce about that isn't . . . you know . . . the unpleasant scandal."

Piers's brow crimped as he felt his wife go tense as a bridge cable beside him.

"Scandal?" he queried.

"She never told you?" Julia lifted a golden brow at Alexandra. "Less than a month before we graduated de Chardonne, our headmaster quite disappeared. There was such a to-do, they didn't even hold a proper soiree for our launch."

"How terrible that must have been for you," Piers did his best to keep his dry sarcasm out of his voice, suspecting he only half succeeded.

If Julia noticed, she gave no indication. "An absolute nightmare, to be sure. There was to be dancing with the boys at le Radon, which included two Italian dukes, and rumor had it, a Romanoff. All canceled. Can you imagine having to return from the Continent swathed in black? I never got to wear my lavender dress commissioned for the occasion. I've never quite recovered from the disappointment."

Piers turned to his wife, thinking her pallor hadn't yet quite improved. "We can attend, if you wish," he offered solicitously. "Lake Geneva is rather diverting in the—"

"No," she said decisively, then took a moment for deeper

consideration, her expression smoothing into a remote, placid courteousness. "No, thank you both, but neither Francesca nor Cecelia can attend, and I promised not to go without them. I hope you understand, Julia."

"Of course," she said graciously. "How extraordinary that the three of you are still so inseparable. I'll at least be able to tell everyone that I went on holiday with the new Duchess of Redmayne. Everyone thought the three of you would remain hopeless spinsters. Now if only we can marry off the other two, though I doubt they'd be able to catch such lofty husbands, if you don't mind my saying."

Piers minded just about every word that escaped her mouth, but he inwardly smiled when Alexandra's grip on his arm tightened with a possessive edge. He would have liked to remind Lady Throckmorton that she hadn't gone on holiday with them, she'd insinuated herself into their honeymoon. Instead, he inclined his head and replied, "Not at all."

"One does wonder, though . . ." She gave her chin a speculative tap. "Whatever happened to Maurice de Marchand? He really was quite a . . . imposing sort of headmaster, wasn't he?"

"Imposing, yes," Alexandra agreed, not taking her eyes from the sparkle of the sea-swept morning.

"Think you he ran off with a lover?" Piers ventured. "Or perhaps stole money from the institution and disappeared?" Or perhaps he killed himself, he added silently. The very idea of wrangling a gaggle of giggling debutantes was enough to make one properly consider wrapping his lips around a pistol and pulling the trigger.

"One hopes." Julia shrugged. "Though the authorities treated it like a murder. There was speculation that a little blood was found along with other evidence."

"None of the evidence was conclusive, if I remember," Alexandra cut in. "The coroner reported that there wasn't even enough to confirm a paper cut, let alone a death."

"Yes, well, men don't just vanish into thin air. There must have been a witness—"

Alexandra leaned forward, her features solemn and troubled. "Witnesses can perjure themselves. Science does not. If you're going to speculate about a murder, you *must* have proof."

"Actually," Julia argued, drawing her shoulders up in a huff. "You don't have to have proof to speculate about anything, darling. That's what speculation is. I don't know why your dander is up, Alexandra, it's not as though anyone accused *you* of murdering him." She laughed giddily. "The very idea!"

That was his wife, a scientist before all things, staunch and passionate in regard to the truth.

Not at all a bad stance to hold, he thought proudly.

"If the headmaster was murdered, Lady Throckmorton, who would you hazard did it?" he asked idly, glad the dig site drew near.

"It's obvious who did it." Julia twisted her lips, blue eyes sparkling at Alexandra. "I've always known."

The fingers on his jacket became talons as his wife leaned toward the smug woman opposite her. "Who?" she demanded.

Julia quirked her lip, gorging on the rapt attention. "Either his lover or . . ."

CHAPTER TWENTY-ONE

Or the groundskeeper.

Alexandra pried her clenched teeth apart and rubbed at her aching jaw. She glanced up from the crate of bones she'd classified and categorized in front of her to watch her husband dip a ladle into the water bucket.

Julia's words had been running through her mind all afternoon.

De Marchand hadn't been killed by a lover, but a victim. And buried by the groundskeeper.

Did Julia know? Or did her words exhume a whisper of truth Alexandra would rather remain buried?

That the groundskeeper wasn't as trustworthy as they'd all suspected.

Jean-Yves had been among the workers at the tombs these past four days, watching her alertly and smiling when he caught her eye.

Just as he did now.

Alexandra did her best to smile back at him, though the

attempt felt brittle and tense. It unnerved her to have the man touch elbows with her husband.

Could his expression of geniality hide a deeper greed or malevolence?

She would find out on the morrow.

With the tunnels and vaulted crypt completely secured, Redmayne and Forsythe hauled the crates she'd packed with various sundries, artifacts, armor, and, as soon as she could finish dusting and chipping away some remnants of the burial shroud, the bones of Ivar Redmayne.

She'd have worked a great deal faster if she'd not been plagued by infernal distractions all day, not the least of which had been her barbarian husband.

He'd been moving stones and earth all morning before aiding Forsythe and the engineers as they fortified the final tunnel into the Redmayne Crypt.

Sweat glistened at his hairline and painted his tawny neck with a lustrous gleam in the lanternlight. One more button of his smudged ivory shirt had come undone, revealing the dramatic swells of his pectorals.

Quite suddenly, she became aware of the dryness of her own mouth, now plagued with a powerful thirst. One the water might not quench.

She refused to watch. Refused to *want*.

There was simply too much to do. Too much at stake. Too much to ponder over and worry about beyond his diverting feats of unbridled masculine strength.

Besides, he'd been absolutely insufferable all afternoon, turning every burdened journey down the tunnel into a rivalry, insisting upon shouldering the heaviest load.

At one point he'd actually foisted upon Forsythe a crate of animal bones, with some snide remark about how bones were hollow and light. Then he'd promptly lifted a crate the size of a small horse packed with iron weapons and jogged—*jogged!*—down the tunnel.

Was it any wonder he nearly drank the entire bucket of spring water?

Alexandra couldn't decide who she was more churlish toward. Him for acting like a self-important, teenaged ass, or her for being impressed by it.

On top of everything, Julia enjoyed the spectacle immensely. That is, when she wasn't insisting upon wandering about the various rooms, touching everything, fiddling with mechanisms, and asking incessant, inane questions of both her and Forsythe.

And speaking of poor Dr. Forsythe, once his masculinity was called into question in front of his workers and two women, he'd done his best to match Redmayne lift for lift and load for load.

Between all of this, the responsibility for a delicate skeleton, and a blackmail letter scalding her through her skirt pockets, Alexandra thought she might expire from the rein she'd held on her temper. Tension coiled her muscles as tight as a springboard, and a headache had begun to crawl from her shoulders and into her neck, threatening to winch a vise around her temples.

Forsythe joined Redmayne at the water bucket, waiting his turn. At this late afternoon hour, he appeared nigh close to death, sweat-drenched and red-faced as she'd never seen him.

Taking pity on him, she offered a conciliatory smile, one he returned with a bit of his old winsome vigor before Julia distracted him.

Noticing their shared moment, Redmayne set his ladle down, stalking toward her with that loose-limbed, feral grace of his.

At the possessive heat in his gaze, Alexandra almost dropped the femur, so she returned her own gaze firmly to her work, refusing to mark his approach even as he leaned down to address her.

"You may offer him your pretty smiles, wife," he growled low in her ear, "because your pretty moans and sighs are mine."

Ignoring the burst of butterfly wings in her womb, Alexandra glanced up sharply to make certain Forsythe hadn't heard his salacious comment on the other side of the cavern.

The doctor's head was bent toward a cooing Julia, seemingly inured to them.

Alexandra whirled on her husband, shaking the femur at him like the finger of an impassioned politician.

And quite forgot what she was going to say.

Must he *insist* on smelling so appealing all the time? Even his *sweat* was alluring. Clean and sharp with hints of leather, earth, and a salty, masculine musk.

Instead of castigating him for tormenting her thus for *four days,* she whispered curtly, "You're being unkind."

His large shoulder lifted in ambivalence as he bent to press his lips to her aching jaw. "I'm being honest," he rumbled.

"You're *being* ridiculous."

"Now who is unkind?" he teased, rooting into her hair to nuzzle at the downy skin behind her ear.

She swatted him away, not because she wanted to, but because she understood the dangers of his intoxicating touch.

"This is the last of it." To distract him, she held out his umpteenth-great-grandfather's impressive thigh bone to him. "I'll admit, the men of the Redmayne line certainly share a remarkable physical structure. Down to their very bones. Ivar would have been mere inches shorter than you, but I'd wager he was equally thick and burly. Also, his teeth were healthy, as I've noted yours are."

He ran his tongue over wolfish incisors, testing their health as his eyes twinkled the color of the Baltic Sea on a clear day. "A man might dine upon such poetic compliments from his lady wife." He sighed dramatically.

She frowned, refusing to be charmed by his good humor. "I've found a few healed broken bones, likely suffered in battle," she continued. "But for one on his tibia from when he was a child. Other than that, he was a robust man, even his knees were intact and his joints healthy. His cause of death would have had to have been something to do with his organs, because his bones show no signs of deterioration or disease. At least not upon initial inspection."

"An impressive ancestor, indeed." He nodded, duly impressed. "I'm fortunate for his bloodline."

"He would have been an excessively strong man," she said with unmistakable meaning. "A leader of men. It would have been unfair of him to expect *any* man to keep up. As to do so would be impossible."

"I understand." He smirked at her just as evocatively, eyes flicking to Forsythe. "I imagine other men were intelligent enough not to challenge him. And if they did, he broke not just their bodies, but their will." He wiped at a smudge of dirt on her cheek, likely making it worse. "Be grateful, wife, that you're married to a duke and not a barbarian, who, for the time being, is only intent upon breaking one and not the other." He leaned in and gathered her lips for a loud, showy kiss that left her speechless before relieving her of Ivar's femur, and carefully setting it in its place within the cushioned crate bound for the examination tent.

"Which one?" she asked, just to make certain she didn't mistake his meaning.

"His body is still intact, is it not?"

Alexandra gaped at him, trying to decide if she were furious or flummoxed as he used his fist rather than the hammer to pound the crate's lid securely tight.

Her first kiss in four days and he'd done it not for her benefit, or even his, but for that of a purely inconsequential man that only *he* considered a rival.

The nerve of him. The unmitigated *gall*.

"I'm taking tea with Julia," she huffed. "Do be careful with your ancestor, though I recently learned bones are of negligible heft."

She picked up her skirts and gathered Julia away from an exhausted Forsythe, who seemed content to saunter beside them, leaving her husband to haul the final crate.

Redmayne's chuckle followed them down the long tunnel before a deep grunt told her he'd shouldered the blasted thing and ambled after them.

If he wanted the burden, he could take it.

Alexandra took a few deep breaths as she navigated the catacombs, calming her blood. It wasn't that she was angry at him, per se. How could she be? He'd been nothing but indulgent of her. Especially this morning, capitulating to her financial suggestions.

No, she wasn't angry. Simply . . . frustrated. Not even at him, exactly. Just at everything. The entire world. She'd spent the whole day railing at the past, dreading the future, and suspecting everyone in her vicinity of being or becoming an enemy.

It wore her down until her bones felt as though they belonged in the dank and dust of this place.

She'd make amends for being so surly at dinner this evening, she decided as she lifted her skirts to climb the handful of steps out of the catacombs and into the sunshine. Perhaps she'd even attempt another intimate overture. She could tell his tether was remarkably close to breaking. It was apparent in his scalding looks. In the whisky-soft depth of his conversations, his voice as silken as his tongue had been upon her.

She climbed past the entrance buttressed by incomprehensibly large beams of wood, squinting as the afternoon sun gleamed off the water below the cliffs of Normandy.

Redmayne had assisted with the installation of those beams not two days prior, after expressing his dissatisfaction with the previous fortifications.

It pleased her that he worried after the workers and their safety.

Every part of her could feel him behind her, and it took a herculean effort, and more than a dose of her feminine pride, not to turn and—

An echo of faint pops and a familiar hiss preceded a deafening splinter of wood and stone.

What the devil—?

"Run!" Forsythe shoved both Alexandra and Julia forward just as the thunderous sound of falling stones drowned out the dismayed cries and calls of the workmen taking their afternoon tea in a tent above.

An explosion of ghostly dust engulfed them all, and the momentum of it pushed Alexandra to her hands and knees as she fought for breath, her chest spasming with bone-rattling coughs.

Chaos overwhelmed her at once. Hands dragged her farther from the tunnel entrance as students, archeologists, and workmen shouted orders at each other.

The chalky sounds of smaller rocks settling between the boulders filled her with such dread, she surged away from whoever was attempting to help her from the wreckage.

What section of the catacombs had caved in? Had everyone made it out?

Had *anyone* made it out?

Where was Redmayne? He'd been right behind her, and she'd been a good several paces out of the tunnel. Surely he'd crossed the threshold before—

Julia stumbled toward her, her entire yellow day dress now an ethereal shade of white. She collapsed into Alexandra's arms shuddering with irrepressible sobs.

"Are you hurt?" Alexandra demanded, searching her for injures with unsteady hands.

"He saved me," Julia wailed. "Forsythe saved me, and now I cannot find him. Is he dead?"

Alexandra handed Julia off to an awaiting student. Swamped with a grave sense of foreboding, she tripped back toward the catacombs' entrance.

Now an impenetrable wall of stone.

Men were already digging at the rocks, yelling and creating a line to pull the earth away from the blocked archway.

Which meant . . .

"No." She lurched faster, attempting to run on legs as steady as a newborn fawn's.

Redmayne. He'd have been the last one out. Where was her husband?

She expected his wide shoulders to melt out of the cloud of settling dust, white as an archangel and just as merciless. He was the Terror of Torcliff. The Amazon hadn't conquered him, nor had the Nile. He'd tamed jungles and forged across pitiless deserts.

A simple cave couldn't possibly defeat him.

The very thought was categorically impossible.

Now that the air had become less choked with stone and dirt, Alexandra found Forsythe as he dragged himself out of the rubble looking dazed. The pallid substance caked in his sweat darkened to take on the appearance of dried blood.

Alexandra helped him to his feet only to shake him. "Where is Redmayne?" she cried, not caring that she sounded just as hysterical as Julia. "Where is my husband?"

Slowly, as though he had trouble understanding her, Forsythe looked to the man-sized pile of stones at his back. "He . . . was right behind us. Wasn't he?"

"No," she whispered. Or screamed. "No, no, no. *No!*"

Forsythe caught her as she shot past him, gripping at her arms. "Alexandra, don't. It's too dangerous."

She struggled against his grip. "He is still in there. I have to get him out."

Forsythe held fast. "If I know Redmayne, I know he wouldn't want you to put yourself in harm's way, not on his account."

"You don't know him. I do. He's my *husband*!" She wrenched away from him. "Either get a shovel and help, or get out of my way!"

She joined the men, grabbing and shoving at a rock she had no hope of budging.

A gentle hand landed on her shoulder, and she turned with her teeth bared, ready to do battle with anyone who might drag her away from the catacombs.

Jean-Yves's concerned gaze didn't hold the comfort it might once have, but she didn't have time to dwell on her suspicions about him.

"I must find him," she panted, unsure of why her lungs still felt tight, or why her heart might burst open. "I *must*. He's my husband. He's my . . . husband."

Sobs drowned the word she could no longer say. A foreign word only a week ago . . . *Husband*. And now, she'd the luxury of one. A good husband. A kind husband. A wounded heart and a generous man. Over the course of eight days, he'd become so much more to her than she'd ever imagined. A mentor. A protector. A knight in tarnished armor. One who rode an unruly, disobedient horse and tamed both predator and prey alike.

He was supposed to father her children.

He'd teased her only seconds ago. Twinkled playful blue eyes at her. Dear God, if she never saw those eyes again. If she never . . . what if he . . . ?

A little despondent noise escaped her, warning of a deeper hysteria threatening to overflow her barely contained panic.

"Petite duchesse." Jean-Yves used the voice one did with the enraged or the infirm as he squeezed her shoulder. *"Mon petit oiseau blessé."* My little wounded bird. "Cecelia led me to believe . . . that is . . ." His face twisted uncomfortably. "I was not given to think this man, your husband, means anything to you."

Alexandra shook her head violently. "I . . . I can't lose him, Jean-Yves," she sobbed. "He brought me to Normandy to be kind. Because he thought I'd find it enjoyable. I can't be the reason he . . . Oh, God . . . He can't die . . ."

Jean-Yves gazed at her with sheer disbelief crinkling the deep groves branching out from his weathered eyes. "This hard man you have only known for days. This duke with a terrible name. You would remain married to him, even after all that has happened to you? You . . . care for him?"

"I . . . I do!" *She did.* God *help* her, but she did.

"Then." He ripped off his jacket, trading it for a shovel someone was handing to the laborers. "Let us dig."

Alexandra let out a grateful sob, snatching a shovel of her own.

How could she suspect dear Jean-Yves? When he was so good. So steadfast. He always seemed to be there in her darkest hours, this enigmatic Frenchman.

Digging into the earth for her.

This time, not to bury a body, but to reclaim one.

Alexandra pried as many boulders away from the entrance as she could, digging trenches beneath them so larger men could roll them away. She broke her nails clawing at the smaller stones that acted like mortar between the large ones. Eventually the straining and burning in her arms gave way to exhausted trembling. Sweat curled the wisps of hair at her temples, trickled down her back and between her breasts. Stones crushed her toes. Blisters smarted her palms. And still she would not stop digging.

Not until she reached him.

Someone called his name. Chanted it. Sobbed it at a frantic decibel that threatened to break her heart. It took her several moments, not to mention the astonished stares of the other laborers, to realize that someone was her.

Beside her, right in front of where Jean-Yves toiled, a stone, triple the size of any man's head, shuddered as though a great weight slammed against it. The masculine bellow from behind it was like a beam of sunlight piercing her panicked desolation.

"Piers?" she called, clawing at the boulder. "Piers, is that you? Answer me. Are you there?"

The earth muffled his reply, as did the sound of her pulse pounding in her ears, but she was certain he'd barked a surly directive of some sort.

Swamped by an unholy elation, she ineffectually chipped at the edge of the boulder, hoping to dislodge it, unable to cognate well enough to translate the words being hurled at her in rapid French.

Jean-Yves seized her, pulling her aside just in time before the boulder gave way and rolled down the mound of smaller stones, bringing a great deal of the blockage with it.

She called his name once more, this time it escaped as a pathetic moan.

Frantic, aware of how humiliatingly agitated she was, Alexandra yanked and pulled at rock and debris, aware that someone worked just as frenetically on the other side.

More so.

Her husband.

His voice reached her. Spouting commands at first. And then his tone gentled with a concerned intonation. And still, she couldn't process the words. Not exactly. All she knew was that she had to get to him.

Finally, it was as though the rock wall between them disintegrated into dust, the smaller stones clattering down the mound as it gave way beneath their collective need.

They clawed only at each other then, driving their bodies together with a wild fusion. As though making certain no barrier of any kind could come between them again.

Alexandra was vaguely aware of a hearty applause. Of voices and cheers and more chaos.

It didn't matter. She didn't care. She heard nothing but the strong, sure beat of his heart beneath her ear. She felt nothing but the molten heat of his skin poured over swells and mounds of steely muscle as he cocooned her in his strength. She didn't breathe air anymore, but she filled her lungs with his scent, took it deep within herself until he overwhelmed every sense she could think of but for taste.

And that could come when they were alone.

She would kiss him. And, dammit, he would kiss her back.

"Alexandra." She heard his voice both from his lips and from deep in the chest beneath her ear. It calmed her. Soothed the uncharacteristically feverish hysterics threatening to overwhelm her logic. "Are you hurt?" He ran his hands down her arms, and up her back, searching for injury. "Sweet Christ. I couldn't tell if you'd climbed the stairs in time. I feared you didn't make it out."

"I thought *you'd* been crushed." Her voice sounded small and plaintive against the wide planes of his chest.

Gentle hands pried them apart. Jean-Yves and another worker guided Redmayne to a rock upon which he could sit and catch his breath. Alexandra trailed after them, anxiously taking in every detail.

He was a mountain of dust and mud. It caked in the thick layers of his hair and even his beard, settling into the shallow grooves of his scars and the slight lines branching from his eyes.

In all her vast and exotic experiences, he had to be the most beautiful sight she'd ever witnessed.

He took the water someone offered and swished the dust from his mouth, spitting it onto the earth before taking another swig.

Alexandra hovered, drinking in the sight of him just as deeply until she noted one of the dirt-caked stains on his thigh was darker than the others caused by sweat.

She dropped to her knees beside him, reaching for the torn part of his trousers. "Oh, blast, you're injured!"

He shrugged. "A rock landed on my leg, but it's of no consequence." He brushed a palm over her shoulder and down her elbow. "Did you sustain any injuries? Your hands, they're raw—"

"Someone fetch me some water," she ordered. "I'll clean the cut and assess—"

"That's not necessary, darling." The patina of dirt

caused his piercing eyes to appear otherworldly as they glimmered down at her, containing both censure, and something softer. "It smarts like the devil, but it's not serious. What I want to know is why you put yourself in harm's way trying to dig me—"

"But you're bleeding!" she interrupted. Nothing else mattered at the moment.

"Hardly." He waved a hand over the wound, declaring it inconsequential.

Alexandra wouldn't allow herself to be appeased. There was too much dirt caked around the tear in his trousers to tell if the wound was deep or not.

"Let me see," she insisted.

"You're not a medical doctor," he reminded her mildly.

"It might need to be stitched." She peeled back one side of the torn material. "I've stitched a wound bef—"

He caught both of her trembling hands in his, engulfing them in familiar, rough-skinned warmth. "Leave it, wife," he crooned gently. "You needn't upset yourself over me. Take a few deep breaths to calm yourself."

At that, she surged to her feet, wrenching her hands away from his as she fought to fill her lungs fast enough. "I *am* calm," she declared. "I'm the very *essence* of calm. If I were any calmer, I'd be asleep!"

Even though he was sitting, he didn't have to reach up very far to place his palms on either side of her face. "I understand, Alexandra. Being spared a terrible death can set anyone's nerves on edge—"

She made a sound of immense frustration at his condescending tone. "That isn't it. I've been nearly missed by death before."

"Then . . ." He frowned, the puzzled lines in his forehead creating cracks in the mud drying there. "I was able to save the bones, you needn't worry that you lost—"

"I thought I'd lost *you,* you enormous Neanderthal!" She knew she sounded shrill, but at this point, she was beyond caring. "Hang the bones! Must you *insist* on hefting the largest box? Upon turning everything into a competition? You could have left it for . . . for tomorrow . . . You could have escorted me out. You . . . You . . . You could have died!"

Dammit, sobs crawled up from her chest and crowded her throat, demanding every part of self-control she had left to grapple them back down again.

"Come now," he soothed with a crooked smirk, rubbing a thumb over her cheek. "Would that really have been so bad? You'd be a wealthy widow. Your problems would have been solved."

Alexandra's hand lashed out and connected with his cheek before she'd realized what she'd done.

In the stunned silence that followed, she seized his face and kissed him brutally. Crushing her mouth to his with enough force to feel his teeth. Hard enough for *him* to feel her rage and taste her terror.

That done, she slapped him again.

Never in the recorded history of mankind had twenty men been so utterly quiet and still for so long.

Redmayne stared at her, stone-faced and eyes glinting. With what, she couldn't tell.

For once in her life, she didn't care.

Then, her husband did something she'd never seen him do before.

He grinned.

CHAPTER TWENTY-TWO

It occurred to Piers that he should stay at the dig site. That he should investigate. Especially since no one seemed to be that suspicious. Old caves collapsed all the time; the men shrugged. Perhaps the fortifications hadn't been as sound as everyone had thought.

What utter. Fucking. Horseshit.

He'd seen to the fortifications, himself. Thousand-year-old cathedrals had less structural integrity.

No. Something had happened. He'd heard it, right before the ceiling had caved in, a different sound had warned him to jump away just in time. Some sort of hiss, and crackle, preceded a pop before the rocks had begun to fall.

Not an explosion, but he suspected gunpowder or a similar agent.

The structural engineer wouldn't return from Le Havre until tomorrow, and it would be folly to attempt to return inside the catacombs without him.

Besides, it would take a miracle to peel him from Alexandra's side.

Now that she might be in danger.

Now that the dynamic had shifted between them. Their bonds strengthened.

"Your wife, she loves you." A medic named Giuseppe had clapped him on the back after washing, stitching, and bandaging his wound. Which hadn't been as shallow as he'd thought, nor as deep as *she'd* feared.

Piers hadn't wanted to argue with the man.

His wife didn't love him. She couldn't. Not only after a few short days.

But she cared. She cared more than he'd expected her to.

It had taken some doing to intimidate her into submitting to an examination in the next tent over. Her hands had been abraded, but what other injuries could she have sustained?

Trying to rescue him.

"What makes you think that?" he asked of Giuseppe.

"Do you not speak of love?" The elder man's impertinence rankled him, and he cast him a warning glare. He didn't dare speak, as his blood ran hot. His temper high. And a thousand foul words sprang to his tongue.

The medic wisely moved on. "It's quite apparent she is utterly besotted with you."

"Because she tried to save my life?"

The older man had eyed him as though he'd never met a man so dense. "If she didn't love you, she would not have slapped you twice."

Piers had looked away then, so the observant man wouldn't see his heart glowing through his eyes.

The medic wasn't privy to the extraordinary circumstances of their marriage. Nor the extent of their denied passion. Nor the unfeasibility of trust between them.

However, he'd been right about one thing.

She'd slapped him twice.

Because she cared.

The sting of her palm still lingered on his cheek. And every time he marked it, an absurd smile threatened to engulf his entire face.

He'd fought it the entire way back to the hotel, unwilling to allow her to see it. She'd be unable to interpret the expression, and he wasn't ready or willing to discuss it.

In fact, they didn't speak much in the carriage, but her hands, more scraped than wounded and thus not warranting bandages, remained firmly tucked within his own.

When he found the culprit, the bastard would pay in five times the blood for every single scratch on her perfect skin.

They sat hip to hip, her head resting on his shoulder. It was as though some polymer or adhesive had grown between them, resisting any separation.

He barely felt a twinge in his leg as he swept her down from the carriage and mounted the steps into the grand lobby.

"Your Grace." The desk clerk called as they passed him, holding out a slim piece of paper. "You've a telegram."

"Later," he barked, mounting the first stair.

He was alive. She was alive. That fact, so often taken for granted, scorched a fire through his veins that he meant to quench with her body.

Ten days be damned.

What mattered other than that she cared? That he yearned?

He'd spend an indecent number of hours bathing her. Bathing with her. All her creamy, sweet skin slick with soap beneath his hands. He could only imagine her slipping her lithe body against, over, and around his. He'd wash every soft and feminine crevice, conducting a thorough examination with his hands, and then his mouth.

Would she do the same? Would she discover him as she

scrubbed the grit from his body? His cock reacted with such violence to the thought, he suppressed a groan and quickened his pace.

He wanted—no—*needed* her hands on him. Small, elegant hands. So efficient and competent, used to intricate work and detailed exertion.

He needed her spread open on the bed beneath him. Wide and bare and without restraint.

Tonight, he was going to—

"But—the telegram, it's from your, Sir Cassius Ramsay," the desk clerk sheepishly persisted. "Marked urgent. Excessively urgent."

Piers gritted his teeth so hard he feared one might have cracked. But he released his wife with a kiss to her grime-streaked forehead. "I've sent ahead for a bath to be drawn, and for Constance to undress you." A privilege he'd burned to claim for himself.

After her outburst, all the fight had drained out of her. She replied with a docile nod.

Piers tried not to think of how young she looked. How much like prey she seemed now with her big gentle doe eyes and vulnerable chin that was wont to wobble.

If only he could slay her dragons. He'd stand over her like a lupine sentinel, snarling at whoever might approach. He'd sear the secrets from her eyes,

Who could want to hurt someone like her? What could she possibly have done to warrant such violence?

Because, whatever had happened in that catacomb hadn't been an accident.

And the results were supposed to have been deadly.

"I won't be but a moment." He wouldn't dare be away from her that long. Not when he must keep her safe. Keep her alive.

If Ramsay had sent him an urgent message on his

honeymoon, it could only mean that he'd found information regarding the assassins from Castle Redmayne. It could mean a clue to unlocking the mystery as to who was behind all of this and bring him one step closer to ensuring the safety of his wife.

Stalking to the desk, he snatched the telegram from the clerk and unfolded it.

If he'd been any less filthy, they'd have watched his skin blanch from swarthy to white. They'd have understood why he turned on his heel and stormed back outside the hotel.

They'd have been less mystified as to why the contents of the telegram caused him to abandon his wife.

> *I consulted my contact in Scotland. Stop.*
> *Falt Ruadh doesn't always refer to red hair. Stop.*
> *It can also denote RED MANE. Stop.*
> *It's you, brother. Redmayne. They're after you. Stop.*

Piers walked toward the sea, fuming. Furious.

The unbound stallion on the train, whipped into a frenzy. The gunmen at the ruins. The accident on the ship. And now the cave-in at the catacombs.

Somehow Alexandra had always been in the way. In danger. And somehow, in his hubris, he'd assumed she'd acquired an enemy along her adventurous and uniquely singular path in life.

How could he have been so blind?

He was the Terror of Torcliff. The Duke of Redmayne. His list of enemies and enmities far surpassed anything Alexandra could even dream of. At the very top were a cousin and a former lover who vastly benefited from his death, and the long inventory only rolled on from there.

She was innocent in all of this. Of course she was.

He'd been the intended victim all along.

And until he wrapped his fingers around the throats of those responsible, the safest place for his wife was as far away from him as she could get.

CHAPTER TWENTY-THREE

Alexandra set out to find her missing husband as the sparkling horizon split the late-afternoon sun in half. She'd had enough with feeling more like a mistress than a wife, waiting patiently in her bedroom until he deigned to come for her.

With Constance's help, she'd bathed away the events of the day, expecting Redmayne to burst into her room at any moment. At first, she wasn't certain she was entirely prepared to meet the erotic masculine promise that'd emanated from every pore of his body since the moment he'd dug his way from the rubble.

After a time, she'd begun to wonder what kept him. She'd wanted him nearby, if at least to bask in the comfort and security his fiendish presence afforded her.

He'd survived. His body was still warm and vibrant.

He was still *her* husband. *Hers.* The possessiveness of the pronoun felt more significant than ever.

He belonged to her. With her. And she needed him.

Dressed in a simple ivory frock, she perched on the bed for as long as her discontent would allow.

When it became apparent a visit from him wasn't forthcoming, she grudgingly admitted a thirst had awakened within her. One not easily slaked by water or wine. She needed to drink in the unparalleled sight of him, to absorb the scent and heat of him.

To remind herself she was alive, that he was well. Because, somehow, he'd become necessary to her.

Her riotous emotions had swung like the pendulum of a great clock. And with each passing minute she spent alone, she'd felt less in control. Of anything.

Her feelings.

Her destiny.

Her very existence.

She'd inquired of the desk clerk as to Redmayne's whereabouts, and he directed her outside, where the porter pointed her toward the sea.

Breezes toyed with her hair like playful fingers, tossing it with soft but unruly chaos as she descended the switchback stairs to the beaches below.

Only to find the evening beaches mostly deserted.

Concerned, she begged the pardon of an elderly gentleman walking a white dog who resembled a puff of cotton. "Perhaps you can help me, monsieur, I'm looking for an extraordinarily tall bearded man. He's . . ." She trailed off. How did one describe the Duke of Redmayne to a stranger? Especially today. Was he still attired as he'd been at the catacombs?

"There was just such a man, madame." The kindly gentleman tipped his hat. "Swimming in the du Val cove tucked back next to Corbeau Noir Cliff behind the dunes." He pointed to where the cliffs cut in sharply, the water disappearing behind shallow crests of sand waving with haphazard tufts of sea grasses. "I thought this man might be touched in the head to swim at such an hour, as the sun will soon be gone, and the wind grows chilly."

"Merci!" she called, cursing the sand falling away from beneath her slippers as she lifted her skirts and hurried toward the cove.

Once she crested the dunes, she hurried across a gentle path through vibrant beach grasses, holding her hands out so the muted breezes encouraged the reeds to paint gentle things on her palms.

The small knoll crested next to the golden face of the cliff, and she found that the other side of the dune crawled down toward the high tide.

Alexandra froze, struggling to fully comprehend the visual cornucopia before her.

The sun's final crescent barely peeked above the curvature of the sea, setting a multihued fire to the various striations of clouds batted around by a gathering evening wind. The summer air blew thick with an approaching storm, heavy and hostile with both heat and moisture.

Venerated by this crimson firmament, Redmayne rose like Neptune from the waves, slicking his wild hair to his scalp with a smooth lift of his chiseled arms.

The consequences of staring at the sun for too long were well documented. Even a glance was inadvisable.

One might go blind.

And yet she stared, unblinking, at a sight arguably more brilliant than that of the disappearing orb. What devastation might befall her, she wondered, if she gaped at him for too long?

The starch abandoned Alexandra's knees and she stumbled to the side, reaching for the nearby cliff face to steady her.

She'd seen naked men before.

In anatomy books, granted, and paintings, and the plethora of sculptures she'd been unable to avoid studying at the Sorbonne.

But nothing could have prepared her for this . . . for him.

He hadn't seen her yet, lurking as she was in the shadow of the cliff.

He'd paused for a moment in a waist-high tide, running his hands down his beard, removing the water.

As though answering an unspoken command, the sea ebbed from him, revealing his nude form with wet, glistening exactitude.

The rounded muscles of his chest, dusted with a fine fleece of ebony hair, flared into immense shoulders which ebbed and crested into long, thick arms. His frame could have been carved from marble before a pour of molten bronze was layered over it.

Another light trail of hair crawled between the obdurate ripples of muscle that made up his torso all the way down to his—

She only caught a glimpse, before he turned in such a way that he was backlit by the sun, casting a shadow over his . . . particulars.

She'd seen enough, though. His lean, tapered hips framed his sex, giving way to long legs carved with a wealth of crests and grooves that shaped and changed as he moved.

She frowned when she noted the bandage on his left thigh had been abandoned, and a small stitched seam marred the muscle there. The wound didn't seem to bother him at all as he fought the receding water toward the shore.

The shadow on his body shifted, offering her another unfiltered view of him. His entire form was like some magnificent sort of machinery, each tendon, muscle, and joint flexing and fluid with both refined movement and unthinkable power.

Pulse fluttering, Alexandra tried not to look. She really did. She endeavored to afford him the same respect and modesty she'd desire.

But then, she'd never bathed nude in the sea with nothing but a small cliff wall and a shallow sand dune for privacy. Modesty seemed to be the least of his concerns as he conquered the stretch of beach and veered toward the cliff.

Toward her.

Or, rather, toward the basket she'd just barely noticed, full of pressed clothing and boots his valet had no doubt left resting against the cliff wall for him.

When he saw her, he scowled. "What the bloody hell are you doing out here on your own?" he barked.

Drat. He'd caught her spying. Wincing, Alexandra met the censure sharpening his blunt features with a pretense of calm.

"I—I came to find you," she explained, inching toward the basket of his clothing and bending to fetch him a towel. "When you didn't return, I worried—"

"You should be at the hotel resting," he clipped, prowling closer with his singular dark grace.

"I don't want to rest." Not when there was so much to say. Not when she'd a million questions perched on her tongue, the first of which being . . .

Why had he left her alone?

He snatched the towel from her, securing it around his hips.

Stung, Alexandra retreated a step, and then another. Realizing she was as unused to his irritation as she was his unabashed nudity. She watched water sluice distracting trails down the grooves of his neck to his shoulders and chest, disappearing into the towel.

"It's not safe here." His veins rolled and flexed above his muscles, larger than before, pulsing with something she didn't quite understand. He seemed impossibly more titanic. His scars, the ones she barely even noticed anymore, stood out in stark relief from features hardened with that well-contained rage she'd always sensed just below the surface.

The girl in her screamed at her to turn. To run. To hide from his displeasure and his strength and the heat he was throwing off in waves, regardless of the chilly swim he'd taken.

The woman in her propelled her feet forward, daring to approach the surly beast. "I know there is danger," she ventured. "It's why I came . . ." Her lashes fluttered low, unable to meet his tiger-sharp glare as she confessed, "Lately, I only feel safe when I'm with you."

"Alexandra." Her name escaped him as a pleading groan before he wet his full lower lip with his tongue. "You could have been hurt today, or worse. It never occurred to me this might be the life we shared. That by making you a duchess, I also marked you for days like this. I don't stay still for long, and I don't always travel the safe roads. I've enemies, and if you remain married to me, they'll become yours as well."

"We both have enem—" She cut off, her puzzlement giving way to astonishment as she digested what he'd just said. "What do you mean, if I *remain* married to you?"

"We've not yet consummated our union." He bit out the words as though they offended him. "You . . . have a choice."

Was he referring to annulment? "You want me to leave you?" she gasped.

"Tell me, wife, is all this worth a life bound to me? The filth, the adversaries, the notoriety. I'm the reason toda—"

"It *is worth it*," she rushed. "I—I know it hasn't been long, but I've felt more alive in the last nine days I've known you than I have in the past nine *years*. This life is what I love, what I've always wanted, don't you understand that? Dig sites and dirt and the dead. I crave travel, knowledge, and adventure, like you. I think we can both find that together, can't we? Granted, fewer attempts on our lives would be preferable. But that's all my . . ." She pressed her lips together just in time.

My fault.

Stunned, she blinked up at him. He still didn't know. He didn't know that every time he'd saved her from a threat, it was one her own past had wrought upon them both. Today, her friends and her husband might have been crushed in the tunnels.

Unless one of *them* had perpetrated the incident.

My fault.

The familiar verdict ripped through her with the strength of a tidal wave.

What could she confess? What should she withhold? He could have been killed. He deserved to know . . . something.

If not everything.

But it wasn't only her secret to tell. Jean-Yves was on his own native soil for the first time in years. They could arrest him right away should his part in de Marchand's death be revealed. Francesca and Cecelia were who-knew-where, and she didn't know how to get word to them should things go awry.

If she told now . . . Redmayne could protect her. He might know what to do.

If she told him now . . . he could react like any number

of men would. He'd take control from her. He'd stampede over a situation she'd balanced so carefully and tear it wide open, dooming her friends and damning himself in the process.

And the worst scenario of all . . .

If she told him now . . . he could condemn her. Turn her in to the authorities and be done with her. Pick another wife, a virgin one, and get as many heirs as he needed upon someone else.

Alexandra searched his face, watching a storm build in his eyes as similar clouds gathered in the north sky.

Surely he wouldn't. Not after the vows he'd made, after the intimacies they'd shared.

She couldn't deny the bond threading through the space between them. She wanted to trust that he wouldn't turn on her.

They were going into Le Havre tomorrow to get her money. Hopefully she could negotiate new terms with her tormentor. She could find out what her blackmailer ultimately wanted from her.

If it came down to it, she'd sacrifice herself for them. For him.

They always spoke of trust, didn't they? Perhaps she could show him a little.

Seized by an agony of indecision, she chewed on the inside of her lip. "I—I wanted to speak with you about the dig . . ."

"I'm not simply referring to the dig, Alexandra," he growled, throwing his arms wide to present her with his magnificent form. "I'm asking you. Demanding of you, an honest answer!"

"I'm trying to tell you—"

"Would you have me like this?" He gestured to his features. "With nothing? Would you be my wife, even if you were not a duchess? Would you still dig for me with your bare hands if you didn't need my heir in order to spend my fortune? Can you remain with me even if it means those who want what's mine might try to take it by any means? Because if you're hurt, I don't think I can—"

"Yes, *dammit,*" she hissed, realizing they were both having a different conversation, but his needed to be addressed so he could calm himself enough to hear her. If he wanted some truths, these she could give. "You're big and arrogant, wicked and bad-tempered, and I . . . I can't help but want to spend every single moment by your side. So, stop being so bloody overbearing and listen to me for just one—"

Redmayne seized her, compelling her silence with his descending lips. His kiss was an erotic demand and possessive embrace as he propelled them both toward the cliff wall without breaking their intimate contact. He devoured her, ravished her mouth, drawing her lips open with his thumb and thrusting his tongue inside.

His big body drove her against the cliff, his arms plunging beneath her arms to cup the back of her head and shoulders, protecting her from the earth.

He was like a human incinerator, immolating her with his carnal heat.

Alexandra felt light-headed, not only disoriented by the swiftness of his kiss, but by the change in him. This was no patient, roguish seduction. This man grinding her against his very powerful, very naked body heeded no rules and brokered no patience.

He'd become a creature of raw, animalian need.

It wasn't until he leaned his hips against her that Alexandra realized his towel no longer remained around his hips. He rotated his pelvis in slow, erotic circles, the ridge of his erection much larger now than when he'd emerged from the sea.

Terrifyingly so.

He broke their kiss to drag his lips down her jaw. "My God, wife," he moaned. "I can't take another moment of this. Of wanting." His hands tangled in her hair as he abraded her sensitive skin with his beard before soothing it with his lips. "The idea that I could have died without making love to you is untenable. Impossible."

Oversensitized and overwhelmed, Alexandra placed her hands on his biceps, hoping to anchor herself into this moment. Trying to keep time from falling away beneath her, merging this moment and another.

The past didn't belong here. Not in his embrace.

She did everything she could to rein in her galloping heart. To gulp air into her lungs. He was her husband. He was kind and considerate and . . . she had nothing to fear.

She did not . . . fear . . . him.

"We can wait," she whispered against his ear, smoothing a hand down the iron cords of his back. "Three more days. I don't want you to regret—"

"I don't fucking care about that anymore, I just need to be inside you. *Now.*" The hand in her hair curled into a fist, tugging her chin higher, exposing her throat to him so he could stroke and lave at the delicate skin there, nipping at it with his teeth.

His other arm lifted her against him, parting her legs so he could settle his hips between them.

Pinning her.

Pinning her down.

Pulling up her skirts.

Cold shards of sharp ice extinguished what heat had built in her womb, dousing it with a terror so pure and absolute, it seized every part of her until even her skin felt scoured raw by it.

She couldn't speak.

Couldn't scream.

Couldn't breathe.

Feebly, she tugged at his arms to no avail. Panic stole the strength from her limbs just as brutally as it had seized her throat.

Her fingers curled into talons, nails biting into the flesh of his arms. He hissed, but the pain only served to inflame him further, causing him to press more insistently against her.

Helpless tears sprang to her eyes. Every one of her muscles locked tight and finally, *finally,* she was able to sob in a breath, dragging the strength into her lungs to push into her trembling limbs.

With a burst of power, drawn from the deepest recesses of her pain, she heaved him away from her.

He stumbled back a step, emitting an oath of puzzled opposition.

Alexandra sprang forward, bolting around him, evading his reach.

"What—Alex—?"

She shook her head again and again as she backed away from him. Injected with an instinct and an energy as old and necessary as life, itself, she turned on her heel and fled.

Fled his body and his unslaked desire. Fled the intimidating sex he'd meant to drive inside of her, and the desperate sound of her name ripped away from him by the wind. Wind that now tore the tears from her eyes and whipped her with loose tendrils of her damp hair, stinging her cheeks and invading her mouth.

She ran until she ran out of beach. Pumping her legs so

swiftly, she wasn't certain her feet touched the sand. She ran until her lungs threatened to burst. Scampered up the stairs even though her ankles ached, and her thighs seized.

She ran away from ten years of grief and pain and guilt and fear. She ran from the almost doglike confusion clouding her husband's savage features. From constant anxiety for her friends, and the persistent threat of discovery. Of death. Of retribution.

And even as she ran hard and fast and long enough to possibly kill her, a part of her knew it was all for naught.

Because she could never escape what she'd done. What had been done to her.

When she had such demons chasing her, she didn't even notice if hotel staff or guests gawked as she raced through the hotel to her rooms, locking the world out.

Every part of her hurt. Burned. Inside and out.

Wanting to go nowhere near a bed, she dove into the corner between her wardrobe and the wall, pulling her knees up into her chest and locking her arms around them, making herself as small as she possibly could. Her trembles became quakes, and then bone-clenching convulsions.

She tried to stop. To breathe. To cry. What little logic she still possessed began to lose hope. To fear that this was her new reality. That she'd been pushed beyond the brink of sanity. Her body was no longer her own. Her fears no longer contained.

She'd become her worst nightmare.

Helpless.

Even against herself.

Burying her face against her knees, she bit down on her skirts, filling her mouth with the taste of salt and wind and silk.

The scream crawling up her throat finally erupted, muffled by the fabrics as her entire soul rent apart in one quivering, bone-shattering cry of pure, helpless, *hopeless* anguish.

She'd thought she was healing. That her patient, tempting husband opened her body and mind, seducing her into the world of carnality.

But no. She was broken. Damaged. Dirty.

No matter how many baths she took. No matter how many tears she offered. How much restitution she paid or forgiveness she begged. No matter how many years were put between her and the night her body had been invaded. She was damaged. Soiled. Unclean and fallen.

She would never again be innocent.

Because she was not an innocent. But guilty. Of murder. *My fault. My fault. My fault.*

Another scream overtook her as she realized what happened next. Once her husband dressed and came after her, he'd demand answers.

And she'd have to confess. Confess or lie.

Either way, she was damned.

CHAPTER TWENTY-FOUR

Piers availed himself of the service corridor rather than the front entrance. He could bear no more telegrams, or "Your Graces," or, Christ preserve him, fucking archeologists.

He wound his way to the laundry, aware he still clenched his soiled towel in a death grip, and he searched for a pile of such grubby linens in which to abandon it. That accomplished, he pumped a trencher of water, and rinsed the sand from his hair over a basin, snatching up another towel with which to scrub his scalp dry.

Straightening, he caught sight of his reflection in the mirror, and was reminded of why he never did that anymore.

He still looked like a monster.

And today, with his wife, he'd acted like one.

He looked above him, as though his gaze could penetrate the stories between them and spy upon his bride in the tower suite. The urge to go to her was a physical drive, tugging and straining until his boots relented and took a step.

His conscience, however, nailed those boots to the floor.

Today had been . . . a disaster. In every catastrophic way imaginable. But until a few moments ago, he'd not realized the extent of the damage he'd wrought.

All this time, he'd been such a dunce. A self-absorbed ass.

He'd thought his wife shy. Or cerebral. Awkward and self-conscious, perhaps. Deliberate and overanalytical.

He assumed she feared him because he was big, mean, and terrifyingly unattractive.

It'd never occurred to him, self-obsessed duke that he was, that her behavior had nothing at all to do with *him*.

Squeezing his eyes shut against the truth did little to help. The pure, unfiltered terror with which she'd regarded him was now branded on the backs of his eyelids. The frantic, extraordinary strength it had taken to shove him away. The desperate speed she'd used to escape him. He'd witnessed that kind of behavior before. In prey animals.

When they ran for their lives.

His breath rattled in and out of his chest as he drew it deep. A thousand possible scenarios barraging him with vivid and hellish vibrancy.

He hadn't known his wife long, but today he'd learned something new. Something devastating.

Someone had hurt her.

And without realizing it, he'd reopened a wound inflicted by another man.

Turning to avoid shattering the mirror with his fist, he caught sight of some of his clothes folded neatly on a table, and several garments hanging on a line, a few of them belonging to Alexandra.

He drifted toward her intimate undergarments, remembering a frustration from the night on the veranda with a sick clench in his belly. He'd tried to touch her through the slit in her drawers, and was unable to.

His fingers shook as he took the delicate item down from the pins, opening the beribboned legs to uncover a row of curious stitches at the seam.

A surge of furious heat overtook him with such force, he thought he might breathe fire rather than give credence to the word battering at every mental wall he could possibly erect.

A figure froze in the doorway. "I'm sorry, Your Grace." Constance Murphy's gentle voice still grated like wind-whipped sand, chipping away his paper-thin veneer of civility. "I—I'll come back."

Recognizing her as someone whose family had worked for the Redmaynes for generations, as someone he'd selected as his wife's lady's maid, he held up a hand to stay her. He didn't look away from the little stitches as he forced the words through his lips. "Did she bid you stitch these, thus?"

She paused so long, he fought the urge to throttle an answer from her. "Nay, Your Grace, my lady does it, herself."

"It is wonderous odd, don't you think?" He finally looked over at her, meeting her young, solemn gaze.

"Wonderous odd," she agreed, staring at what he gripped in his hands with a stark sort of sadness.

"What do you make of it?"

She looked back at him as though he were daft.

As well she should.

Piers begged her with his eyes, pleaded with her to give him some explanation other than the black, ugly conclusion now amalgamating in his mind, adhering like tar and pitch.

"Your Grace?" she breathed.

"Why would a woman do this?" he bit out through clenched teeth.

He already knew. Of course he did. Before Constance's chin wobbled. Before her eyes welled, turning an unflattering shade of pink. He knew what she would say, because he'd been rejecting the gut-wrenching, unthinkable truth with every step he'd taken toward the hotel.

It was why he hadn't chased Alexandra when she'd fled.

Abruptly, he changed his mind. He didn't want the girl to answer his question anymore, but she did, goddamn her.

"Mayhap, Your Grace, her only worry in regard to her"—she gestured to the garment, unable to find the words—"inn't convenience, but protection."

Protection.

A wave of emotion inundated him, threatening to pull him under a violent tide of grief and fury. He flushed hot, then cold, shivers of goose pimples breaking out on his skin even as he thought he might burst into flames when a brilliant, almost luminescent rage surged through every fiber of his being.

Was he fire? Or was he ice?

What he was, was an idiot. A blind, selfish, fucking worthless rutting imbecile.

"I'll . . . come back, Your Grace."

He barely marked the maid's watery offer, nor her exit as he examined the painstakingly perfect rows sewn into Alexandra's undergarments.

She'd never taken a lover.

But a man had taken *her*. Against her will.

Everything about her, since the first moment they'd met, clicked into place like a terrible, blood-chilling puzzle.

When Mercury had almost crushed her, she'd winced away from Piers's touch. Not because he was the Terror of Torcliff, ugly and scarred, but because he was a *man*.

Alexandra had kept the gun at her side while they'd walked together on Maynemouth Moor, her finger close to the trigger.

For protection.

Not against assassins, but against *him*.

Frustrated wrath welled within him as her endearingly artless seduction the night she'd proposed now became something altogether insidious.

He'd thought her an overwrought, spinster virgin who'd had too many years to research, contemplate, and *complicate* a very simple act of pleasure.

But no. Yet again, he couldn't have been more mistaken.

The thought of their wedding night had caused her so much distress, she'd come to "get it over with."

Her list . . . Those conditions he'd found both absurd and adorable. Dear sweet contemptable *Christ*! The entire fucking time, she'd been trying to figure out a way to not relive a past nightmare.

She hadn't wanted him to use his tongue.

Because someone had used theirs against her, somehow.

She'd wanted them to disrobe.

Because someone hadn't bothered to take their clothing off before—

He stared down at the garment in his hands. The stitches blurred by a narrowing of his vision as red began to bleed into his periphery.

How many times had he made use of the convenient opening with a mistress or a lover?

He'd endeavored to do the same with Alexandra the other night.

Anger tightened his shoulders, then his chest, the tension rippling down his arms until he dropped her undergarment as though it scalded him.

Turning, he searched for something to break.

The table closest to him did nicely. He kicked at it, sending it colliding into the crank press. Then he proceeded to dismantle it violently with fists and boots, fighting the horrific portrait forming in his mind.

She'd requested that they face each other . . .

Because she'd been taken in some dreadful, demeaning fashion.

He ripped something off the wall and smashed it onto the ground.

He'd been too aroused, too utterly entertained by her to truly wonder why she'd asked him to be gentle so as not to do her intimate damage.

Because . . . Because someone . . .

He roared as his gorge rose, and he had to swallow several times, using iron will not to heave the contents of his stomach on to the floor.

Something else violently disintegrated beneath his gathering madness.

He tried. *By God*, he tried not to allow the clues to conjure the images of her . . . like that. But alas, he'd narrowed down her ordeal to a few lurid and unthinkable circumstances.

The portrait screamed at him, and he wished she could rip open his skull and scrub the image from his mind.

So he ripped other things, clothing, linen, rending them so they matched the tattered shreds of his humanity.

God! The things he'd accused her of. The ruthless seduction he'd all but forced upon her on their wedding night. She'd requested the lights off, not so she couldn't see his face, but so he couldn't see her fear.

He'd been so uncompromising about her shyness, so relentless in his all-consuming desire.

And so unforgivably cruel when he'd thought she'd lied about her virginity.

She'd not been acting the innocent, she'd truly not known what to do. She'd never experienced pleasure before, only pain.

You claim you've never been kissed? Well, you sure as hell have been fucked.

A raw, torturous breath hissed out of his throat as a fathomless, abysmal pit of regret, shock, and self-disgust threatened to buckle his legs from beneath him.

Like the monster he'd never wanted to be, he'd tortured his poor wife.

The games. The teasing. The agonizing anticipation of ten days, when all she wanted was to be done with her wifely duties. To have the untenable obligation in her past, instead of looming like a sword over her head.

Because the expectation of a terrible thing was often worse than the reality of it.

And how had he finally approached that situation this evening? By pressing his inflamed, naked body against her. Kissing her with all the savage lust unleashed by a brush with death and exacerbated by her exquisite feminine beauty.

He'd pinned her to a chalky cliff, imprisoned her with his oafish body, intent on wrapping her strong, lovely legs around his waist so he could fuck all the life-affirming desire roaring through him into her.

No woman deserved that for their first time with a new lover, no matter how many she'd had before, let alone a woman with her particular trauma.

The crimson-hued wave of rage receded, and another tide of exhaustion overtook him as he surveyed the devastation he'd wrought on the laundry room.

It shamed him that he'd acted thus, but he couldn't have faced her filled with such impotent, violent, passionate hatred.

Never. He'd never frighten her like that. Never face her with the fury contained within him. Not as long as he lived.

He needed this fatigue in order to maintain the gentility she'd require of their next interaction. Because, even now, a cold splash of murderous haze lingered inside of him. Longing to demand answers from her.

Like who? And how? And where could he find the— he dare not even call him a man—the mud-sucking villain?

Because every breath he took was borrowed from the devil. Every day since the terrible day he'd put his hands on her would be carved out of his flesh.

Yes. A Redmayne's revenge was slow. It would be wet. It would be messy. Methodical. And ultimately lethal.

But now was not a time for that. First, before he could hunt down and take apart a true monster, he must do his level best to put his wife back together.

She deserved that, at least, to feel safe with him. From him.

Carefully, he retrieved her drawers and hung them just as they'd been before, his hands visibly trembling. They seemed so small and pretty and clean in a room afflicted with such disarray.

Turning, he went to find her, prepared to answer for his crimes against her, whether intended or not.

In the hallway, Constance single-handedly held back a bevy of wide-eyed clerks, porters, and his favored maître d'. They all gaped at him, some with wariness, and others with apparent concern.

"I'll replace all that is broken on the morrow, and pay for any extra work I've caused," he offered wearily. "I couldn't . . . go to her—"

"Do not you worry yourself, Your Grace," Constance

said in a small, kind voice. "They only know what they need to, but they understand."

"They understand what?" he asked, not wishing to have brought any embarrassment to his wife.

Constance opened her mouth to reply, but a young, swarthy porter beat her to it.

"Quelqu'un a essayé de nuire à la femme qu'il aime."

Wearily, Piers turned to take the back stairs up to her room, not allowing himself to contemplate why he didn't bother to correct the boy.

Someone tried to harm the woman he loves.

When Piers didn't immediately find Alexandra upon opening the door to her room, he called her name, allowing his eyes to adjust to the dimness.

No lamps had been lit, and daylight had almost faded entirely, giving way to an early gloom. Other than the cream damask curtains performing a ghostly dance at the open balcony doors, everything in the cozy suite remained still.

A magnetic awareness tuned the fine hairs on his neck and arms. A charged pull as subtle and as potent as that of the moon on the tides drew him around to find her. On the other side of the bed, tucked between the wardrobe and the wall, Alexandra stared stone-faced and unmoving, her arms around her knees and her gaze fixed on the far wall.

This time, when he said her name, it was in an aching whisper.

She flinched, but didn't look at him. Not until he made his way around the bed, slowing to attempt a careful approach.

Countless questions and platitudes sprang to his lips, the first of which was: *Are you all right?*

But he bit down on his lip, refusing to ask the insipid question. Because, of course, she wasn't all right.

And part of that was his doing.

In a swift but oddly graceful motion, she pushed away from the wall and stood, stepping out to face him. Her back straight and shoulders squared, like a martyr readying to meet her fate. He yearned to help her, to hold her, but wasn't certain she'd even want him to touch her just now.

The soft blue of an overcast gloaming painted her a paler shade of ivory than he'd ever seen. Tears smudged bruises beneath her eyes and pain etched hollows below her cheekbones. Her lips, swollen with her grief, with *his* kisses, glistened as they shook.

Someone had turned her beauty into her tragedy. Despite her simple attire and her serviceable style, she was possessed of a poise and proportions that were eminently desirable.

To look at her was to appreciate something rare and irrevocably flawless. A brilliant, mercurial woman with a smile full of secrets. More of a masterpiece than the *Mona Lisa*.

Lovelier. More seductive.

What made a man think that he could do aught but appreciate such a work of art? What sort of fiend would help himself to her innocence without her consent?

When her pleasure was so radiant, how could anyone stand to cause her pain?

Even though two identical rivers of tears unceasingly flowed down her cheeks, her voice remained steady when she spoke. "I owe you an explanation."

"Alexandra." He took a step toward her, and shriveled a little inside when she retreated a step away. "I know."

The preparatory breath she took shuddered through her entire body. "Let . . . let me start by apologizing . . . for—"

"Don't you dare." This time he advanced, but curled his fists firmly at his sides to keep from holding her. The effort took more restraint than he credited himself with.

"I *know,*" he repeated. "I know your secret. The one you've desperately been trying to hide from me all this time."

Her breath hitched as she went from pale to gray, then stopped breathing altogether.

"Someone . . . raped you, didn't he?"

He said it.

The word he'd been avoiding for what felt like *hours.* It scraped his throat like shards of glass, leaving his tongue with an acid taste of disgust and regret. But it had to be uttered. To be aired, this secret they had between them.

Her face crumpled first, followed by her body.

She folded over, curling around herself as her legs completely failed her and she sank to the floor in a pool of ivory skirts. Her arms locked around her middle, as though doing so could somehow keep her together. She rocked back and forth as a low, awful sound burst from her mouth. Followed by another, forcing its way through her clenched teeth.

Sobs, he realized, terrible reverberations of anguish. She fought a losing battle against them, doing her best to bite them down. To swallow them. Going so far as to clamp both her hands over her mouth.

But they rose. Like demons they rose, ripping their way out of her and into the night.

Piers dropped along with her, hitting his knees. Reaching, but not touching. Aching, but not speaking. Because language hadn't yet invented words for this sort of pain, and therefore neither had it words far comfort.

Despite this, or because of it, a miracle happened.

She surged forward, falling into his arms in a storm of tears and pain and a mass of mahogany hair.

He gathered her to him, settling her in his lap right there on the floor, folding over her as she wept and shuddered, sobbed and clung. Her face buried itself against his heart as it broke alongside hers, drenching it with her tears.

He cupped her head to him, not wanting her to see the wells of his own emotion. His tear didn't take the track it should down his cheek, but was interrupted by the grooves of his scar, diverted somewhere into his beard.

He'd trade his castle just to erase her memory of the deed. He'd offer his name, his title, his fortune to turn back the sands of time, to prevent it from ever happening. Nay, he'd give his life for it.

For her.

Christ, how brave she'd been. Selling herself to the Terror of Torcliff, trading her ill-treated body to a monster in order to save her family's honor.

She'd built a life before him, filled it with unique and singular accomplishments.

There was no one like her, and *she'd* asked *him* to be hers.

He'd not seen the offer as the gift it was, not at the time.

What an undeserving fool he was. An utter, unmitigated ass. Why had he been so worried about his legacy in the first place? What small and ridiculous thing would his revenge against his cousin accomplish? Come to think of it, what had *he* ever accomplished? He'd done little more than be born to please himself. His birthright was nothing more than an unbroken line of barbarians who'd once killed enough people to indebt a king to them.

He may be a duke, but *she* was the prize. A doctor, a linguist, and a lady. Someone with purpose and meaning.

As her tempest of grief and rage fizzled down to a misting, hiccupping cry, he crooned softly to her, humbled in a way he'd never before imagined.

She was his.

Beyond that, he was hers. And, if she wanted, he would remain so, no matter what.

For he'd blessed few virtues, but faithfulness was one of them.

"I'll never touch you like that again," he vowed, lifting her chin with the crook of his finger, thumbing away a stray tear. "Alexandra, you'll never have to fear me. I'll be your husband in all ways, but I'll never require you to share my bed."

She gave a watery sniff as more tears leaked into her hair and it took her several shuddering breaths to speak. "Wh-what about . . . your title?" she whispered. "Your heirs?"

"Let Patrick have the whole bleeding thing," he murmured. "I care not anymore. These past few days with you have showed me what really matters, and my legacy, such as it is, is of little consequence."

"R-really?" She dashed away some of the moisture on her cheeks, moisture he longed to kiss and taste and soothe with his lips and body. For that, unfortunately, was how he communicated, what he understood. Things that were unspoken. Conveyed with touch and looks and gestures.

This would be a sacrifice. One he gladly made for her.

"I know the past is important to you, and the future was just as much an obsession of mine. But after today, I've come to realize that it's right now that matters." He searched her dear face, daring to brush at her cheeks with his knuckles.

"The man in that tomb, my ancestor, he never saw the glory his son brought his name. And the strangers who buried him cared not for his traditions, they simply walled him away on unholy ground. And all I can think is . . . does it even matter? What will I care for my castle and my title when I am gone? Why live only to make my holdings greater when I die? Why not, instead, spend my life, my fortune, giving you the life you want? The experiences you deserve."

Some of the warmth of epiphany left him as his dark thoughts turned to the reason they were sprawled on the floor thusly. "Right after I reap a very Viking form of justice on the man who—"

"I can't—I can't talk about that just now." Her voice broke, and Piers swallowed a surge of a temper he thought he'd exhausted.

"I'm sorry."

"Piers?" she whispered, her voice hoarse with emotion. "I—I don't want you to stop touching me. I liked it. I needed it. I didn't know that about myself before. But you were so gentle—and skilled . . ." She ducked her head low again, hiding her features from him. "You made me feel beautiful," she said against his chest. "You made me forget."

Her words ignited a spark of hope not only in his heart, but in his body. One he quelled with brutal will.

"I frightened you today . . . and I know I have been pitiless with you before. I accused you of lying, when you were only protecting a painful secret. All I could see were the reasons I had to mistrust you. I never considered your reasons not to trust me might have been even more powerful. And for that, I am more sorry than you know."

She gave a shaky sigh, expelling the exhaustion of a good cry and, he liked to think, the relief of an unburdened conscience. "I don't want to have a secret. Any secret. But for so long, I've felt much like an open book with a page torn out. I appear completely ordinary. But if you try to read me, to know me, it's impossible, because there's something missing. Something lost."

Pressing his lips to her damp hairline, Piers savored the fragrance of her. "You, my wife, are anything but ordinary. You're perfect."

She pulled back a little, gazing up at him with those dark, assessing eyes. He wondered what she could see in the gathering shadows. Probably more than most could at noonday.

She swallowed twice before she could bring herself to speak. "I'd like to hope nothing much has changed between us. I still want a family. Children. *Your* children, I mean. I want to . . . to make love to you. I just don't . . . I don't know how."

He let out a long, strained breath, both elated and humbled. "Alexandra . . ."

She tensed. "I understand if . . . if this alters your desires. I'm not a virgin. I'm an entire mess, and if you no longer want—"

"Dear God, no!" He trailed his lips over her forehead, down her temples. Pressing little chaste, worshipping kisses to her cheekbones, her nose, the corners of her lips.

She turned her face to him, pressing her still-wobbling mouth against his own.

He let her, soaking in the kiss until she broke it with a great sniff.

He'd give his soul for a handkerchief.

"I feel better now." She sighed. "I think . . . I think I can try . . ."

He lifted her, carrying her to the bed and settling her upon it. He stretched out next to her, behind her, tucking her body gently against his, and scooping out a protective cocoon for her.

"Tomorrow," he said.

"What?" She lifted her head, but he guided it back to rest on his arm.

"Tomorrow." He traced little symbols of comfort over her arms. "Or the next day. Or whatever day you are ready. Once the tears have dried and the fear is departed . . ."

And he felt a little less like murdering someone.

Once someone had ceased trying to murder him.

Relaxing, she nodded, her lithe form shuddering a few more times.

"Tomorrow," she whispered around fresh tears. "Piers?"

"Yes, darling."

"What do I do now?"

"Now," he rumbled, doing his best to match his breath with hers, touching her with comfort rather than need. "Now you allow me to hold you. To watch over you as you sleep in my arms."

She nodded, leaning deeper into his embrace.

Piers held her the entire night, searching the darkness for answers he knew were not there. He wouldn't rip information from her she wasn't ready to give. He wouldn't touch her unless she asked him to.

He would search out his enemies and put them in the ground, for they posed a threat to her as well. Then, when she was safe, he'd tear the world apart until he found the man who'd done this.

And avenge her.

CHAPTER TWENTY-FIVE

Alexandra had expected to suffer through the following day, to spend each moment dreading her midnight reckoning. Likewise, she'd feared a heavy and melancholy change in the dynamic between her and her husband after the overwrought, if emotionally intimate, night they'd spent in each other's arms.

However, as she and Redmayne trundled along the scenic cliff road from Le Havre to Seasons-sur-Mer in a coach burdened by a veritable treasure trove, she felt lighter than she had in years.

A smile broke over her as she enjoyed the brilliant sunset and laughed at her husband's own brand of wry humor. Was this what joy felt like? A cluster of hours nearly free of care, every moment filled to the brim with delight, each one a distinct flavor and all of them sweet.

Their first stop in Le Havre had been the bank, where Redmayne withdrew a mind-boggling amount of money and relinquished it to her as though he'd given her a mere trinket.

On the subject of trinkets, she'd never realized that a man could have the emotional and financial fortitude to shop like a Redmayne. Pillaging coastal villages and such was a trait handed down to him by his ancestors, and evidently, her husband awoke hell-bent on honoring his lineage to the fullest. The notable difference being, of course, he paid rather than plundered.

Paid handsomely, in fact.

Never mind hacking through foreign jungles and forging lethal rivers. Redmayne conquered the entire market street and beyond with a singular focus, spoiling her as though it was a mission given him by the queen.

He plied her with costly gifts, insisting on a garnet set of jewelry he claimed matched her hair and eyes. The earrings, brooch, bracelet, and watch cost more than she thought it should, but he'd not even bothered to barter with the jeweler.

After a few disconcerting extravagances, Alexandra had begun to contain her appreciation of anything, worried they'd end up going home with it. If she exclaimed over an intricate telescope, he bought it and the matching sextant and compass. If a scarf caught her eye, he commissioned it in every color. He didn't restrain his purchases to those she admired, but procured her French and foreign things he thought she might like, such as a jewel-encrusted Moroccan lantern, or a book written by Sir Grégoire-Pierre Leveaux, the famous sixteenth-century explorer. It charmed and delighted her how easily he matched her tastes without needing to ask.

He insisted she pick several ready-made skirts and blouses from a shop window, and he obtained a few new articles of clothing, himself, mentioning something vague about an incident in the laundry room.

It embarrassed her a little, how many times he vowed

to take her to the dress shop in Rouen Julia went on and on about.

"These will do just fine," she said, hoping the shop-keeper didn't speak English, for fear he'd offended her. "I have no need for Rouen."

Alexandra had never considered herself a materialistic woman, as a frequent traveler must select her things with economy, but she couldn't say she didn't enjoy herself immensely.

She could barely contain her gratitude when he recommended she select a gift or two for Cecelia and Francesca. She found a vastly expensive decorative abacus for Cecil, and agonized over Frank until he suggested a new riding crop with a lovely and intricate but eminently practical handle.

He whipped his own thigh with it, testing its merit.

Alexandra knew she'd forever keep that moment locked in her memory, the most precious acquisition of the entire day. The Terror of Torcliff, a bearded menace with the reputation of a demon, lost in a distracted, boyish fantasy, swiping at the air with a riding crop as though it were a fencing sword.

"I'll thank you to school the ridicule from your regard, Doctor," he bade with a lopsided smile upon noticing her intent gaze. "I was merely conducting a thorough scientific analysis."

"And what has your analysis concluded?" she inquired, suspecting she was unable to school much of anything from her features, not even the strange, aching profusion of luminescence in her heart.

He held the crop before him with as much fanfare as Arthur's Excalibur. "I proclaim this item an excellent offering for even the most discerning outdoorsman, or outdoorswoman, as is the case."

She plucked it from his hand, tapping him on the arm with it. "We scientists do not proclaim, we deduce."

He merely laughed. "Now that you're a duchess, you should indulge in the odd proclamation. Much less work than a deduction, and yet often just as startingly effective."

She wondered if the world would ever recognize that the Terror of Torcliff had never been a terror at all. But a man. A man possessed of so much wit, skill, charm, intellect, and humor, he was forever surprising her. Often delighting her.

Enchanting her, even.

If she did anything for her husband, she vowed, it would be to make certain everyone else accepted that, as well.

Finally exhausted after hours of shopping, they strolled along the waterfront, where he'd drawn her into idle conversation about her family. They'd wandered into a café offering the most delectable pastries filled with delicacies both savory and sweet. As their nibble became a gorge, they spoke of her antics with the Red Rogues as an impetuous girl.

For once, her girlhood memories weren't tainted with what came after. She could look at the joy and the innocence she'd shared with her dearest friends and appreciate it for the treasure the relationships had been.

That they still were.

He'd been appropriately charmed and chagrined at her account of the time Cecelia had been caught reading a lurid novel in a deportment class. The mistress had forced her to read a passage aloud, and then almost expired from the vapors as poor Cecelia read a particularly salacious scene between two star-crossed lovers.

They'd savored sumptuous custards as they spoke of Francesca's dark wit, inflexible will, and impetuous temper, painting horrific alternate futures wherein he'd actually married her.

He'd wiped tears of laughter from his eyes, and held patiently still as she picked a spot of cream from his beard with her handkerchief.

It was almost as though they had no secrets from each other.

And they almost didn't.

On the carriage ride home, the currency in her purse was heavy at her side as she tucked her arm into Redmayne's and rested her temple against his shoulder.

He pressed a short, temperate kiss to her forehead and patted her gloved hand indulgently.

It was the first time he'd touched her all day.

The thought drew the corners of Alexandra's mouth into a pensive frown. He treated her as though she was a precious antique, already chipped and on the verge of breaking. Though she enjoyed his more relaxed and charming company, and was grateful for his tender care of her, she wasn't certain she liked this new dynamic between them.

The restrained, almost virtuous edge to his need.

It very much resembled distance.

She missed the Terror of Torcliff. Rougish, wicked, assertive barbarian that he was.

They required a veritable train of porters as they swept into the hotel, and the concierge met them at the bottom of the stairs with a message.

The laborers had tirelessly dug out the entry of the catacombs, enough for the engineer to safely go in and investigate it in the daylight on the morrow if Redmayne desired to be present.

The reminder of the danger smothered their good humor.

They didn't speak of it through their tense dinner, as a

mighty wind curled the whitecapped waves high against the beach. Nor did they mention anything of import as they mounted the three flights of stairs to find their suites at the end of the evening.

They didn't speak about much of anything, in fact, as there was too much to say, and nowhere to begin.

He kissed her at the door, and bade her a solemn, tender good night. "Come to me," he invited. "If you need anything."

Alexandra stood in her doorway, an invitation perched on her tongue as she watched his broad, straight back until it disappeared into his rooms.

She'd so much to ponder and to dread. The meeting. The money. The murder. All the possible outcomes of a confrontation.

It settled her mind, somewhat, to learn the catacombs were now open. Though she battled nerves about ever setting foot in there again, she also hadn't received any new notes about an alternate meeting place.

Now that she had the money, she was anxious to get on with it.

She obsessed over the identity of who would reveal themselves to her as Constance dressed her for bed with an extra attention that both bemused and moved her.

Once they'd bade each other good night, she selected a skirt, wide belt, and simple blouse from her purchases she could hide beneath her dark cloak.

That accomplished, Alexandra perched on her bed and glanced at the clock. Quarter to ten. She still had over three hours. Three hours to allow the howl of the wind to slowly drive her mad.

Drifting to her husband's door, she heard the murmur of voices and the faint rustles of footsteps over the din of the night. She pressed her ear to the cool wood, listening to the masculine percussions of his friendly but perfunctory conversation with his valet.

Though it made her feel pathetic, she stayed like that, letting his voice and proximity create a welcome distraction. The steps faded, and the light was doused, but for the faint glow of what she assumed was a bedside lamp.

Alexandra heard the protestations of the bed as he settled his heavy frame into it. Finally, she drifted to her own bed, collapsing onto her back.

His presence thrummed through the wall with an almost palpable vibration, and Alexandra occupied herself by picturing him beneath the enormous canopy, his brawny limbs stretched long and splayed in indolent repose.

Her body came alive at the image that invoked, tingling with a restless, anticipatory sensation she summarily rejected.

What did he do before sleep claimed him? Did he read? Or ponder the view of the hectic sea? He didn't strike her as a man who would keep a journal, though often explorers such as they were known to do so.

Did he think about her? Or write about her? What would he say?

Did he still want her?

Tomorrow, he'd offered. *Or whenever you're ready.*

Tomorrow was never guaranteed, for anyone, especially them. The threat to her life hadn't passed, and she faced a possible enemy tonight with obscure but obviously nefarious intentions. What if the money wasn't enough anymore? What if the entire world discovered her crime?

Could Redmayne protect her then? Would he? It was one thing to keep the secret of a victim, but another thing, entirely, to perjure oneself for a murderess. One who'd put your life in danger on multiple occasions.

Redmayne suspected his own enemies to be responsible

for the recent attempts on their lives, but he'd also noted that it was her appearance that started the happenings in the first place.

It didn't make sense that a blackmailer would want their target dead.

But she wasn't, was she? She'd never truly been harmed.

Could he be so insidious, so ingenious, that he'd meant for her to survive everything?

Could it be that his aim was to terrorize her, to illustrate just how easily he could take everyone she cared about from her if she failed to pay?

Which now included her husband. A man she'd only known for nine days.

Ten, at the stroke of midnight.

She tossed and turned, wresting herself into a sitting position as a memory of something he'd said tore through her.

The idea that I could have died without making love to you is untenable. Impossible.

She made a sound of pure disbelief as a not altogether foreign ache settled low in her belly. Lower. Intimate muscles clenched around a slick sort of emptiness the moment before she sprang from the bed.

No time for contemplation, not when there was still a chance she could change her mind.

The idea that de Marchand might be the only man to completely have her. That her husband might learn the truth. Or worse.

That she might die before making love to him . . . *was* untenable.

Impossible.

Especially now, when her desire surged with more intensity than her fear.

She padded across the floor and pressed her ear to the

door once again. The dim light of a lantern still glowed beneath the seam, but all sound was smothered by the blustery night.

Drawing in a deep breath, she gripped the door latch and inched it open with the flat of her hand.

She heard her name before she peeked her head around, an answer—an invitation—poised on her lips.

At the sight of him, all her wits deserted her, the powerful tableau stealing what breath she had in her lungs and what words her mind could form. She gripped the latch of the door tighter, steadying herself as a dizzying rush of blood invaded her head.

Redmayne was, indeed, recumbent upon the edge of the bed, eyes closed, head tossed back, throat exposed. A strapping leg stretched along the snowy linens of his mattress, the other foot anchored on the floor. One hand curled into the sheets, gripping rhythmically.

The other around his sex.

Her heart leaped into her throat, and she had to swallow several times, gaping as he dragged his fist down the thick, sleek shaft, pausing at the thatch of onyx hair, before pulling the opposite way.

His features twisted into a grimace of something akin to pain, but not quite. The grooves at the edges of his eyes deepened with strain, as though his lids would never part again.

The wind, welcomed in by his open window, noisily tossed that one recalcitrant forelock over those sealed lids as his breath hitched and released.

For a second, or maybe an eternity, Alexandra stared at the organ he stroked between his legs. Duskier in hue than the hand around it, it jutted proud and thick and . . . long enough to make each fall of his fist quite the journey.

It would never fit inside of her, there was simply no possible way—

Her core tightened, almost insistently, releasing an alarming rush of moisture.

A dark pleasure sound dragged from his chest, a perfectly timed rejoinder to her body's invitation.

The sculpted contours of his torso bunched and released, knotting with slow thrusts that could have hypnotized her if he'd not growled her name.

Then groaned it.

She glanced back up his body to find his eyes still closed.

He didn't know she stood there.

And still he said her name.

Was this how he wanted her? She marveled, mesmerized by the play of the lantern light, gilding the roped crests and valleys of his abdomen as he slowly rolled his hips in long, torpid motions, pausing with a labored breath before he pulled back.

Above him, perhaps? Not pinned beneath. Not from behind.

Unbidden, she remembered the pistoning slams of her attacker's hips. Short, quick, dry, tearing. That was how she'd assessed men must be inside a woman. How they moved in order to—to finish.

But this . . .

She took an unbidden step toward him, then another. This gentle glide of his hips was like some magnificent, primal dance, his every muscle perfectly controlled. No violence or frenzy.

This won't take long.

Alexandra blinked several times, blocking the words.

What if it did with her husband? Come to think of it, none of her previous encounters with Redmayne had been abbreviated. And, so far as she could tell, he'd already pleasured himself for longer than her entire ordeal with de Marchand had taken.

He seemed in no great hurry to finish. As if he'd learned to become patient with the agony gripping his expression.

Almost . . . as if he enjoyed it.

The breeze brushed her nightgown against her body, abrading nipples so puckered and sensitive, she could bear it no longer.

She peeled it away with a humbled sense that she might be the only creature ever to creep so close to the Duke of Redmayne without him knowing it. He was always so ready. So aware. But in the throes of this wicked, beautiful act, he was utterly vulnerable and yet preternaturally male.

"God," he breathed, his hand sliding faster, his fingers tightening. "Alexandra."

"Piers."

CHAPTER TWENTY-SIX

At the sound of his name, Piers bolted upright and dragged the sheets across his lap. The sight of her did nothing to curb the climax gathering in the twin weights beneath his cock.

He'd have thought her a vision he conjured, a lust-shrouded fantasy. Naked. Ethereal, ephemeral. Possessed of a delicate, unearthly beauty.

If not for the insecurity flickering behind the heat in her burnt-whisky gaze.

Stymied, he closed his eyes and opened them again, just to be sure.

At the sight of her, his cock was beset by an insistent, painful throb so agonizing, he ground his teeth together.

In his fantasy, she'd been sliding her slick body down his shaft, those perfect, pert breasts swaying in a most tantalizing manner every time her hips met his.

And, miraculously, there they were. There *she* stood. In his bedroom. Pale and proud and nude, shivering in the breeze that fluttered at her heavy locks, making them shimmer like the tresses of some pagan goddess.

He dragged his eyes away from her pink nipples. "Alexandra. What are you—what do you—?"

"You said my name." She swiped a nervous tongue across her lower lip, just the one, as her eyes locked on the sheet barely concealing the ridge of his erection.

He grimaced. How long had she been there? How long had she watched as he stroked himself to an illusion of her?

God, but his mind couldn't have conjured anything close to the magnificence of reality.

"Did you say my name because . . . because you imagined me doing . . . that to you?" She nodded to his hand, now clutching the sheet to him.

Panic surged above his lust as he searched her frustratingly placid features. Was she disgusted? Aroused? Afraid?

What should he answer?

He decided upon the truth. At the very least, it would drive her back to the other side of that door. Because he could think of no reason on God's blighted earth that she would be in here with him unless . . .

"No, Alexandra. No, you weren't stroking me with your hand, not in my mind."

"I was—you were—inside of me."

His breath stopped. His heart stuttered, stalled, and then started again, pounding against the cage of his ribs. And still, he answered her with complete honesty. "Yes."

She stepped closer. "I was on top of you?"

He held up his hand. "Don't."

Her composure flickered, unveiling a hurt.

"Alexandra," he rushed around a hoarse throat. "If you come any closer—" Bloody hell, that sounded like a threat.

"I mean . . . You don't have to do this. I told you I wouldn't touch you."

"I know." She stopped right in front of him, her breasts inches from his mouth. Her knees almost touching his. It was torment. Torture. It was pure, spike-riddled hell. But he kept his word, bunching his fists in the sheets.

"I want you, Piers."

His mouth watered, his muscles gathered, and his cock gave an insistent jerk against his thigh.

A wayward strand of hair fluttered over her face, and he yearned to tuck it away, to stroke the downy softness of her cheek. "Are you sure? You have to be sure."

"I wasn't," she answered, her eyes shy and gilded with so many things, not the least of which was sex. "Not until I came in here and saw you . . . like that."

He swallowed a flare of embarrassment at being caught in such an honest moment of need.

It was her fingers that smoothed his errant hair back from his forehead, her touch cool on his lust-fevered skin. "All I know from before you is . . ." She searched for words, her eyes drifting from side to side. "*Was* forceful and fast."

Some of the heat wilted out of him, replaced by a well of sorrow and anger. He thought he'd wanted to know what happened to her and how.

How wrong he'd been. The mere mention of it slayed him.

"But you were . . . slow, just now," she continued. "Deliberate." She bent to him, sliding her hand down his arm until she captured his wrist.

Mesmerized, and frankly petrified, Piers remained mute, his lids peeled wide as she guided his hand to the soft mahogany hair between her legs. She pressed his fingers there, and they easily slid between the plump folds, encountering warm, wet silk.

They each gasped, sharing a shudder of disbelief at the sparks that ignited between them.

"I want you to be the last man inside of me." Guiding his wrist, she rolled his finger over the bud hidden between her closed folds, her gaze turning as liquid as her desire. "I want it to be you. My husband . . ."

He'd heard enough.

Piers lifted himself, reached for her, and dragged her down over him. This he could do. This he would do, what he'd promised from the beginning. Replace the memory of another man with nothing but soul-shattering bliss.

Alexandra didn't realize what it had taken from her to offer this, to request it, until he'd taken the mantle of seducer from her shoulders.

Redmayne remained seated and kept the sheet over his hips as he guided her legs to split over him.

They sat like that, sharing breaths of disbelief, his eyes searching hers as though looking for a reason not to.

He found none, because she gave none.

Alexandra steadied herself on his strong shoulders as he anchored one arm behind her, wrapping her legs around him. She liked this, being above him. Looking down at the scarred and primal beast pinned beneath her. There was power here, potent and feminine. One that caused a tremor in his limbs and unfocused his gaze as though the sight of her inebriated him.

When he fused their lips, her very grip on reality shifted beneath her. Other parts of them merged, as well. Their hearts. Their souls. Perhaps their destinies.

It was she who tangled her tongue with his, tasting him, stroking in wet circles. Penetrating him.

With a low, primal growl, his hands went to work.

Though his kiss grew in ferocity, his fingers stroked her

leisurely, reacquainting himself with the warm folds of her sex, spreading the wet desire he found there to the hard pearl throbbing above it. He oh-so-gently pressed the hood between his forefinger and thumb, rubbing at it with such slippery skill, a shower of sparks exploded behind her eyelids.

"Piers," she gasped against his mouth. "I'm already . . . I'm going to . . ."

"I know." His reply was so incredibly male. So full of ardor and arrogance, and she didn't have the chance to be incensed by it, as he did something else eminently more infuriating.

He stopped.

His fingers left the swollen, aching bud, and reached beneath, to circle the intimate opening, abrading it softly with the work-roughened pads of his fingers.

Feminine muscles convulsed beneath his touch, clenching at him, inviting him in.

He probed at first, pulling back to watch her expression as his finger sank deep. Deep enough to fit his palm against the cradle of her thighs.

"You're so wet," he whispered with a broken reverence. "But I want more. I want to make you ready."

"I am ready," she panted, fighting the urge to squirm and writhe.

He answered her challenge by withdrawing and entering her once more, another finger joining the first.

A stretching sensation startled her, but she felt no pain as he sank in deep once again, pressing the heel of his palm against her throbbing peak.

Magic. Those magic hands.

She whispered his name. Gasped it as he created delicious friction in a soft, rhythmic motion. His fingers felt both foreign and fantastic inside of her, but it was the heel of his hand, pressed against her quivering bud, that elicited the most intense response.

With her legs split as they were, and nothing but his arm to keep her from falling, her instincts to twitch and writhe were little more than frustrated little jerks of her hips. The lurches became lithe rolls, until she rode his hand with an almost shameless need as a sweet and adamant tension gathered between her legs.

He claimed another kiss as her thighs locked and trembled, releasing another rush of moisture around his fingers as he brought her to that beautiful, straining, almost-there place.

And again, drew away.

She whimpered against his lips, bereft, her hips curling forward, searching for the magic.

"I know, darling," he rumbled, his voice laced with a similar tenuous suffering. "Are you afraid?"

"No." She was terrified. And tantalized. And so utterly in need of the release he could provide, she might die from wanting it.

His eyes glowed almost silver in the light as he searched hers, finding the fear she did her best to conceal.

Steadying her with gentle hands on her thighs, he reclined away from her, lying back on the bed.

The wind felt marvelous on her skin, already slicked with a sheen wrought of both apprehension and passion. It tightened her nipples and lifted her hair from the back of her neck.

"If you want me inside of you, wife, you may have me at your leisure." His eyes glistened with a need almost fanatical. A hunger akin to worship. He prostrated himself beneath her, an offering of flesh and blood. A sacrifice and a prayer.

She stared at his magnificent body, an answering hunger surging through her.

It never occurred to her that he wouldn't do the taking. The thrusting. That he wouldn't pin her down.

That she could take him.

Alexandra looked down to where she straddled his thighs, where the formidable shape of his sex tented the sheet.

"I—I don't know how to please you," she confessed, suddenly daunted.

He gazed up at her with a patience so tender, so genuine, it released a swell of emotion inside her. "Don't you know by now, Alexandra, that everything you do pleases me? To look at you pleases me. To touch and kiss you pleases me. The scent and taste and shape of you is the greatest pleasure I've ever known. Anything you do beyond that . . ."

His words died on an indrawn hiss as she reached between them and uncovered him, curling her fingers around the jutting base of his erection. It was warmer than she imagined. Hotter, even, than his fevered body.

Transfixed, she drew her hand up the column toward the engorged tip, marveling at the smoothness of the skin as it slid over unyielding steel beneath.

Big, she worried. Breathtakingly big. And yet, so unlike the weapon she'd expected to find.

How could such a blunt, silken appendage cause the sharp, tearing pain she'd experienced before?

It couldn't, she decided. Wouldn't. Not this time.

Piers would never hurt her.

She knew by the reverent way he whispered her name. By the careful grip he kept on her thighs. By the power over this act he'd placed entirely in her hands.

By the way he closed his eyes, attempting to hide the vulgarity of his primal desire for her.

He didn't have to, she wanted to tell him.

She burned just as hot, somehow. He'd brought her to such a place, had found such a needful, shameless, brazen part of her that an obsessive desire for his body overwhelmed the lingering fears and doubts she might have.

Maybe it would be different if he were above her. Or behind her. If he restrained her and pulled her hair.

But like this . . . with his tremendous body stretched beneath her, his lust contained by iron chains held in a tremulous grip.

All she wanted was to come apart over and around him. To slake his need and fulfill his desires.

She ran an inquisitive finger over the sensitive bulb at the top of his sex, finding a curious, silken moisture of his own making.

He turned his head to the side, his chest heaving with labored breaths, his muscles locked with the herculean effort of his restraint.

It was time. Time to release them both from their chains.

She lifted herself, placing him against her opening, spreading dewy heat on the crown of his sex.

As she lowered slightly, breaching her body, neither of them breathed.

She froze. For an eternity she trembled above him, paralyzed, unable to go forward, unable to turn back. It felt . . . It felt . . .

She didn't know how it felt. It didn't hurt. But neither did it feel good. Or right. Not like this, with her body exposed and his face turned away.

He thought to give her autonomy. To save her from his gripping hands and his powerful lust, and astounding strength. And she'd thought she could do it herself.

They'd both been wrong.

She retreated, letting his sex fall against her thigh.

"Piers," she gasped, hating the desperate note in her voice. "I—I need you." Needed the comfort of his arms around her. The protection of his body against her, even if that protection was merely from her own mind. Her own memories.

He was there the moment the words left her. Right there, twining his arms around her, his forehead pressed to hers, his breath feeding her tight, struggling lungs.

"I—I need you to do it," she confessed in a small voice.

He stilled, a mantle of veneration settling around them as he reached between their bodies and guided himself back toward her swollen, damp flesh. He prodded at her entrance, settling there before he released his organ, both his arms burrowing beneath hers to anchor at her shoulders.

"What do I do?" she pleaded.

"Hold on to me, Alexandra," he whispered, folding her against him. "Just be here. Just be mine." He cupped her head to his shoulder, his own face burrowing into her hair as he urged her trembling thighs to relent.

And finally, they did.

It wasn't as though he impaled her. Not exactly. It was more like her feminine flesh molded over the turgid length of him as she melted down and around him. But only to a point. After he'd made it so far, her inner muscles seized, locking them in a sexual battle he dared not fight.

"Holy God, woman." He wheezed as though in pain. "You're so . . . tight."

She wanted to ask him if he was all right. To soothe and strengthen him as he had done for her, but all she could do was focus on the stretching, straining pulse of her intimate flesh as it struggled to contain the length of him. She wriggled a little, hoping it would pull him deeper, only gaining perhaps another inch.

He let out a few foul curses on a long breath. "Tell me to stop," he begged. "Don't let me hurt you."

"Don't stop," she panted, pressing her hips down, seeking the relief she knew existed at the end of this. "Just . . . just . . . *please.*"

He understood her plea, and his fingers curled up and around her shoulders, pulling her down to meet his hips in one strong, lithe push.

She cried out, unable to stop herself.

"I'm sorry," he said tightly, making to retreat.

"No." She locked arms around him, grinding her hips down against his. "Don't. Move." Her order was a hissed whisper, given through a throat clogged with a million opposing emotions.

He obeyed.

At first, all she could feel was him inside of her. This foreign, fierce, pulsing shaft of unyielding flesh and heat. She stayed like that for a moment, just feeling. Experiencing. Analyzing.

No pain. No tearing. Just this uncomfortable pressure at first, which rapidly gave way to an exquisite sort of fullness.

Breath began to infuse her again as she latched on to that one fact.

No pain. Just Piers.

This man, who was so much more than what was inside of her. He was the gentle breath at her ear. The smooth skin stretched over the iron cables of his shoulders and spine as she gripped him like a woman about to fall away from herself.

The tender, banked power of the arms ensconcing her in a cocoon of comfort, supporting her entire weight. The coarse hair and dense muscle of his chest, abrading her sensitive breasts as she crushed them against him.

The softer hair of his solid legs tickling at the thin, sensitive skin of her inner thigh.

He was all of these things, and so much more than she could possibly have fathomed.

Her protector. Her husband.

Her lover.

Even though every primitive instinct Piers possessed screamed at him to move. To thrust. To fuck. He fought himself with all the ferocity of an adversary.

Because the instinct to protect his woman from any and all threats had become the strongest of all.

Even if that threat was his own primal need.

Besides. He was inside of her. Finally. Locked within a body more sweet and tight and wet than even his fantasies could have devised.

It was enough.

And it would never be enough.

It was more than he dared hope for. More than he deserved, this exquisite gift of her trust.

And still he longed for more.

If it was as far as she could go tonight, he'd understand.

If she withdrew now, she'd take a bit of his soul with her.

It was the most difficult thing he'd ever done, preparing to let her go should her fear overtake her.

Let me show you how sweet it can be, he silently urged. *Let me claim you as mine, so you no longer belong to the past.*

Slowly, in infinitesimal increments, she relaxed against him, around him, her sex becoming a sheath shaped to the length inside. Her grip slackened, her breath strengthening even as her muscles melted against his.

Her small, delicate hands began a feather-light exploration of his back, running along the columns of muscle bracketing his spine, dipping into the valley between.

Piers returned the caress, smoothing his rough hands over her shoulder blades, charting the dip of her waist, reveling in the silken cream that was her skin.

He wished he could see her face, and yet he wasn't ready for her to look at him just yet. He treasured the breaths against his neck, the trust inherent in their pose. The intimacy.

"All right," she whispered.

"All right," he answered. She needn't say more.

He arched his spine slightly back, pressing down into the mattress, easing only the base of his cock out of her before rocking forward in a smooth, gentle thrust.

The friction was negligible, but it was all they needed for an aching, remarkable pleasure to bloom between them.

She sucked in short breaths as he rocked her with slow, stinging curls of his hips, remaining deep inside of her, pressing against her womb.

He thought he might die from the pleasure of it.

Finally, she pulled back a little to look at him, her features a mixture of awe and bewilderment.

And pleasure.

More. She needed more. He could give her more.

He licked his thumb and brought it between them, to where she was so small and soft and yet spectacularly tight around him. He brushed at the crest of the distended, swollen nub at the hood of her core.

She made a sound so low and lovely in the back of her throat it might have been the purr of a lioness. Her fingers drew up the column of his neck and slid into his hair.

When he thrummed her again, she tightened her grip, allowing a soft sound of encouragement to escape her.

Reflexively, she pressed a hand to her mouth.

"No," he said huskily, kissing her fingers without once breaking his steady, slow rhythm. "There is no need to silence your pleasure. Sing it to the night, my lovely wife. Let it know you are mine, and that I, alone, can make you feel this way."

He licked at the seams of her fingers, and they fell away, returning to grasp at his hair.

God, he loved it when she did that. Anchored his neck so she could control their hot, slippery kiss.

A triumphant joy welled within him when her hips began a tentative dance. Flexing and rolling to the rhythm of his.

He timed the thrusts of his tongue to that of his hips, the feather-soft brushes of his thumb an off-beat percussion that set her thighs to quivering. Her eyes darkened, becoming decadent, dark pools of fathomless longing.

"Piers," she warned, little concussive tremors building along the feminine flesh now clamped around his cock.

"Don't wait for me," he whispered against her mouth, laving at her with heated kisses and strong thrusts of his tongue.

In truth, he could have come the moment she'd wrapped her slim fingers around him.

But he'd be goddamned if this was over that quickly. He'd previously vowed to make her drenched and exhausted before he finished with her, and, at the moment, she was only one of those things.

Gloriously wet.

He dipped his finger lower, wickedly testing where their bodies were joined, gathering the abundant moisture there and swirling it around her throbbing hood.

Her lips tore from his as her spine arched and flexed, her head dropping back on her shoulders as a hoarse, guttural cry broke from her.

She convulsed around him, over him, her sex milking at him in voluptuous, rhythmic waves. Her unbound hair brushed the small of her back, and her clasping fingers tore at his own locks as she shivered and shuddered in a long, extravagant release.

Christ, her pleasure was the most beautiful sight on this entire fucking globe. If he never saw another exotic mountain vista, or volcanic eruption, or even the unparalleled paradise of shores both familiar and foreign. If he was cursed to stay in one place, forever in the dark, he would gladly do it if only to watch the graceful arch of her body as it locked in the throes of the bliss he could give her.

His own release pulsed into his cock, ready to rush into her, and he bit down on his tongue hard enough to make it bleed. *Not yet.*

Not until she begged him to stop.

Alexandra collapsed against her husband, curled around him, allowing the voluptuous pulses of liquid pleasure to drift away.

Awestruck and humbled, she marveled at the freedom and profundity of what she'd just experienced. What beauty she'd seen behind her eyelids as she'd come apart with hm inside of her. The dances of light and that electric enchantment that was part of him, part of what he did to her.

It took her only a few deep breaths to realize that he remained inside her, hard and hot as ever, his body still corded taut and features straining to remain civil, and rapidly losing the battle.

"You . . . you didn't . . ."

Though his muscles built upon themselves beneath the weight of his self-possession, his hands were gentle as they took her face. "Are you through, Alexandra?" He forced the question through a straining throat before lowering his lips to her neck, sampling the salt and musk of her skin.

"What do you mean?"

"Let me spread you beneath me," he requested tightly, lips drifting down her throat, and across her chest. "I need to see you. To see this." He rocked once more into her still-quivering flesh. "I need to taste . . ." A hand lifted her breast, covering her nipple in the decadent, wet heat of his mouth.

The indecency of his request, along with his position, was enough to build a languid excitement within her loins.

"Yes," she sighed, as he moved his attentions to her other breast.

Her eyes popped open as he withdrew, and she was suddenly on her back, her legs spread wide by the weight of his hands.

"My God," he groaned. "You're so pink and perfect."

With an ice-blue glint in his eyes, he descended upon her, applying his tongue to her delicate flesh, flaying her open with long, flat licks until, miraculously, a new and insistent desire built within her womb. Once her hips began to lift from the bed, he concentrated his ministrations to the one place she knew would soon implode with a hot thrill of bliss.

And, once more, he pulled away just before she came, prowling up her body like the dark panther who'd stolen his beauty, or gifted it to him.

He slid into her with one fluid, beautifully deep motion, settling into another deliberate, controlled rhythm. His alert eyes searched her face, gauged her expressions.

She felt his hesitancy. His lingering restraint, and she brought her hands around his waist and lower, pressing him deeper.

"More," she whispered, feeling him tense, seeing the question in his eyes. "More," she repeated, lifting her hips to meet his.

His thrusts quickened, driving deeper, pressing her higher.

She loved this, the softness of the mattress at her back, the hardness of him on top of her. She felt safe. She felt . . . glorious. She found she could control the rhythm with her hips, lifting faster, harder, taking all of him inside, all his animalian ferocity, his noble grace.

The lust that drove him to the edge of his control.

He swelled inside of her, growing impossibly larger, finding a place within her body just as prone to pleasure as the little pearl without.

Pleasure gripped her once more, this time deeper than before, an all-encompassing pulsating riot of thrills tearing through her veins until even her fingers and toes were infused with the sparkling, shimmering whole of it.

It didn't take her from herself. Not this time. She watched with fascinated awe as he followed her to that place. Gasping her name, groaning it, then roaring as liquid jets of his release bathed her womb.

He was the most beautiful like this, she thought. Helpless against pleasure, held in the heat and thrall of her body. His every sinew rippled with a bliss that seemed to match hers, perhaps even exceeded it as sumptuous shudders overtook his large frame before he finally gave one last, deep drive inside of her.

Rolling to the side in a controlled collapse, he brought her with him. Draping her over his chest and spreading her hair along his torso, unworried by their sweat-slicked skin or the leavings of their pleasure.

They breathed together in the silence, allowing the wind

to cool their bodies as they each took a moment to contemplate the cataclysmic enormity of what had just happened between them.

After a moment, chill bumps began to ripple along her skin. Redmayne kissed her shoulder and heaved himself off the bed, dipped a cloth in the basin of clean water, and returned to minister gently to her.

That accomplished, he gathered her beneath the blankets to face him on her side, creating a cocoon with his body before drugging her with lavish kisses.

He gave her a long, searching gaze, "Alexandra, tell me honestly. Are you all r—"

"I think it's possible that I love you." One might think she'd gone and blurted something without thinking. But she hadn't. Not this time. She simply didn't want to answer the question he was about to ask. Because the answer would be both yes, and no.

He couldn't have appeared more stunned if she'd stabbed him in the heart. "You think . . . it's possible . . ."

She sighed, looking heavenward. They were back to the repeating again.

"I've never had a definition of love before." She brushed her hand through the fine fleece of hair on his chest, finding the quick, strong beat of the organ beneath it. The one she wasn't certain belonged to her. Or ever would. "But I think if I can't imagine my life without you. If I feel so attached—so dedicated to you. So powerfully possessive of you. That must mean something, mustn't it? If I trust you like this. To do this." She let out a wry laugh. "I've only known you nine days. Ten come midnight. But I have ceased being able to imagine my subsequent days without you in them. Doesn't that seem like love to you?"

"Alexandra, I "

She placed three fingers over his lips, one against the

seam of her favorite scar, silencing his reply. "You don't have to say anything. In fact, I wish you wouldn't. Not tonight. I just needed you to know."

She burrowed into his body, and was heartened when he pulled her close without hesitation. A new emotion had likewise seeped into his embrace.

Possession, she liked to think.

Alexandra watched the arms of his mantel clock, content to time the rhythm of his slowing breaths. Just over an hour before she had to go.

She fought a sense of doom at the thought of leaving the safety of his arms.

The sensation of his limbs became lush and heavier upon her, twitching with dreams. A quiet, masculine snore rumbled through him. Just the one.

She smiled, glad he could sleep.

At least one of them should.

CHAPTER TWENTY-SEVEN

A portent of dread sang through Redmayne's blood, yanking him from a blissful, languorous sleep. He clutched at his head, feeling like the very devil had woken him.

Needing comfort, he reached for his wife, disconcerted to find himself alone in bed.

He sat up, calling her name as the covers drifted away from his naked body.

The wind no longer cooled his fevered skin but added an insidious chill to a gathering sense of doom.

Don't be a melodramatic fool, he admonished himself. He mustn't allow the events of the past fortnight to weaken his constitution. He needed to remain sharp. Self-assured. To enhance his instincts and keep his wits about him.

It was the only way to keep his wife safe until he dealt with the threat.

Her sheets were cold enough to have been empty for some time. Too long for a visit to the washroom. The fact pierced him with no small amount of displeasure, and something eminently darker.

He stood, intent upon finding her.

Perhaps she'd gone back to her own room, unused to sleeping with another. Certainly, they'd made strides toward healing, but that didn't mean she wouldn't require a great deal of space and patience. She was so used to her own sovereignty, and he'd no mind to take that from her.

Most noble couples slept apart; perhaps that was her preference.

Well, it bloody well wasn't *his*. He'd do what he could to change her mind forthwith.

He reached out to close the window, lost in his thoughts.

His hand froze on the pane, the other joining it as he watched a cloaked figure haloed by a lantern scurry through the intemperate night. The wind blew the hood away from her head, uncovering a long braid of the most extraordinary color.

He'd known who it was before he saw her hair. Of course he had. He'd memorized her walk, her height, her movements. He'd studied everything about her without even meaning to.

He wanted to fling the window wide and call after her.

In his drowsy stupefaction, he almost did.

But the facts immobilized him. She'd left his bed at— he checked his clock—nearly midnight, dressed, and now made her way toward the catacombs alone.

Catacombs he'd meant to scour for clues as to who was trying to kill him.

Mind racing with a million thoughts, suspicions, and subsequent denials, he yanked on trousers, a shirt, a dark jacket, and his boots.

What the veritable fuck was she up to? At this hour, she could only be about one of a few things, and each scenario that filtered through his thoughts was more sinister and offensive than the last.

He'd given her a fortune in cash this morning. Could she possibly be leaving him? Could their mind-altering sex have been nothing more than a grateful fare-thee-well?

Had she meant to abandon him all this time?

A bleak thought sent him reaching for his pistol and tucking his knife into his boot.

She might be meeting someone.

A friend in need? A coconspirator?

A lover?

A growl ripped its way out of his chest. He'd been *so* careful, so suspicious.

He sifted through their every interaction since they'd met, searching for a clue, stopping to stare at the bed as his breath sawed in and out of him.

She could have pretended a great many things. Her affection, her story, her kindness.

But not this. A woman's affectation could falsify her pleasure, but not her body. The trembling. The need. The wide-eyed awe of it. The wet, pulsating releases.

But what of everything else? What about . . .

I think it's possible that I love you.

Why would she say that, if she'd meant to leave? If she was meeting another man?

Was it possible she wanted to throw him so completely off course she'd stoop to such a heartless confession?

She'd been a weakness of his since the moment he'd met her. A dazzling, alluring, infuriating, *confounding* woman. One he'd been so desperate to claim as his own.

All this time, could her heart have belonged to another?

He refused to believe it, that she would break him so thoroughly.

Icy fingers of doubt and dread slithered their way around his heart, freezing it, turning it brittle and still.

Women did what they had to do, didn't they? In lieu of

honorable duels, lucrative vocations, and socially sanctioned means of survival, they had to find a way to seize
their power through any means necessary, didn't they?
They were adrift and prisoners of the social mores of men,
and so to get what they wanted, they often stooped to stunning feats of brutal manipulation.

His mother, his former intended, his mistress . . .

His wife?

He fought the urge to slam out of his rooms, creeping
through the hotel and veering toward her path in a steady,
silent jog. He took no lantern, accustomed to navigating
in the dark, using the sliver of the moon and the swing of
the distant lantern as a guide.

His wife had a reason to hate all men. For, no matter
how suspicious he became, he couldn't deny that her
trauma had been real.

He'd held her as her heart shattered. Had her sanity
gone, as well?

What a brilliant woman he'd married, and hadn't it been
socially and medically acknowledged that there was a fine
line between madness and brilliance? Was it possible she
was both victim, and mastermind? Could she have married him intending to become his wealthy widow all along,
waiting for the final strike until she'd at least a small fortune with which to disappear?

She wasn't harmless. She knew how to wield a pistol.

He could be walking into a trap, even now.

Even as all these suspicions drove spikes into the cof-
fin of ice surrounding his heart, he violently rejected them.

The more he desired to trust her, the more his mind
seemed to sway with riotous suspicion bordering on para-
noia.

He didn't believe she would try to hurt him.

This was Alexandra. As compassionate as she was

determined. As honest as she was enigmatic. Logical, levelheaded, and lovely.

Except she'd had secrets, hadn't she? He'd seen them lurking in the shadows of her eyes. But he thought they were done with that, that he'd uncovered them all.

Apparently not.

You've only known her ten days, his reason whispered.

Another sensation raised the hairs on the back of his neck, causing him to duck behind cover and squint into the night.

It still felt as though the devil walked here, looking to smother what little light he'd found in darkness. Piers's hunter's instincts sensed danger out there. Not a being, but a void. Something or someone hollow, abysmal, hungry.

Another predator?

With his hand on his weapon, he stalked his wife in the dark, as he had so many other creatures, intent on following her to the source of her mysteries.

Alexandra trained her pistol into the shadows beyond where the illumination of the lantern danced upon the damp walls of the catacomb. She might be willing to sacrifice herself for her friends, but that outcome certainly wasn't her first option.

Especially now.

Now that she'd fallen in love with her husband.

No, not fallen, per se. But drifted into it in barely recognizable shifts of her heart. He'd become necessary. A curator of healing and joy. The idea of him finding out. Of rejecting her. Or worse, of falling victim to her tormentor, was simply untenable. She had to do what she must to keep something like yesterday's cave-in from happening again.

Alexandra hoped to meet her nemesis in the first antechamber past the crypt entrance, the stability of which remained dubious in her estimation. But as she'd tripped over smaller rocks still yet to be cleared from the causeway, she'd discovered a note stuck between the temporary buttress and the seam of the cave.

The Redmayne Tomb.

She swallowed the harsh, metallic flavor of panic as she made her way down what now seemed to be an eternal, windowless hall. The dank stone, cracked by the insistent roots of grass and vegetation, threw every one of her footsteps back at her in an eerie echo. She'd the sense she was being watched, or followed, and she couldn't help but wonder what lurked in the shadows beyond her feeble light.

She couldn't say why she lowered her pistol when she turned the corner to the Redmayne crypt. Perhaps because the thought of shooting a friend seemed so ludicrous.

Of course she would never. She didn't have it in her to kill.

Except she did. *She had.*

That's why she was here.

"Julia?"

The woman reclined against the mound of dirt where the Redmayne skeleton had once rested, still attired in a dinner gown and bedecked with diamonds. The diamond comb in her golden hair glittered in the light of the lamp resting at her elbow. It must have cost more than any one of Alexandra's payments.

"Oh, don't let's pretend to be astonished, *Alexander.*" Julia tipped her head to the side, eyes narrowed like a serpent's. "You're just so exceptionally clever, you had to have at least suspected it was me."

Alexandra flinched, but mainly at Julia's use of the Red Rogue nickname for her.

She *had* suspected Julia. That is, the woman had been

on her list of possible suspects, though she'd never truly believed it simply because . . .

"You don't need my money," she puzzled. "And yet, you've taken mine all these years . . ."

"Of course I didn't need your money, but *you* did. Everyone knows your family has been in financial decline for decades. I simply enjoyed the idea of your suffering."

"But . . . we're friends." She realized how insipid the statement was; they obviously were anything but. However, she couldn't seem to stop listing reasons why her blackmailer and persecutor couldn't *possibly* be Julia Throckmorton.

Even though she stood right before her, admitting it.

She'd always been rather timid as a girl. Dainty and gullible and, forgive her, intellectually hopeless. Had she changed so much in ten years? Enough to mastermind a cave-in, hire assassins, instigate the accident on the ship, and also time the catacomb cave-in just right so she hadn't been caught in the wreckage. It seemed improbable. Impossible.

But then, Julia had been flitting from tomb to tomb the day before, hadn't she? Touching everything, bothering people just enough that they'd purposely ignored her. She must have tampered with something.

She'd been on the ship deck when the load had fallen. At the wedding where the assassins had been. On the train platform.

She'd been everywhere that something had gone wrong.

"Friends?" Julia toyed with her necklace, pinching her lips tight against her teeth. "*Friends? Friends don't fuck each other's fiancés, Alexander.*"

Stymied, Alexandra stepped back. "I—I never . . . whatever rumor you heard, it was wrong. I've never taken a lover."

The woman's skin tightened over her bones with a terrifying look of pure malice. It was the ugliest expression Alexandra had ever seen. "You had *one,* didn't you, *Alexander?* And don't bother denying it, I watched you that night. I saw what you did. I witnessed *everything.*"

Struck dumb, Alexandra gasped cold, dank air into her lungs. Julia couldn't mean . . .

"Maurice de Marchand." Julia whispered his name like that of a saint. "For two years *I* was his muse." A look of nostalgic rapture overtook her, transporting her, no doubt, to the past. "He stripped me bare and worshipped my body. He showed me how to tempt and please a man. Taught me how much pleasure could be found in pain. I was his obsession. The only object of his desire."

"If you truly believe that, you are a fool." Alexandra shook her head, the tableau before her inconceivable. She'd assumed the blackmailer would be an opportunist at best, and at worst someone with a grudge against her family.

But never someone who actually missed the man she'd murdered.

With a blink Julia returned to the present, pinning Alexandra with a glare of hatred so poisonous, it curdled the contents her stomach.

"He *loved* me," she spat. "You were nothing but a diversion. An opportunity. He spent hours worshipping at the altar that was my body. And I at his. All he did was bend you over his desk and shove up your skirts like a cheap whore. Don't think you were special to him, *Alexander.*"

Alexandra's hand tightened on her pistol. She *really* wished Julia would cease using that name. She didn't know which she found more shockingly abhorrent, the woman's cruel words, or the madness glittering like her diamonds in her hard, hard eyes.

"De Marchand hurt me, Julia. Don't you understand

that?" Anger rose within her, welling from a place so old and dark it frightened her. "If you witnessed what you claimed to have done, then you know that we were not *lovers*. That I didn't want him anywhere near me."

Julia threw up her hands in a gesture of disbelief as old as time.

"Oh, don't make me laugh. *Everybody* wanted him. You snuck into his rooms and took his most intimate things for *years*. I'm the one who told him, you know."

"You. *What?*" Alexandra's finger caressed the trigger of her pistol at her side, reeling with disbelief. "Did you know what he would do to me? Did you throw me to him hoping he'd steal my virginity?"

Julia rolled her eyes and kicked her hip away from the empty dais ledge. "Oh, don't be dramatic, of course I didn't. I thought he would strap you a good one and then come looking for me . . . How could I have known you would practically ask for it."

"I did nothing of the—"

"You let him spank you first, when everyone knew how aroused he became when he did so. You even admitted to him that you knew he liked to cause pain. That it made him harder than a—"

Alexandra cocked the pistol and pointed it at Julia's chest. Or somewhere thereabouts; she shook so violently, she couldn't be sure. "He . . . he raped me, Julia. Why didn't you stop him?"

"I can't tell if you're lying to me, or to yourself." Julia eyed the pistol pensively, without fear, but like a puzzle in need of solving. "You barely fought him. God, once he got inside you, you just lay there like a cold fish—"

"Stop. Just *stop* it!" Alexandra screamed.

She could pull the trigger.

If she did, Cecelia and Francesca would be safe. Her

husband would be free. She might bring the entire tomb
down upon them, but what did it matter? This nightmare
would be over.

Her finger brushed the trigger, her breaths shortened.
Focused.

And then she dropped her arm, emitting a wounded
sound of defeat.

She couldn't do it.

Because, the truth of the matter was, Julia was just as
much a victim of de Marchand as herself. Arguably more
so. If he'd been with Julia two years before the rape had
occurred, then he'd begun to prey upon a girl at just fifteen. He manipulated her in her formative years. Had created a zealot out of a simple adolescent.

She hoped he was burning in hell.

"Julia," she began, hoping to reason with the unbalanced
woman. "I've brought the money." She held out the purse,
a veritable fortune inside.

Julia eyed it like she offered her a serpent. "I decided,
now that you're a duchess, a mere fortune will no longer
do."

"What more could you want?"

Julia regarded her contemplatively, adopting a posture
of scrupulous study. "I thought your husband would be a
torment to you. The Terror of Torcliff, a dominant, disfigured lech. I thought he'd make you suffer, that I could
watch you squirm like a worm on a hook. But, alas, it
seems the two of you are disgustingly well suited."

"Is that why you tried to hurt him?" Alexandra began
to change her mind about shooting the woman. "To make
me suffer?"

"Hurt him?" Julia scoffed. "I've devised something
worse than that, I think. I want you to tell him. To confess
what you did."

"There's no need for that."

Alexandra whirled around, dropping her purse as Redmayne melted from the shadows of the crypt entrance, an immense specter of quiet fury.

At first her soul soared, elated at the very sight of him, at the safety and strength he brought with him. She was no longer alone. So utterly alone and afraid.

Then, as though shot out of the air by a masterful marksman, her joy plummeted to despair.

He knew. He'd heard everything.

"Your Grace," Julia greeted him like an old friend. "Do come in, your wife has such a compelling story. Should you tell it, Alexander, or should I?"

"Stop. Calling. Me. That," Alexandra commanded. It was folly to antagonize the woman, but what did that matter now?

Redmayne's winter-cold gaze scanned Alexandra for a moment and then turned on Julia. "Listen to me." He enunciated his words through his teeth, waves of malevolence rolling off him. "I've never in my life hurt a woman, but I will see to it that you—"

"I'm sorry, Your Grace, but if anything happens to me, it's your wife who will be locked away." She pursed her lips into a pretty pout. "Tell him, Alexander," she cajoled dramatically. "Tell him what you did. How you bent over for our headmaster, how you lay there and enjoyed it until your shame drove you to—"

Redmayne lunged past Alexandra toward Julia, stabbing a warning finger toward her. "Shut your mouth, you mad bitch."

"I killed him." They both stopped to stare at her. Julia's expression was rapt with triumph and Redmayne . . .

Alexandra swallowed, drawing the courage to look at him from wells she hadn't known she possessed. She couldn't identify his reaction, not exactly. Horror, maybe. Anger, surely.

Condemnation?

"I—I murdered de Marchand when he—as he—" She couldn't say it, she couldn't admit that her seventeen-year-old self hadn't been able to stand the idea of him finishing inside of her. "He—he'd a razor on his desk and . . . I took it. I turned. And I slit his throat."

Neither of them moved as Julia crowed from behind her. "Tell him! Tell him all of it. How you gathered your clique of snobbish wretches, and the bastard gardener, and you all buried him in the garden like so much fertilizer."

Her husband stood abnormally erect, his fists clenched at his sides. "*That's* your secret. *She's* why you requested the money today."

His voice was so remote, so utterly devoid of emotion, she couldn't delineate a statement or a question, but she nodded anyway.

"That's the whole of it."

"She's a murderer!" Julia screeched. "She took the man I loved from me, and I will pay her in kind!"

The very idea bled what life she'd left out of her.

Redmayne lifted his eyes to Julia, speared her with the full effect of his cold, monstrous regard. "I wish she'd not have killed him, Lady Julia, only because I've been denied the chance to butcher him, myself."

"What?" Julia gasped.

"What?" Alexandra echoed.

"Consider yourself, and your lover, fortunate that he died so quickly."

Alexandra found herself locked in his arms with such fierce tenderness, she collapsed against him, grateful sobs welling in her throat.

"My God. My wife . . ." He clutched her tighter, shaking

with a barely leashed rage. "To think what you've suffered. I can't—"

"The world will *know*." Julia's voice climbed to a manic,
hysterical pitch. "I can prove it! You'll both be ruined."

"What evidence do you have?" Redmayne demanded.

Julia addressed Alexandra. "The three of you Red
Rogues considered yourselves so perfect. So much more
brilliant than everyone else." She laughed as though no one
had stated a more ridiculous notion in her life.

"I had naught but the razor and my word, at first," she
admitted victoriously. "Which would have been little in the
way of proof . . . until *you* started wiring me money. Now
I have a paper trail. Letters from you as a girl, begging me
not to tell. It's all as damning as a confession." She turned
on Redmayne. "One that will be sent to the authorities by
my solicitor should anything happen to me, condemning
both you and your ridiculous Rogues."

"You forget, Lady Julia, that my brother *owns* the authorities." His voice was laced with a similar black victory.
"I'm the bloody Duke of Redmayne, my line and my name
is older and more unbroken than that of the queen. Against
mine, your word will hold as much weight as a whisper in
a whirlwind. And if you breathe a word against my wife,
you'll never see the outside of an asylum. Now get. The
fuck. Out of my sight."

Suddenly—*blessedly*—speechless, Julia pushed away
from the dais, skirting the edge of the room. "I'll find a
way . . ." she said tightly.

"Not if you know what's good for you," her husband
warned. "Or I'll have you arrested for the attempts on my
life. You'll hang if that's what it takes."

Alexandra lifted her head from where she'd buried it in
her husband's chest, a question burning through her.

"How did you do it, Julia?" she asked, stopping the

woman from slinking away. "How did you orchestrate all the mayhem? Did you really want to hurt me so much that you'd threaten innocent lives?"

The glint of a shotgun barrel preceded another set of wide shoulders into the chamber. Julia stumbled backward on her bejeweled, heeled slippers, staggering toward Alexandra.

"Do you think this simple cunt could pull off such clever machinations as that?" Thomas Forsythe raked Julia with a withering, dismissive glance that reduced her to tears. "She couldn't even manage a passable fuck."

Alexandra lifted her pistol, feeling her husband turn from warm muscle to cold steel at her back as his arms tightened around her.

"Thomas!" She gaped at the man she'd considered her friend. He'd deserted all sense of affability, adopting a stark and hard mask.

"Put that ridiculous weapon away, Dr. Lane." He sighed with a note of feigned boredom. "And kick it over here."

"I will not!"

"Do it," Redmayne asserted from behind her.

Stunned at his capitulation, Alexandra gaped. "But— but."

"Your husband is wise." Forsythe stepped deeper into the crypt, circling for three paces until he was in between the door and the dais. "He recognizes an L. H. Parker field grade shotgun. This ingenious piece of handmade machinery is able to drop an elk at fifty paces, and has been rumored to stop a charging bear. If I were to pull the trigger now, not one of you would escape being wounded." He adjusted the weapon on his shoulder.

"But you, dear Doctor, would be blown to shreds."

CHAPTER TWENTY-EIGHT

If Piers ever had a nightmare scenario, this was it. His wife between him and his enemy, a delicate shield. His own pistol tucked in his jacket.

If he were to reach for it now, Forsythe would fire. The blackguard wanted to. The desire for blood was written all over him.

Unused to feeling helpless, Piers glared at him over his wife's head, silently promising a slow and painful death. Vowing retribution. This man had awoken this morning, unaware that it was his last.

But before he could kill the fucking blighter, Piers needed to get Alexandra out of range.

Because even if the bastard doctor put a hole the size of Blighty in Piers's middle, he'd take Forsythe to hell with him before he gave up the ghost.

"Piers?" Alexandra whimpered, her pistol still trained forward.

"Drop it, Doctor." Forsythe took a threatening step forward, stopping five paces away. "Or I drop you. You know

I don't want to do that, Alexandra. But I think you know that I will."

Leaning down, Redmayne whispered into Alexandra's ear, as Julia's shrill voice fractured against the dome of the crypt, shouting, "How could you say such awful things after what I did for you last night? You weren't moaning words like 'passable' as I was swallowing your disgusting—"

"Shut up for once in your life, you ignorant slut!" Forsythe inched the barrel of his weapon in her direction, only an arm's reach to Alexandra's left.

Alexandra bent her knees, lowering to the ground as she placed her small pistol in the dirt. "You don't want to shoot that in here," she warned. "We're not certain it wouldn't cause another cave-in. We'd all be crushed into the dust."

"Push it toward me," Forsythe ordered, ignoring her.

Alexandra did, and in her panic, she fell. Scrambling backward on the ground, she didn't stop retreating until she ran into Piers's legs.

Julia made a desperate, humiliated sound. "How dare you insult me like this! Was it her you wanted all along? Tell me, you craven bastard! Did you use me to get to her?"

Piers bent down, helping his wife to her feet, accepting the hilt of what she'd surreptitiously pulled from his boot.

"There's no need for jealousy." Forsythe sneered at Julia. "My tastes never tended toward boring little bluestockings always prattling on. Correcting me, condescending to me." Forsythe's lip curled into a sneer of disdain. "What man wants to fuck a woman who thinks she's smarter than he is? Though, now that I know you have blood on your hands . . . I have to admit you're much more interesting."

"What do you want, Forsythe?" Piers demanded, his hands itching to close around the man's throat. To watch the life drain from his eyes as he strangled an apology from the smarmy bastard for disrespecting his wife.

"My passion for history pays little, I'm afraid," Forsythe admitted blithely, eyeing Alexandra's purse. "And so one does what one must . . ."

"Here," she said, tossing it at his feet. "Take it and be-gone."

He didn't even glance down. "I've been promised so much more than that . . ." He lifted the shotgun higher, drawing a bead and closing one eye. "To kill the Duke of Redmayne and make it look like an accident."

Piers didn't have to ask by whom. He already knew.

The only people who would profit from his death. Patrick and Rose Atherton.

"A gunshot wound is impossible to pose as an accident," Piers said drolly.

"These catacombs are secure enough to withstand the noise, you saw to that yourself, didn't you?" Forsythe re-minded him. "It took more finesse with the gunpowder than I expected to even create the first disaster. I can do it again. Except now, by the time they dig you out, I'll be long gone."

It was never going to get that far. "What would it take to let the women go?" Piers demanded.

Then it would just be him and Forsythe.

Then he could go to work. Because as devastating and severe as the gun in Forsythe's hands was, Piers could be spectacularly more lethal.

This crypt was close quarters, and a rifle of any kind had very distinct disadvantages in such a place.

But he couldn't act, couldn't think, couldn't relax enough to perform the dangerous maneuvers he needed to, if his wife was in the least bit at risk.

"I'm sorry." Forsythe's finger grazed the trigger. "But the duchess is now a part of the job I was hired to do."

Patrick Atherton glided into the room dressed in a finely woven gray suit, a six-barreled pistol pointed at them both. "A job you've failed at, enormously."

He turned to Piers, the spite glittering in eyes a pale reflection of his own. "How does the cliché go, cousin? If you want something done right . . ."

Patrick had always been a little bit less. Less tall. Less handsome, young, or vigorous. Less powerful both in title and in stature.

Which is why he'd hired a mercenary. The nancy fucker had never liked to get his hands dirty.

"You two followed me here," Piers deduced. Patrick had been the void in the night. The prickle at his back. But Piers had been too intent upon his wife to pay the instinct the heed he should have.

She was his weakness, and now his cousin knew it.

"When I received word the cave-in had failed, I caught the next ferry to Normandy," Patrick explained with a droll sigh. "Since you seem to have more lives than a cat, I figured it might take more than one of us to finish the job."

Piers jeered at his cousin, hatred boiling to the surface. "Christ. Is Rose out there, also? She might as well join us."

Patrick's gaze sharpened. He'd hit a nerve. "Of course not. Rose wouldn't let me kill you, not when she's still madly in love with you. She hasn't touched me since you've returned from the dead."

"It's because you're weak," Piers snarled. "You haven't the bollocks to kill me yourself. You had to hire this incompetent to do it."

"I'll show you incompetent!" Forsythe bellowed, his trigger finger twitching.

Piers had known Patrick his entire life, had counted on the fact that his jibe would rankle his cousin, who pushed the barrel of Forsythe's gun to the side. "Lose your composure, and you'll lose your payment, Forsythe."

The doctor's mouth tilted into a mulish frown, but he pressed his lips closed.

Patrick's pistol glinted in the lantern light, less dangerous than the shotgun, but still lethal. "You're right, of course, this should have always come down to you and me. It's rather poetic, is it not? That I prove myself worthy of the savage Redmayne title here in our ancestor's tomb?"

"You'll never be worthy of the Redmayne title," Piers taunted. "You're too pathetic."

"Not so pathetic as your father."

Redmayne stilled, his lips pulling back from his teeth in a silent snarl of warning.

"He granted me access to this project years ago, you know, back when you were a boy and I a young man. It's been a great venture for the glory of the family. One I resurrected when I thought I was to become duke. When you were supposed to die in that jungle."

Patrick inspected the tomb. "Your poor father, always seeking solace in his idiotic schemes, forever leaving them unfinished. This was one of the few I encouraged. I stood beside him while you and Ramsay were off getting your education, while your mother fucked her way across Europe. I helped him manage both his funds and his grief. Helped him tie the knot in the rope from which he hung himself."

Lanced with a lightning bolt of rage, it was everything Piers could do not to vault over his wife and tear the man apart.

"Send the women away and we'll have it out right here,"

he demanded. "Man to man. One of us will be laid to rest in the Redmayne crypt for good."

"Piers!" Alexandra protested.

"I'm not an idiot," Patrick remonstrated. "I know I'd not best you in hand-to-hand combat. It's one of the reasons I know I'd be a better aristocrat. A duke shouldn't *have* to go into battle. Other men do it for him." Patrick shook his head slowly, true sorrow tightening the Redmayne features he didn't deserve to display.

"There's no saving the duchess this time, I'm afraid. There's a chance she carries your progeny." He leveled his pistol right at Alexandra's stomach. "And that just won't do."

Piers had never known true fear, not before that moment. Time became a construct, slow and disjointed.

He switched the knife Alexandra had taken from his boot to his left hand, reaching across his body to shove her toward the dais. The moment his wife was out of the way, he drew the pistol from beneath his jacket, levered his arm up, and squeezed the trigger three consecutive times.

Patrick's shot went wide, and he never had the chance to attempt another, as two of Piers's bullets found their mark in his heart. He crumpled to the ground, landing on his face with a sickening crunch.

Alexandra would have tripped over Julia, had the woman not dived for the pistol on the ground, snatching it and taking aim at Forsythe.

Forsythe, who'd leveled his shotgun at Alexandra, noticed Julia's intentions in time, and a great, concussive boom deafened them all as he pulled the trigger.

Diamonds glittered as they disseminated in a truly awe-inspiring radius, along with gore that didn't bear consideration. By the time they fell to the floor, Alexandra had taken cover behind the three-foot-tall mound of earth and stone, her head down, hands covering her ears.

Piers pivoted, squeezing the trigger thrice more, narrowly missing Forsythe as he dove behind the opposite side of the burial platform.

Forsythe immediately began to reload, stalking Alexandra around the other side of the dais. She saw him in time, and dove away from the cover of the dais, scrambling for the pistol still clutched in Patrick's hand.

Apparently adept at counting bullets, Forsythe stood, pumping the now-loaded shotgun, sliding the shell into place.

Piers abandoned his empty pistol as he took a running leap and vaulted over the earth to land between the gun and his wife.

No one heard Forsythe's last words as Piers gripped the barrel, wrenched it out of his hands, and shoved his dagger through the man's throat, gorging on the primal elation of dispatching the villain up close.

Of watching the life drain out of his eyes.

When he turned around, Alexandra had retrieved his pistol, and stood in the middle of the crypt slowly turning in a bewildered circle. Her unfocused eyes shifted restlessly as she pointed the gun at Patrick's facedown corpse, then to what little was left of Julia, before landing on Forsythe, whose blood still gurgled from his neck.

Piers dropped him like the sack of refuse he was, a grateful euphoria weakening his knees at the sight of her. God, but she was precious. She was alive.

She was his.

And she loved him.

He put his hand up, reaching for her. "You're safe," he said, rounding the dais and approaching her cautiously.

She gripped the gun, staring at him as though his presence startled her. As though she'd only just awoken from a nightmare to find herself surrounded by this chaos.

"Piers?" she mouthed, then winced, putting a hand to her ear.

He went to her, the ringing in his own ears only abating slightly as he slid his hand down her arm and relieved her of the pistol before abandoning it to the platform. "Can you hear me?" he asked gently. "Are you hurt?"

"I can hear you . . . barely." Her body trembled like she'd spent the night in a snowdrift, and her pallor began to worry him. "What a mess," she exclaimed, her voice breaking as she truly took in the aftermath of the horror.

"Don't look," he admonished her, reaching out once again.

She flinched away, staggering a little.

"What a disaster," she murmured, a crimp appearing between her brows. "A tragedy. I'm sorry they wanted to hurt you, Piers. I'm sorry. I should . . . I should help clean it up. I am used to the dead. But I think I might be sick if I tried. My stomach couldn't take it . . . it's so unsteady. It hurts so much."

Piers paused, disconcerted by her nonsensical torrent of words.

Tears streaked down her face when she looked back up at him, and he could stand it no longer. "I'm going to hold you, Alexandra." he warned. "Probably tighter than is comfortable. And you are going to let me."

"It's all right," she said in a voice belonging to a girl much younger. "I don't need . . ."

"I do! Dammit," he all but roared. "Now be still."

He dragged her against him, cloak and all, not realizing until she was safe in his arms that he trembled just as mightily as she did.

She leaned into him, slightly at first, and then heavier, burrowing her arms into his jacket.

He couldn't stop saying her name. He chanted it like a

song, a psalm, a prayer, enfolding himself around her, over her, stroking her hair, dragging her scent deeper into his lungs with every breath.

He swept her out of the room, taking her a few strides down the catacomb tunnel before resting his back against the dank stone wall, allowing themselves a dark place to fall apart for a moment.

To know nothing but each other.

To feel alive.

They'd always connected here, in the darkness. It was a place they could be honest. Truly, finally honest.

"You . . . you know everything about me now," she whispered. "All my secrets. I'm a murderer."

He made a derisive noise. "And I don't bloody care," he said fiercely. "Alexandra, if you didn't notice, I've killed more men today than you have in your lifetime. I meant what I said, the only reason I would take back what you did is so that I could do the deed myself. So it wouldn't weigh on your conscience, so the blood didn't stain your hands, because I'd be happy to bathe in it."

She wept softly against his chest, and he belatedly realized he might have said too much, might have shown her more of his ferocity than she was capable of enduring at the moment.

"B-but . . . de Marchand wouldn't have killed me, he said as much." She gathered a wretched breath. "It isn't the same as fighting for your life."

"Yes it is," he hissed, squelching the urge to shake her. Or kiss her. Or . . . Or . . . whatever would keep her from giving in to her pain or her guilt. "You saw what he made of Lady Throckmorton. There is no question you fought for your life, Alexandra, no fucking question. There are fates worse than death, and he could have made what was left of your childhood a living hell. More than he already has."

She was silent for a time, sniffing in hitching breaths. Burrowing deeper against him, as if she couldn't get close enough to his warmth.

He understood the feeling, more than she could know. He wanted to absorb her, somehow. To shackle her to his side so they'd never again be parted. He'd the most absurd desire to whisk her home. To lock her in the tower at Castle Redmayne so he could always be assured of her safety.

Because this inexhaustible emotion gathering inside of him threatened to completely dismantle him. He knew, then and there, that he'd walk through hell for her. He'd slay dragons and face entire armies. He'd circumnavigate the globe to lay her foes at her feet. And the power of whatever suffused him would assure him victory.

Even though he was naught but a man. What coursed through his veins as he held her was mightier than mortals could expect to conceive of. There was a word for it, but it somehow didn't seem long enough, or potent enough, to truly convey the breadth and scope of it.

His entire life, he'd never quite had a sense of belonging. Had never known what the words "home" or "family" meant, or why they meant so much to others.

Until here. Until her.

As he buried his face in the tangled skein of her braid, he exhaled all the anguish, distrust, and misery he'd clung to for so long.

And inhaled a courage he'd never before possessed to say the words he'd never before considered. "It's possible— probable—that I love you." He repeated her confession back to her. "That I've loved you since the first time I saw you in the mist on that train platform. I love you, my brave, beautiful wife. God, how I love you."

She leaned back, and in the darkness he couldn't look into her eyes. "Piers?"

"Yes, my love?"

"Piers. I . . ." She stumbled back, and the rush of cool, underground night air made him terrifyingly aware of a wet, sticky substance on his shirt. "Piers, I'm cold."

He caught her as she fell, scooping her into his arms. Saying her name. Howling it as the sounds of boots and the flicker of lanterns made their way up the tunnel entrance.

Patrick's bullet *hadn't* missed, he realized as he ran with her down the hallway. It was the cause of her pallor and her shocked insensibility.

As he ran his every heartbeat became a prayer. His every breath a plea.

Don't take her from me.

He wasn't sure to whom he begged, but for all the adversaries he was willing to vanquish for her, there was one he was helpless against.

Death.

CHAPTER TWENTY-NINE

He loved her.

It was the first thought Alexandra had as soon as she drifted out of the miasma of pain and the dreamlike stupor that had seemed to banish that pain to another place for a time.

She pried open recalcitrant lids, testing the light in the room before managing a proper look about her familiar hotel room.

She felt as though Mercury had stampeded over her middle.

But Piers loved her. And she loved him.

So . . . where was he?

She attempted words, but only a slight croak escaped a throat dry and hoarse from disuse.

A figure bent over her. A man. A dear, familiar face.

But not the one she yearned to see.

"Petite Duchesse. Drink this," Jean-Yves slid a strong hand behind her head, lifting it enough for her to take a sip of water. "A bullet passed through your side, just above

the hip," he explained. "You are fortunate to have survived. Fortunate, indeed, that the medic was a surgeon in the recent Franco-Dahomean War. He is familiar with bullet wounds."

The memories assaulted her sluggish thoughts with astoundingly vibrant accuracy. Julia. Forsythe. Viscount Carlisle.

All the blood.

She sputtered over a sip, and Jean-Yves patiently wiped her mouth, as if he'd been a nursemaid all his life.

"Oh, God," she groaned, tears pricking at the backs of her eyes. "So much death, Jean-Yves. More bodies. More secrets."

"Do not think of this." A paternal hand brushed over her hair, light as the fall of an autumn leaf. "I am sorry I did not follow you that night," he said earnestly. "I thought you were safe in your husband's arms. In his bed. I did not think you'd slip away." His eyes held a mild censure, one that pricked her with guilt.

"I'm sorry," she whispered, the apology encompassing more than he would ever realize. She'd never bring herself to admit to him that she'd suspected him of blackmail. That her guilt and terror had caused her to treat everyone in her sphere with the same distrust. "I'm so sorry."

"It is over, *Duchesse*. The authorities know the duke's cousin tried to kill him, and that Forsythe killed Lady Throckmorton and that you would have been next had he not dispatched them." His kind gaze crinkled with a sad smile. "Your secrets are now safe. Your husband is now safe."

"But—"

"These bodies, I helped to bury, as well, and I always will if called upon to do so. For you, and for them." He motioned with his chin to the door. "Your life may begin anew with a man who loves you most desperately."

She grasped his hand and held it, her throat too full of emotion to express her gratitude, though he squeezed her palm, his smile full of tender comprehension.

Releasing her, he went to the door, motioning someone inside.

Not Redmayne, but the "them" to whom he had referred.

The Red Rogues descended upon her in a flurry of silks and exclamations.

"You're awake!" Cecelia leaned down and hugged the air around her as if she were too fragile to even touch. "Oh, thank God, Alexander, we were so bereft when we heard you'd been shot, we nearly rowed the length of the entire Channel rather than wait for a ferry."

Francesca dropped a single kiss on her forehead. "Luckily, Cecelia was able to charm a fisherman into chugging us across."

"And by charm, she means pay." Cecelia nudged her spectacles farther up onto the bridge of her pert nose, hovering like a worried hummingbird swathed in cobalt silks.

Francesca bustled about, her butter-yellow skirts swishing across the floor efficiently as she filled Alexandra's water glass, adjusted the drapes for optimal light, placed her shawl close by, selected a book for her to read, and scrutinized the label of the tonic on the bedside table as though prepared to give her medical opinion.

"How long have I been asleep?" Alexandra wondered.

"Oh, a few hours, not to worry." Cecelia picked up a hairbrush. "Would you like me to untangle your hair?"

"A few hours?" Alexandra looked to Francesca for the truth.

"A few dozen hours." Francesca sighed. "One and forty, to be exact, if you count the time it took your husband to get you here."

Almost two days? Alexandra marveled as she drank in the sight of her lovely friends and did her best to push herself into a seated position. Pain incised her, and she hissed a foul word.

"Oh, no, you mustn't move," Cecelia admonished. "Your stitches might tear, and then poor Redmayne would—"

"Where is he?" Alexandra asked, wishing for him with an ache that surpassed the one in her side.

"Oh, in the next room." Cecelia threw a flippant gesture to Redmayne's suite as she lowered herself to the mattress and began a cautious unknotting of Alexandra's braid. "Francesca poisoned him."

"What?"

"I did *not,*" Francesca insisted. "He's still breathing, or was, when I checked an hour ago."

"She slipped a sleeping tonic into his tea," Cecelia tattled, running the silver brush over Alexandra's tangled tresses. "But I think she gave him too much as he's been unconscious for nigh on ten hours."

"That had nothing to do with the draught I gave him," Francesca argued. "And everything to do with the fact that he hadn't rested for the thirty hours prior." Dropping into the chair beside the bed, Francesca smirked. "He forced my hand, I'll have you know. If he'd not have been pacing like a caged lion, growling at the staff and interrogating the surgeon every twenty minutes, making a general nuisance of himself, I'd have let him be. But the longer he stayed awake—the longer you remained unconscious—the more insufferable he became."

Cecelia leaned in conspiratorially, her blueberry eyes sparkling with rapture. "He's hopelessly besotted with you, Alexander. Now that I'm not terrified for your life, I find his behavior rather romantic."

It buoyed Alexandra to no end to hear it. For she would have been the same. Insensible. Incoherent with worry for him. That's what love did to a person.

"Yes, the poor lummox," Francesca agreed. "What the devil did you do to him? You've only known each other ten days."

"And yet I love him," Alexandra admitted, meaning it with every part of her soul. "I love him so terribly much."

They regarded her with identical expressions of disbelief.

Francesca snatched the tincture from the bedside table once again. "How much of this did they administer to you?"

"I mean it," Alexandra said around a laugh, cut short by a searing pain. "I'm as hopelessly besotted as you say he is."

Cecelia seized her hand, holding it to her abundant bosom. "Oh, Alexander, I'm relieved—no—thrilled to hear it. You deserve such a love. Such a man. He might be fearsome and more than a bit . . . untamed for a duke, but I feel that he'd find a way to snatch a star from the firmament if you requested it of him."

Francesca leaned forward intently. "Did everything—I mean the wedding night—when you two— Blast it all, I'm wondering if he is kind?"

Alexandra had to smile. It wasn't often Francesca found herself without words, and the obvious care in her friend's discomfiture warmed the cockles of her heart.

"He's kind." She smiled, remembering their lovemaking with a tinge of a blush. He was not only kind, but carnal and wicked and sensitive and so much more he hadn't shown her yet. "He's . . . rather marvelous."

"Good." Francesca sat back like a queen reclining in her throne, appeased for the time being.

"To think it was Julia blackmailing you all this time." Cecelia brought a hand to her décolletage, toying with the pearls there as a melancholy touched her gaze. "Jean-Yves tells me she didn't survive."

Alexandra was in the middle of recounting the events of that night to her enraptured friends when the door between the two rooms exploded open, startling them all.

Redmayne stalked inside, pulling up short when his eyes locked on hers with an alarming intensity.

He looked appropriately terrible, one side of his wild hair smashed to his head, as though he'd slept in one position the entire ten hours. The gashes of his scars appeared deeper, angrier, as did the grooves branching from his eyes. His beard was fuller, stretching down his neck, unchecked for a few days. His shirt was only halfway fastened, the swells of his tawny chest dark against the white garment.

Alexandra had never thought anyone so unutterably beautiful in her entire life.

An invisible thread of emotion wove through the space between them, propelling the tension to an acute peak. His face could have been chiseled from granite, his eyes swirling with the most intemperate of storms.

She wished she could say something, but the sight of him quite struck her dumb. Any words that came to mind seemed either trite or insufficient.

He speared her friends with that fearsome gaze of his, pointing to the door. "Out."

Cecelia complied after kissing Alexandra's cheek and giving her hand a reassuring squeeze.

Redmayne stopped Francesca at the door. "I'll deal with you later."

"That's what you think." Francesca shouldered past him, tossing a saucy wink over her shoulder.

He slammed the door behind them before turning back to her, his expression ravaged. Gutted.

Furious.

"Are you all right?" Alexandra cringed even as the words left her mouth. She'd always detested the question, and now she absolutely understood why people asked it.

Instead of answering, he dragged his eyes away from her, locking them on the gilded arabesque wall above the headboard as he visibly battled a plethora of emotions.

"I've had nearly two days to build up a temper against you," he finally snapped. "You slip away to meet with a blackmailer—the sex and lethality of whom was unknown to you at the time—without a word to me? Of all the dangerous, witless, reckless—"

"I thought it was my blackmailer who was responsible for the attempts on your life. I was trying to protect my friends, myself, and ultimately *you* from what I'd done," she explained.

That brought his gaze back down to clash with hers. "Protect. *Me?*" His features rearranged from bemused to disbeliving. "Alexandra, I am your *husband*. It is my call—no—it is my *right* to protect you. And if you ever deny me my right again, I'll lock you in Redmayne Tower and lose the key, do you mark me?"

A spurt of defensiveness shot through her. This wasn't the romantic reunion she'd expected to share with her so-called besotted husband. "What makes you think you can—"

"I cannot!" His sonorous voice cracked raw upon the word. "I cannot stand at your bedside and watch you struggle to breathe, wondering if you've enough blood left in your body to sustain you. Wishing I could tear my veins open and offer you mine. I cannot watch someone threaten your precious life. I cannot—*will not*—allow you out of my sight into a world where you might be taken from me."

He stalked to her bed, dropping to his knees beside it, his features ardent and his eyes pinched with anguish. "You don't know what it will cost me, Alexandra, to love you like this. It consumes me. It obsesses me. You've somehow, in less than a bloody fortnight, become more integral to my sustenance than the very air I breathe or the water I drink."

He gathered her hand to his mouth, dragging his lips against her palm. "All I'm asking is for you to have mercy on me, wife. If there is a battle to fight, a villain to face, I beg you to allow me the honor. Because the cruelest thing you could do, is sentence me to a world without you in it."

Moved beyond words, Alexandra drew her fingers through his beard and up the scar on his cheekbone before reaching to sift through the layers at his scalp. He leaned his head into her touch like a great cat receiving his due.

"I love you, too," she finally managed.

His mouth tightened at the sides, compressing into a tight line. "Promise me, dammit."

"I promise," she said, welling with a devastating tenderness.

"No more secrets between us," he amended, rising to perch on the bed next to her, threading his fingers through hers. "I want all of you, Alexandra. I want your pleasure and your pain. Your sins and your secrets. Your past and your passions, your opinions and your pretenses. I want to know everything. All of it. To be the only one with whom you share them. I'm a selfish bastard, wife, and I'll thank you to indulge me. I want you without limitations and beyond suspicions."

To her surprise, Alexandra found a similar desire within

herself. "No more secrets," she agreed. "Though you'll have to share me somewhat, with them." She tilted her chin toward the door through which the Rogues had gone . . .

. . . and were likely listening on the other side.

He frowned, pretending to consider it. "If they are essential to your happiness, then they are to mine, as well."

"Kiss me, husband," she said.

He bent over her, careful not to press or jostle, laying his mouth against hers with a fervent sound vibrating in his throat.

A surge of love trilled through her, not unlike the pleasures from his magical hands. But softer, spilling across her heart with an exquisite glow, bathing her in warmth and wholeness.

When he pulled back, she witnessed the same glow in his eyes.

"You're perfect," he whispered. "My brilliant, beautiful wife."

She laid her hand against his scars. "So are you."

She knew each of them to be deeply flawed, wounded, and imperfect beings, but she understood what he meant. They were perfect for each other. Two restless souls that would never be still.

And would no longer have to wander alone.

EPILOGUE

It'd taken Piers exactly two years to get to this moment.

"Are you sure?" he asked one last time, remembering her blanch as the Polynesian midwife had instructed her to make love with him like this to hasten the birth of their child.

He might have known something like this would happen, but when Alexandra had suggested that she give birth halfway around the world with a midwife she'd met while excavating an ancient aquifer, he'd readily agreed.

Neither of them had wished to suffer the boredom and isolation of an English confinement during her pregnancy. And her lively stories of paradise, of a tribe where pregnant women were respected, revered, and pampered—not to mention scantily dressed—sounded like a most capital idea.

For months now, it had been paradise. They slept in a raised open-walled hut, made luxurious by fluttering curtains and plush rugs. The ocean lulled them to sleep every night and bade them awake every morning.

They feasted on exotic fruits and coconuts, fresh fish, pork, and hearty grains harvested or butchered that day. They swam in crystalline coves and played beneath waterfalls. And, as she became weighted down by the child in her belly, he rubbed her feet while she floated in salt water.

A few days a week, Piers would hunt with the men, learning their skills and teaching them a few of his own. The tribe often had visitors from many foreign places, and they welcomed each with broad, beautiful smiles and vigorous trade.

Paradise.

Regardless of where they were, every day with her was a utopia. And every night was heaven.

Though they'd always been blessedly compatible lovers, her pregnancy granted her an insistent and, at times, rather ferocious libido.

If he had his way, he'd keep her as pregnant as she wanted to be. They'd sire an entire litter of dark-haired, amber-eyed darlings. If only he could enjoy the rapacious glint of hunger in her eyes.

Alexandra was in bed, as in all things, a curious, enthusiastic lover who'd eventually become a master, her skill unparalleled by the most celebrated of courtesans. They'd bonded as husband and wife, and Piers had been able to push the boundaries of even the most salacious acts.

Except for this. Never this.

"We don't have to do this," he said. "There are other ways."

"I want to." Alexandra padded to their bed, and he lifted her upon it, gathering the pillows to support her belly as she bent over. "I trust you."

Those words were like a balm to his heart, and a tinder to his cock.

"You tell me if you're afraid," he said.

"I'm never afraid. Not with you." She rested her forehead on her arms. "This is the last memory I want to be rid of. The last barrier I want to shed. How better to do it than this?"

He both heartily agreed and obsessively worried. Thus far they'd been lucky enough to avoid a negative sexual experience. With communication, humor, and understanding they'd been able to breach her fears and bury many of her memories. What a treasure it would be, to free her of every pain. He knew she'd never completely forget, but perhaps she could release as much of her burden as was possible. Relinquishing the hold of the past on her present existence.

He moved behind her, caressing her spine, savoring the feel of her hip in his hand, fuller than before, sensual and soft.

The sight of her was almost too beautiful to bear. The plump globes of her ass extended toward him, the luscious trove below already dewy and damp.

Piers split the folds with a probing finger, hunger knotting in his belly as he bent to feast. When his tongue slipped along the lovely pleats and pliant petals he reveled in her little mewls and hitches of breath. He teased her with little darts of his tongue, coaxing the folds to become full and hot, engorged with desire. He searched her sex in all the intricate places, delving inside with his tongue, wanting to drink at the well of wanting he found there.

He'd never cease hungering for her flavor. Never would he be satiated.

Tormenting her with slow, swirling motions, he made her give up her dignity to him as she writhed and wriggled and pressed her hips backward, rocking against his lips. Finally, he centered all his attentions on her clitoris, flicking it in feather-light strokes, knowing that was all it would take to send her over the edge.

She arched and cried out, dousing his tongue with her release. Her body clenched and trembled, her hips jerking until he brought her down slowly, disseminating her climax into soft-spun shivers that bloomed goose pimples over her naked flesh.

Piers pulled back, wiping his beard and licking his lips like a cat who'd been caught in the cream. He'd never tire of her gratification, of the satisfaction it granted him.

Rising to his knees, he drank in the sight, loving the glow of her pregnancy, the luminescence shimmering beneath her skin.

"I love you," he growled, when he meant to murmur.

"I love you," she replied dreamily.

Reaching down, he palmed himself, rubbing the head of him against her vulnerable opening, expecting her to tense. To stiffen.

She didn't.

He bent over her, pressing heated kisses to her spine, whispering love words as he pushed into the velvet cove of her body. Once he'd locked himself as deep as he could go, he stayed there, enjoying the wet, tight feel of her around him. The little pulses and aftershocks of her climax a heavenly feeling around his sensitized flesh.

"God, this feels so . . ." He stopped, drawing back. "Are you all ri—"

"If you finish that question, I'm going to geld you." Her threat held no real heat, and Piers grinned as he felt the impatient wriggle of her hips.

He flexed inside of her, and then began to move. The position afforded him the most wicked sight. His cock, slick with her desire, impaling her again and again, joining them in strong, rhythmic thrusts. Her delicate pink skin, soft yet tight, exerted the perfect pressure, welcoming his thrust, clenching upon his withdrawal.

Her sweet sex was shaped to accommodate only him, and by God did it ever.

After his first initial thrusts, she began to rock back against him, opening herself to him, matching his rhythm in little demanding nudges. Urging him deeper.

He obliged, reaching between them, beneath himself, to flick at the beaded nub he knew would respond. His other hand spread her ass, his curious fingers twirling wet circles around the tight opening he found there.

Her astonished gasp was followed by a pulse of her inner muscles, goading him onward. He breached the gathered place only slightly with his fingertip, delighted when a swift and unexpected orgasm ripped through her, clamping her flesh rhythmically around his, milking him until he could stand it no longer.

His breath caught, then ceased as his release broke his rhythm, locking him in clutches of liquid fire. Her name poured from his lips in several broken syllables, the pulses of ecstasy so wildly overwhelming he almost yearned to escape them.

It was all he could do not to collapse upon her afterward, but he controlled a descent that somehow found their limbs tangled together. Her belly nestled between them, he cocooned her body with his, caressing the places he'd grown to recognize as her favorites. The undersides of her breasts, her clavicles, the swell of her stomach.

"You didn't seem to mind that," he ventured, wickedly.

"It was the best," she panted, slick from exhaustion and exertion. "The best . . . ever."

He chuffed. "You say that sentence so often, I'm starting to suspect its verity."

She lolled her head to the side. "You doubt me?"

Sweeping above her, he pressed a kiss to her nose. Her eyelids. The corners of her soft mouth. "No. I don't. I trust you."

It was a terrifying thing, to trust someone so entirely. It did not come easily at first. But as their marriage grew, he came to accept that her penchant for honesty wasn't merely an endearing trait, but an inexhaustible virtue. She had to be the most loyal person he'd ever met, and that loyalty was returned by those who loved her in kind.

Sighing, she wrapped her arms around her middle, nuzzling into him as he rested beside her.

"You can come out now," she prompted the baby before huffing away a strand of her hair. "So many people are eager to meet you." They each stared for a moment, though he wasn't certain what they expected.

"Probably is a boy," she muttered. "One as stubborn as you are."

"I hope it's a girl."

She lifted her brows. "Oh?"

"A little girl with black hair and amber eyes. Someone who calls me 'papa' and trails rivers of ribbons all through the castle."

Her smile could have lit the night sky. "You'll spoil her, terribly."

"That's the idea. She'll be the new Terror of Torcliff. A more fearsome creature than I could ever be."

"Don't you dare!" She jabbed at his ribs with a cruel finger. "If you create a monster, you'll have to deal with the raising of her. I'll have none of it."

His happiness flickered. "Do you think she'll fear me? Looking as I do?"

Alexandra caressed him with all the tenderness the world contained. "She'll love you, as I do. Your face will be the dearest sight, because to her it will represent home and love and safety and acceptance. Our children will be proud to have such a handsome, fearsome father."

Piers cleared a gather of emotion from his throat, deciding to lighten the moment. "We can call her Katherine," he suggested. "Kitty. After the animal who changed the course of my life for the better. Without him, I'd have married Rose."

He caught her jab this time, not that it wasn't deserved. "Don't even speak like that," she admonished him. "I can't fathom it." Her features fell. "I almost pity her. She's lost everything. Her reputation, her title, what little fortune she had."

He made a face thinking that Rose could rot in the drafty dowager house she'd been relegated to in some cold corner of Blighty. Just so long as he never had to see her again.

Freeing her hand, Alexandra ran a finger down the scar on his jaw, distracting him. "The beast that put this here was more than a mere kitty."

"You're right, as always," he acquiesced. "Would you allow me to name our child Panther? Or Jaguar?"

She made a face "You're right, Kitty is perfect."

"You're perfect." He kissed her.

"We both know that's a lie. I've been an absolute beast to you for a month." She struggled to turn over, to find a comfortable spot.

"Only two weeks by my count," he teased, chastised when her brow pinched into that endearing frown. He reached up to smooth it away. "You're an adorable beast."

She leaned her cheek into his palm. "When the baby can travel, where would you like to take her?"

He pulled her in tightly, fitting her lovely bottom in the crook of his body. "Let's go home for a while. Let the staff meet our child and invite your parents from Hampshire.

I'd like to take some time to see Mercury's new foals. Besides, the Redmayne remains will be returning from the museum."

"I love that idea," she readily agreed. "I think I'll miss a Devonshire summer by then. Less hot." She brushed a damp curl back from her brow.

She shifted again as the distinct outline of a foot rippled above her navel and he pressed his hand to the little thing, wishing he could meet its owner more than anything in the world.

"I think I'll go find Cecelia." Alexandra yawned and stretched her naked body with an indolent grace. "We're both going to swim beneath the waterfall today. The feeling of weightlessness is indescribable. It's the only time my back doesn't cause me conniptions."

"I'll come with you." He heaved his body from the bed with great effort.

She threw him a saucy smile. "You weren't invited. What if it's just a swim for us ladies?"

"Do you really think Cecelia's domineering, insufferable husband will be any farther than ten paces away?" He rolled his eyes. "If not coiled around her like a sea serpent?"

Another brilliant smile nearly blinded him with happiness as she scooted off the bed, her full breasts bouncing in such a way his mouth watered.

"And you're any better than he?"

"Of course I'm better," he snorted. "I can make it a good fifteen paces before I miss you and have to return."

"There you go," she teased. "Turning everything into a competition." She kissed him, wriggling into a colorful little shift in such a way that made him glad they'd be at the water again, where she'd be wearing as little as possible.

"Before we return to Castle Redmayne, we'll have to

stay long enough for Cecelia to give birth. She could be as much as a month behind me. Perhaps she'll have a girl, as well." The idea seemed to thrill her. "They'll be great friends. A second generation of Red Rogues."

"Is the world ready for such a thing?" Piers slid his arms around his wife, humbled at the simplicity of their happiness. The all-encompassing entirety of it. "I shan't mind remaining in paradise with you as long as you want to be here." He cuddled her belly. "Besides, I'm anxious for Kitty to meet her Ramsay cousin."

Don't miss the next novel in the
Devil You Know series

ALL SCOT AND BOTHERED

Coming in Spring 2020

Don't miss the other sensational
novels from *USA Today* bestseller
Kerrigan Byrne

Victorian Rebels series
THE HIGHWAYMAN
THE HUNTER
THE HIGHLANDER
THE DUKE
THE SCOT BEDS HIS WIFE
THE DUKE WITH THE DRAGON TATTOO

Available from St. Martin's Paperbacks